D0839580

Visions
of Mary

DEDICATION

As the central theme of this novel is bravery, it is fitting that I should dedicate it to Mr. Rick Corman, the bravest man I have ever had the privilege of meeting. Though every bone in Rick's body is riddled with cancer, he continues to run three miles every day. I can't begin to imagine the pain that he endures. As a physician I have never encountered a person less afraid to die nor more determined to live. Rick, just like the valiant soldiers of WWII, your bravery in the face of adversity is truly inspirational. I am proud to call you my friend.

I owe a special debt of gratitude to several people without whom this book would have remained unwritten.

To Judy, the love and light of my life. For thirty-five years, through thick and through thin you have been my soul mate. No one else on the planet would have put up with half my insanity and yet remained such a loyal, loving, and forever patient companion. Thank you Judy. My love for you alone will never die.

To Reese, Graham, and Jillian, my children and joy of my life. I am so very proud of each of you.

To my parents Melvin and Betty, who gave me life, taught me how to work hard and to live with dignity.

To David Leddy who gave me wings.

To Lee Lauderback and Erik Frazier who helped me tame the Texan and the Mustang.

To R. Kenton Nelson, Artist and Friend without whose encouragement and gentle prodding I never would have summoned the courage to put this story out there. Kenton, you once told me, "Sharing an artistic endeavor is like being the only naked guy in the room, but either get over it and get on with it, or go home." Great advice! Thanks pal.

VISIONS OF MARY

A NOVEL OF ONE MAN'S WAR

Joseph Richardson, M.D.

two harbors press | *minneapolis, mn*

Two Harbors Press
212 3rd Avenue North, Suite 290
Minneapolis, MN 55401
612.455.2293
www.TwoHarborsPress.com

ISBN-13: 978-1-938690-62-4
LCCN: 2012923757

Distributed by Itasca Books

Cover painting by R. Kenton Nelson.
Editing by Tom Eblen
Typeset by Steve Porter

Printed in the United States of America

CHAPTER ONE

The dense, low snow clouds made the January morning all the more black as they dumped their freezing load on the vacant countryside. Moonless and eerily dark, the snow had yet to start falling when I backed out of the drive only fifteen minutes ago. As if making up for lost time, the clouds now seemingly emptied en masse. The snowflakes were large and wet and frequent, each taking a measure of burden reflecting the headlights back into my unadjusted eyes. My forward vision limited to only about ten feet, the gleaming flakes created a swirling white miasma made whiter by a backdrop of nearly total blackness, a veil rendering me encased and claustrophobic. Timidly driving on, I experimented with a couple of different headlight settings before finally deciding the OFF setting afforded me the best view of the road ahead. Unfortunately this choice also turned off the dashboard lights, leaving me without a visible speedometer. No matter, since I couldn't safely drive over ten miles an hour even if I was crazy enough to do so.

"Damn it, I'm gonna be late." Being late, or rather I should say *not* being late is very important to me. While I'm always late if my wife is involved, she seems to have her own internal clock that has no basis in reality, my wife is not involved in the task of getting me to work. As such, I've not been late for a shift in the ER in over twenty-two years, a fact in which I take considerable pride. The unforeseen snow was about to change all that. I know from experience that there are few things in life more disconcerting than waiting for one's replacement after a busy twelve-hour stint in the ER, especially after working all night. A typical night shift ends at 7:00 a.m., usually outlasting a spent ER doctor's ability to think. Never go to an ER between 6:30 a.m. and 7:00 a.m. as during this period the average doctor's brain will inevitably have turned to mush, capable only of holding on, waiting to be rescued by the next doctor reporting for duty, all the while praying nothing requiring any semblance of advanced cognition rolls through the door. Sometime around 6:50 a.m., even through the muddled haze of exhaustion, notice is taken if your rescuer has yet to appear, a minor irritation, but noticed just the same. By 6:55 a.m. this minor irritation will have escalated into a full-blown panic. "What if they forgot they're on the schedule today?" A major hassle both for the doc going off duty and the doc who gets a call at 7:05 a.m. jarring him/her from a sound sleep with the awful news that he/she was expected twenty minutes ago. "No worries… Just get here as soon as you can," a sentence usually followed by "Asshole," muttered under the caller's breath as soon as the phone is hung up. "The very least I could do is warn the night shift doc I'm going to be late," I thought, dialing my cell phone.

"Hey, Scott, this is Dave."

"Yes?" he said. I could almost hear his sleep-deprived mind begin reeling, revving up to meet a challenge.

"Hey, I'm on my way, but I'm gonna be late. I've never seen it snow so hard."

"Snow?" he asked.

"Yeah. Go look out the back door. It's really coming down. Anyway, I'm on my way so don't pick up any more charts. I'll be there as soon as I can… Thanks, and sorry!"

"No worries. See you when you get here."

I was all but sure I heard him curse me before the phone line disconnected. I felt bad, but consoled myself with, "Oh well, it couldn't be helped. How am I supposed to predict a blizzard when the experts on TV declared the weekend would be partly sunny with only a ten percent chance of precipitation?" With ten miles between me and the hospital and forward progression limited to only ten miles an hour, the math was easy. "At least it's not sticking to the roads…not *yet* anyway."

As per usual my mind began to wander. They say I'm a bit ADD, a gross underestimation of the true measure to which I am afflicted. Attention Deficit Disorder really sucked when I was in grade school because I seldom made it through an entire hour without getting lost in a daydream, totally missing whatever the teacher was saying in a vain attempt to educate me. As such, I did very poorly in public school. ADD has been a boon to my professional life however, enabling me to care for multiple patients at any given moment, even in the midst of all Hell breaking loose. I kind of thrive on chaos. It's an adrenalin rush of sorts, similar to the exhilaration of skiing or flying. The downside being I require almost constant stimulation to stave off boredom. I'd much prefer being busy, overwhelmed with sick people all day, than to sit waiting for something, anything to happen.

As a child I remember living for *snow days*, for the brief reprieve from the monotony of daily routine they provided. There were few things in life more joyous than awakening unexpectedly late in the morning, toasty warm under the covers, my mother letting us sleep in after learning from the radio that school had been cancelled for the day. Instead of misery, the spelling quiz for which I was perpetually unprepared, or any other of the myriad of homework I had failed to perform the night before, the day would turn into fun, sledding and snowball fights, noses red from cold, and hot chocolate. Best of all I could delay making up a creative, albeit dubious excuse, my usual substitute for any school assignment until the bus ride the following day. Ah, such was my childhood.

As an adult, I've chosen a job that requires my physical presence regardless of extenuating circumstances. The remainder of the world can be buried under twelve feet of snow, but because people could die if I failed to show up for work, not melodrama, but righteous fact, I always manage to find my way there on time. That said, I've grown to dread snow days for the claustrophobic, lethargic pall they cast upon the civilized world. My mood sinks as I begin to consider what the day ahead will be like. Even in the crazy, disorganized realm of the emergency department some things are predictable. I've been doing this work long enough to correctly anticipate what's in store for me.

Because of the unanticipated snow the volume of patients will be relatively low, limited to, for the most part, legitimate emergencies, the kind of patients I thrive on. Tomorrow will be crazy regardless of the weather, but since this storm has caught all of mankind including the Weather Channel off guard, today will be reasonable. The morning will be filled with car wrecks, especially if the roads get slick, which they most assuredly will before noon, but the majority of them should be minor fender benders, as the snow will limit maximum driving speed, thereby reducing the energy transferred between two colliding objects.

"Lets see, F=ma, the average car weighs 3000 pounds so that's...?" Catching myself, I laughed aloud saying, "Geez I'm a geek!" Around 10:00 a.m. there will be an influx of older people with broken hips acquired going to or from the grocery store to get milk. I've never understood why people who don't even drink milk are compelled to get out in the first few hours of a winter storm just to purchase a gallon or two. It's as though people believe milk is the universal antidote for snow. Goodness knows my mother has never weathered a snowfall without a gallon of milk in the refrigerator, acquired by sending my brother trudging out through the blizzard, only to throw out that same gallon unopened a few days later. I wonder if dairy farmers see a huge upswing in sales with the advent of a winter storm?

By noon we'll see the first heart attack, a portly middle age man who, prior to the commencement of his crushing pain, was sucking on a cigarette as he shoveled wet snow. If he's lucky he'll have only pain en route to the ER. If not, it's a function of how far away he is when his heart arrests that will determine for him how he'll spend the remainder, if any, of his life.

After noon we'll get people from east elsewhere with large envelopes of their previous MRIs in hand, all hoping this will validate their request for narcotic pain medication, "Just enough to get me through till I see my surgeon in six weeks." They seem to come by the busload on days like this, purposed to dupe some unwary ER doctor into giving them pills. The newbies to this culture will come in feigning back pain after moving stoves or pianos. There always seems to be a lot of furniture moving on stormy days or Sunday nights. I am convinced that the federal government should put warning labels on all furniture weighing more than one hundred pounds. "WARNING. The surgeon general has determined it may be harmful to get drunk and naked and move heavy furniture around your home." Gotta get a fix somehow, I suppose. From Napoleon to Hitler, bad winter weather has had disastrous, adverse effects on supply lines. It's not surprising that prescription drug trafficking is no exception.

If school is cancelled, moms with feverish kids will begin showing up around 4:00 p.m. having been unable to get their children into the pediatrician's office. Today the kids will be legitimately sick, as opposed to tomorrow when just the sniffles will be a reason to get out of the house and take junior to the ER.

Around 5:00 p.m. there will be an influx of nursing home patients, none of whom will be any different than they have been for the last two weeks, but who have, despite being nonverbal from their incapacitating strokes, all inexplicably developed the ability to communicate their crushing chest pain to the nurse. Exactly how a nursing home nurse divines the nature of this complaint will always remain a mysterious art to me, but I guarantee at least three such patients before 7:00 p.m.

At 7:10 p.m. I'll get a call from Bob, my replacement, who will use the snow as his excuse for being thirty minutes late even though he's been at home all day watching it snow and had plenty of time to prepare for what any idiot would realize would today be a longer drive to work…. Asshole!

Okay, I'm probably taking this a bit too far as I'm getting angry at a guy who's probably home in bed and yet to do anything wrong…yet.

The roads were beginning to get slick. "Better be careful," I thought, "or I'll be the first of the car wrecks to hit the ER." It's funny, but a few years ago we stopped calling car wrecks "accidents" because the term implied a known lack of willfulness on the driver's part. Was it really an accident, or an elaborate scheme to defraud insurance companies out of a few bucks, or more seriously, an attempt to end one's own life using an automobile as an easy escape? We now refer to wrecks as *Motor Vehicle Collisions,* a little cleaner terminology in a court of law. "I hate attorneys! They've ruined the whole country as far as I'm concerned," I say aloud to no one, then laughed at myself for ranting like a mad man.

My mind's banter paused long enough for me to realize I'd not passed a single vehicle since leaving home, at least not that I could recall seeing. As I pulled into the parking lot, I could see a red blur through the opaque wall of snowflakes. I assumed it was the large sign above the ambulance portico announcing to the world that this is the Emergency Department, and so aimed my slipping, sliding car in that general direction. "Man, it's gotten treacherous!" Driving under the portico, I could immediately again see the outside world and braked abruptly to avoid hitting an ambulance, parked crewless under the portico, its rear doors agape. I wondered aloud what they'd brought me to start the day when, to my delight, I saw two paramedics pushing a gurney, transporting an elderly patient out of the Emergency Department. "Great! They're sending someone back for a change," a good omen, as it represented someone already evaluated and treated by my partner and deemed stable enough to go back to wherever it was they came from. Rolling down my window to say hello, the oldest paramedic, a long-time friend of mine, beat me to a greeting.

"Morning, Doc. Looks rough out here."

"Yeah, it's getting dangerous. How is it in there?"

"Empty now. Looks like it'll be a slow morning till rush hour."

"That's what I'm hoping for. Maybe a chance for some coffee and read the paper before the fun begins. You guys be careful out here today."

"Thanks, Doc, you too," a polite, though thoughtless response exhaled as he and his partner lift the litter and its content into the back of the ambulance. Parking my car, I brace myself, girding my loins for yet another shift.

Scott is waiting at the door, satchel in hand.

"About damn time," he says half in jest, but only half.

"I'm sorry, but you'll see in about two minutes what you're up against. I've never seen a storm as intense." Seeing he was in no mood to chat, I asked "Anything to check out?"

"The board is clean. See you tonight."

"Tonight? I thought Bob was scheduled tonight."

"Nope, we traded."

"Well if that's the case, take your time coming in. Looks like I owe you an hour. See you then."

Scott wearily raised his hand goodbye in response without looking back. He had only recently returned to Tennessee from northern Michigan and I'm sure he thought I'd been a total wimp about driving in less than the horrific weather he was exposed to in the wilds of the northern frontier. To hear him tell it, he's a veritable *Nanook of the North*. I felt vindicated when only two minutes later he poked his head into our work cubicle and said, "Man, you weren't kidding, were you? I'm gonna call Joan and tell her I'm sleeping here. Call me if it gets crazy."

"Like that will ever happen," I said sarcastically. Scott knows a cry for help is a sign of weakness. No ER doc worth his salt would ever call a partner in early unless it was a major catastrophe, a plane crash or an earthquake with hundreds of victims. Even then the call would be seen as less than manly.

"Do we even have on-call quarters?"

"Yeah, next to ICU North. Just ask one of the unit nurses and I'm sure she can bed you down."

I see the smirk wash over his face as he said, "Wow, this is a full-service hospital."

I rolled my eyes, looking over the top of my glasses as he walked away, his sleep-deprived brain believing he'd just made a witty comment worthy of a Nobel Prize. When he wakes up later and recalls this conversation he'll feel more embarrassed than witty.

Settling in, I began my shift by nesting, ridding the desk of last night's patient charts, a pizza box containing a single slice of pizza, cold, but tempting, as this was my primary means of sustenance in medical school and remains my favorite choice of quick meals. I set the pizza on top of the keyboard and filled the box, empty except for a few crumbs, with multiple empty or half-full cans of Diet Coke, and the wrappers from two or three candy bars. Scott is still young enough that his youthful metabolism overrides any tendency to put on pounds. I couldn't tell if this represents a concerted effort on his part, or rather reflected a blessing received by his choice of ancestors. In either case, Scott looked pretty damn good for a man of forty. Certainly better than I looked at fifty-five, and probably better than I've ever looked if I'm honest with myself. It's just too bad he can't figure out how to use a garbage can.

With coffee and the morning paper to entertain me, I lost track of the first two hours of my shift, not a single patient checked in. There was a little chatter on the med radio alerting us to the potential of burn victims from a house fire on North Broadway, but apparently the house had been vacant for some time so no injuries were reported. The hours and minutes ticked past before my first patient of the day, an elderly man sent from a nursing home who earlier had fallen against a dresser, nearly severing his right ear. I waited for a CT scan of his head and cervical spine to rule out a more serious injury before beginning to repair his laceration. He was a pleasant enough fellow, too demented to know the day or the year, or to laugh at my joke when I called him "Mr. Van Gogh," but he seemed kind and quiet. He hummed while I busied myself reattaching his ear. He didn't wince as I injected the Lidocaine, a local anesthetic, but continued mumbling incoherently in singsong fashion, a soothing background music to my task.

As I finished putting in the last few throws of suture I heard a ruckus at the ER entrance immediately outside the sliding glass door of the treatment room. Two local police officers had just arrived unannounced, escorting a man whose arms had been handcuffed behind him. He appeared elderly, eighty at least, and, though stooped from age, he towered over the accompanying younger men. It was clear the older gentleman was not willingly coming to seek my attentions. "John Murphy, captain, 47-2630," he repeated over and again.

"What have you boys brought me?" I asked through the partially closed door, "Another too drunk for jail?"

"It's John Murphy, captain, 47-2630," the first officer said sarcastically.

"Is he sick or hurt?"

"He's neither."

"Then why have you brought me Captain Murphy?" I asked, peering over the top of my glasses. The nurses always hated when I did this, as the gesture silently infers the question, "Are you really that stupid?"

"Because we found him wandering in the snow out by the highway. No winter jacket and no ID."

"Sounds to me like he's given you his ID, what more do you need?"

The bound man again shouted, "John Murphy, captain, 47-2630," and began trying to wrestle free of the police officers' grip.

"Easy, Captain, we'll figure this out. I'm almost finished here." Addressing the policemen, I asked, "Why don't you stick around in case we need some help containing your pris… err…friend?"

"No can do, Doc. We've just been dispatched to a robbery out on the bypass."

"Well take him with you, then. I don't see how this is my concern," I shouted after them.

The policemen both returned my derisive look before running out the door.

"Damn it! Knoxville's finest strike again." I stood at the door, my gloved hands clasped together to remind myself not to touch anything non-sterile.

Seeing his captors retreating through the opening automatic doors, the old man seized the opportunity and frantically started running down the corridor in the opposite direction.

"Grab him, Steve!"

Steve, a mountain of a man with twenty years ER nursing experience had already sized up the situation and sprung from his chair. Without a word he stepped into the man's path, becoming a two-hundred-eighty pound barricade of human muscle. Upon seeing the futility of that path, the old man looked about furtively as would a cornered beast, unaware he was about to be grabbed from behind by two female nurses.

"I guess we should go ahead and book him in, Betty. He's a runner, so call security to come stand by his door, and put him in room twenty-seven if you would please, so we can keep our eyes on him."

"Do we take the cuffs off?"

"Oh damn, the cops are gone with the key."

"I've got one, Doc," Betty said, retrieving a small silver key dangling from a chain beneath her scrub top, hidden within the crevasse of her cleavage.

"Why would you have a handcuff key?" I asked. Betty shot me a sweetly wicked smile.

"Never mind. I really don't want to know," I said, shaking my head in mock disgust. Returning to sewing, my demented patient continued sweetly mumbling incoherently, totally oblivious to the recent commotion.

"John Murphy, captain, 47-2630," could be heard repeatedly echoing down the hall, and then surprisingly, he said something different, something that sounded like Japanese. *"Watashi wa amerika-jin, watashi wa anata no yujindseu."* As I knotted the last suture my demented patient whispered its translation, "I am an American. I am your friend," the first intelligible words I'd heard him utter. Probably the first intelligible words he'd spoken in years, a phrase hidden away in the deep crevasses of his grey matter, now erupting to the surface of consciousness, bidden forth by the hearing of an unexpected foreign tongue. I stared at him in mock surprise.

I watched John Murphy pace about the exam room as I finished the charting on my previous patient. The glass door of the enclosed cubicle allowed me to observe from a distance while keeping Mr. Murphy from running, for run he most assuredly would if given the opportunity. I'd seen and examined confused patients every day for the last twenty-five years, but something about this man was different, a puzzle that intrigued me. Even stooped by age he was a tall man, six three, perhaps six four. At a hundred and fifty pounds, he was painfully thin for a man of his height, but there was no indication that he had ever weighed much more. His head was crowned with a still-thick mane of stark white hair, which though now disheveled, I could tell was usually quaffed without a strand out of place. His skin had not fared the ravages of time well, with age spots mottling flesh so thin it was almost transparent. The sun at some time over the last century had taken its toll, rendering that skin and, more strikingly, his eyes forever tattooed. Pale blue, but bluer once, now effected less vibrant by a greenish white ring of arcus senilis, those eyes wore the wizened patina of one who had seen much, the same eyes now betrayed his naked panic. He moved sprightly about the room with an agility that belied his age.

Backing this man into a corner had probably been a mistake, transforming a docile old man into a physical force that now begged to be reckoned with. I watched him stiffen as the registration clerk attempted to perform her duties. At her question he again stated his name, rank, and serial number, stalwartly refusing to either provide more information or sign consent forms authorizing us to evaluate him. Steve attempted calmly to reason with him, but when that proved futile, started removing the man's jacket to search for any identification. John Murphy took a bare-fisted swing at him, barely missing his cheek before wrapping his arms tightly across his chest, purposed to prevent any further attempts at taking his jacket.

"Careful, Steve. If he's brave enough or crazy enough to take a poke at a man twice his size, he's dangerous."

"Well what are you gonna do, Doc? We can't let him tie up a room all day."

"Let him pace. He's old as hell, eventually he'll wear himself out."

"I'm okay with that for the moment, but if we get busy you'll have to come up with another plan."

"Are you saying it's slow?" I asked with a grin. My question was met by audible gasps, most exhaled in jest, but some were the guttural responses of a true believer.

"Damn it, Doc, now you've done it," Steve said, angry my statement was more calculated joke than faux pas. There is widespread lore in emergency departments perpetuating the belief that both the number of patients and the degree of craziness of those patients is controlled by fates, unseen forces, ER gods, if you will. To say aloud in an ER words like "slow" or "quiet," even if those words are accurate descriptors of present reality is considered blasphemy, tempting the fates to rain down terror in the form of innumerable patients, each crazier or sicker than the last. There are true believers and Steve is one of them.

"Just kidding," I said, still grinning. I could see Steve was not amused, as my sacrilege was threatening to destroy the nicest day we'd had in months.

"Look, if it gets crazy, I'll let you take him down, but right now he's not hurting anybody and he's not under arrest. Besides, he's already given you what you need. Call the local recruiting office and see if they can tell you who in the Army can provide us information about a former officer."

"Good idea. I don't think he's a bum. If he is homeless, he doesn't look like he's been on the streets too long. His clothing is well kept and well to do."

"I agree. Try calling the local nursing homes as well, see if they have any escapees to report."

"Yes, Doctor."

Intermittently observed over the next twenty minutes, John Murphy's agitation faded as the old man's body acquiesced, giving way to exhaustion. He didn't lie on the exam table, I assume because this position would render him too vulnerable, but instead took a chair from the back corner and moved it and a steel IV pole to the center of the room.

"He's smart!" I said to no one in particular. "He's found a weapon and now holds a defensible position." He sat in the chair, intent to be at the ready with his hand firmly clutching the IV pole, but sleep was threatening soon to subdue him. His head began to bob as his brain vacillated between sleeping and wakefulness before finally succumbing completely. I recognized that head bob, having done it plenty of times myself in an 8:00 a.m. class, lulled to sleep by the endless drone of a boring professor. I'll have to be careful not to startle him later when I go in, but for now I'll let him rest.

Two patients and twenty minutes later, he was still sleeping, snoring loudly now. Seeing he was no longer a danger I asked, "Hey, Steve. Any word on our captain?"

"Not yet, Doc. The Army is trying to help out, though. They're going through some files and say they'll call me back by day's end."

"Hmm. Okay, I guess. Now that he's had a nap, I think I'll try to talk to him." Figuring I should be as non-threatening as humanly possible, I'm all of five foot four and a hundred forty-five pounds, so not too much of a physical threat to most people, I softened my image further by entering his room with a cup of coffee in each hand.

"I hope cream and sugar is to your liking. I'm fond of sissy coffee myself," I said, sotto voice to gently awaken the slumbering man. He didn't respond immediately, so I said, "Captain Murphy?" a little louder this time. He awakened with a start, quickly re-establishing his grip on the IV pole. "Easy, Captain. I'm your friend." He appeared panicked yet dazed at first, as if awakening in surroundings different than those in which sleep was first met. Taking a drink of my coffee, I offered him his. He looked first at the cup, then my smile, then the cup. After several seconds of study he decided to accept my offering, tentatively taking a sip after sniffing the steaming liquid. He seemed pleasantly surprised to find the coffee was genuine, then looked at me apologetically.

"It's okay. You can't be too careful," I said, letting him sit quietly and drink in the warmth before saying, "Tell me about yourself." He looked puzzled, so I said, "Where are you from?"

He considered my question for a few moments then said, "I don't know."

"Well where do you live?" After some thought he again replied, "I don't know."

"You don't remember where you live?"

"No...I... I can't seem to recall." Nonchalantly, he took another drink of coffee, nonplussed by his amnesia.

"Where were you going in this storm?"

"To the dentist. I have an appointment at 11:00 a.m."

"What's the name of your dentist?"

"I don't know."

"The police found you wandering out in the snow."

"They did? I don't remember that," he said, genuinely surprised.

"It was only two hours ago."

"Oh?"

"Yes sir. Let's try this another way. Uh, do you have a wife or children?"

"Mary," he said smiling at last, the warmth of a pleasant memory.

"Where is Mary?"

"At home, I guess. Yes, that's where she would be."

"And home is?"

"I don't know."

"How about children? Do you have any?"

"I have a son," he said. "Johnny."

"And where does Johnny live?"

"I don't know. If he's home from school, he's with Mary I suppose."

"School? How old is Johnny?"

"Sixteen at his next birthday."

"What year was your son born, Captain Murphy?"

"1943," he said matter-of-factly.

"That would make him, uh, let's see, sixty-six, right?"

"Yes, I guess so," totally unaware of the incongruity of his statements.

"You gonna let me go?" he asked.

"Where are you going?"

"To the dentist, like I told you," once again beginning to get agitated.

"How are you going to get there?"

"In my car, of course," he said as if this was the stupidest question he'd ever heard in his life.

"Where is your car, Captain?"

"I don't know, but I'm gonna be late if you don't stop your interrogation."

"I'll tell you what, if you can show me where your car is, I'll let you go."

"It's right outside."

"Okay, Let's go see. I suspect it's still really coming down out there, so wrap this blanket around yourself."

"I don't need a blanket, young man," he said, his male pride insulted at being patronized.

"I'm sure you don't, but do it for me please?"

"Okay, fine, but I think you're making way too much of a little snow."

Grabbing my jacket, we walked to the parking lot. To my surprise the snowfall had all but stopped compared to the storm that met my morning commute, reduced now to just a few large flakes lingering on the breeze. We discovered my Porsche nearly buried under a foot and a half of heavy, wet snow, as were the other three cars in the lot. The swift, cold wind was blowing the accumulated snow into massive drifts but was also giving us some reprieve as the storm was driven ahead, retreating to the northeast. The straggling, broken clouds parted widely in patches, revealing the amber glow of an early-winter afternoon sun.

"Okay Captain, which one is yours?"

The old man looked around but saw nothing that resembled his vehicle.

"I…. I don't see it. Somebody must have taken it."

"Well what kind of car is it?" I asked, knowing full well there would be no automobile of his describing here to find.

"It's a 1949 Pontiac Torpedo with a flathead eight. I love that car. It should be here, but I just can't seem to find it."

"Well let's go back inside and see if we can find another way to get you to your dentist appointment."

Visibly disappointed, Captain Murphy nodded his head in agreement as we both retreated to the warmth of the ER.

Barring the discovery of any structural lesions in this man's brain, I had my diagnosis. It was clear to me that Captain Murphy was temporarily if not permanently lost in the past. What's more, he was totally oblivious to his inability, yet another poor soul imprisoned, separated from present reality by his incapacity to form new memories… the classic symptoms of Alzheimer's dementia.

In a perverse way, establishing a diagnosis is strangely gratifying to a physician, kind of like the pleasure one gets upon completing a puzzle or complex task. Unfortunately, while putting a name on his malady made me feel good, it did little to help the captain. Alzheimer's is not curable, and it's primary symptom, that of recent memory deficit, is making our immediate dilemma of getting Captain Murphy home next to impossible.

"Captain Murphy, I want to help you. I think the whereabouts of your car is locked in here," I said, tapping my finger on his forehead.

"Will you allow me to do a few tests? A CAT scan perhaps, and see what we can find out?"

"Seems to me like a waste of time and money, but you obviously have your heart set on it, so I guess that will be okay. We just can't take too long, though. I've got to get home to supper. Mary really fusses if I'm late."

"It shouldn't take too long, I promise."

I ordered the tests, and in an act of efficiency borne on the fact that Captain Murphy was the only patient in the ER, he was quickly whisked away to the scanner. As I sat writing, Steve approached and in hushed tones says, "Hey, Doc, we heard back from the Army." Giving me a puzzled look, he continued saying, "Captain John Murphy, 47-2630, a navigator in the Thirteenth Air Force, was killed in action in the South Pacific, June 4, 1945…."

CHAPTER 2

I've practiced Emergency Medicine in a large tertiary care center ER for twenty-five years. In doing so, I've enjoyed a front row seat to that freak show known as the human condition. To say that nothing much shocks or surprises me would be an understatement, but news of the death of Captain John Murphy, now some sixty-five years past, shocked me, a jolt as palpable and surreal as it must have felt to friends and family all those years ago.

Stunned, I finally asked, "Okay, who the hell is this guy? He's answered to Captain Murphy since he's been here." The loss of personal memory, name, birthday, "Who am I" is a late finding in Alzheimer's. This man was far too functional to be at that advanced a state of disease.

"Maybe he's just crazy?" Steve said, proffering a new diagnosis.

Shaking my head in disagreement I said, "He doesn't appear psychotic. He certainly doesn't have the body habitus of a schizophrenic. He's clean, well dressed, recently shaved. That doesn't add up."

Steve shrugged his shoulders saying, "Well, I'm all out of ideas." We both watched as our *John Doe*, the name assigned any unidentifiable patient in the ER, wheeled by, returning from the scanner. Continuing to address him as Captain Murphy, Steve encouraged him to take a seat in the same exam room he'd occupied most of the day while I reviewed his test. As anticipated, the CT scan revealed a youngish-looking brain, some mild atrophy, but remarkably healthy.

"I suppose that's how you live to be this guy's age and still look so vigorous."

Pondering at my desk as more and more normal test results returned from the lab, I watched Captain Murphy or *John Doe*, or whoever he was, pace about the room. He'd removed the blanket when we returned from the parking lot, but had gotten cold I suppose and was now putting it back on. Perhaps he was planning on leaving?

Preemptively I asked, "Going somewhere, Captain?"

"I'm going home," he replied in a voice that sounded more like a pouting three year old than an adult man.

"Captain, I'd like to ask you a few questions, if I may, to evaluate how well you're thinking." He starred at me incredulously as though this was the most ridiculous request he'd ever heard before saying, "Doesn't look like I have any choice. Go ahead, ask your questions, young man."

"Okay, Captain, can you name the president of the United States?"

He laughed and said, "Of course I can!"

"Well?"

"It's… I can't seem to recall, but I'll know it when I hear it."

"Okay, let me give you a clue, he's a tall, handsome black man."

"Look, Doctor, I don't know what ridiculous game you're playing, but the president of the United States is most certainly not a black man. I'm finished with your absurd little experiment here. I'm going home!"

"And just where is home?" I asked, sincerely hoping he would recall.

"Can you give me an address? A telephone number perhaps?"

He squinted his eyes, desperate to recall, but could bring nothing to the surface. Then surprised at a flash of discovery, he said, "Three-fifteen Bond Street."

"Bond Street? There is no Bond Street in town. Where is Bond Street?"

"Cincinnati, Ohio," he said triumphantly.

"Cincinnati is hundreds of miles from here. Are you sure?"

"I'm sure," he said confidently.

"That's great. Can you tell me your name?"

He looked at me surprised and said, "I've already told you, John Murphy, Captain, 47-2630." Setting his jaw, his eyes again acquired a steely, faraway look.

Taking a calculated gamble that I might shock him and potentially jog his memory, I coolly responded, "Captain John Murphy died… June 4, 1945."

He again stated flatly, "John Murphy, captain, 47-2630." His eyes remained distantly focused, but tears began to form in the corners and soon were dripping onto his cheek. He began shaking, becoming mute.

"It's okay, I just want to help you," I said, taking his hand. That's when I took notice of his lapel pin; red, yellow, and blue, it was the emblem of the Thirteenth Army Air Force. Rubbing my index over its smooth surface, I quietly asked, "Is this yours? Is this what you did in the war?"

Softening, he nodded affirmatively, "Yes. Fifty missions without a scratch… then…"

He became very quiet, his eyes once again focused as if seeing a distant specter, a ghostly image emerging from a fog.

"Were you in Europe?"

"The Pacific, son. The Thirteenth Air Force served in the South Pacific."

"Tell me more. What did you fly?"

"B-24s."

"*Liberators*?"

"That's right," he smiled, pleased that someone else knew. "Best damn airplane ever made, if you ask me."

"From what I've read, the men who flew them loved them."

"We did! She was a great ship. Could take a whole lot of punishment and still bring you home safe."

"I guess I thought the B-24 was only used in Europe."

"Well mostly, I guess, but we used them in the Pacific as well. We bombed the hell out of Jap shipping."

I was intrigued. This man was clearly confused, but not psychotic. He was intelligent enough to subtly try to disguise his memory deficits, but like most people with early Alzheimer's, his distant memory, recollections of an earlier time period, seemed completely intact. Perhaps if he could tell me his story I could piece together enough information to get him home. Not that it was normal ER procedure, mind you, as I rarely had this much time to devote to any single patient, but here on this unusually slow day sat the only patient in the ER, affording me all the time in the world. We were snowbound and unlikely to get too much busier. Besides, I sensed that before me sat a man whose story was worth retelling. I always enjoy a good story, and all of a sudden he seemed delighted to share his.

"So tell me, where did you grow up?"

"Valdosta, Georgia," he said in a soft Southern twang, a characteristic that I should have picked up on before.

"What do you remember of your parents?"

"Everything about my daddy, not too much about my momma, not my real momma anyway. She died in childbirth."

"With you?"

"No, my brother Davey. She died when I was three years old."

"I'm sorry. Tell me more about your father," I said, not wanting him to stop and reflect on anything too painful, deterring our little bit of progress.

"Daddy was an attorney, a small-town lawyer, one of only two in the county at that time. He came home from the war and married my momma. They moved to Atlanta so he could go to school. I was born there in 1922, just a few weeks before he finished. I don't remember much about Atlanta because we moved to Valdosta when I was a baby. My granddaddy, my momma's daddy, had a big place on Main Street, right in the middle of downtown, and my momma and daddy and me moved in there with him."

"Was your granddaddy in law as well?

"No, he was a doctor like you, but not so fancy, I suppose. He practiced out of that house on Main Street for over fifty years. People were always coming and going. It was a pretty exciting place to grow up because nothing went on in the whole county that my granddaddy didn't know about. Everyone thought my granddaddy hung the moon. I was pretty proud just to know him, let alone be his kin. He raised Davey and me like we were his own children."

"What happened to your daddy?"

"Oh, he was around, physically at least, but I reckon when my momma died his soul just sort of shriveled up and died right along with her. Folks say he was pretty much outgoing and friendly before that, but that's not how I remember him. He wasn't mean or nothing, he just wasn't interested in us boys. I think he blamed us for taking Momma away from him. My granddaddy, on the other hand, was a different story. He took up the slack and raised Davey and me up proper. He took us fishing and played baseball with us. He was always firm but kind, honest in his dealings with folks. He made us toe the line, but I don't remember him ever spanking us, though I'm sure we deserved it a time or two. He just didn't have the heart, us boys with no momma and all…"

"What about your grandmother?"

"I never knew her except from a painting over the mantle. She died when Granddaddy was in France during the war. He said she got Spanish Influenza in 1918, the same disease that killed all them soldiers. She got sick and died in just two days. Granddaddy never forgave himself for not being at her side when she passed." Silent tears welled in his eyes, tears of pain for a much-loved grandfather who had lost his *raison de la vie*, now all these years ago.

"She was quite beautiful, at least that's what everyone who knew her in Valdosta told me. Granddaddy used to take Davey and me out to the cemetery to talk to her. I didn't understand back then, but I do now. He just loved her so much he wanted us to love her too." He sat quietly for a moment, a quirky, sad smile on his face.

"I haven't been back there in years," he said as way of explaining his pause.

"What about school?"

"Mine or Granddaddy's?"

"I meant yours."

"Oh? Well I went to Valdosta High School," he said without further elaboration.

"Were you a good student?" I asked, pushing him onward.

"I had to be. Granddaddy wouldn't tolerate anything less. He was a very goal-oriented man and demanded the same of us boys. He grew up dirt poor and still managed to go to medical school at Harvard. That was a pretty miraculous feat at the time. I remember at a very young age a burning desire to be the best at whatever I did, just so I could be like him. He was my hero and excelled at anything he put his mind to. Good or bad, I have Granddaddy to thank for instilling that same attitude in me. He taught me to peruse my dreams with everything I had. I can still hear him saying, 'Johnny, if you aim at nothing you'll hit it!'"

"So he was strict?"

"Not really, he didn't have to be. Davey and me were pretty good kids and we loved the old man too much to ever embarrass him. We both came to understand early that we were reflections of him. Everyone in town would know of any shortcomings, and we could be sure they'd be quick to tell him."

"How about sports?"

"Yep, did them too."

"Football?"

"Yes, but I didn't get to play much. Too scrawny. I was always the tallest and the skinniest kid in class. Not too good for football, if you know what I mean. I was pretty good at track, though. Cross-country. I was first in the state in '38, '39, and '40. That got me an athletic scholarship to Princeton. I got an academic scholarship, too, but not nearly as good as Davey's. I don't think he ever made less than an A his whole life.

"That's pretty impressive."

"Not too bad for a boy from a little backwoods Georgia town."

"Tell me about Davey. Is he still living?"

"That's a pretty shitty way to ask that question Doc," he said, obviously getting heated.

"I'm sorry. I meant no offense."

"None taken I suppose. Its just Davey isn't living. He died in 1944. Battle of the Bulge they called it. He was shot in the leg and pinned down by gunfire after he'd gone out to help an injured buddy. They both froze to death within earshot of their friends who couldn't get to them to help. I got a letter from one of them after the war telling me what really happened, how Davey died and all. I didn't know he'd been killed till after I got home myself."

"I'm sorry. He must have been quite a guy."

"Davey was the best. He could do anything he put his mind to better than anyone. He was always the best student, the best athlete. No telling what he could have done had he lived."

The old man suddenly wept openly, nightmarish memories more than half a century old still raw, wounds too painful to dwell upon once the scab had been picked away. After several quiet moments he said, "I blame myself. Davey couldn't wait to follow after me. He wanted to sign up when he was seventeen, but Granddaddy wouldn't let him. He snuck off and tried to sign up, but the recruiter in Macon called Granddaddy. He drove up and got him and brought him home. Davey finally agreed to wait till after graduation. He finished as class valedictorian and had a brilliant future, but he was determined to join the Army. He signed up the day after graduation, going back to Macon to that same Army recruiter. That was the spring of '44. By Christmas he was in the Ardennes." His voice cracked with emotion, "Jesus, he was only eighteen…"

"It sounds like he admired you very much."

The old man nodded, clearing his eyes of tears. "That's why he was hell-bent on signing up. If he had only waited a month he probably would have gotten to have a life."

"We just don't know, I guess, how profoundly a simple decision will affect our lives."

"You're right, son. I'm eighty-nine as of my last birthday and I still don't understand it all."

Seeing another opportunity to get some useful information I asked, "When is your birthday?"

"April 28, 1922."

I jotted this down on his chart then asked, "And how did you find yourself in the Army?"

"I was at Princeton at the time, thinking I was gonna be an architect. I was in the library studying for finals on December 7th when Johnny Walters, a friend of mine, ran into the lobby and yelled out, 'The Japs just bombed Pearl Harbor.' I just stood up, speechless. I've got to admit I didn't know where Pearl Harbor was, but I was pretty sure it was ours. Well, finals be damned, we all enlisted in the Army the next morning, every one of us."

"Just curious, before Pearle Harbor did you have any clue that a war was coming?"

"I guess if I'd been paying attention I would have. There was talk of war all that fall, but I was too preoccupied to take much notice."

"School?"

"Should have been, but no, it was more Mary."

"Ah, your wife," I said with a knowing smile.

"Well she wasn't my wife at the time. She was still Mary McPhee. The prettiest girl I ever did lay eyes on," his eyes twinkled at the mere thought of her.

"Red hair, green eyes and an hourglass figure that was just too much, if you know what I mean, son."

I smiled and nodded.

"She was dating Dave Allerdice that fall. Dave was Princeton's big man on campus, quarterback of the football team. He set a passing record at Princeton that still stands to this day. I met Mary at a bonfire the night before a big game with Yale. I was smitten instantly, but I figured I didn't have a chance when I saw whom she left with. I'll never forget the date, Friday, November 14. Well our team beat Yale twenty to six the next day. Dave came back to campus on Monday looking bigger than life, but by that time I couldn't stand it anymore. I knew I had to have Mary or die trying. I sat and waited all day in the commons, just hoping I'd catch a glimpse of her. I guess I hadn't planned much past that, what I'd say and all, so when I finally did see her I stumbled all over myself asking her out. When she said yes, well I must have been the happiest guy on earth. It turned out that she was just as smitten with me, but I didn't know it at the time. The next three weeks were a blur; my studies went right out the window. Well, when Johnny Walters ran through the library going on about the Japs, the first thing I did was run and find Mary. She wasn't too keen on me signing up, but she understood why I had to. She agreed to marry me the next week and we got married on December fifteenth, just two days before I got on a train bound for Texas."

"Texas?"

"For flight training. When I signed up the sergeant asked what I wanted to do. I didn't really know, so I said pilot. Being a college man and all I got my first choice. Next thing I know, I'm on a train bound for Texas with two hundred other fellas, several of us leaving our new brides behind. It was odd, one of the saddest days of my life, but strangely exciting. I'd never flown before, never even been in an airplane. It sounded like a grand adventure. I felt like a warrior and there was blood, our blood, to avenge. I...*we* were gonna make them Japs pay. Extracting justice wasn't a fair trade for a new bride, all I was leaving behind, but I felt honor bound. It was an overwhelming, gut-level response, a calling I couldn't ignore."

"I can only begin to imagine, Captain. I remember my father expressing those same sentiments although he was too young to have served at the time.

He did his bit in Korea a few years later. I guess that's why your war has always fascinated me. It's thrilling to hear about it from the perspective of one who actually lived it!"

"You would have done the same," he said knowingly.

"I think I would," I smiled proudly, honored he believed we shared this value. Sometimes I feel like I was born in the wrong generation," my wistful statement made me sound like a child eager to consume another morsel of a bedtime story. Seeing he had a captivated audience, happy to have someone interested in his tale, he decided to bargain.

"Look, son, I'll tell you more than you want to know in exchange for another cup of that coffee and perhaps a doughnut?"

"Captain, you've got yourself a deal!"

CHAPTER 3

Upon finishing his doughnut, dipping the last of it in his coffee, he paused, dabbing a napkin to his mouth with a flourish of his wrist. Then coughing to clear his voice, he began to recite his epic with all the aplomb of a veteran showman.

"There was electricity in the air that day," he began with a flare, the timbre of his voice suddenly changed from our previous conversation.

I chuckled, "I see you've regaled others with this tale."

"Didn't your granddaddy teach you not to interrupt your elders?"

My face reddened, "Yes, sir, he did. Sorry. Please continue."

He harrumphed and began again…

"There was electricity in the air that day, a current, invisible to the naked eye, but real and palpable just the same. It was unseasonably cold. Exhaled breath quickly crystallized, wisps to be dissipated by the blustery wind. The clouds were low and dense, added to by the billowing effluent, a hot metallic smoke, the tinny tasting amalgam of vaporized water and steel and oil and coal soot being spewed skyward by multiple huge steam engines, vehicles assembled to carry us, the newly conscripted first to training and then to war. Mary was there and she clung to me, clung to me like she would never let go, oblivious to the hundreds of other folks on the platform around us. This same scenario was being repeated in every metropolis across the nation. Families and loved ones congregated on railroad boarding platforms and in bus terminals, embracing their beloved young men, all proud and fearful, a strange visceral brew, the emotion of war, an emotion shared by wives and parents for countless generations of mankind. Damned if you do, damned if you don't. Consoling words of perspective, for a greater cause, a cause worthy of the sacrifice. I found myself wondering what percentage of those gathered were looking upon their loved ones for the last time. It never once occurred to me that Mary might be doing the same.

The previous forty-eight hours were a blur. I'd asked Mary to be my wife and amazingly she'd said yes. Mary was only seventeen at the time and we couldn't legally get a marriage license in New Jersey without her parents' consent. Fearing the answer would be no since we'd only known each other six weeks, we decided it was easier to beg forgiveness than to ask permission. Taking matters into our own hands, we took the train into Manhattan after my roommate, Bob Meyer, a history major who was hoping to go to law school, advised us that New York's laws were a bit less restrictive. We found a justice of the peace within two blocks of Grand Central Station who'd of late been doing a booming business performing wedding ceremonies for couples finding themselves in the same desperate position in which we found ourselves. We paid our fees and said our vows before kissing and rushing to the sidewalk to hail a cab to take us straight way to the St. Marks Hotel on the Lower East Side. Again, Bob, who'd grown up in the city, recommended the St. Marks as cheap but clean. Mary insisted that I carry her over the threshold, so I picked her up on the sidewalk and carried her through the door only to be met by a steep staircase that ascended a flight and a half to the desk. When I started to put her down she said playfully, "No way, Pal. Not until we're officially across the threshold of our room am I going anywhere."

"Okay, fine, if that's the way you want it," whereupon I threw her over my shoulder like a sack of potatoes and carried her up the stairs. The top step was a fraction of an inch taller than all the previous and my toe caught it. We came precariously close to falling down all the steps when she said, "You can put me down while you register... you're gonna need your strength."

"Nothing doing. You tossed the gauntlet," I said, shifting her to my left shoulder as I signed the register. The clerk got in on the act, assigning us a room on the fourth floor. "Thanks pal," I said, sarcastically rolling my eyes at him before turning so Mary could retrieve the key. They exchanged pleasantries as I darted across the lobby before turning back to ask, "So, where is the elevator?" He just laughed and pointed me to the staircase where I began the trek up three more steep flights of stairs. I was pretty winded, but there was no way I was about to back down. When we got to room forty-three, top floor, end of the hall, I turned and let Mary unlock the door. Officially crossing the threshold I dropped her on the bed and mocked fainting, falling on top of her. We spent the next forty-eight hours entangled with one another, barely coming up for air, let alone food. I remember those days as the happiest two days of my life. Also as the fastest, because it seemed like only minutes till we found ourselves standing on the platform saying long, sad goodbyes.

"I promise," I said, making an X across my heart, "I'll send for you as soon as I can. At least we can be together before I ship out." She smiled, but I could see my words were small consolation. She made no sound, but large tears rolled from her eyes and down her cheeks before falling to the wood planking of the snow-dusted platform. Her reddened nose was running from both the cold and from crying. Sniffing, she held on to me until well after the conductor announced, "All aboard," and the train lurched forward and started to move. It accelerated faster than I anticipated so I had to tear myself away and run to catch the last hold before it was past the end of the platform and out of reach. "I love you!" I yelled back, unashamed of my public declaration, darting past other well-wishers to catch the rail. Standing on the step, the rail firmly in hand, I leaned out and watched Mary vigorously wave goodbye until I was well out of sight. Past all hope of catching another glimpse of her, I swung myself into the vestibule between cars and entered the rear door of what I soon discovered was a full Pullman car. The mood of the passengers was segregated into two camps; one loud and boisterous, almost celebratory of the inevitable victory, and the other subdued and reflective, yet mooning over loved ones left behind. I had to walk forward, passing through five cars, every seat occupied by men of my own age, before finding a vacant seat next to a shy, red-headed kid who sat staring at the floor. "Hello," I said trying to make small talk. "Is this seat taken?" He gestured silently with his hand as if to say, "Be my guest."

"Thanks. Where you from?" I asked, parking myself in the proffered seat. I was determined that, though sad over leaving Mary, I was going to fall in with the boisterous camp. He looked up at me as I stowed my small bag, the wheels of his mind spinning, trying to decipher if he were annoyed at my intrusion.

"Boston," he finally said.

"I'm Johnny," I said, offering my hand. He returned my handshake weakly and said, "Robert...Robert Cowen. What part of the South are you from?"

"Is it that obvious?"

He chuckled, "Yeah, pretty obvious."

"I suppose I do have a bit of a drawl. Valdosta, Georgia. You probably never heard of it.

"Can't say that I have, Johnny. Where you headed?"

"Texas! I reckon ol' Uncle Sam's gonna make a flier out of me. How about you?"

"Me, too... Texas, I mean. Going to Camp Walters for basic. I just finished high school so I guess the infantry is the best I can do...that or the Navy, but I can't swim so I picked the Army. My pop did the same twenty years ago and he did alright."

"Europe?"

"Yeah. He got gassed at the end of the war and spent two years in a hospital in France. He told me some about it for the first time just last night. He said it was hell on earth but if I followed orders, kept my head down and my feet dry I'd be fine. He still can't walk across a room without wheezing." At his words, as if conjuring up concealed demons I could feel a palpable fear rising, first in him, then in the boys around us listening to his words. As the train rolled southward the bluster and bravado of the day was slowly being eroded by the realities of going to war. Combat remained an abstract concept for all but a few professional soldiers, but the last generation of Americans, my father's generation, still remembered, still bore scars both physical and emotional. I turned and watched as a kid who couldn't possibly be more than sixteen exchanged his unusually pasty complexion for even greater pallor as he listened. He began to rhythmically rock ever so slightly, forward and back, his unfocused eyes latching onto me as I offered him my hand asking, "What's your name?"

"Jimmy, sir."

"Well I'm Johnny, but I'm no sir, not yet, anyway." Jimmy didn't say more so I asked him, "I hope you don't mind the question, but how old are you?"

"Eighteen," he said sheepishly, his eyes widening like a kid caught in the act, a grubby little hand in the cookie jar.

When I questioningly raised an eyebrow in disbelief he defensively responded, "Eighteen sir, I swear!" Given his quickness to bristle, I clearly was not the first to question his honesty on the matter. Robert Cowen came to the poor kid's rescue saying, "Relax kid, we believe you," a gracious lie, as no one around believed him.

There were similar conversations throughout the cars, subdued but excited, anxious to see what the next few weeks would hold. We were off to be soldiers, or sailors, or airmen, all with the same calling, that of kicking our enemy's, first Japan's and now Germany's collective butts. The whole world was officially at war. America was unprepared for a fight on this unprecedented scale and we had a lot of ramping up to do in order to catch up with the people who had declared war upon us. To that end it seemed the whole country was on the move by train or by bus.

Our train had started in Boston before proceeding to New York where I had boarded. Next stop was Baltimore, and then on to Philly, taking on several hundred more men at each stop. The train was soon filled to overflowing and so didn't stop again after Washington until we were in Texas. Houston was like a giant sieve where men from everywhere were being separated and segregated into this unit or that. The majority of men accompanying me on this journey south were put back on that same train to be dispersed to training facilities, both old and newly established throughout the American Southwest.

The sixty-five degrees that greeted us in Texas felt balmy in comparison to what I had left behind forty-eight hours ago, a bone chilling eighteen degrees, made colder by a stiff, blustery wind. Exchanging modes of transportation, instead of a train I soon found myself on a bus with forty other boys who chose or had been chosen to become pilots. The segregation process at the train stop deluded us with our first taste of feeling elite, though in retrospect I don't know why we should have had any notion of superiority. We were every bit as green and unproven as any of those men who were to be relegated to the trenches. Only one guy out of the forty on the bus had ever flown in an airplane let alone piloted one. What we on the bus possessed in common was our education. A college degree, or at least some college, was the minimum requirement to get into ranks of those to be trained as pilots. This proved early to be a deceptively inadequate measure, as merely attending college did not necessarily assure a new recruit possessed the intelligence, eye-hand coordination, cunning, bravery, or any other quality requisite to success as a military pilot, but on the bus that day we remained gloriously oblivious to those requisites.

At this juncture we rode along together through the scrub-littered West Texas countryside with an unsubstantiated notion that we, the chosen, were all frightfully superior. We reveled in this notion, albeit timidly at first of false modesty, but over the next four hours this modesty gave way to full-blown grandiosity. When we took to the skies the Axis would capitulate out of fear of our imagined prowess. We would prove our mettle and change the course of both warfare and aviation. We believed we would change the world, a feat to be accomplished in short order, dreams easy to conjure while we were yet oblivious, unknowing of the challenges Uncle Sam had in store for us. En route to Abilene our bus stopped and we were billeted for the night at a small hotel on the outskirts of San Antonio. All forty of us were now fast friends. The natural jockeying for top billing, inevitably looming on the horizon, had yet to commence. We walked together, still sporting civilian clothing and haircuts, to a small bar where a grizzled, gap-toothed older lady, and I use the term lady to convey her sex and not her demeanor, took our drink orders. The arrival en masse of such a large group in an establishment accustomed to serving perhaps three or four patrons at any given time appeared to both surprise and delight her. She was quick to let us know she would not tolerate any "rough-housing or tomfoolery from a bunch of snot-nosed, barely-out-of-diaper recruits." When we all agreed to behave ourselves she happily began pouring drinks, serving us the nastiest rotgut whisky I'd ever tasted, not that I'd tasted much whisky at that point. After a few drinks the foul brew seemed to go down smoother and by 1:00 a.m. it tasted pretty damn good. There were no women present other than Daisy that night, not that I was looking for women, being only days married and still mooning over the lack of my bride, but Daisy was a caricature, not unlike an Al Capp cartoon, that I couldn't fail to notice. Daisy Mae Porter at seventy-three was clearly a survivor, a tough old bird who, though fifty plus years our senior, was still tough enough to kick most of our asses in a fair fight. I just knew I wasn't man enough to challenge her even if I had been inclined to do so. Under Daisy's watchful eye we drank and laughed and got drunk and laughed louder and got drunker and laughed louder still, but we all behaved as promised, being young and unsure of ourselves and even more unsure of how harshly Uncle Sam would punish us if we dared to get into trouble. These were uncharted waters for the majority of us, being the first time we had been on our own, away from home or schools or sweethearts and in the companion of only men. There were seven among us who had been married less than two weeks who were still trying to figure out how we were to behave as husbands, let alone adult men.

I don't remember much about how that night ended, but somehow I awoke the following morning in bed with a tremendous headache, still wearing the same clothes I had worn the day before. At 5:00 a.m. the heavy fisted bus driver was banging on our door, laughing mercilessly at our shared plight. I now hated this guy more than anyone I'd ever known. I wanted to kill him just to stop his relentless pounding, as did everyone else in our group. He remained agonizingly persistent and somehow, almost miraculously it now seems, got us everyone loaded on that bus and headed for our destination in Arizona, all before 6:00 a.m. I discovered later that he and Daisy were in cahoots; he'd been passing this way with busloads of new recruits for some time now. We thought we represented the first wave of volunteers after Pearl Harbor, but Uncle Sam had been quietly building his air force since the advent of the war in Europe. Our civilian bus driver had been making weekly runs for two years now. Daisy paid him a dime at first, then a quarter dollar a head as the size of each arriving bus's passenger list grew.

The bus ride was quieter that morning; the only sound the winding of the diesel, the tires on the pavement, and the son-of-a-bitch driver whistling some new tune. As the day heated up, as days do in West Texas, even in winter, I was as dry as the scrub shrubbery we were passing. I must have drifted off, waking around noon when we pulled into a lone filling station diner where the bus took on fuel. All forty of us piled out and quickly emptied the ice chest of any liquid we could find. I thought the dime I spent on that Coca Cola, twice the going rate at the time, was the best money I'd ever spent in my life. I purchased a second and a packet of Goody's Headache Powder in the hopes of purging myself of the evil now possessing my body. It worked well enough that I bought a ham sandwich and the last piece of pie in the store before boarding the bus for the last leg of the trip. It occurred to me that everything I needed at that moment, though grossly overpriced, could be found waiting for us at that little oasis in the middle of nowhere. It was as though this was a planned, well-orchestrated descent into hell.

Once again aboard the bus, the driver whistled a merry tune. I suppose I would be jolly too if I possessed such a well-oiled machine to make money. Regardless of the fleecing, I felt like a man reborn after the Coke and headache powder, but still didn't feel much like talking. I guess the other boys aboard felt the same way because the conversation for the remainder of the trip was pretty subdued, becoming even more so after it got dark, the sun setting early as it was almost the winter solstice. I snoozed again, only to be jerked back to consciousness by the harsh voice of one Sergeant Richards, a snarling, imposing presence I soon discovered was to be addressed only as "Sergeant Richards, sir," his barked instructions before ordering us to get our sorry butts off the bus. We arrived at the camp around 11:30 p.m. By 12:30 a.m. my already short hair had been shorn and my civilian clothes stuffed into a khaki duffle bag, replaced with a set of new, itchy green fatigues. We followed Sergeant Richards to a Quonset hut-type barracks and were told to take a bunk. Lights were out at 1:00 a.m. and I lay there wondering what the hell I had signed up for. The recruiter told us that as pilot candidates we would be commissioned officers and not have to go through basic training, but my present circumstances seemed an awful lot like what I expected basic training to be. I didn't lay there too long before reveille sounded awakening me at 5:00 a.m. We all dressed quickly, and then haphazardly lined up to wait whatever might happen next. At precisely 5:05 a.m. Sergeant Richards came in bellowing "Good morning, girls! Time to rise and shine."

His demeanor had mellowed ever so slightly as he sat down and explained why we were being treated differently than we had been led to expect.

"You boys are in the pipeline and there's a clog downstream. The last class doesn't graduate from Classification for two more weeks, so I've been given the job of entertaining you boys in the meantime."

Joe Barnes, a skinny red headed kid from Queens who had been in the backseat of the bus and not said three words since we left Houston spoke up saying, "I thought we didn't have to go through boot camp like the infantry, at least that's what I was told."

Several others chimed in "Yeah, me too."

Sergeant Richards snarled, "Well you little girls can go right on back to your mama's teat, but if you ever want to see an airplane in this man's army you've got to get there through me. Anyone man enough to become a real soldier haul your ass out front and line up. The rest of you sissies can go report for KP since the kitchen is all you're good for." I was smart enough to keep my mouth closed, and was really glad I did because Sergeant Richards rode Joe Barnes unmercifully from that moment on. We all lined up in front of the barracks without further comment. Stepping out of the barracks that morning it was still just as dark as it had been when we arrived the night before. We stood at attention, trying our best not to shiver in the morning cool while the sergeant explained that we were to be trained, as would any other recruit while we waited to be transferred to Classification. As the sun rose on our workout I finally got a good view of the camp. There were hundreds of men about, all going through the same rigors we were, but conspicuously absent was the evidence, sound, smell, or sight of an aircraft of any sort. My heart sunk as the reality of Richards' words, more promise than prophetic, became increasingly clear. That morning I did more push-ups than I had done in all the rest of my life combined. Calisthenics were followed by a little five-mile run before lunch. After leaving the chow hall we were introduced to the 1911 model Colt .45, a fine weapon that, before we were allowed to shoot, we had to demonstrate our ability to disassemble, clean, then reassemble for inspection by Sergeant Richards. Later in the afternoon we took another five-mile run, then showered before supper. The group shower proved to be a bit unnerving for the most shy of the group, me included. I left the shower with the knowledge that all men were *Not* created equal, a little secret I kept from Mary for years to come. After supper we were to report to the quartermaster to be issued gear; military equipment we were to have stowed in a precise manner prior to lights out. I slept more deeply that night than I ever imagined possible in spite of the fact that I was seething with anger. I hadn't known what to expect in training, but this was clearly not it. In fact, this was the exact opposite of what I'd been told by the recruiter, but we were at war and I was determined to do whatever it took to get the job done. We all were.

The following morning at precisely 5:00 a.m. we were awakened to start another day of grueling physical exertion and training. The reverie of superiority we'd felt at being selected for our elite group was quickly and deftly being transformed into anger. The more I endured, the angrier I got, but my anger was misplaced, aimed not at the Germans or the Japanese, but rather at Sergeant Richards. This intense, worthless gauntlet all seemed completely futile, a cruel and unusual punishment inflicted on us by an envious inferior solely because we had been singled out as special. I wondered then, as I still do now, if Sergeant Richards was trying to compress the usual eight weeks of basic training into the two weeks he had available. We were to be aviators, why did we need to know the finer points of hand-to-hand combat? Who cared if I ever mastered the art of caring for an M-1 rifle? I doubted I'd ever even see another after the two weeks are up. I believed then, and still do, that Richards was a sadistic pig who seemed to delight in our physical pain. The more he pushed us, the more I was determined to endure, if only to have the satisfaction of returning some day as his superior officer and eating him alive.

Our group endured the two weeks. Even Joe Barnes, who Sergeant Richards had singled out from day one as his whipping boy, survived. On the last day I was rewarded with three letters from my sweet Mary, God, how I missed her. Especially at night when it was quiet and I had time to think.

I heard much later that Joe was killed, shot down on his first mission in Europe by an experienced ME-109 pilot. That would have made him twenty-one... twenty-two at the most. I always liked Joe. He was one of those guys who never seemed to get a break.

CHAPTER 4

The morning was cool and crisp, the low rising sun invading a cloudless sky as we boarded the bus for Arizona. Our same group of forty was all aboard with the addition of three more guys who had joined our group a little late. They had straggled in, arriving a full day later than most of our group, having missed the train out of San Francisco. True to form, Sergeant Richards had not been terribly forgiving or forgetting of this indiscretion. We all felt worse for those three than we did for ourselves. Just like Dante, there were levels to Richards' hell, but rather than sin or evil for which the departed were justly punished, Richards assigned one to a given level for seemingly the most innocuous transgressions. Poor Joe Barnes found himself in the deepest level while the three new guys were assigned just slightly higher. To this day I still don't know if Sergeant Richards was truly evil or if he really believed his harsh treatment of us was a means to an end, better preparing us for the fight we would soon enter.

Bob Sullivan was from Fresno, the sweetest, most pleasant guy you could ever meet. We became instant friends the moment we first met. He was a law student at Loyola prior to heeding Uncle Sam's call. His two companions, Jim Thorpe and John Bell, were classmates at Cal Poly, both training to be engineers. Upon learning of their intent to leave school and enlist, the dean of Cal Poly's College of Engineering invited both to stay on campus in San Luis Obispo. The university was feverishly preparing to open classes aimed at training naval and army aviators. Jim and John, both being known commodities on campus, were promised positions in their new program. They declined, thinking they might enter the fray sooner by joining the Army and going straight away to flight training in Arizona. The three had met on the train en route to Phoenix and, as had we, boarded the train fully expecting to begin flight training at an undisclosed camp. Originally transported to an overcrowded airbase, they were turned away for their own little unscheduled descent into hell.

Like men freed from prison, we were all elated to the point of giddiness, but unlike our ride two weeks ago, this bus ride was devoid of any false sense of bravado. If nothing else our stint at basic training made each of us keenly aware that we were no more special than any other young man who had answered the call to duty. Happy to have run the gauntlet, though humbled by the experience, we contentedly rode on a bus through a beautiful New Mexico morning to what we hoped would be our introduction to flight training. After stops for both lunch and supper and an unscheduled delay for a flat tire, we rolled into Glendale, Arizona at about 0230. I liked saying that, "0230." A new way to communicate the time of day that Uncle Sam insisted we all must use as it removed the ambiguity of 2:30 a.m. versus 2:30 p.m. I'd never considered the potential ambiguity having never before had the need to communicate the hour so clearly. We were met by a brand new facility opened in January of 1941 under the auspices of the AAFTC or Army Air Corps Flight Training Command. Thunderbird Field, as it was called, was built not by the Army but by private contractors and financiers, many of who were popular movie stars enticed to invest at the behest of General Hap Arnold. I remember reading in the *New York Times* about him before the war. Lots of folks thought General Arnold was a nut job, but it turns out he was a visionary who saw the looming clouds of war and realized how woefully underprepared America was to defend itself. He engaged the private community, convincing them there would soon be money to be made training pilots to fly in a war he foresaw as inevitable. He must have been pretty persuasive, because different groups of well-heeled folks around the country began building flight-training facilities with little more than General Arnold's word they would indeed be repaid by a grateful American nation as collateral. Enlisting as soon as we did after the US declared war on the Japs, we thought we would be the first to be trained. As it turned out, we weren't even in the second wave of pilots to be trained. Men had begun signing up in ever-increasing numbers since late 1939, some so eager to enter the anticipated fight that they joined the air forces of foreign nations. They were not without precedent but following in the footsteps of the *Escadrille de Lafayette*, a group of American men who had joined in the defense of France prior to the US officially declaring war on the Central Powers, igniting a volunteer spirit in the Great War a mere twenty years earlier.

We were surprised to find hundreds of men already engaged in various stages of training, and to our delight that training was in learning to fly airplanes rather than in learning to march in the blazing sun or do calisthenics to the point of exhaustion. As I got off the bus I couldn't take my eyes off the silver and yellow two-seater airplanes repeatedly passing overhead. These airplanes seemed to be everywhere, an almost constant, circuitous line of cadets taking off and landing in the brightly painted trainers. A respectful sergeant welcomed us to Thunderbird, and while accompanying us to the officer's mess for supper, explained the nature of the show going on above us. The men up there flying were student pilots all performing touch-and-go landings. They were nearing completion of the first stage of their flight training, which he pointed out was obvious because they were alone or "solo" in the planes. He also pointed out a crowd of men he identified as flight instructors nervously watching en masse from the ground. The aircraft were Ryan PT-22 Recruits, "The basic flight trainer here at Thunderbird." I watched in amazement for several minutes. We all did, feeling a flush of excitement, realizing it soon would be us up there showing of what we were made.

Over supper, and I might add, a better supper than what we had recently been accustomed to, we were welcomed to the field by Colonel White, the base commander. Everyone at Thunderbird seemed to be according us with the respect due a fellow officer, an honor that we all hopefully were destined soon acquire. It was a marvelous change from how we had been treated that same morning. Colonel White seemed to be an agreeable enough fellow, but I hoped that, with any luck, he would never have reason to know my name. After pleasantries he turned the welcomes over to Captain Mike Wallaby, the chief flight instructor who outlined the schedule, a curriculum that would occupy our waking hours for the next one hundred and eighty days. The first three weeks would be a period of rigorous testing, designed first and foremost to determine if we were both physically and intellectually fit to be Army aviators. The second goal of testing was "To determine at what post we best fit." He laughed aloud at this comment, pointing out this segregation could be accomplished with a ruler. The cockpit of a fighter could only accommodate a man so tall. Any man over six feet three inches in height had better be happy about becoming a bomber pilot, just as any man under five feet five inches tall was destined only to fly fighters, "as his little legs couldn't reach the rudder pedals." This brought hoots of half-hearted laughter as most men in my group had joined up with the idea of becoming fighter pilots. Since the Great War, books and radio had invested the fighter pilot with a cachet of glamour and romance. I was glad I was only six feet three inches tall and still had a chance at a fighter, but either way, at least I'll be flying and not sloshing through the mud.

After we had been tested, Ground School would begin. That would involve navigation, mechanics, and aerodynamics, a term I'd never heard, but which was described as the science of flight. It would be a full six weeks before we would actually touch an airplane, a statement that brought groans from the crowd. "Don't you worry boys, we'll have you in the air and killing Japs and Nazis in no time," a comment that elicited cheers from the group.

The second six weeks was Primary Flight Training, a feat to be accomplished in the little Ryan PT-22s. If we were successful in passing this obstacle, and at present ninety percent of cadets were, we would advance to the next stage of training called Basic Flight Training. Here the airplane used would be a BT-13. Bigger, faster, stronger than the Ryan, these airplanes, built by Consolidated-Vultee, were affectionately dubbed the Vultee Vibrator. It didn't take much of an imagination to figure out why. More complicated and difficult to fly, the washout rate would on average remove another twenty-three percent from our ranks. Those who survived this obstacle, and survival was increasingly becoming an appropriate word as cadets were killed in flying mishaps on a weekly, if not daily, basis, then matriculated to the final level, Advanced Flight Training. Flying at this level was accomplished in a plane produced in Texas by the North American Aircraft Corporation known as the AT-6 and aptly called the *Texan*. Again a quantum leap in both power and complexity, the *Texan* would prove to be a difficult taskmaster. The room grew quiet enough to hear a pin drop as Wallaby reported the attrition rate at this level from either washouts or fatalities were another twenty percent. For a while we sat silently and let that statistic sink in. We had a dangerous challenge ahead of us, a challenge very unforgiving of any inadequacies. For the first time, the gravity of my chosen occupation became real to me. Was I up to the task? Clearly forty percent of the men who came before me were not. What would prove the deciding difference? Was I smarter or merely as smart? Was I even smart enough? I mulled this over, not hearing much more as Wallaby went on to describe what lay ahead for each group after our time here at Thunderbird. He gave us one last opportunity to seek other assignments. No one accepted. We were then dismissed for the evening after Wallaby announced, "Class starts at 0730. Enjoy your last night of freedom."

Outside the officers' mess there was a bank of about ten telephones where men were already lined up to make calls home to wives or loved ones. Mary had written me every day and I had returned letters, though not as frequently. This would be my first chance to talk to her since leaving her standing on that boarding platform in New York three weeks ago. I couldn't wait to hear her sweet voice, but it looked like I would have to, as I was about the twentieth guy back in line. I was excited to tell her that once I had made it to advanced training she could come and stay with me, living in one of a group of small houses off base the Army had constructed for just that purpose. It might only be for five or six weeks, but at this point I'd settle for any time with her I could get.

As I waited I thought about the newfound admiration I had for the men at this camp. More so than rank, as most of the men present would soon equally be commissioned as first lieutenants, this staging created a pecking order rendering those who had survived the full prescribed course of training without either washing out or being killed at the top of the heap. Though I was a little scared I was also excited. Now, more than ever, I desperately wanted to make it to the top of that heap.

CHAPTER 5

Sleeping to 0700 that first morning felt decadent. Bob Sullivan and I shared a small room, a far cry from the Quonset hut we slept in the night before. In spite of the madness of war driving this training frenzy, we felt as though the Army was now going out of its way to treat us as the officers and gentlemen they were grooming us to become. Like a bad dream, the perceived unfairness of the preceding two weeks, all of the hardship and pent up anger was quickly fading away in the light of the manner in which we were now being treated. I actually began to feel lucky having run the gauntlet and suffered the blows, as they created an appreciation for all that I now possessed.

Classification testing and ground school proved to be both rigorous and demanding, with a whole lot of information being presented to us in a very brief period of time. Though the process was intense, I consistently excelled, and upon completion found myself at the top of my class by a substantial margin. I don't really think I was that much smarter than the guys around me, rather I just seemed to understand the secret art of how to take a test. Modesty aside, perhaps it was a little of both, especially because I didn't feel like I was working nearly as hard as the majority of my classmates. Regardless of the reasons, God, my brains, or to whatever I owed a debt of gratitude for the nature of my success, I was dead on track to achieve my new ultimate goal, Fighter Pilot. It was kind of funny to now have this as a goal since only three short months prior I wouldn't have given the notion of becoming a pilot a second thought. Of course, neither was I married three months ago.

The war had dramatically altered the lives of every person I knew. Now Mary and flying fighters were my entire world, all I could think of from sunup to sundown.

Mary moved back in with her parents to save money while she waited to come join me once I got to Advanced Training. All in all, it was probably a good thing she couldn't come right away. Even though I wasn't necessarily working as hard as I could have been, Mary would've been a distraction, a beautiful, voluptuous, amazing distraction, but a distraction nonetheless. I probably would also have worried about the distraction a beautiful gal like Mary would naturally be to a camp full of virile young men, especially given the paucity of any women, beautiful or not, in the vicinity. Jealousy? Perhaps, but my growing jealousy made me miss her all the more. Fortunately I was able to call her twice a week, and though it cost me a big chunk of my pay, it was worth every penny.

Upon finishing all of my classes in the ninety-ninth percentile, I had delusions of grandeur. "The Army should consider giving me command of my own training facility," I quipped over beers at the officers club. This was said in jest of course, as I still had a long way to go before earning my wings. Despite my success, I harbored secret fears and doubts. Had not better, smarter men than me finished in the top of their ground school class only to wash out in the cockpit? Just because I was great in the classroom did not make me a fighter pilot. I still didn't really know I if I could fly; I'd not, as yet, even touched the controls of an airplane. All that would change Monday at 0700 when we began primary flight training.

The weather was perfect that morning, low humidity, not a visible cloud in the sky and best of all, no wind. In all my life to that point I had not thought about the weather as much as I had this past weekend. I'm not sure why I was so fixated because the weather had been perfect since my arrival in Arizona four weeks ago, perfect, that is, except for the wind. There were days when the wind had blown steady at twenty knots with gusts as high as thirty-five knots. Statistically those were the days when most of the fatal mishaps occurred on the flight line, the days that made novices wince, especially those so nouveau as yet to have flown. It was an escalating anxiety, this fear of the wind, shared by all, though spoken of by only a few and then only in short, knowing sentences so as not to broadcast one's own fear. The war would not wait for optimum flying conditions, so neither did nor could flight training, wind or no wind, fear or no fear. The American flag hanging from the flagpole at the entry gate of Thunderbird was visible from my quarters. It was the first thing I looked at upon awakening every morning, its response to the wind immediately alerting me to the conditions of my invisible opponent, brisk or calm, blowing from one direction or variable, was the speed constant or were there intermittent gusts? It was the gusts, the wind's treacherous, unpredictable thrusts and parries that were the most feared. Praying for either calm or consistent winds, seeing a limply hanging flag this morning brought me solace as it represented the best of all possible circumstances, no wind.

After breakfast and an initial briefing from the chief flight instructor, which included some inevitable jokes about new cadets returning our meals later in a bag, we walked together to the flight line. Though all of us were excited, conversation remained sparse in anticipation of this our first test, real and tangible, not merely ink and paper. We walked to a line of Ryan PT-22 trainers, their nearly new aluminum fuselages glistening in the morning sun. At each airplane stood two people; the crew chief, an enlisted man, corporal or sergeant who was responsible for the mechanical workings of the airplane, and an instructor, an officer, lieutenant or captain, who would be the man responsible for teaching me to fly. Every trainer had a unique designation, a three-digit number painted in twenty-inch numerals on the rear of the fuselage. Every student had been randomly assigned to a specific aircraft and crew. Mine was Ryan 056, so I walked down the flight line tentatively looking for my mount. Finding it ninth in a row of thirty I was greeted by Sergeant Mike Cox, a man ten years my senior and quick to let me know that this was *his* aircraft and I'd better take care of it if I knew what was good for me. The other man awaiting me in front of Ryan 056 was my flight instructor, Lieutenant Dan Scott. In stark contrast to Sergeant Cox, Lieutenant Scott appeared to be fresh out of high school. He smiled and offered me his hand and then as an afterthought saluted. We began a *walk around* of the little airplane with Sergeant Cox pointing out several mechanical items that would be my responsibility to inspect before each and every flight.

"It's not your job to *fix* anything, I don't care how handy you are. Just inspect it and report any problems to me or one of my guys."

"Yes sir," I said.

"I'm not the sir, he is," pointing to Lieutenant Scott.

"Sorry, just my upbringing," I said.

At this he offered me his first smile revealing wide gapped teeth.

"I think we've got ourselves a winner this time," he said to Dan.

On completion of his comments he turned the show over to Lieutenant Scott, who was putting on his parachute. Checking his own chute, he then calmly proceeded to instruct me on how to buckle mine on. I climbed into the front cockpit and he crouched on the wing, reaching in to point out various controls before instructing me how to fasten my seatbelt and shoulder harness. Satisfied I was safely belted in, he said, "Let's go fly!" I responded by grinning from ear to ear.

"One last thing, we have no real way for you to ask me questions once we fire it up." He must have seen this statement shake my confidence, because he quickly added, "Don't worry, you'll be able to hear me talking to you. See, this is a rubber hose connecting my mouthpiece to your helmet. Just listen and do what I say and you'll be fine. If you feel me rattle the stick that means let go, I've got the airplane, understand?"

"Yes sir," I said sharply.

"Well let's go then."

I waited as he climbed into the back cockpit and put his helmet on.

"I'll walk you through this first start up," he said, then shook the stick at which I let go of mine.

"Just wanted to see if you were paying attention."

"Yes sir," I answered then remembered he couldn't hear me.

He laughed, "I heard you but only because the blade isn't spinning yet."

I gave him thumbs up.

"Atta boy," he responded. "Reach up and give the engine two shots of primer like I showed you." I quickly complied, then watched the airplane come alive. The controls in the front cockpit, attached by cables or rods to the controls in the back cockpit, began moving as if by magic. One by one, airplanes up and down the row belched oily smoke and sprang to life in a cacophony of asynchronous engine noise. Mike Cox stood at the ready awaiting Dan's signal, a salute, and then briskly snapped the prop down. The five cylinder Kinner radial engine responded with a pop POP pop, an ungainly song created by the engine's uneven number of cylinders, two of which ported to the right side of the airplane and three of which ported to the left. This gave the Ryan a distinctive sound not unlike my grandfather's gasoline-powered washing machine when the load in its tub became unbalanced. Funny the things you remember from your childhood.

Dan had me throttle the airplane up to 2300 RPM, which took me several seconds as I scanned the unfamiliar instrument panel for the tachometer. Once the engine settled at the required setting, Dan checked the magnetos, first right, and then left.

"Take note of the engine settings, especially the oil pressure, then pull the throttle back to idle." Wordlessly I complied, and then we waited as this same ritual was being repeated in various iterations up and down the line.

"That's called a run-up. You'll do a run-up in every airplane you fly before you leave the ground. Every flight, every time, understand?" I nodded yes.

One by one, beginning with the airplane farthest to the right, then proceeding in sequence down the line, each plane took its turn pulling up to the taxiway, turning left, then passing, as if in review, each of the other airplanes awaiting their opportunity to move. I watched as the eight planes to my right passed before me, each making shallow turns right, then left, then right again. Intuitively Dan said, "You have to serpentine. You can't see over the nose and you'll hit the airplane in front of you if you don't. Operating as a group we always start with the airplane parked furthest to the right rolling first. We do it this way, so you only have to worry about traffic coming from one direction."

"That seems smart," I said, then realized it was said to myself.

As the ninth airplane in sequence, our turn finally came. Dan said, "Throttle to 1500 RPM and drive us out." Timidly I advanced the throttle and the airplane began rolling. I pushed the stick hard to the left, but the Ryan didn't respond.

Dan laughed and said, "This isn't a car, cadet! You steer with your feet," at which I felt him push the left rudder pedal and the plane quickly followed command. "Now *you* steer, gentle right and left turns, please." I did my best to comply, but moved slowly and with trepidation, as steering with my feet felt completely foreign to me. I quickly discovered that Dan was correct; each time the nose passed through the centerline I lost sight of the aircraft in front of me.

We taxied in this fashion the half mile to the end of the runway, then watched as each plane in sequence assumed a position at runway's end, opened its throttle full and began accelerating down the runway. It occurred to me that I would not be able to see over the nose going straight down the runway and I felt a little panicky. Thankfully Dan shook the stick before we pulled out, saying, "Sit back and enjoy your first airplane ride." I must have been pretty excited and scared, because I had a death grip on the stick and I didn't hear a word he said. He got my attention by rapping me on the knee with the stick. Jarred from my brain lock, I complied, letting go. "You can fly it next time," he said as a way of consolation. I gave him two thumbs up and did my best to relax and allow him show me what I was getting myself into.

It was somewhat comforting to know that I was not the only person having fears or anxiety at this juncture, as many men asked for transfers to other realms of service immediately following their initiation flight. In some schools this early attrition rate was as high as two percent of all cadets. Though I feared the next few moments, I was determined not to fall into that group before giving flying my best shot. My anticipation heightened as we taxied to the end of the runway and stopped. "Here we go," he said, smoothly advancing the throttle. "Keep looking straight ahead but follow the edges of the runway with your peripheral vision," he shouted over the now roaring engine. The airplane bowed to his wishes and began rolling down the runway, slowly at first overcoming inertia, but quickening gradually to a lively pace at which the tail began flying and lifted off the ground. With this shift in attitude I could see the rapidly oncoming world over the nose, the airplane careening faster and faster. I initially thought we were flying at this point, but a couple of bumps let me know that the main wheels were still attached, albeit loosely, to terra firma. One breathless moment later we were flying. I will forever remember this moment as the second most exhilarating experience in my life, not as good as sex, but good just the same. It felt and looked and smelled amazing. Like many people I'd had dreams of flying, but this reality was so much better. I could now comprehend why so many pilots waxed poetic upon seeing God's world from a vantage point previously known only to Him.

Once free of earth I was amazed how quickly skyward the airplane climbed. Leveling off at around five thousand feet above the ground, we began some gentle turns, first right then left. I'd expected to fear falling from so great a height, but it never once entered my mind, completely lost after seeing the view from this vantage point. I was too excited, too enthralled, too overwhelmed, and even perhaps too stupid to feel afraid. Everything below seemed so small, so distant, ground features appearing almost toy-like. The mountains to the west, so imposing on the ground, became miniscule in perspective. As best I could, I turned in my seat to let Dan see the delight in my eyes. "No fear here, no sir! I'm going to be a pilot," I wanted to shout to him. Seeing I was enjoying myself Dan upped the ante a bit, first by doing tighter and tighter turns requiring more and more bank. The feeling of g-force pushing me deeper into my seat added a visceral zing to my giddiness. My excitement must have been contagious, eliciting a barrel roll, first left then right, diving a little bit before each to pick up enough speed. "I see you like this." I responded with two thumbs up held at arm's length into the onrushing slipstream. "Okay then, we'll have a little more fun. Put your feet on the rudders and take the stick. Try and keep her straight and level." Eagerly I did as instructed, my early success at doing this little task filling me with a sense of pride and accomplishment, albeit a bit prematurely. After several minutes of this we were closing in on the western mountain range so Dan suggested, "Now try a shallow turn to the left." As I complied the airplane began not only to turn but also to ascend. "A little forward pressure on the stick to keep her level. Just aim to keep the nose on the horizon, and don't forget the rudders." He was correct as my feet had yet to move. When I did, the airplane again started a gradual turn, but this time was descending. "Now just a hint of back pressure... atta boy!"

We continued turns, right and left for the better part of an hour, my confidence growing by leaps and bounds before Dan said, "I've got the airplane." The airplane immediately becoming more energetic and coordinated in Dan's capable hands, we banked to what seemed more than ninety degrees as Dan pushed us into a steep descent. Pulling level at two thousand feet he asked, "Do you see the field?" Looking about briskly for several seconds I finally had to admit I didn't with a headshake. "Look about twenty degrees left of the nose." When again I didn't respond, he added, "About five miles." Searching the given coordinates I finally caught a glimpse of the waiting airstrip, pointing it out in response.

"Good, cadet. That's where we came from and that's where we're going. Get a good mental picture of where it's located in reference to the town and roads and the mountains. That's your home for the next several months." As we got closer to the field I saw Dan's head in the mirror, darting back and forth as he searched the sky for other cadets. Spotting one he said, "Traffic at your nine o'clock. There are lots of other folks in the sky today. Keep your eyes peeled and point out any other planes you see." I nodded and began searching for traffic in earnest. Oblivious to their presence only seconds ago, I quickly spotted eight airplanes, as all the Ryans seemingly converged on the airport at once. "See the wind sock on the tower? It points the direction the wind is blowing. Always land and take off into the oncoming wind if you can. The wind is out of the south, which is true about ninety-five percent of the time here. We're going to fly south over the centerline of the runway at about eight hundred feet above the ground. About mid-field we're going to take a steep right turn. Put your hands on the controls, but let me fly the airplane. Just feel what I do and follow." Again I nodded understanding. We joined into the procession, a conga line of five other airplanes, two over the runway and the other three turning to follow an invisible circuitous path to the ground. I watched the parade of small airplanes with trepidation, but even without communication between these aircraft our simultaneous arrival still appeared a well-choreographed dance. The throttle moved and I felt in my throat the dramatic slowing of the aircraft that followed. Parallel to the runway we began our descent with Dan ratcheting down more and more flap surface in ten-degree increments. Once aligned with the runway he began gradually decreasing the throttle, finally arriving at a full aft position in coincidence with the main landing gear touching the ground. Firmly planted on earth, the airplane slowed and the tail gradually settled, rendering me once again unable to see anything over the nose. Rolling down the runway Dan asked, "Can you see the end of the runway? When I answered no, he laughed saying, "That's why you get your ass off the runway just as soon as you're slow enough to make a safe turn." Once we had made that turn and joined the parallel taxiway he said, "You take it from here." At this my feet came alive and I began turning left, then right, then left again, a serpentine dance, careful to keep a safe distance from the airplane in front of me. Even shallow turns on the ground were more difficult than I had imagined, as using my feet to steer felt foreign to me. I turned too sharply at one point and the tail did its best to swing around to take the lead. Dan used the throttle and brakes to recover the situation then allowed me to continue, albeit watching me a little more closely from that point on. On the tarmac, pleased that I had not repeated my ground loop, let alone struck anything, Dan again took the controls and briskly turned us into the same parking position from which we had started. Holding that position with the brakes he revved the engine up to ten inches of manifold pressure for several seconds before closing the throttle completely, pulling the mixture control to full lean the engine sputtered an asynchronous pop POP wheeze, a last gasp as if offended to be dismissed before falling silent. Before Dan could say a word I shouted, "Whoopee!" like a kid after his first carnival ride. "Glad you liked it. Lets hope you feel the same way after I ride your butt hard for the next six weeks," I heard Dan say through the rubber tubing still connecting his voice to my ears. Without the obscuring engine noise that voice boomed like the voice of God. Though I knew he was serious, I clearly had some major trials and tribulations in my immediate future, not the least of which was the steep learning curve for the act of flying an aircraft. I had no further illusions. I was hooked from that point on, fully believing I was destined to be a flyer. Looking up and down the row at my classmates I mostly saw faces alight with elation, but clearly this was not the case for everyone. I watched from my cockpit as poor Jim Thorpe jumped from the wing of his plane and ran to a shallow drainage ditch just off the tarmac. Falling to his knees, he vigorously offered up his breakfast to the Arizona landscape. "Maybe he's just sick," I thought, hoping for him what I believed was the best. He transferred out two days later without ever again going aloft. I later learned that Jim was killed in action only minutes after landing on Omaha Beach, an infantry captain leading troops in the first wave of soldiers to storm over Normandy on D-Day. I can't help but wonder if he'd have survived had he been in the air…

CHAPTER 6

0600 came awfully early the next morning, even the first blush of midwinter sun having yet to appear in the eastern sky when I rolled out of bed. I had not been able to fall asleep the night before, as visions of the sequential steps involved in landing the Ryan were projected like an animated film on the inner lining of my closed and increasingly frustrated eyelids. Over and yet over again I reviewed the process. I probably made a thousand landings last night, all prompted by Dan's hint that today would be the day he would turn me loose to solo.

All cadets were expected to solo at around ten hours of instruction, some successful only with more flight time logged, some less. If a cadet wasn't deemed ready by fifteen hours he would be dismissed from training and his flight instructor would be evaluated to ensure that his instruction techniques were "by the book." Dan must have been impressed with me. Although in the course of the first week I had amassed only six hours of flight time, he still proposed to turn me loose with an expensive piece of military equipment. Rightly or wrongly, I was honored. Secretly I did feel like I was a natural at flying. The basic skills of coordinated turning and banking, holding assigned altitudes, and returning the aircraft to the ground undamaged all seemed to flow from me increasingly without effort, unfettered to course through the compliant airplane. Flying felt intuitive, as though I had been born to this calling and no other. Dan recognized early my innate talent, leaving me determined not to let either of us down.

I had started to tell Mary last night on the phone that today would be the day, but I figured there was no reason to worry her more than she already was. Being separated, it was easy for me to forget how she must feel. I wrote to her every day and spent a good deal of my paycheck calling her every time a telephone was available, but it just wasn't as good as being there. Fate had given us only three nights together as man and wife, a tempting morsel of what our lives together would be like, just enough to make us both desperately fear the loss. I was able to bury those fears in the rigors of training and learning, but I had left Mary with nothing other than the memories of the hours we spent together, uncomforted by any mundane distractions like those that afforded me solace. Lacking that shelter, Mary's fear was real and palpable and constant, yet forever and always unspoken. Mary was a trooper, brave and supportive as were most of the brides of our generation who found themselves left behind. Realizing her constant exposure to the various novel catastrophic ends to which her mind always led her, she had taken a job as a secretary at the local bank, hoping for a distraction while at the same time gathering for us nest eggs. Her employer gave her the position knowing it was only temporary at best, as Mary proffered her intent to join me wherever I may be just as soon as the Army would allow. Mary being Mary, she had thrown herself into the position with such abandon and competence that he now deemed her indispensable. She was excited to tell me the time spent coming to join me would be considered vacation time, paid vacation time at that, provided she promised to return when I left for my initial assignment. "It will give us cash. Something to start our lives with just as soon as this war is over." While I liked the idea of starting our life together with a nest egg, I wasn't happy with her plan at first. Having a wife who worked outside the home made me feel like a failure, somehow less of a man. Husbands were supposed to be the providers, the natural order of things in 1942, but Mary was just so jazzed I couldn't say no. I swallowed my pride and agreed, never letting her know I had reservations. Besides, this job afforded her a distraction from worrying about me. I wasn't going to bust her bubble by telling her some fool was conspiring to send me up alone today in a flying machine. Conspiring proved to be the appropriate verb as I later learned Dan had bet two of the other flight instructors twenty bucks I would be successful. I'm glad I didn't know that when I got into the airplane that morning. Ignorance was bliss all around.

Dan was quickly in the airplane that morning, and when he remained in the rear cockpit on firing up the engine my immediate enthusiasm waned. He'd failed to mention it in the morning preflight briefing, so I assumed he'd changed his mind and I was yet on this side of my fifteen-hour deadline to solo. He didn't say a word aloud until we had taxied out to the hold short line and were waiting for our light signal giving us permission to roll. Seeing the flash, I pulled out and only then did Dan say, "Turn to a 180 degree heading and climb up to 5000." Nodding understanding, I complied. Soon we were alone in the sky flying southward. After thirty minutes of straight and level Dan said, "See that strip over there about five miles to the west?" Looking and finding, I nodded. "Put us down there just like you would at home." Again, I nodded and turned to begin a descent to what I approximated to be eight hundred to a thousand feet above the terrain. From that altitude I crossed the runway and banked hard right, initiating the landing sequence I had been performing in my dreams. I landed a little too high which produced a bounce or two, but I recovered nicely by adding just a hint of power. I noticed it was an uninhabited concrete strip in the middle of a parched field. Slowing as we approached the runway's end Dan said, "Just shut her down here." I pulled the mixture and the engine sputtered before stopping. Dan got out onto the wing and crouched at my cockpit. "You ready for this, cadet? You'll be my quickest start yet."

"Yes, sir, I think I am… If you think I am."

"I think you are. Hop back here in the rear and we'll give it a go. It will feel different back there. Different visibility, different stick pressures, so don't let that fool you. Just watch your airspeed and fly the airplane. Make it your bitch," he laughed. I didn't return his laugh, being too focused on the task at hand. As I got out and climbed into the rear, he said, "I want three takeoffs and landings just like you did yesterday."

"Yes sir," I said saluting smartly, my signal to prop the engine once I'd announced, "Mags on!" With one throw of the prop the engine again quickly ignited, springing to life. As I taxied to the end of the runway I don't think I've ever in my life been more focused, intent not only upon passing this obstacle, but also on living to brag about it. Scanning the sky for other aircraft, I swung the little plane around offering a little prayer, "Please, Lord," before giving her the throttle, releasing the brakes and beginning my takeoff roll. Dan was right, the visibility was dramatically worse and I found I had to add a little forward pressure on the stick to fly the tail off the ground, but once there, everything else felt pretty much the same. I remember thinking, "I'm committed now," as the wheels left the ground. I was fine, going through the motions step-by-step, pretty much oblivious to the world around me until I turned final and saw the runway stretching out into the distance before me. My hands were sweating, my heart racing and my mouth so dry my tongue stuck to its roof as I flared for that first landing. It was so smooth I didn't even know I was down. Calmed by my success, I repeated the process twice more then pulled the plane to where Dan stood waiting and shut the engine down again. He tried to appear nonchalant, but I knew he was just as pleased and proud as I was. "So, what'd you think?" he asked with a huge grin, patting the metal fuselage affectionately.

"I think the plane flies a whole lot better without your fat ass in the back." A joke I could get away with as Dan weighed all of one hundred, thirty pounds soaking wet. He laughed, "Well done! Now trade me seats. This time you have to prop the plane. Let's go home, cadet."

"Yes, sir," I said saluting. Flying back to Thunderbird that day the sky seemed bluer, the sun brighter than I'd ever before noticed it. I'd cleared the first hurdle, feeling both satisfied with myself and frightfully superior to my classmates being the first of our group to solo. My success gave renewed confidence to my mates, all of whom would soon accomplish the same feat thus putting us back on equal footing, but for a week at February's end I was the undisputed king of the hill.

After I'd successfully soloed my life became somewhat mundane for the next few weeks. My day started with calisthenics in the morning, which after our brief stint at real basic training I realized was nothing more than a cursory nod to all that military training was supposed to entail. My workout was followed by breakfast in the officers' mess, which was also significantly more civilized than what Uncle Sam served up to basic recruits. Here the Army didn't try to disguise the lack of quality by dishing out massive quantities of powdered breakfast staples. No, we had a choice of real eggs with beefsteak or bacon, biscuits and gravy, pancakes, all to be washed down with fresh milk or black coffee. I was quite impressed, as I'd never eaten better than this at home. I am told my culinary experience at Thunderbird was an aberrancy, as food at other training facilities was not nearly as good. After breakfast we had two hours of lecture followed by a briefing with our flight instructors. At the onset of the war there was a ratio of one instructor for every four students. Chuck Marshall, Bob Sullivan, Bill Armstrong, and I were all assigned to flight instructor Lieutenant Dan Scott. Ours was a good group and we did our best to take care of one another, learning a lot about flying by hearing firsthand the mistakes and failures each of us were making on a daily basis. After our briefing, we took turns in the airplane, each going up with Dan for flights of an hour and a half apiece. Basic flight training in the military took few if any detours from a very rigid curriculum, and thus members of our little group were introduced to various flight maneuvers on an almost simultaneous basis. After all four of us had a chance to either prove our mettle or embarrass ourselves with Dan in the back cockpit, we met again to debrief the flying of the day. This was pretty informal and usually occurred over supper, unless we finished too late, in which case we talked over beers at the officers club. After the first three weeks, the flights were more often than not made without an instructor in the back. Nothing against Dan, but I loved these flights alone. As the winter days lengthened, so, too, did our solo flights. On Sundays there was no formal instruction, but with your flight instructor's permission you were allowed to check out an airplane, much the same way one would check out a book from a library and fly it to your heart's content. While most of the fellows didn't avail themselves of Uncle Sam's generosity, I certainly did. Free gas and an airplane to fly, I was like a kid in a candy store. The more I flew and learned, the more I was convinced after the war I would find some way of turning this wartime obligation into a permanent profession. Dan was the person who first planted the seed of this dream in my head or in my heart or wherever it is that dreams are supposed to reside. Before him I thought myself here to learn how to punish the enemy, a worthy goal, but shortsighted at best. Dan's after-hours musings had a profound effect upon me. I came to respect him very much despite the fact that he was two years younger than me. We all did. At only eighteen years of age Dan had already demonstrated his superior abilities as a pilot. Of course Dan had been flying most of his life. His daddy taught him to fly and let him solo the family crop duster when he was only eight years old. After that, in the growing season he flew all day, every day. Upon enlistment he'd already logged more flight hours than anyone else in the Army Training Command. In typical military fashion, the Army decided to misuse those skills, assigning him the stateside role of flight instructor instead of wielding him as the formidable flying weapon that God had clearly hardwired him to be. Dan was the undisputed leader of our little band and given his abilities, would have been so regardless of his age or rank. As such we all hung on his every word. Off duty, with tongues and minds both loosened from convention and lubricated by beer, Dan shared his vision of the postwar future. He dreamed aloud of the day when travel by air would become the norm rather than the exception and rightly predicted the need for skilled pilots, armies of them, to make this dream a reality. I liked his vision and liked the idea of flying airplanes as a profession. Mary seemed to like the idea as well, at least she professed to like it whenever we got to talk long enough to dream together about what our future life might be like. Separated now for months, dreaming of a future together was our favorite pastime, the only thing that kept us sane. Though in 1942 it wasn't proper to speak of such things, I dreamed nightly of more than our future together. Every evening without fail I was met by visions of Mary's warm, inviting body, a veritable paradise that had pleasured me intensely for only a brief two day period and now represented for me home and comfort and all that could possibly ever be right in this world. The promise of our future together was sustenance just like food or water or oxygen. It left me wanting. It gave me drive, an appetite for success. To deprive me now of a future with Mary and with…dare I risk saying it let alone wanting it….children, would deprive me of life, at least any life I could imagine wanting.

Yet another element of this wanting was soon to be introduced, that of merely surviving to meet my conspired future. On March 15 my good friend Bill Armstrong was killed attempting a dead stick landing after his engine failed a short half-mile from the runway's end. He was returning from a long cross-country solo flight, the last leg of which had been thwarted by a strong headwind. Flying against that headwind, Bill spent more fuel than he anticipated, ultimately costing him his life and the rest of us a friend. That such a seemingly small indiscretion, Bill's inattention to a minute detail, could cost so dearly shook all of us to the core. There were no insignificant details in this venture. From the beginning we'd all talked about the threat, the inherent danger of our occupation, but Bill's death made that threat palpable, gave it teeth and glaring eyes, a huge black dog that ruthlessly anticipated the taste of each of us as it crouched silently in the dark waiting. I would say patiently waiting, but the untimeliness of this loss argued that death was indeed an impatient bitch. It steeled me, giving me an immovable resolve to survive this conflict if only for the promise of one day providing for Mary. To that end I worked all the harder, determined to be the strongest, the smartest, the best.

Bill's death affected Dan more than any of the rest of us. Feeling he alone bore the whole weight of responsibility on his shoulders, he asked for a transfer to a combat unit. The unit commander requested that Dan consider staying for just two more weeks, allowing his three remaining students to complete their primary training. Reluctantly he agreed. I'll never forget what he told the commander in response, "The best pilots are those who fly as though they have nothing to lose. These men hinder me because I've discovered that they are indeed mine to lose."

From a purely military standpoint it was a stroke of genius putting Dan in a combat position. By the fall of 1944 he was well on his way to becoming a triple ace when he was shot down by flak, defending a flight of heavies from the Luftwaffe's marauding onslaught. Injured by shrapnel, he bailed out and survived the loss of his Mustang, then evaded capture for three days. The Germans executed Dan in January of 1945 for his part in an escape attempt from Stalag Luft One. I have little doubt had he survived he would have owned his own airline.

CHAPTER 7

With our primary flight training complete, our group was to be transferred to Louisiana for basic flight training. I've always thought the name misleading, because though the term basic seemed to imply just that, basic, the instruction we would receive was actually the intermediate step between primary flight training and advanced flight training. Dan was to depart for England on the same day we were to be transported to Louisiana. Thankfully Dan agreed to stay on as our instructor until Chuck, Bob, and I had completed our primary training, affording us the benefit of his watchful eye. Bill's death just three flight hours short of completion rendered our graduation celebration stifled and anti-climactic, a bittersweet affair replete with excessive consumption of alcohol. To a man we considered ourselves lucky. We had survived our primary flight training, a feat Bill's loss demonstrated was something to be thankful for. Dan proved the best possible instructor we could have encountered, a talented pilot with a unique combination of gifts. Patient and compassionate with a superb ability to communicate, Dan also was blessed with enough bravado to be the consummate warrior pilot. Shaken though he was by Bill's loss, he was thrilled to get his chance to jump into the fray. We all had developed a romantic notion of what war and valor and honor were to be, a delusion shared until the reality of experience would teach us otherwise. Our initial training complete, our valued comrade-in-arms lost, and our leader off, bound to gather his own measure of glory, we drank heartily to each, and not our usual libation of beer, but of fine, well-aged scotch. Bill Armstrong's father was a wealthy attorney. We had a memorial service for Bill in Arizona after his body had shipped home for burial. We didn't have the pleasure of meeting Mr. Armstrong, but he sent us a case of his best scotch, contraband that we kept hidden. Cadets were forbidden to consume alcohol, a prohibition that was largely ignored by cadets and thankfully overlooked by officers, but I have no question that this valuable package would have been commandeered if the brass had discovered the nature of its contents or its whereabouts. I've gotta tell you the scotch, Glenfarclas I think it was called, went down awfully good that night, but didn't wake up so good the following morning. The last time I ever saw Dan was through pained, bloodshot eyes, tainted red by that same scotch, as we were lined up waiting to board a C-46 transport. I had a blinding hangover from the last night's celebration and would swear that the combination of sunlight, engine noise, and exhaust fumes were conspiring to be the death of me, but I couldn't very well complain. Cadets were not allowed to drink, and sympathy for my condition could very well lead to punishment for my condition. As I had chosen this pain for myself, I was determined to keep my mouth shut. I saw Dan through the perimeter fence where he sat with a driver and jeep. He waved, then saluted before I climbed aboard. Even from a distance I could see that he felt no better this morning than I did. Chuck, Bob, and I returned his salute and while tempted to laugh at his misery, we all felt as bad as he did so stifled the mocking. He said something to the corporal driving the jeep and they sped off toward town, leaving me with foreboding, that melancholy ache of forever loss. I could only hope my next instructor would prove to be as good.

Climbing aboard the C-46, this was my first encounter with a large, multi-engine aircraft. This beast was a brand new airplane, fresh off the assembly line in Louisville, Kentucky. Utilitarian, drab military green in appointment, its color was stark even in contrast to the eternal blue of the Arizona sky. At idle, the twin Pratt & Whitney radial 2800s emitted a roar of deafening proportion. Engine noise and oily exhaust reverberated around the airplane's cavernous interior, both amplified to the threshold of pain and attendant nausea even without a hangover. Twice I choked back down the thickened remnants of last night's scotch and White Castle hamburgers, twenty of them I seem to recall, and climbed an extension ladder up to the open cargo door. That door was a good ten feet above the ground, but queasy green and carrying my eighty-pound B-4 bag it seemed more like a fifty-foot climb. The burly corporal standing in the entrance laughed at my misery before reaching down to grab the bag and me, effortlessly pulling both over the threshold. "C'mon *sir*, you're holding up the line," he shouted. Given my condition I'm sure his derisive "sir" was more respect than I deserved. "Thanks," I said weakly and climbed the inclined floor to a seat in the front of the airplane. Chuck and Bob were both at least as miserable as me if not more so. Neither said anything as we exchanged glances of commiseration. I knew I would be ok as long as neither of the other two puked. I closed my eyes and waited only about thirty seconds before I heard Bob running to the cargo door, dodging other guys trying to get to their seats.

"Don't you puke in my airplane!" the corporal shouted to no avail. Bob was just short of the door before falling to his knees, heaving the remnants of last night's celebration to the wooden airplane deck. I couldn't hear the sound of his embarrassment, but its odor wafted forward and shortly thereafter I followed suit, mercifully managing to hold it till I made it to the door, leaving the former contents of my stomach to dry on the ramp, baking in the Arizona sun. The corporal began cursing, "I ain't smellin' this shit all the way to Louisiana," to which Bob wordlessly retrieved a towel and did his best to clean up after himself. He stuffed the vomit-soiled towel back into his bag and zipped it tight.

"Never again," he whispered to himself under his breath. I nodded agreement and let my head drop back, closing my eyes and begging for the respite of a little sleep, but sleep was not to come. The very second the cargo door slammed shut with a resounding crash, the pilot throttled up and taxied. I would have sworn the engine noise could get no louder, but it more than tripled when the pilot advanced to take off power. Locking my head in a vise could not have proven more painful. The three of us grimaced, holding our ears to muffle the roar, which did not lessen until we were at altitude.

The ride over Arizona, New Mexico, and Texas was thankfully smooth, but as we flew ever closer to the Gulf of Mexico the moist air became more and more turbulent, the aircraft's respondent bouncing inducing waves of nausea and scant, bilious vomiting. My self-induced misery made that flight feel like an eternity. Each turn and bank and bounce amplified my torment to torturous proportions. Arriving over the Gulf Coast before initially approaching the airport, our pilot had to navigate around three towering thunderstorms. Mid-afternoon, the daily cycle of convective storms was just beginning to gather steam. To my gastronomic relief, he did a masterful job of planting the big cargo ship smoothly on the runway. Upon landing in Louisiana, the three of us were spent, mutual in our agreement never again to so debase ourselves. Before leaving the airplane I vowed never again would I willingly bring upon myself such torment. I wish I could look back upon that first ride in a big airplane with fondness but that never has nor ever will come to pass.

We gathered our bags and waited as each cadet disembarked, again with the help of the surly corporal, climbing down a ladder to the tarmac below. The receiving pavement was refreshingly firm yet odd in composition. The ramp at Thunderbird was constructed of small gravel and compacted sand while the pavement here was an odd mixture, composed of both rocks and the small shells of some long ago dead aquatic creatures suspended in a matrix of tar. The slow evaporation of the recent rain into saturated air from the tarmac surface rendered it slick, even to surefooted young men. In my debilitated state I was neither sure nor fleet of foot, and I quickly found myself on my ass surrounded by hooting young men all laughing at my inglorious stumble. "What more could possibly go wrong today?" I thought, lying prone on the wet ground. Bob even snickered as he offered me his hand to help me up.

Almost immediately we were ordered into lines of twelve each and called to attention by a captain standing in the back of a jeep. All fifty-eight of us immediately complied. With an accent, dripping thick of a Brooklyn heritage he said, "Raise your right hand and repeat after me, I, your name (no one jumped upon the obvious joke – everyone stated his own name...okay, I'll admit I thought about it), having been appointed a first lieutenant in the U.S. Army under the conditions of war, do accept such appointment and do solemnly swear or affirm that I will support and defend the constitution of the United States against all enemies, both foreign and domestic, that I will bear true faith and allegiance to the same; that I take this obligation freely, without any mental reservation or purpose of evasion; and that I will well and faithfully discharge the duties of the office on which I am about to enter, so help me God." We all repeated in monotone the chant-like oath. For as rotten as I felt, saying those words sure made me feel proud. I, we were about to have a hand or, should I say, a foot in kicking those Jap and German bastards to the curb. The captain smiled and said, "Gentlemen and officers, welcome to the United States Army and to Lake Charles. I'm Captain John Gilbert. Your CO is Colonel Jamie Gilbert, no relation." It was clear that this was not the first time he had given this speech. "In the next forty-five days we're going to teach you how to be more than just pilots. We're going to train you to become Army aviators. It's going to be tough. If recent history repeats itself, more than a third of you standing here will discover to your dismay that you do not have what it takes. Work hard and give it your best shot. Believe me, we don't want any of you to wash out. We desperately need pilots on both fronts, but we've got to be sure we're sending our best if we're going to win this war. I can assure you that both Mr. Hitler and Mr. Hirohito have already sent their best. Your quarters for the next forty-five days are the Quonsets on the far side of the ramp there," he said, turning to point. "Find an empty bunk, stow your gear, and meet for chow and orders at the mess hall at 1700. Any questions?" Finding there were none, he shouted, "Dismissed!"

First come, first serve, some of the guys took off in a run to best position themselves in bunks. Bob, Chuck and I took our time. I figured the Army would have plenty of beds and worst-case scenario, we could sleep on the floor. At that moment I could have slept anywhere.

The buildings, though relatively new, were already showing signs of heavy use and decay. The unrelenting Louisiana sun and humidity were taking their toll as mold and mildew could be seen on any surface that had managed to escape being slathered in paint. The wood and corrugated steel buildings were a far cry from the facilities we had left at Thunderbird. Those had been constructed using private funds, and no financier in an environment fueled by patriotism would have dared give our armed services any less. These facilities, however, had obviously been hastily cobbled together, probably by inexperienced hands hastily hired to facilitate getting as many pilots trained and on their way to the front as quickly as possible. I didn't really mind. None of us did. We were here to learn to fly combat, not take a spa vacation. In retrospect, I did feel like one of a large herd of cattle being quickly plumped up for the slaughterhouse. I had no idea…

The following morning I met my new instructor, one Captain Joe Marcum of Madison, Wisconsin. Joe's persona exuded mean; his scowling glare broadcast to the world that he was one cold-hearted son-of-a-bitch. I assumed this was for his own emotional protection as I once overheard him saying something about not naming a horse that he might have to kill and eat. Unlike Dan, Joe was a stoic guy who spent absolutely zero time outside of the classroom or the airplane conversing with his students. He showed up at precisely the time scheduled and spoke as few words as possible to explain what he desired me to do. I was a pretty quick study and never gave him cause to be upset at my deficiencies, but the same could not be said for some of my cohorts, whose misstep or misfortune turned Joe from a quiet, asocial person into a fuming maniac.

The airplane we were to fly at Lake Charles was the BT-13. Manufactured in ever-greater numbers by the Vultee Aircraft Company, it was heroically named the Valiant. Student pilots before me had renamed the trainer dubbing it the Vultee Vibrator because the damned thing had a habit of vibrating violently right before the stall. I still remember Joe telling me, "That's a good thing because you always have plenty of prior notice before the stall occurs." I really liked the Vibrator. Compared to the little PT-22s from which we had just graduated, the Vultee was spacious, outweighing the Ryan three to one. It had a tube radio and intercom providing us our first exposure to radio communications. A birdhouse canopy enclosed the cockpit making the aircraft a bit quieter, a necessity to allow its pilot to hear radio transmissions. Powered by a Pratt & Whitney R-985 four-hundred-fifty horsepower radial engine, it cranked out more than twice the power of the Ryan's five-cylinder Kinner. Though clearly utilitarian, the designer still managed to embellish the tail cone by incorporating a little flash of deco flair. Other than that sole bit of whimsy, the airframe was business all the way. The Vultee sported beefy, widely spaced, fixed landing gear, much more forgiving of botched landings than other trainers, a good thing because botched landings were certainly in style the first two weeks of basic training.

Unlike primary training where we had talked ad infinitum prior to touching an aircraft, here we jumped right in. After an hour walkaround, Joe had me in the cockpit ready to taxi. The BT-13 was far more complicated than what I was used to, but as Dan was fond of saying, "An airplane is an airplane is an airplane. The basic skills don't change." I soon found out what he meant. We were second in line for take off that morning, and I was airborne before I had much chance to ruminate and get nervous about flying something new. The stick and rudder pressure required a bit more muscle in this heavier aircraft, and things certainly came at me quicker, flying fifty miles an hour faster than I was accustomed, but, all in all, I finally understood what Dan had tried to tell me.

Spring weather in Louisiana is a volatile affair as the state lies entirely within the boundaries of the Gulf coastal plain. The alluvial land is saturated swamp, inhabited by only the hardiest of creatures from alligators to humans. When Louisiana weather was good it was spectacularly good, at least on the ground. When it was bad it could in an instant become flat-out dangerous;

gusting wind and towering thunderstorms that frequently spawned tornados. Being from the nearby state of Georgia I had never imagined Louisiana as windy, but it certainly was that spring. Perhaps I was now more keenly aware of the wind's invisible presence due to my new avocation. Blowing perpetually out of the south, roily, boiling, and humid to the point of discomfort, it carried in its embrace a somehow comforting primordial smell of wet earth and mold, an aroma stimulating remembrances in a fold of my mid-brain harboring inherited primitive memories. That scent was diminished but still detectable even at 20,000 feet above the wetlands producing it. Mornings were the time to fly if you wished to avoid the bumps. As the climbing sun heated the day, a new round of turbulent air and thunderstorms became energized, unleashing the aggravated atmosphere to wreak havoc. Awash in the ensuing turbulence, an airplane bobbed like a tethered cork in a stream, every flight an exercise in keeping the churning aircraft upright. This was somewhat disconcerting at first, but we quickly became pretty adept at ignoring the bumps.

We flew every day, twice a day. After the first week, which was spent mastering idiosyncrasies of the new aircraft, we were introduced to the art of formation flying. This new skill was approached timidly at first with lots of room to spare and err separating the aircraft. Being the lead aircraft in a formation had its challenges, as the lead pilot had the responsibility of navigating to or from a specific target. This had to be accomplished while maintaining basic flight parameters such as holding specific altitudes and headings. Even simple intuitive things such as avoiding terrain or fixed obstacles became of paramount importance because everyone else in the flight group relinquished those tasks to the lead and could easily follow a careless or inept leader right into the ground.

I personally found being a follower in trail of a lead aircraft much more difficult. First there is the trust factor. Do I trust the person I'm following to keep me safely in the sky? Sometimes yes, sometimes no. Secondly, flying the aircraft was much more complicated from that position. Things as simple as a ninety degree turn required precise power changes. If you were on the outside of the turn, more distance had to be traversed in the same period of time if separation from the lead aircraft was to be maintained. This required an increase in speed and therefore more power. Similarly, being on the inside of a turn required a power reduction. Every cadet pilot was required to develop and demonstrate proficiency as both a flight leader or *lead pilot* and flight follower or *wingman*. Over a week to ten days we each honed these skills, allowing us the confidence to fly tighter formations, followers venturing ever closer to the leader.

After mastering formation flying we were introduced to night flying. I thought it was funny how differently things sounded and felt at night as opposed to flying in daylight. A perfectly good engine always seems to sound only milliseconds away from giving up the ghost anytime the ground is not easily visualized. That same irrational notion applies to flying over open water as well. I suppose its human nature to be more anxious any time our options become limited. Hyper-vigilant is probably a better word than anxious. If you lose an engine in a single-engine aircraft your choices are narrowed down to "Where am I going to land?" If it's dark when an engine loss occurs, you find yourself at the mercy of the terrain below, a vast unknown. All a hapless pilot can do in such an emergency is keep flying the airplane until his wheels meet the ground, all the while praying he doesn't hit anything else in the process.

By the end of our time at Lake Charles we could confidently fly close enough to each other to exchange spit. We could navigate over significant distances and find increasingly smaller, more complex targets then turn around and find our way home. Missions such as these required teamwork and an esprit de corps. We learned to trust each other with our very lives, a bond not shared by many and not soon to be forgotten. My flight instructor Joe Marcum never did become my friend like Dan, but that doesn't mean I didn't respect him. He was gruff, an all-business kind of guy. His job was to teach me how to fly and survive, not become my friend. He performed his duties very well, teaching me several valuable lessons.

I'll never forget my last flight with Joe. After a hard day of flying we droned home at 8000 feet above terra firma. About ten miles south of the field Joe said, "I've got the airplane. Its time for your final lesson, is your parachute properly packed?"

"Yes sir," I said, a gnawing fear growing in anticipation of his next words.

"Good! Get out on the wing."

"Excuse me, sir?"

"You heard me, get out on the wing."

"That's not part of the curriculum, sir."

"I know it's not, but it *is* an order. Get your ass out on that wing or I'll wash you out." With no choice but to comply if I wanted to complete my training, I unplugged my headset, then slid the birdcage back and tenuously stepped out onto the wing. The onrushing slipstream made securely holding on difficult, a task made even more arduous when Joe started making steep turns. "This idiot is gonna make me jump," I thought, but to my relief he invited me back into the cockpit after ten minutes of riding precariously on the wing, holding on for dear life. Quickly climbing back into the cockpit, I plugged my microphone in and angrily shouted, "What the hell was that?"

"My final lesson to you. You now know you have the courage to bail out if the situation arises. Combat is not the time or place to find out you don't have the balls to get yourself out of the aircraft. You do, and now you know." As usual, Joe was right. I doubt he really would have washed me out, but he did teach me a valuable lesson.

"That's a pretty unorthodox way of showing me, but thank you," I said, meaning it sincerely.

"You're welcome. You've got the plane, kid, take us home."

"Yes, sir!"

By this point in training we all had similar tales, magnified by time and hubris into feats of derring-do to be regaled at the bar or over chow. Each had a story better than the last. To be sure, there was competition among the ranks. You can't put two human males in the same space for any length of time and not expect some jockeying for position. It's the nature of the beast, the skin we men live in. We all wanted more than just to survive the training; we wanted to have a choice in our destinies. Almost to a man we dreamed of becoming fighter pilots. That was the glory job! Both the cinema and popular fiction had glamorized the exploits of the fighter pilot, the fearless, almost superhuman men who fought in the skies of the last war, heroes forever galvanized in the minds of the American public. Every schoolboy in the country knew the name of America's "Ace of Aces," Eddie Rickenbacker. We would fight over the right to play Eddie in our playground wars as children. As an impressionable child of eight, my granddaddy let me see Howard Hughes' *Hells Angels* four times. Released in 1930, it chronicled the daring flying adventures of two brothers, Roy and Monte Rutledge, defending God and country from the evil Hun. For reasons I couldn't understand or begin to verbalize at the time, Jean Harlow left parts of my prepubescent body tingling. The adventure and flying and sex were all too alluring, the harbinger of wet dreams to come. Around the same time a Douglas Fairbanks movie called *The Dawn Patrol* was released. I liked that one fine as well, but I really liked it in 1938 when Errol Flynn and Basil Rathbone starred in a remake of that same movie. I wasn't the only kid in the country that stood transfixed by those shimmering images. It was all so romantic and chivalrous just like King Arthur and his Knights of the Round Table. We took in this romantic myth hook, line and sinker. Sure there was danger, but as long as one acted with nobility and gallantry, one would prevail. Yet in the event that one should die, at least one would die with honor. I liked the prevail scenario better. Prevail and go home to the inviting arms of beautiful women. I had my beautiful woman, my lady-in-waiting; my Mary was Guinevere to my Lancelot. All I had to do now was sally forth and confront evil, and God knows we were overwhelmed by the perceived evil of the Japs and Nazis. I couldn't wait for the chance to join the battle in the sky to display my bravery and avenge the evil being waged against all that I believed was right. None of us could.

It seemed as if time was moving too slowly, for while we were stuck here learning our war-craft the evil was growing, metastasizing, even winning, perhaps. With each passing day our moods and indeed the collective mood of the entire nation grew darker and more anxious. We had responded to the call to arms. Most young men of my generation responded by signing up, many mere teenagers, lying about their ages, all for the honor of returning fire to the Japs and the Germans. We were training, gearing up for an inevitable conflict, the entire nation's collective anxiety lacquered with a thick coat of hubris and the romance of Arthurian legend, but the response just wasn't fast enough for most. It certainly wasn't fast enough for me.

We shared our camp with a contingent of Brits who, like us, were being trained as aviators. They had seen up close and personal what the German enemy was capable of, investing them with a sense of urgency that proved contagious. It gave them an un-lacquered zeitgeist, their view of the world tempered by reality rather than the romantic notions of war tempering our own. They had seen realities of loss, the finality of death, the wanton destruction of things once deemed eternal. Our hubris made it difficult to comprehend what they shared with us. We were Americans, cocksure of our strength, of our place in the world. Hadn't we already beaten the Brits twice, as well as coming to their rescue in the last great debacle, soundly defeating the Central Powers? Surely the outcome would again be the same if we could only get there, but the Brits' firsthand account of the battle we would soon join influenced how we believed we best could serve. They reported accurately the staggering loses being suffered by the British Bomber Command, making us want all the more to be fighter pilots. The press continued to hide those losses from the American public. We pitied those poor bastards, the bomber pilots. "Better to be the master of your own fate rather than a sitting duck in a giant flying tin can." We even took to calling those guys "tinned duck." I believed the harder I worked, the more skilled a pilot I could become, the more likely it was that I would have a choice in how I might best serve.

The news that spring rendered our moods even more black and disheartened as the Japs were successfully kicking our asses all over the Pacific as the United States struggled to even mount a response. All that was about to change, however. In a daring, almost suicidal mission General Jimmy Doolittle, already famous in the United States as a race pilot, added to his measure of fame and glory by leading a group of American bombers in a raid on Tokyo. Galvanizing our pride as a nation, the seemingly invincible nation of Japan felt the first blow of our steel. We were coming, by God, and there would be hell to pay. Thank God someone among us had the resolve to finally strike back. Maybe being a bomber pilot wouldn't be that bad a position after all? Those guys clearly had guts!

CHAPTER 8

I finished my training in Louisiana, again at the top of my class. While I was both happy and relieved by this honor, poor Chuck was neither so fortunate nor so skilled. He washed out in the last week by balling a perfectly good BT-13 into a wad of mangled tin. I watched helpless as he bounced the landing and then as we had been trained to do, gave it the gas and did a go-around. He probably could have salvaged the first landing by adding a little power prior to letting the airplane settle again and been just fine, but the go-around gave Chuck time to psych himself into defeat. The next time around he greased the main gear onto the runway but for some reason, a sense of relief I suppose, he stopped flying the airplane before he set the tail wheel on the ground. The result was a spectacular ground loop and the destruction of a piece of expensive military hardware. Uncle Sam was neither forgiving nor forgetting. He was offered a couple of options and finally chose to go to bombardier school. He would later be lost along with the balance of his B-24 crew on a mission to bomb the Ploesti oil refineries.

My success was soon to afford me some choices, though not the choices I wanted. Before the graduation ceremony at Lake Charles, a meager ceremony, certain to be devoid of any pomp and circumstance, the CO called me into his office to have a little chat. We'd had occasion to speak a couple of times during my stint at Lake Charles and he knew how desperately I wanted to go to fighter school. Graciously, he staged a little demonstration for me before announcing what decision he had made regarding my advancement.

A pair of P-51 Mustang fighters had landed at Lake Charles en route to the West Coast and he jumped at the chance to use them.

"Come with me," he said. "I've got something I want to show you." I had no idea what was up, but when the CO says walk, you walk.

"You're maybe the finest natural pilot we've had pass through this facility since the war began. Hell, anyone that can impress Joe Marcum must be a pretty good stick!" I felt my face redden.

"Joe was impressed with me? He never told me," I said, surprised.

"He wouldn't now, would he?"

I laughed, saying, "No, I suppose he wouldn't."

As we walked and talked, I noticed we were heading toward the flight line. My jaw dropped when I saw the Mustangs sitting there, pretty as a picture.

"Wow, look at those," I said, almost drooling. "We've all heard the rumors, but this is the first Mustang I've seen."

"Beautiful planes, aren't they?"

"Yes, sir! Is this the part where you tell me that these are my next mount?"

He smiled weakly saying, "Go ahead and climb in." I didn't have to be told twice and was quickly up on the wing lifting the canopy hatch. Wiggling into the seat I said, "Tight fit," words I immediately regretted. Damn it all, too late, I saw what he was up to. I slipped my long legs past the rudder pedals and slid in a little further, trying to appear as comfortable as possible without revealing my dismay.

"Go ahead son, close the hatch," he said, knowing that I knew his intent. I pulled the hatch down and crouched forward enough that my head only grazed the top of the canopy. He opened the hatch and crouched down on the wing beside me. Turning, I gave him a stupid, shit-eating grin.

"Not gonna work, is it?"

"Don't you have anything in a larger size?"

He laughed saying, "No, I'm afraid not. Look son, lots of men would kill to be as tall as you. I know you could be a great fighter pilot. The important thing now is 'you know' you could be a great fighter pilot… maybe even the best if you could only fit in the damned thing, but you can't." I nodded sadly in agreement. "But that doesn't mean you can't fly combat. You've done so extraordinarily well in your training I'm prepared to give you a couple of options, but fighter school isn't one of them."

To say I was heartbroken would have been a gross understatement. I had never failed at anything in my life. His words, though true and wise, made me sad nonetheless, sad and angry at the same time, angry with the CO, angrier still with myself.

"Then why the hell have I been busting my ass?" I shot back at him, surprised that I had let my frustration escape my mouth.

Very calmly he replied, "I assume that just like the rest of us, you want to serve your country. Isn't that ultimately why you're here?"

"Yes sir," I said, digesting his wisdom.

"You have a great many gifts, Lieutenant. I suggest you take stock of them and put them to their best use."

"Yes sir, thank you sir."

Ultimately, I just had to face the fact that this was not a personal failure; it was just a reality check. I was too damned tall to fit comfortably in any of our fighters, so in spite of a training performance that the Lake Charles base commander described as "legendary," I was destined to become a bomber pilot. Maybe it wouldn't be so bad, although the words *tinned duck* kept ringing through my mind.

The completion of Basic Flight Training was a branching point on the road to Advanced Training. Those chosen to become fighter pilots would go to an advanced school to prepare them to fly single- engine aircraft and ultimately fighters, while those chosen to become bomber pilots would be sent to multi-engine advanced training. The choice the CO offered me, should I complete the final chapter of my training with the same aplomb, would be either combat, or a position as an instructor with the training command in Texas. As I yet had the final hurdle to clear, I was not pressed to give an answer that day, though I already knew in my gut what my choice had to be. I figured that flying bombers was a sure ticket to the ETO (European Theater of Operation). I now not only had to convince myself, I had to convince Mary, which would be no small feat.

That same afternoon we had a commencement ceremony and then were dismissed without further fanfare. Bob and I went to the officers club and had a steak dinner. Bob celebrated while I moped. I'd learned my lesson about alcohol well and had a single beer in celebration, watching as Bob downed several. He had scored high and given his size, all five foot five of him, a fighter plane fit him like a glove. Tomorrow he would be off to central Florida to complete his advanced training. He ultimately found his way to Great Britain, where he was to fly P-47s. Quite successful, Bob finished the war as an ace with seven confirmed kills and not a single scratch to show for it. We said our goodbyes and I turned in early after packing my limited belongings in my B-4 bag.

The following morning I boarded first a bus, then ultimately a train bound for Cincinnati. I had a lot to look forward to, as Mary was at that moment also en route to Cincinnati. As an officer, I was allowed the privilege of cohabitating with my wife in a small, private, single-room apartment off base. To say I was ecstatic was a gross understatement. I had not laid eyes upon her since last December when I left her on the train platform frantically waving goodbye. We wrote every day and I managed to call her at least once a week, but it was small consolation for not being with her. She was now a constant in both my waking and sleeping thoughts, memories of our honeymoon leaving me with a nearly constant hard-on.

That matter did not improve when I finally saw her in Union Terminal in Cincinnati. She looked ravishing and I was not the only man in the station to think so. She got several wolf whistles dashing past a group of sailors upon spotting me. That tomfoolery stopped when we finally reached each other and stood for a good five minutes kissing in full sight of God and anyone else present in the station that day. I could barely walk after that, but I hardly gave a good damn. We had rings on our fingers, little golden permission slips from a gracious God granting us full and unfettered access to each other's bodies. We hailed a taxi and went post haste to the Netherlands Hotel in downtown Cincinnati. Mary had shed her shy little bride persona and now was like a hungry lioness on the prowl. She could hardly have matched my own desperation. We were out of our clothes and making love before we even made it across the floor to the bed. We had sex three times that night before finally remembering we had yet to eat, so we ordered up a room service breakfast and had sex again. After breakfast, completely spent by our night of calisthenics, we fell asleep. Mid-afternoon I was awakened by Mary's playful nibbling on my earlobe, her warm naked body draped languidly over my left side. "C'mon Sparky, time for another go," she purred. Not waiting for a response she straddled me bringing my male member, unaccustomed as it was to such ministrations, to life yet again. "You're insatiable," I laughed, trying unsuccessfully not to stare at her beautiful body. A real, live, breathing, gloriously naked woman making love to me was just almost too much to take in. Her body was unbelievable, better than my best imaginations of the same. Trim and athletic, I could almost encircle her waist with my hands. In blind reverie I watched her, gently moving her body on mine, picking up both tempo and passion. I finally noticed her eyes smiling down upon me, admiring me as I admired her, before rolling back under fluttering eyelids as she came yet again. I increased the pressure between our bodies by holding her even tighter as I moved hers, now paralyzed by the intensity of her orgasm, against mine. After her third she stopped me, which was good as my recently pleasured member was losing its tumescence. I laid back triumphant, my hands between my head and the pillow. "You're quite a skilled lover," she said breathlessly. "You know you're the only woman I've ever been with, don't you?" I asked, suddenly alarmed.

"Of course, silly, it's not an accusation, merely an observation. A compliment, nothing more," she smiled.

"I suppose I've given the subject a lot of thought over the last five years, and I mean a *lot* of thought. It's just that most of the guys in the unit have.... how should I say this?...availed themselves of forbidden pleasures with the women around the camp. I just wanted you to know..."

"I know... I know you. That's why I love you so much," she said, reaching up to peck my cheek with a kiss before laying her head upon my chest. I closed my eyes and drifted off again content, the world right and beautiful, a temporary amnesia, perhaps anesthesia would be a better word for our momentary disregard of the looming war.

When I awoke she was still in the same position. I curled her red locks around my finger trying my best not to disturb her sleep.

Without looking at me she said, "I was afraid to break the magic."

It was then I noticed she'd been crying.

"I'm just so afraid."

"Afraid of what, honey?"

"Afraid of losing you...this..."

"I know, but I promise you," I took hold of her face bringing her eyes to mine, "I promise you I'm coming back.... I guess that's what makes my news harder to tell you."

"What news?" Sitting up, she gathered the sheet to cover her nakedness.

"Well, I've been offered a position."

"What position?" she asked, excited yet apprehensive.

"I've done a pretty good job in training. Good enough that some folks noticed... They said that providing I complete my advanced training, again at the top of my class I could have my choice of staying stateside and working for the training command, or..."

Stateside was all she heard before jumping up to tackle me, "That's wonderful, darling, I'm so happy!" She kissed me again hard through tears of joy.

How on earth could I tell her?

"I've got to finish at the top of my class."

"Oh silly boy, is there really any question that you will?" she laughed.

"No, I don't guess there is, but that's not the point," I said searching her face for a clue of what I was trying to convey.

Now alarmed she asked, "Well what is the point?"

"My other option is combat…"

Reading from my eyes that my decision was already made, she slapped my face and wordlessly gathered the bed sheet around her before walking to the bathroom, slamming the door. I waited a good long while before getting up and slipping on my pants. It was late afternoon when I drew back the blinds to look out at the building across Fourth Street. A gentle breeze blew north, shepherded along the man-made canyons, carrying with it the smell of the river. It seemed an eternity before I heard the doorknob turn. She opened the door just a crack and said, "I'm so sorry. Can you forgive me?"

"I'm the one who should be asking your forgiveness. I'm sorry Mary, but I just can't see doing anything else. We didn't ask for this fight, but we sure as hell gotta finish it. I just don't think I could live with myself knowing that my friends were in harm's way while I sat at home fat and happy. I've got to do my job and be a part of this."

She put her fingers to my lips to stop my words, saying, "I know. That's one of the many reasons I love you so. I don't understand why men feel they have to fight to prove their worth, but my daddy did twenty years ago and now here you do, too. I believe it must be something God weaves into a man's heart. The need to be a warrior. The need to protect your family. I don't really understand, but I'll try to. I'm just sorry I slapped you."

"I deserved it. I should have let you have some say in the decision. It's just that I didn't think there was really any decision to be made. My gut is telling me this is something I must do… I just don't have a choice here." We stood in silent embrace at the window, wrapped loosely in the sheet and watched the early summer sky turn from dark blue to night.

CHAPTER 9

I started out my advanced training, as did all contemporaneously trained military pilots, flying the North American AT-6. In the Army Air Corps we called them "Texans" while the Navy called them "SNJs." Different nomenclature, but the exact same airframe produced by the same manufacturer on the exact same assembly line. The Navy pilots liked to brag their SNJ version had beefier landing gear for carrier landings, but that was not truly the case. I know of what I speak because my grandfather and me by default were friends of Bob Schultz, one of the engineers who designed the *Texan* for North American. Kind of funny the things guys will fight over in a bar once they've had their tongues lubricated by a beer or two or twelve. They also called this airplane the "pilot maker" for what I would soon learn were very good reasons. Compared to what I had previously been flying, this airplane was a big, butt-ugly brute with its own set of idiosyncrasies, quirks purposely included by design as obstacles to either overcome or be devoured by. This was not done callously or maliciously, but rather to prepare us for similar idiosyncrasies that we would encounter in heavier, faster combat aircraft. A Pratt & Whitney R-1340, 650 horsepower radial engine powered the *Texan*. A metal, variable-pitched prop gave it a distinctive, deafening sound, because at full power the prop tip speeds exceeded the sound barrier with a deafening roar. An electric inertial starter, retractable landing gear, radios and navigational equipment, and best of all, machine guns, three .50 caliber Browning, made the *Texan* a perfect trainer for the airplanes we would soon be called to fight in. I would soon be expressing both love and hate for the bastard in the same breathe.

Because of the complexities of this new aircraft we spent the first week of advanced training doing all our flying on the ground. I was like a caged feral cat, pacing my enclosure, awaiting escape. It helped that Mary was close by, filling every night with pleasure. There was between us an unspoken sense of urgency, an immediacy of foreboding, the pretense of loss. We laughed and loved and carried on all the while knowing separation was imminent, our reverie soon to be shattered by the mission at hand. We made the best of the moments we had together, sucking the marrow out of each last second. When at last it was time to mount up and go tame the *Texan,* Mary stood outside the perimeter fence along with some of the other wives to watch me take off.   Even though we had been warned of the phenomenon, it took a whole lot more right foot to keep the accelerating airplane tracking the runway centerline. Giving it the power, I was quickly up to fifty knots and pushing on the stick to fly the tail off the ground. The airplane was so massively wide I had only a small bit of runway edge at the limits of my peripheral vision to guide me. With the tail up I saw that I was nowhere near the centerline but was in fact about to depart the left side of the runway. I mashed on that right rudder enough to track the runway's farthest left border before rotating. Clear of the ground and accelerating skyward, my next job was to retract the landing gear, a feat easier said than done in the *Texan.* The landing gear and flaps were each powered by a hydraulic system that needed to be manually energized, requiring the pilot to depress a lever prior to operating either the gear or flap controls. The hard part was reaching down and backward to energize the system, then down and forward to pull the gear handle as these calisthenics distracted the novice pilot, requiring he look down into the cavernous cockpit rather than forward at the horizon. The end result was that I, the still-novice pilot, was all over the runway and then all over the sky.

From the ground it must have looked comedic, like a careening circus clown car. Knowing that Mary was here watching me fly for the very first time made me feel ill. I was red-faced embarrassed until Jim Cleveland, my new designated instructor said, "Not bad for a first time. I didn't have to touch the controls even once."

"Really? I thought you'd wonder if I'd ever been in an airplane in my life after that takeoff."

"Did you hurt yourself or the airplane?"

"No, sir."

"Then that's pretty good. Not too many guys that I don't have to help a little on the controls with their first takeoff and landing. I'm pretty forgiving on the first couple, after that, not so much. If you can put her back on the deck with the same skill you just showed me you'll be the best student I've had to date."

"Well now you've jinxed me."

"I doubt that. All the reports up to this point say you're a natural. I'm gonna find out today for myself. Why don't you turn thirty degrees right and climb on up to 10,000. We'll start off by finding the edge of the envelope."

We spent the next hour and a half doing stalls and spins. The *Texan* proved to be an amazingly nimble airplane for all its ungainly appearance. I bounced the first landing a bit trying to find the ground, but I kept good directional control and exited the runway feeling pretty good about myself. Mary and her new friends were still at the fence cheering for me as I taxied in. Jim pointed them out asking, "Do you know those girls over by the fence?'

"Yeah, the redhead is my wife." She looked great standing there in a new blue dress that made her eyes appear even more vibrant. Her heels made her legs' oh so perfect… even from a hundred yards away she was stunning. I was so proud.

"Wow, she's a looker. You're one lucky son-of-a-bitch!"

"You bet I am. She's great. How about you? You married?"

"I got a girl back home that I've been writing to, but kind of hard to figure all that out with the war and all." Sounding embarrassed, he quickly changed the subject.

"Shut this bitch down and we'll go debrief the flight."

"Yes, sir!"

I spent the next two weeks flying twice a day with Jim Cleveland. He turned out to be a really nice guy. Some of the other cadets griped about him, but I never had cause. I logged thirty hours flying during that period, in addition to several hours a day in ground school discussing multi-engine procedures. Jim got me feeling pretty comfortable in the Texan and ready for the next hurdle.

I got the weekend off, so Mary and I borrowed a buddy's car and drove to Cincinnati to take in a baseball game at Crosley Field. The Reds were hosting the Brooklyn Dodgers in a doubleheader on Sunday. It was my 22nd birthday and Mary wanted to do something special. I would have been happy to check into a hotel room and spend the weekend ravaging each other, but she said we could do both. We checked into the Netherlands Hotel and found ourselves in the same room we had shared two weeks earlier. By eight p.m. we had made love in both the bed and the closet. After showering together, I put on my dress uniform and she wore her blue dress with her mother's pearls. We were quite a handsome couple when we appeared in the hotel restaurant for our dinner reservation. The following day we slept in late. Mary read a novel, Ernest Hemingway's *For Whom the Bell Tolls*, which had just been published, while I read *The Enquirer* from cover to cover. For a late lunch we walked to the park. Mary had found out about a deli located between the park and our hotel, so we stopped along the way and bought two corned beef sandwiches with tomato and mustard and two Coca-colas. She brought the blanket off the bed and we had a picnic in a spot secluded among some grand old trees on the hill overlooking the city. After lunch we continued our reading, I with my back against the tree and she with her head in my lap. I dozed off for what seemed a great restful nap only to be awakened by Mary playfully nibbling on my crotch. I was pretty quickly awake, but not before Mary could undo my belt and unzip my trousers. Her dress on and panties off, she straddled me. Beneath the enclosure of her dress she guided me with her hand into her wet warmth then proceeded to bob up and down on my shaft, never once dropping the book from her view.

"Well this is certainly turning into my best birthday ever," I said, amazed at her boldness.

Mary just giggled. I reached for her breast but she slapped my hand away.

"Someone might see, silly," she stage whispered. "You can do that later tonight."

I acquiesced and put my hands behind my head as she nonchalantly brought me to a shuttering, silent climax. She smiled and continued to read as I gradually went soft inside her. She finally rolled off and curled up under my arm and we watched the sunset over the hills south of the river. After dark, we strolled casually back to the hotel. I remember feeling more content than I ever had in my life.

The next day we walked to Crosley Field for the games. We ate hotdogs smothered in Cincinnati chili and covered with pickle relish, mustard and chopped onions. We drank Hudepohl beer from amber bottles and cheered as the Dodgers beat the Reds 4 to 1 in the first game. I'll never forget looking over at Mary that afternoon. The way the sunlight played on her auburn hair, transposing it into an amber halo. The soft beauty of her face, the ampleness of her curves, her contagious smile and poise, the gracious ease with which she both strode the earth and lived in her skin. I knew I was the luckiest man on earth. I fixed that image in my brain like a photograph, knowing on some primitive level it would one day bring me sustenance.

The Reds got their revenge under the lights in the second game, winning two to one. As the sun was setting we saw a contingent of five B-17 bombers in close formation fly over, leaving the magic of an unforgettable weekend shattered in their wake. They were awe-inspiring, but droning northward over the city they broke the magic reverie of the weekend, reminding us of the arduous task at hand. I had to report for duty at 0700, so we drove back to Dayton holding hands in the dark, a night made all the deeper by our quiet contemplation.

The next morning I was still pretty sleepy as I walked to the flight line at dawn. All the talking was over. Now it was time to break and saddle a new mount. Awaiting us sat a line of relatively new Beechcraft AT-10s, dubbed the "Wichita." Manufactured in Wichita Kansas, the twin-engine trainers had been painted bright yellow so that no civilian observing them from the ground would mistake them for an enemy bomber. Wisely anticipating the looming shortage of aluminum, Walter Beech designed the trainer to be constructed almost entirely of wood. Even the fuel tanks were ingeniously constructed of plywood, lined with a coating of nitrile rubber. Mr. Beech's genius stopped there. Though powered by a pair of Lycoming 285 horsepower radials, the little airplane was woefully underpowered. Even with both engines churning full bore, the little airplane felt deficient, deprived of all it could have been with just a little more muscle.

It seemed odd sitting in the cramped cockpit to the left of my instructor, whom I could see eye-to-eye rather than sitting in tandem where the only measure of the instructor's displeasure was a rap on one's skull. In the Wichita I could gauge my performance by observing facial expressions, subtle nuances of his satisfaction or disappointment. My first multi-instructor was a captain, David Owens of Portland, Oregon. He walked me through the start-up procedure on the right engine, and then asked that I perform what I had just learned on the left. He said, "Don't get too used to flying with more than one engine on this airplane. The secret to flying multi is learning how to fly with fewer engines than are hanging out there on the wings." I didn't understand immediately, but I soon did. We flew for a couple of hours doing stalls and steep turns, getting a feel for the flight characteristics of a new airplane. Dave then asked, "Are you ready?"

"No time like the present," I answered confidently.

"We'll start with a left engine out. Get your foot ready," he said, pulling the power on the left. The airplane veered leftward as anticipated then began to shudder as if entering a stall. With the right rudder pedal held to the floor I could yaw the airplane back to some semblance of normal flight.

"Now make a 360 degree turn to the left," Dave said, watching to see if I could figure it out. To turn left, I banked left and let some of the pressure off of the right rudder.

"Good job," he said, surprised. "Now turn right." I banked right, but without rudder I started to skid. Intuitively I pulled back a little on the power and stopped the skid.

"Very well done!" he said, truly impressed.

"I can see how this would give your legs a work out."

"Imagine flying home from Germany like this. Hours from home would give you quite a workout. Now picture doing it injured," he said grimly.

"God forbid!"

"It's happening every day now. Get good at this. It may mean the difference between life and death for you and your crew," he said emphatically. We flew for another hour doing shallow turns with one or the other engine at idle, its prop feathered.

"Tomorrow we'll do some stalls and steep turns with the same configuration. You did very well today. I think the buzz about you being a natural is probably true," he smiled. I felt myself blushing, then suddenly embarrassed at doing so. "Let's go home," he said with a nod of his head. I added power and equalized the engines while turning back to the base, awash in a sea of pride.

For the next eight weeks I logged more time flying the AT-10 with a single engine, right or left, than I did flying it with both. As training progressed I began flying more and more complex missions which, though personally satisfying, had the unhappy consequence of my seeing less and less of Mary. Although I was with her every spare moment, it just wasn't enough for neither she nor I, but she never once complained. Instead she repeatedly reminded me, "Do your best! Learn to fly that thing better than anyone else so you can come home to me." I knew she was right. My reward, getting to grow old with Mary, would become the greatest single motivator in my life.

Our entire group completed the first weeks of advanced multi training without a hiccup. It now was time for the real thing. Two-thirds of us were assigned to fly B-24 *Liberators* in Dayton while the remaining were being sent to Langley to fly B-17s. I took this as a pretty sure sign that I would be serving in Europe and started wrapping my mind around the fact I would soon be killing Germans. Somehow I found it harder to see white, northern Europeans as an enemy than it was to see Asians as an enemy. The Germans were enough like us, white, Christian, civilized, that it was easy to feel empathy at some level. My grandmother was from Germany and I was sure I still had some brace of kinfolk there, kinfolk that I would anonymously be killing by dropping bombs upon them from 20,000 feet. I didn't seem to have those same reservations about the Japs. They attacked us, after all. They were foreign and mysterious, and after Pearl Harbor it seemed obvious to all Americans that the mystery surrounding them was nothing more than a disguise, a thin veil that cloaked hearts of pure evil. Unlike killing Germans, I felt no moral ambiguity about killing the sneaky bastards. They were an enemy I found easy to hate, a hatred ignited by their own treacherous actions, a hatred that became a passionate call to duty. Was it now not only our right, but our duty to deliver the war to their doorstep? The more I thought about it the angrier I became. It roiled in my gut for the remainder of my training, a daily topic of contention with anyone willing to listen.

My first encounter with a B-24 came on July 6 of '42. It was such an astounding beast I shall never forget first laying eyes upon it. There were twenty of them spread out upon acres and acres of concrete ramp, awaiting us in the hot morning sun. They seemed massive at first glance, big as boxcars. These machines were brand spanking new, fresh off the Consolidated Aircraft Corporation assembly line in San Diego. We would be the first class to fly these new trainers, guinea pigs in the Army's experiment to streamline bomber pilot training. The Allies desperately needed to get pilots to the front faster and in ever increasing numbers. The whole country was gearing up production of everything from pilots and soldiers to airplanes, tanks and ships. These bombers would soon be produced at the unfathomable rate of one per hour thanks to production line techniques garnered from the likes of Henry Ford, an astounding feat given the sheer size and technological complexity of each aircraft. Unfortunately, it took much longer to train a pilot to fly the airplane than it did to produce the weapon itself, a fact that irritated the top brass who for the most part had no experience with aviation.

All twenty of us gathered in the shade of the wing of the closest airplane to discuss the day's training activities and await the arrival of the chief instructor. Arriving ten minutes late, he profusely apologized, standing in the back of the jeep to lecture us on the merits of the *Liberator*.

"Gentlemen, welcome to your new home. This lady is the Consolidated B-24 and she's your new mistress. You'll either love her or hate her, but if you don't respect her the bitch will take everything you own including your life." There were a few chuckles at the captain's allusions, but they quickly hushed when his face did not sport a smile. "You laugh, but you're gonna find out that she will kick your ass and take your lunch money quicker than any bully you ever had nightmares about." He waited for comment, then satisfied that there was none, continued. "These planes are fresh from the factory at a cost to Uncle Sam of $300,000 apiece. He expects you to take care of and return his property. We are providing you with the most technologically advanced weapon in the history of mankind. She can fly faster and farther carrying more payload- ten crewmembers, ten hours of fuel, and 2000 pounds of ordinance- than any other aircraft in service today. All her powers come at a cost. She is the most difficult-to-fly aircraft in our fleet, designed for performance and not your comfort or even your survival. Remember, she was designed with one thought in mind, killing, and today she's gonna try and kill you. The tricycle landing gear makes her easier to land, but harder to taxi. Her ground handling is a nightmare. You'll find your accommodations inside surprisingly cramped for such a large bird. No space was wasted on you. The only way out is through the back, walking the narrow catwalk over the bomb bays. When I say narrow I mean narrow at only twelve inches wide. The bomb bay doors retract like a rolltop desk, eliminating drag from a door hanging out in the slipstream. This is good because it does not slow you down over the target. The downside being the door itself is light, only supporting about a hundred pounds of weight. If you fall off the catwalk in flight you're gonna fall through the door to your death. Don't fall!" he said, looking about to see if his words were achieving the desired effect. He then jumped from the back of the jeep and began to walk around the airplane pointing out various features to all of us who were following, hanging on his every word. His cynicism had indeed fostered our undivided attention. "This engine is the Pratt & Whitney R-1830. Turbo supercharged, 1200 horsepower apiece. They leak oil at a phenomenal rate. The three-blade prop is a Hamilton-Standard, fully featherable, hydraulic controlled. The wing above you is called the 'Davis' wing after some engineer at Consolidated, designed to flex without breaking. The wingspan is one hundred ten feet, the length sixty-seven feet, eight inches. She weighs 35,000 pounds empty. Maximum take off weight is 65,000 pounds." Walking around the tail of the aircraft, he pointed out the size of the massive rudders. "It takes all of that to turn this gal and there is no mechanical assist, it's all you. Even with that she's slow to respond to inputs, making close formation flying nearly impossible." Grabbing hold of a gun barrel he said, "Here's your rear protection, two Browning .50 caliber machine guns. You'll find a total of ten of these guns as we walk around, four pairs in turrets and one on each side at the waist positions. Notice that there are no windshield wipers for the pilot or copilot. You see forward on the ground by sticking your head out the window and taking a look."

"And getting wet or cold," I added.

"Exactly right! Like I said, not much thought was given to making you comfortable, which is unfortunate given your missions may last ten hours or more. That's a long time to be stuck in an ill-fitting seat. Did I mention there is no heater and it gets pretty fucking cold at 40,000 feet?"

"Sounds cozy," I quipped. He clearly was not amused, but continued on without missing a beat. It was clear this talk was scripted. He'd given this speech many times in the recent past and was now on a mission to complete it again without interruptions.

"She cruises at 215 miles per hour with a maximum of 290. She stalls dead at exactly ninety-five miles per hour. Stall recovery in a B-24 is a skill all its own, an art that we will teach you over the next week. Any questions?" Seeing there were none, he pointed out the small group of officers, none over the age of twenty-four, who stood waiting behind us.

"Gentlemen, split into groups of three or four and join up with one of the instructors there. Today you'll each get a turn at the controls. During the flight I want each of you to spend some time in each of the stations aboard. We want you to have some idea of the tasks you'll soon be asking your crews to perform." He saluted and we returned the salute in unison before he shouted, "Dismissed!"

I ambled over to a friendly looking fellow who had just popped a stick of chewing gum in his mouth. He introduced himself as, "Jim Truitt of Walla Walla, Washington." We introduced ourselves and exchanged small talk for a few minutes before Jim pulled down a ladder and the four of us climbed through the rear hatch, making our way to the cockpit. As a group, Jim walked us through an introduction to the B-24 instruments and start-up procedure. We then played rock, paper, scissors to see who would have the honors of being first in the left seat. I won, but I wasn't sure I was happy about it. After a brief pep talk, Jim pulled back the window, making sure a lineman stood at the ready with a fire extinguisher. Beginning with the left outboard engine he fired them up one by one, waiting for each to be humming to his satisfaction before moving to the next. He would do the first takeoff, then we would trade positions in flight. We were third in a line of six taxiing out to the runway. It was nearing 1130, the temperature rapidly rising, projected to top out at eighty-five. It had to be ninety-five in the cabin already. Jim was sweating profusely, getting quite a workout simply manipulating the controls to taxi.

"Looks like fun, doesn't it?" he quipped. I couldn't hear his voice over the din of the four radial engines, but I could read his lips.

"It looks like a lot of work," I shouted. It was a lot of work. A ninety-degree turn required a whole body effort on the pilot's part, having to be both anticipated and commenced well in advance of the required maneuver if he hoped to avoid obstacles in his path.

Aligned with the runway at long last, Jim simultaneously advanced all four throttles. Each of the throttles could be moved independently if the need arose but were arranged so they also could be moved as if a single unit. The mixture and prop controls had a similar configuration. All three groupings were on a central console along with the trim control wheels, which required the pilot to fly left handed, keeping his right hand free to change power settings.

Jim rotated at 105 mph, and the big bomber lumbered into the sky in trail of two others. We climbed up to eight thousand feet, and joined up with the other *Liberators* before separating to go our lone ways. Once well clear of any other aircraft, Jim turned on the autopilot, or "Charlie" as he called it, and we switched positions, allowing me to assume the role of pilot, left seat. Turning "Charlie" off proved to be somewhat of a shock. Thinking I was prepared, I was quite surprised to discover the effort required to accomplish something as simple as changing directions. I flew for almost an hour doing shallow turns, ascents and descents before giving command over to the next student, amazed at the fatigue in my left arm upon getting out of the seat. Flying this baby was going to be a physical workout, no doubt about it.

Once again a passenger, I climbed through the door and spent some time in each of the other stations as ordered. As advertised, walking heel to toe over the eighteen-foot expanse of the narrow catwalk in flight proved a bit unnerving. A bit of turbulence could transform the trek into an almost impossible feat. My first stop was the lower turret ball. In the Liberator this was, of necessity, a retractable affair allowing for ground clearance beneath the airplane. Opening the hatch, I peered inside the cramped quarters. My lanky frame couldn't have fit inside even if I were greased up. Once inside the ball, the gunner was forced to endure sitting with his knees to his chest for hours on end. It must take a small man with a tremendous amount of courage to fight the war from this vantage point.

Unlike the ball turret gunner, the waist gunner could move about freely, but he did have his own set of difficulties. His only armor was a helmet and heavy flak vest. Even worse, he was constantly exposed to the unceasing blast of wind through a large open port in the wall, which, while in summer may have been a blessing, in the winter was a curse. Above 40,000 feet it would be pure torture regardless of the season or special apparel. The view from the waist however was spectacular. I stood behind the mounted machine gun and like a child pretended I was shooting at German 109s attacking from above, secretly happy that no one else was about to see or hear my *ak-ak-ak* machine gun imitation. I could see how easy it would be to loose a *bandit*, the name given attacking enemy fighters, in the sun's blinding glare. I could also see how a gunner, distracted in the heat of battle, might potentially shoot and damage friendly aircraft or even his own aircraft. Perhaps a wider formation would be a good thing. At least it will be harder for my own people to shoot me down.

Finished daydreaming, I slid through the tunnel to the tail gunner seat. Though not as snug a fit as the ball turret, the man occupying it would find himself in pretty tight quarters with a very limited view. This was the only position in the airplane from which an attack from the rear, whether from above or below, could be reasonably defended. I shuddered to imagine needing to escape from either this seat or the ball turret in the event of a catastrophe. My bet was chances of getting out alive were few to none from either. With that thought in mind, I began considering emergency egress from the position I would assume. The pilot, co-pilot, and bombardier all had to pass through a narrow port then cross the catwalk to reach the exit. Trying to accomplish that trek as a crippled airplane accelerated, tumbling uncontrolled out of the sky would clearly be almost impossible. As the captain of this ship, my crews only hope of survival would require me to stay at the controls, keeping it upright for as long as possible. I also would have to anticipate our demise and order the crew out. Once the death spiral began all hope was lost for everyone aboard. I couldn't let that happen. I wouldn't let that happen. This was an epiphany. It had previously been a passing thought, a nod to the standard conventions and expectations of leadership, but here it was, real and tangible and overwhelming. I would personally be responsible for the survival and well being of nine other souls, a responsibility that may well require the sacrifice of my own life. In an instant I felt brave and determined yet exceedingly small and timid, a mouse against a lion. I spent the rest of the flight in quiet contemplation, sitting in the navigator's seat until a buzzer sounded, a signal I assumed meant to come back up front.

Jim, now flying from the right seat, allowed Bob Hirschman, the last guy flying left seat, to stay where he was. We joined up with the other five bombers, and then headed for home. As we turned final, Jim walked Bob through the landing sequence, and he did a great job, the wheels barely squeaking as we rejoined the ground. Bob was feeling pretty cocky until we reached the turnoff point where he underestimated the turn. Thankfully we were going pretty slowly by that point and the airplane was not damaged. The same could not be said for Bob's pride. Jim taxied us out of the dirt and back on to the tarmac. It had been a very eye-opening day. Though I clearly had my work cut out for me learning to fly this thing, I knew I could do it. More than just do it, I was confident I could excel at it. I liked this big ugly crate, this weapon of inestimable destruction, this symbol of death. I shouldn't wonder so much about such things. Had not Christians for centuries loved and cherished emblems of their faith that at face value was no more or less than the same, like the cross, a tool with which to kill other people? The airplane felt substantial yet ethereal in much the same way as the cross of Jesus. Not to sound too fruity, but this plane indeed had a spiritual quality, a soul if you will. Many Native American peoples imbued inanimate objects with souls and I think on some level they must be correct. From the moment I passed through the hatch I sensed this airplane had a soul or a heart or whatever you may want to call it, a sensation that just did not go away. A heart that greeted your heart, entwined with it, a presence real yet invisible, just like the winds that carried it aloft. Something that promised to protect you, a promise to bring you home if you would but learn to respect her. I didn't really know her yet, but already I respected her. These thoughts were not something I felt comfortable sharing with another man, but my Mary listened and understood and even loved the airplane before she ever laid eyes upon one. God, I loved that woman.

I spent the next four weeks learning the *Liberator*, inside and out. I could fly it with only two of the four engines cranking. I could land it in a forty-knot direct crosswind. I could land it at night and in the rain. The only question that remained, the one most haunting one; could I fly it in combat? Could I keep a cool head when the flak shells were bursting around me, when enemy fighters were swarming like bees, shooting at me, all the while evading our own defenses? When friends were dying all around me, being shot from the sky like so many fowl? I thought I could, but really I could only barely begin to imagine how it would be. At twenty-four, it was still easy to feel invincible, even immortal. Dreams of glory were as common as stars, but on dreary nights even those stars had to be taken on faith, being hidden by clouds as dense as one's immediate reality. I would find out soon enough, I supposed.

At last the big day, Friday, August 7, 1942, came and I graduated from flight training. I was happy as was our entire group, but the celebration was mechanical and false, no pomp and circumstance. There was a war on and we were just products, much-needed widgets produced for the war machine in ever increasing and therefore more mundane numbers. I was, in a word, common, a single soul among thousands and soon to be millions, all with a single common purpose. Only Mary believed I was more special than a common Joe and I loved her for it all the more. We were given a weekend pass after being instructed to report for orders on Monday at 0800.

All my classmates were heading to the officers club to celebrate, but Mary and I, assuming this would be our last weekend together for the foreseeable future, were determined to make the best of it. There would be plenty of time for drinking with my buddies later. Mary had already packed and was waiting for me. She looked pretty as a picture in her new dress. It was white Swiss with red polka dots and did little to hide her beautiful form. I wanted to ravage her then and there but she just laughed saying, "Hold your horses, cowboy. Anticipation is half the fun." Anticipation was a euphemism for a cruelly sweet torture. She really expected me to wait, but what could I say? Mary had a real knack for knowing just how to turn my crank and I loved her for it all the more.

We caught a train bound for Chicago along with at least fifty other uniformed guys. The Drake Hotel on Michigan Avenue had a special deal for servicemen. Mary had once stayed there as a child and remembered it as magical. After asking me if we could afford it, she made all the reservations. We couldn't really, but I wasn't about to tell her no. She said the Drake was "grand and beautiful" and was giddy as a schoolgirl at the prospect of staying there. I, too, was excited, but it had nothing to do with the hotel. As far as I was concerned all we really needed was a bed and a place to eat when we came up for air, which I hoped wouldn't be too often.

As I said, Mary looked great. A couple of soldiers, kid private recruits I recognized from the train, must have agreed because they whistled as she got out of the taxi. They had turned and were walking back to the curb just as I got out on the opposite side. Both stopped short when, over the taxi, I smiled and pointed to the bars on my shoulder then the wedding band on my finger. "Sorry, sir," they mumbled before making a hasty retreat. I couldn't blame them really. Mary was indeed beautiful, and a guy would have to be dead not to notice her, especially the way she looked that day. This encounter was the second time I had witnessed such testosterone-fueled admiration of Mary. *My* Mary. *My* wife. The operative word in both of those phrases was *my*. Mary was mine and no other had dared aspire to have her. I've got to confess this sort of incident, this innocent little interaction was made me jealous and constantly more possessive. I was proud of Mary. Damned proud just to be with her, but the things that made me so proud of her also attracted other men just as surely and powerfully as they had attracted me. The nature of this thing was basic animal attraction, an irresistible pull like moths to a flame. This natural order of things made me afraid. Afraid that in my absence Mary would find someone else, someone stronger, smarter or more handsome than me. Someone a calloused world would naturally choose as a preferable mate for a prize like Mary. In short, someone better than the likes of me! The more I thought about it the crazier it made me. My jealous paranoia grew exponentially by the minute. It threatened to overwhelm me and bring ruin to this, our last weekend alone together before I went off to war, leaving her for months, if not years, unprotected from the advances of other men. It was only a matter of time before that *someone better* would be the one to make an overture.

Over supper I found myself vigilantly scanning the room looking for anyone brazen enough to cast a leering glance her way. Mary noticed my distraction and asked, "What's wrong?" I'd been found out. I didn't want to tell her the truth, which was the fact that I was becoming a jealous idiot, so I just said smiled my best fake smile and said, "Everything's great, why?"

"You just seem to be somewhere else."

"I'm right here sitting three feet away from the prettiest girl in the world." I meant every word of it. Her smile began to break down my defenses. I should tell her what a loony I was becoming, but before I could begin the waiter arrived at the table with our dinners.

"Eat up there, cowboy. You're gonna need your strength," she said, taking my hand with a leering smile of her own. The touch of her hand shot through me like a million volts of electric current. Yet again I found myself enchanted, bewitched by her womanly charm, a hormonal flood that washed over me, tumbling me head over heel like a tsunami. Forget everyone else in the whole wide world. Mary was my wife and I her husband, her man, her *only* man. This was going to be one wild ride of a weekend. It was clear Mary intended to send her warrior off to battle dripping with the war paint of her very essence, a carnal tattoo declaring her ownership to anyone who might look my way. I was lucky enough to be that warrior.

CHAPTER 10

"I'm not going to Europe," I announced upon opening the manila envelope containing my orders, the look on my face announcing surprise at the news seconds before my words. Mary and I along with a few fellow graduates and their wives had gathered on the steps outside of base command headquarters to open our orders, one by one disclosing our fates to the group. I was the only new graduate in our group assigned to the Pacific, news that both shocked and thrilled me. The other guys slapped me on the back with the heartiest of congratulations, some with not too well disguised jealousy, but Mary's eyes revealed she did not share their elation. Until now Mary and I had little doubt I was destined for England to fight the Nazi Hun bastards, anticipating the same assignment received by ninety percent of all newly minted bomber pilots. Mary had packed me a couple of pairs of long johns, heavy woolen socks, and the sweater she knitted me for Christmas in preparation of the cold, damp weather of the English isles, but I wouldn't be needing any of those luxuries. The tropics was where I was bound and a totally different enemy, the Japs were dug in awaiting me. Paraphrasing, I shared the remainder of my assignment. I was to board the 9:20, a troop train out of Chicago, bound for San Francisco where I would be assigned and meet my crew. From there we would board another train to San Diego to pick up a brand new B-24 from the Consolidated Aircraft Corporation's assembly plant. After two days of flying to wring the bugs out of the bomber, we would shuttle the bomber to the South Pacific by way of Hawaii. The thought of flying over that vast expanse of ocean made me anxious. I hoped the navigator assigned to my crew would be a good one, though I didn't share that thought aloud. No reason to make Mary more anxious for my safety than she already was.

We were all packed, expecting to leave that day, but the other guys, everyone bound for Europe, got a short reprieve as they did not ship out till the next day. I, on the other hand, would be on the 9:20 for Chicago that very morning, in little more than an hour. A lone jeep and driver pulled up to the curb, my transportation to the train station. I begged the guy to let Mary ride along so we could say goodbye at the station. At first he said it was against regulation, but when he saw Mary doing her best faux pout and looked around to see the group happily dispersing, lacking anyone who might care about those regulations, he relented. "Thanks pal, I owe you one," I said tossing my B-4 bag then myself into the back of the jeep. Mary sat up front with him. I vowed to myself never to forget the image of Mary's red hair blowing in the breeze, a dancing veil to the delicate features of her ever more beautiful face. Mary was determined to be a trooper. She looked back, smiling at me almost constantly as we drove along, but despite her brave facade, I could see the moisture collecting in the corners of her eyes, the faintest betrayal of her heart's true desperation.

This goodbye was going to be painful. Mary and I both knew it was the prelude to a minimum of a yearlong separation. At least I had the promise of the adventure I was embarking upon to distract me. Poor Mary would soon be left alone to ruminate on the sorrow of our separation, not to mention the ever-present specter, that of an almost palpable fear and the anxiety of loss. An irretrievable loss. An unfathomable loss. An unsurvivable loss, the forever loss of me, her husband and lover. She never shared as much, but I knew what she was thinking for I was thinking the same.

Pulling up to the train station I offered the corporal five bucks if he would wait and take Mary home. He declined the money but agreed to wait for Mary as we said our goodbyes.

"Good luck and God speed sir," he said offering me a crisp salute.

"Thank you," I said returning it. "This shouldn't take too long."

"Take all the time you need, sir."

I tossed my bag to the curb then took Mary's hand to help her down. She put her arm around my waist locking her hip to mine and tucking her body and soul under my arm, we walked to the platform conjoined as one being, a condemned being consigned to walk to its imminent execution. Awash in the noise of the busy terminal, neither of us said a word. We didn't have to speak as all the words had already been spoken, any others would prove superfluous and empty. At the platform's edge we stopped and clung to each other in frontal embrace, a grip held until the conductor called the final "All aboard!" At this we acquiesced to the inevitability of our separation. Tearfully whispering, "I love you," her voice broke, fragmenting into multiple simultaneous pitches too dissonant to be musical.

"I love you, too!" I took her face in my hands and, peering into tear wet eyes, took one long last drink from the dregs of her soul before turning and jumping aboard. I didn't look back, afraid that seeing her alone, sobbing and bereft on the platform would reduce me to tears, a vulnerability I did not want to display in the company of other men. I set about choking those emotions down by sheer will. I would concentrate on something else, anything else, *anything* other than Mary.

Stowing my bag under the first available seat, I sat there transfixed for what seemed like hours, lost in oblivion, ignorant of others around me. I gazed intently at the flat Illinois horizon thinking this, as it would vertigo, might soften the hollow ache in my soul. Hypnotized by mundaneness, the surrounding countryside lacking any feature to which I felt akin, I soon fell asleep, and not just any sleep, but a deep chasm of impenetrable sleep where the unhappy world melted away. That is how I survived those first few days of separation from Mary. Rightly, I don't remember much about that thirty-six hour train ride to San Francisco. I retain vague images of other uniformed men around me, men strangely animated, even raucous as they intermittently invaded the numbing cloud enveloping my brain, but I don't recall a single name or conversation.

Poetically, my mental fog and mood lifted as we rolled into San Francisco's train yard, greeted by a dense miasma, that phenomenal fog that each morning rolls in off the sea to shroud the city within its legendary billows. I'd never experienced a fog quite so dense, but I'd read about San Francisco's unique weather since I was a child and now here it was to greet me. It seemed almost magical, fulfilling the fairy tale proportions that my juvenile brain had envisioned. Surprisingly cool for a mid-summer day, the damp cold gave me gooseflesh. I opened my B-4 bag and retrieved the sweater Mary had packed for me before realizing I would be unacceptably out of uniform if I donned it. I inhaled of it deeply in hopes it might retain Mary's scent before pushing it back into the bag.

It seemed the whole of the United States Army was milling about the platform and adjacent terminal, scurrying about seeking direction. I had no clue as to where exactly I should report, nor how I was to get there. A sergeant with a clipboard by the main entrance appeared to be the oracle of all information military, so I waited in a long line for the opportunity to ask his direction.

"My guess, and it's only a guess, is you're to report to headquarters out at Hamilton in Novato. Take the Fulton Street trolley to Union Square. Get off in front of the St. Francis Hotel. You can either take a taxi or wait for the bus. There should be a city bus that comes by every hour or so. It can get you out to the airport. Next!" he yelled before I could say, "Thanks. You're right, it's Hamilton." Although impatient for me to move along, he acknowledged my "thanks" with a nod.

I caught the trolley as instructed to Union Square, hopping off in front of the hotel. Unknown to the rest of America, this place was a real hot bed of military activity in the summer of 1942. As I waited for the bus at the curb I saw two admirals and lots of other Navy brass coming and going. I considered asking what the deal was, but figured too many questions might arouse suspicion in light of the war and the ever-present fear of invasion permeating the psyche of the West Coast. If I didn't already know I probably didn't need to know, but intrigued, I followed a group of sailors inside. The lobby awaiting was beautiful and I'm glad my curiosity had gotten the better of me. Inside was an impressively large case clock I romanticized as having watched over all who stayed as guests, its incessant ticking echoing across highly polished floors of travertine marble, above the din of numerous patrons, military or otherwise. The walls were of a beautifully patinaed walnut burl that must have cost a blue fortune when the hotel was constructed. You just don't see such opulence, such attention to detail anymore. I later discovered that beginning in 1942 Admiral Nimitz directed the Navy's Pacific operation from the second floor of the St. Francis, an impromptu command center he continued to use throughout the war. This only added to the legend and mystique of the old hotel with many stories and secrets to share if one but bothered to look. One such secret; the St. Francis had once been the venue of a now infamous scandal in the 1920's when silent film star Fatty Arbuckle's young female companion had been found dead following a three-day bacchanal. A corrupt newspaper, bent upon selling the provocative story, true or not, fueled the ensuing scandal by suggesting the starlet died at the hands of Arbuckle in a botched rape attempt. It rocked Hollywood, riveted the reading public, sold newspapers and ruined Arbuckle's career. In the end it took three separate trials to finally acquit Arbuckle, but really only the hotel and God knew the truth. I sat in the lobby savoring the architectural elements of a bygone era, anticipating a wait of several hours when after only thirty minutes the bus for Novato came along. Lucky for me I saw it as it pulled up.

Rushing outside, I boarded along with a dozen or so other passengers just as the fog was beginning to dissipate, intermittently revealing patches of a sunny azure sky that only minutes before could only be imagined. The bus ride took about an hour and included a crossing of the Golden Gate Bridge. By the time we reached the bridge, the fog had completely vanished, not a single cloud or wisp of moisture to be seen. The spectacular view of the bridge as well as the view of the city from that vantage point made me determined to acquire a camera before I left the States. Mary would have loved to see this. I wanted a way to share these images with Mary when I got home, though only God himself knew when that would be.

Hamilton Army Air Field was architecturally interesting in its own right. It seemed too fancy to be a military base. The buildings were of concrete block construction hidden beneath a façade of white stucco. Red clay tile roofs completed the bases mascaraed as a Spanish villa. A sign at the gate said the base had been constructed in 1932 and was named for aviation hero Lieutenant Lloyd Andrew Hamilton of the Seventeenth Aero Squadron. Lieutenant Hamilton had been killed in action, flying near Lagnicourt, France. Though I'm sure it was a well-deserved posthumous honor any man would relish, I couldn't help but see the irony. Was this not an omen, a misplaced portent of the mishap soon to befall many of the airmen passing through these gates? Hamilton was a staging point for airmen Pacific bound. Who in their right mind would send them off with this bit of bad luck? Funny, in contemplating the potential inappropriateness of naming the base for a deceased airman, it never once crossed my mind that a similar fate might lie in wait of me. I'll bet not many people regarded the name as a prediction of demise, even if they took the time to read the plaque.

In the command building the entire first floor of the north wing was populated by row after row of desks, each home to a terse enlisted man trying to maintain his sanity as he was daily beset by an onslaught of new, soon-to-be deployed airmen. To their credit this process had become remarkably efficient, a well-oiled machine that soon had me in a room shaking hands with the best eight guys I've ever had the privilege of knowing. I was instructed to report to the mess hall at 1400 hours to meet my crew. They all knew the name of the pilot to whom they were assigned, while we pilots remained clueless. I entered the mess hall to find 400 uniformed men milling about; boisterous conversations appeared to be the order of the day. All fell silent when the base commander took the podium. The pilots were invited to the podium one by one and introduced, allowing the other men to see and identify them. After the last was introduced, the pilots were instructed to stay put so crewmembers could find the pilot to whom they had been assigned. The room soon turned into a swirling mass of male humanity as guys began looking for individual faces in the crowd. The frenzied search lasted about fifteen minutes before calm ensued. Eight guys, each eager to say hello, each as concerned about my qualifications as I was of theirs, soon surrounded me.

Of my crew, the first to find and greet me was Lieutenant "Jack" John C. Lafarge of Lafayette, Louisiana. Taller and thinner than me, two years my senior, Jack spoke with a Cajun drawl that was both pleasant and comic to anyone not from the Louisiana swamp country. Dark skin and blue eyes, Jack was a handsome man, a descendant of a mixture of cultures and races that had freely exchanged bloodlines in the Deep South over a hundred years ago. Jack would be my co-pilot on more than twenty missions before being assigned his own ship. He smoked a corncob pipe and effortlessly blew smoke rings just like my granddaddy. I liked him immediately.

Next was Lieutenant Carl Murphy. "Call me CJ," he said shaking my hand vigorously.

"Okay, CJ. Where you from and what are you gonna be doing for me?"

"I'm from Milwaukee and I just finished navigator school."

"You any good at navigating?" I asked in jest.

"Don't really know yet. You any good at flying?"

"I guess I don't really know yet either. I did finish at the top of my class, if that means anything to you," I chuckled.

"Not in the least but I guess it'll have to do," he smiled. I'll tell you what, you don't get me killed and I won't get you lost."

"That sounds like a good deal to me. Just keep in mind that if you do get us lost it's a long swim home and I'm not gonna be responsible if a shark eats your ass!"

"Fair enough," he agreed.

"What did you do back home in Milwaukee?"

"I worked in a brewery like my father before me and his father before him."

"Your dad took a little vacation?"

"What? Oh yeah, prohibition. Yeah, he worked for a bakery till Schlitz reopened in '34."

"Beer huh? Did you bring any with you?"

"Nope, sorry, but the officers club has the local stuff on tap. It's not Schlitz, but its not too bad either."

"We'll check that out later," I said offering my hand before turning to meet the next.

"And Sergeant, who are you and what is your specialty?"

"Joe Spencer of Hoboken, sir," he said, saluting.

"And what is it you do, Joe?"

"I'm a gunner sir, me and Jordy here are your waist gunners."

"Jordy?"

"Short for Jordan, sir. Jordan Fouts."

"Where you from Jordy?"

"Lexington, Kentucky, sir."

"Bourbon and horse racing, huh?"

"Yes sir, but I ain't never tried neither. Before the war I was planning on going into the ministry. I signed up for the Army right after school let out."

"So you graduated high school?"

"Well, uh, no, sir. Not exactly. I lied about my age, you see? I know it was wrong, but I figured it was for good reason."

"Well done, soldier. I'm pretty sure God can forgive you."

"He already has, sir," he said confidently. Not wishing to hear the exposé of Baptist theology that I sensed was imminently forthcoming, I quickly moved on.

"And you must be the ball turret gunner," I said offering my hand to the shortest man in the room. Immediately incensed, he quickly shot back, "And what makes you think that?"

Aware of my faux pas, I casually responded, "Because you look like the bravest guy in the room."

He began to smile, but suddenly stopped, thinking better of it. "Nice save, sir," spitting the *sir* out, more a facetious curse than a title of respect. "I'm Leonard Markowitz and I'm a Jew," he said, placing the chip back squarely on his shoulder, his eyes clearly daring me to knock it off. Leonard was accustomed to being victimized, battered so frequently by a society that mocks the weak, the lame, the *different* that he decided long ago to reject that behavior from anyone or anything. I had inadvertently struck a raw nerve. Leonard, being street tough as he was, decided to reveal all his exposed nerves and see what I'd do about it. I'd met people like Leonard before and spent some time considering why they acted as they did. Being different from most, a person can decide to embrace that difference and fight those who dare bring it up as a point of contention; do nothing, cowering in fear and accepting of the beating; or reject the difference altogether, doing everything in their power to disguise it by assimilating, blending in, sometimes to the point that they become the first to bully or mock others. Leonard had chosen the first and had spent most of his formative years in a defensive posture, a posture that, at only five foot three inches, still loomed menacingly before me. He was a dangerous little man, a man weary of being defined by his stature or his religion. Exposing both, he dared me to respond that either was anything less than a noble characteristic. He was tough and quick and I liked the idea of taking such a man to a street fight as long as he was on my side.

"Are you Ashkenazi or Sephardi?" I asked, knowing the question would defuse a tense situation. His eyes softened.

"Ashkenazi. My grandfather came from Russia. How about you, sir?" he asked respectfully.

"I'm from Valdosta, Georgia," I said, aware I was not answering his real question.

"No, I mean are you a Jew as well?"

"Well, my grandmother was Jewish so I guess that makes me a Jew too, at least in the eyes of the Nazis, and probably the Japs as well."

"How about in your own eyes?"

"You don't waste any time, do you?" I chuckled. "I'm circumcised, if that's what you mean, but that has less to do with religion and more to do with the medical beliefs of my grandfather. He was a doctor and he raised me. He was Baptist so I guess that's what I am, too, but I'm not exactly sure what I believe."

"So you don't have any qualms flying with a little *Heeb*?" a term of derision he'd grown accustomed to hearing.

"None at all. And I sure as hell couldn't fit into that ball and don't know if I'd be brave enough to do it even if I could. You've got real *chutzpah*," I said, hoping my choice of words from the small cadre of Yiddish I knew an appeasement.

"You're a real *mentsch*!" he said, smiling at last. Seeing my puzzled expression he explained, "It means you're alright in my book."

"Thanks! Where you from Leonard?"

"Call me Lenny. I'm from Queens, sir."

"Okay, Lenny. Queens huh? That's where my grandmother was from."

Oddly, I thought, his questions had struck a nerve, a hibernating ganglion, a collection of neurons for decades bereft of stimulation. "Am I a Jew? Do I even have a choice in the matter?" Is it a matter of faith or the mere fact that I have a drop of Hebrew blood coursing through my veins, blood that looks, feels, tastes, and smells indistinguishable from the blood of any other living soul on the planet? Knowing my grandmother's heritage I'd given the question considerable thought, especially after befriending several guys who were Jewish in my first year at Princeton. I had not been raised up with any education of the Hebrew part of my heritage so I decided to do a little research. I discovered that in the eyes of the world I was in fact Jewish, not by choice but by virtue of whom my ancestors were. I was Baptist, not by my choice, but by a choice made for me by a loving grandfather who wisely wanted to spare me all the pain and stigmata Judaism would undoubtedly have purchased me in a backwoods Georgia town. Being Baptist in Valdosta Georgia was less a system of faith than it was a southern social convention. America was a 'Christian' nation and we, by God, were good Americans. When my grandmother married my grandfather, a *goium*, a non-Jew, her parents disowned her. Odd I thought as her mother had done the same marrying a Navajo. I knew little if anything about neither her family nor their cryptic religion. There were no Jews in Valdosta. My grandfather had met her, Lydia, at Harvard and fallen in love. They married in spite of the open disapproval of her parents. Granddaddy brought her home to the south with him where he cherished her right up to the day she died, and continued to cherish her to the day he died. Now here, all these years later, a deceased grandmother I never knew continues to influence my life in ways I had never imagined nor considered. I guess by default I did know something about her, I knew that she must have loved my grandfather enough to give up her family, to be considered dead to them and move to Georgia.

The next fellow in line said, "Uh, sir," retrieved me from my immediate identity crisis.

"Yes? Oh, hello! You are?"

"James Moberly, sir."

"James or Jim? I asked before taking liberties with his name.

"I prefer Jim, Sir. I'm from Kalamazoo, Michigan. I'm your bombardier."

"Nice to meet you Jim. You any good?"

"The best sir! I can drop one in a pickle barrel from 20,000."

"Great! That's what all you guys say so I'll expect nothing less, Sergeant. What'd you do before the war?"

"College, sir. I was almost finished with a degree in architecture."

"Fascinating. I was working on an architecture degree myself."

"Really? Where'd you go to school?"

"Princeton," I said, suddenly proud. "How 'bout you?"

"University of Chicago. I was working on a fellowship at Taliesin with Frank Lloyd Wright when the war broke out."

"Really? I'm impressed."

"Don't be. I spent more time peeling potatoes than I did drawing. I was his kitchen slave and the war was a convenient means of escape. Of course, after signing up my first job in the Army was peeling potatoes," he laughed. "I really wanted to be a pilot, but I washed out in basic. I just couldn't get the knack of landing. It all ended when I ground-looped a *Vibrator* and destroyed it. The Army decided I'd make a better bombardier, so here I am."

"Don't feel too bad. I know lots of talented guys who washed out for one reason or another."

"Oh I don't feel bad… Okay, I did at first, but I like what I'm doing now and I'm good at it."

"Just curious, do you think your training in architecture has any bearing on that?"

"I'm sure of it! Finding the target in the site is all about pattern recognition, a skill that's second nature to an architect."

"Interesting! I'm sure we'll have plenty of time to talk about this further."

"You bet, sir," he said as we shook hands.

Assembled by the whims of fate, this crew was turning out to be pretty good. Initially unhappy that I wouldn't be allowed to handpick a crew, the guys assigned to me were probably better than what I would have or could have picked for myself.

The next guy before me was another smaller man who I rightly guessed was the tail gunner.

"What's your name soldier?"

"Wooster, sir. Bill Wooster."

"And where are you from Bill?"

"Columbus, Ohio."

"I've been there! Rickenbacker Field, right?"

"That's it, sir."

"I landed there several times in training. I never made it into town, though."

"It's nice. There's lots of pretty girls there," he said with a grin. Bill had penetrating blue eyes that conveyed both sensitivity and intelligence. I'm sure he was popular with those girls.

"Nice to meet you, Bill. What'd you do before the Army?"

"I worked at my dad's filling station and went to night school."

"Night school? What were you studying?"

"Women mostly, but writing as well. I want to be a novelist."

"That's great. Are you keeping a journal?"

"Yea. I figure the war should give me some good stories in exchange for my time."

"That's a great way to look at it."

"Just today I heard a name I'm gonna use in a novel some day. How about Bledsoe? Bledsoe Courage for a name?"

Unabashed, another man joined our conversation, "I'm Bledsoe Courage. Did I overhear my name mentioned?" Bill was clearly embarrassed at being caught so I bailed him out.

"You did. Neither of us has ever heard the surname Courage before. Bill here is a writer…"

"Wants to be a writer," Bill interjected.

"Wants to be a writer and liked the sound of your name. Says he wants to use it in a book some day."

"Is that so? Well, don't that just beat all? My momma would be so proud. She's the one that gave it to me. Made it up all on her own seeing she wasn't exactly sure who my daddy might be, an occupational hazard of sorts, you might say. Anyway, she said I'd need a strong name to make it in the world with no daddy. I reckon she was right, 'cause people do seem to take to it and all."

"So you wouldn't mind if I used it?" Bill asked.

"Not a bit! In fact I'd be right proud and honored."

"Where you from Bledsoe?"

"God's country, Atlanta, Georgia."

"I might have guessed that from your accent, the Georgia part at least. I hail from Georgia as well. Valdosta to be exact."

"And I might have figured you for a fine Southern gentleman as well," he said shaking my hand firmly. Who you looking for today?"

"Funny you should ask that," he said looking at my nametag. "I'm lookin' for you! I'm your radio man."

"Well great! We're all here then." The other guys had started to wander off so I asked, "Hey Jack, can you round up all the guys and we'll meet as a group over in that corner for a few minutes."

"Will do, Captain," he said. Jack had been trying to keep an eye on all the guys that passed our way before they dispersed into the larger group of men. Everyone collared, we met for the first time together as a group just outside the mess hall doors.

"Gentlemen, feel free to light up if you care to." I didn't yet smoke but everyone else did. Jack pulled out an old brass trench lighter his father had carried in Europe and obliged everyone else with the gift of fire.

"First just a bit of housekeeping. Officers and enlisted men are not permitted to fraternize. Not my rule, but Uncle Sam's. Here in the States we'll comply, but once we get to the PTO I'll have no trouble relaxing those rules a little as long as my word is always obeyed. You don't know me yet and I have no right other than my rank to have your respect. I hope over the coming weeks and months to earn that respect. I won't ever ask you to do anything I wouldn't do myself and I pledge to you I will do everything in my power to bring each and every one of you home safe to your loved ones. I expect the same of you. We're all combat green here and I'm man enough to admit to you I don't think I know every answer. Suggestions, as long as offered respectfully, will always be appreciated. Likewise, there is no such thing as a stupid question. It's only stupidity if you don't know something and still don't ask. Jack, excuse me, Lieutenant Lafarge and I will be here for the next few days getting lectured on things particular to our mission in the PTO. We leave Friday for San Diego where we'll pick up our ship. We get a day or two to wring the bugs out of her before we set off over the Pacific as a group. I don't know yet where were headed other than the PTO, so don't bother asking. I'll tell you where were going after we're airborne. Any questions?"

Bledsoe spoke up, "Yeah, Cap'n, we gonna name our ship?"

"Damn right we are."

"Can we get us a naked lady painted on the side as well?" he asked with an almost childlike glee.

"You bet, but we've got plenty of time for that. You guys be thinking of a name, Okay?"

"Yes, sir," they said en masse, seemingly delighted at the prospect of this first task.

"Gentlemen, we'll see you in San Diego. Dismissed! Lieutenants Murphy and Lafarge, come with me." Once out of earshot of the enlisted men I said, "CJ, you said something about the officers club having a good brew on tap?

Over the next four days Jack and I attended what was being called PTO school. PTO was the military's title for the war being waged in the Pacific, an anagram for Pacific Theater of Operation. The classes were an intense, in-depth indoctrination of everything the military thought a pilot needed to know to both function and survive in the PTO. A lot of it was Army bullshit like organizational structure and chain of command. As I had serious doubts that I would ever lay eyes on Douglas MacArthur or Chester Nimitz, the Army and Navy's top commanders in the pacific, I'll never understand why it was deemed important to hear about their military careers for an hour each. The afternoon lecture was a bit more useful to my way of thinking, but still boring to the point of anesthesia. Presented by a little, bespectacled doctor, he droned on for two hours about the mind of the enemy. Let's face it, if we knew so much about the mind of the Japanese, how did we let Pearl Harbor happen? I guess hindsight is always twenty/twenty. To be fair, what he was really trying to impart to us was the tenacity of our enemy, an enemy who valued honor and tradition more than the sanctity of human life. Such an enemy would stop at nothing to be victorious. He encouraged us to develop a realistic view of our foe rather than one tainted by hubris. Propaganda posters not too subtly suggested the Japanese people were barely civilized, mentally deficient, and morally bankrupt. Nothing could have been further from the truth. Their culture was thriving long before Christopher Columbus set foot on the shores of this hemisphere. The Japanese soldier had for centuries had a culture of warrior priests known as Samurai who raised the art of war to almost religious proportions. The soldiers we faced in 1942 were descendants, schooled in that tradition. They had been well trained and were dedicated, motivated by a quasi-religious nationalistic fervor and impervious to personal hardship. They could live for a month on food we would not consider suitable for the garbage pail while hidden in caves or buried in mud and mire. Many were experienced, battle-hardened veterans of the Japanese Manchurian Campaign. The Japanese soldier was a formidable enemy and we had better garner respect for him before engaging him in a fight or we would most certainly lose that fight.

In terms of practicality, the first day seemed like a total waste of my time. The remainder of the week, however, proved both interesting and valuable. Some of what was presented was of supreme importance. I paid particularly close attention to the lecture on how to ditch a B-24 in the ocean and live to tell about it. A forced landing in the ocean was a possibility about which I had bad dreams. The skill had to be learned in a classroom setting, as there was no way to manually simulate such a catastrophic event for each new pilot. How to survive in the water should you find yourself and your crew stranded there would be a hot topic of discussion for the foreseeable future. The need to always wear a *Mae West* life jacket while flying could not be stressed enough. How to navigate over open water with no discernible landmarks and successfully find your way home was a valuable skill to possess should your navigator be killed or incapacitated. Many of the topics were skills any good boy scout would have been taught and should remember, such as how to find fresh water if island bound, how to start a fire, and how to control bleeding along with various other basic first aid skills.

We were introduced to several simple phrases in Japanese under the guise of needing to communicate to civilians. Phrases we all hoped would never need to use because saying them would mean the unthinkable had occurred and we had fallen into the hands of the enemy. Phrases such as "*Watashi wa amerika-jin, watashi wa anata no yujindseu*, I am an American, I am your friend." Hearing this particular phrase, I remember joking that the Army was teaching us to lie in Japanese. My quip got a hearty laugh from everyone in the room except for the instructor. Either he was humorless or I was not as original as I thought as he dryly pointed out that he had heard that joke before. I suppose he was right, it was a little too easy. We all practiced saying the phrases aloud for the next hour, each praying that he would never have to utter them in any context.

There were forty of us in the class and over the course of the week we became fast friends. After a day of lectures we hit the officers club, talking and drinking until the wee hours of the morning, basking in what it was to be *comrades in arms*. Jack was quickly becoming my best friend. He was witty and had an easy charm, which made him comfortable to be around, fitting like a pair of old shoes, the ones you would wear to church if only your mother, or in my case granddaddy, would let you. A man of few words, when Jack did speak, his words were well chosen and considered. Like me, he had learned moderation in drinking. I couldn't say the same about CJ. He was loud and boisterous to the point of being obnoxious when he was sober. When he was drunk he was a holy terror. The evening would begin with him seated at the bar regaling a gathering crowd with a seemingly endless litany of ribald jokes. CJ was a natural comedian and quickly became the venue's nightly floorshow. The barkeep kept his glass topped off and CJ kept drinking and telling jokes. By 1:00 am CJ was typically too drunk to walk, so Jack and I would help him back to the barracks and pour him into bed. The mornings after, he looked and felt like death warmed over. Jack and I, after multiple attempts, would finally roust CJ from his bunk before the two of us would head to the chow hall for breakfast. Still looking puny, he would meet us at the classroom door to begin the process anew. CJ was a great guy, but I could tell being his friend was going to turn into a lot of responsibility.

"It's going to be a long war," I said, following him in.

"Yep!" was Jack's sole reply.

The final day at Hamilton was devoted to a pair of topics, evasion and escape. Rumor of exceptionally harsh treatment at the hands of Japanese captors was slowly leaking out of the South Pacific jungles, being confirmed by a handful of American soldiers who had somehow managed to escape. This should have come as no surprise. The world had watched in silent horror the treatment Japanese soldiers had inflicted upon conquered Chinese soldiers and civilians over the last decade. An enemy captured or conquered was deemed less than human by a Japanese psyche eons in the making. Japan was one of two nations that had refused to sign the 1929 Geneva Convention, but had, in 1942, reluctantly agreed to abide by the regulations. The new rumors begged to differ. Our soldiers who found themselves in the hands of the bastards were being tortured and killed for the slightest infractions. Starvation was the norm. Mistreatment of Americans was rapidly becoming a sadistic sport. It was the sworn duty of any American officer or enlisted man to attempt and continue attempting escape. He was obligated to only reveal his name, rank and serial number to his captor even under the threat of torture or death. Many men were dying to fulfill this obligation. Many men cracked. At the most primitive of levels, escaping one's captors became a basic need, a man's only hope of survival. He didn't have to be ordered to escape. He couldn't ignore the primal urges compelling him to do so. The need or obligation to escape was discussed in great detail. It was the *how to* of escape that was lacking in this discussion. It seemed to boil down to a concoction of daring, courage, and dumb luck.

The art of evasion was somewhat easier to convey. "Stay hidden. Do not confront an overwhelming contingent of enemy forces, but stay hidden and evade them. In this situation you're the victor if you survive. In fact, your survival robs the enemy of his victory if you live to fight another day," words of wisdom from a man who knew firsthand of what he spoke. Sergeant John Slaughter had three months earlier escaped from a Japanese compound. He had been forced to endure weeks of starvation and intermittent torture. He bore fresh scars, his fingernails having been ripped out by a sadistic guard wielding a pair of pliers. The military was now using the testimony of men like Sergeant Slaughter and a lucky handful of others to better equip men headed for the front.

In addition to standard issue weapons, a Model 1911 .45 caliber semi-automatic Colt pistol and an M3 sheathed fighting knife, both of which were to be worn at all times, Uncle Sam provided us with some clandestine toys aimed at evasion and survival. Each flight crew member was issued a survival pack that included a small bottle of water purification tablets, a brass compass, a mirror for signaling, fishing hooks and line, and a collection of medical supplies such as bandages and aspirin, all contained in an olive drab cotton duck pouch. "A man could keep himself alive in the jungle for a long time with its contents." More stealthy were topographical maps printed on silk scarves that were easily concealed in a pocket. "Knowing where you are is half the battle in evading an enemy force and escaping." The maps could easily be overlooked by a captor and would prove invaluable in planning an escape.

"None of this equipment will make a bit of difference if you don't have it on your body when you leave the aircraft. You are responsible for your crew's safety and lives. They will complain incessantly about having to wear the equipment in the unforgiving heat of the tropics. Ignore their complaints and order that they wear the equipment. It could literally be the difference between life and death." I knew firsthand the aggravation of which he was speaking. We had been issued sidearms early in our training, along with a leather holster that hung across the chest. At that time the weapons were more toys than tools. Most men of my age had played with toy guns as children. My favorite was a Buck Rogers Liquid Helium Ray Gun. It was a bright yellow and red squirt gun; constructed of metal, it had the heft of a real weapon. I loved that thing, a birthday gift from Granddaddy and carried it with me everywhere because you never knew when the bad guys or alien creatures lurking around every corner might beset you. At eight years old, carrying it made me feel manly and invincible. When Uncle Sam issued us the Colt .45 sidearms, I'd dutifully worn mine for the first week, feeling that same manly sense of invincibility, but no longer eight, the novelty soon wore thin. The gun seemed perpetually in the way and its weight surprisingly burdensome. I abandoned the notion after only three days. Sergeant Slaughter had just brought the war to real life. The training over, I was about to jump into an unforgiving fray heretofore only imagined. Unlike the bad guys and alien creatures of my childhood, my enemy was real, a flesh and blood human being with a heart's desire to kill me. The pistol was a real tool and I resolved to go nowhere without it. Looking about the classroom I could see that I was not the only man deeply moved by the lecturer's words. We gave the good sergeant a standing ovation, not only for his message of wisdom, but for his bravery, confirmed by his service and sacrifice. Beyond anyone's question a strong and brave man, he wept.

The following morning, having completed our brief indoctrination to the PTO, Jack and I along with thirty-eight of our new friends boarded a train bound for San Diego. The Army was using us as guinea pigs in an experiment, as we were to be the first group to try a new program designed to efficiently transport aircraft and crews to the front. Previously the B-24s were ferried to the South Pacific by skeleton crews who dropped off the aircraft, then returned home to repeat the cycle. As more and more aircraft and pilots were rapidly needed the inefficiency of this system was recognized. To test the efficacy of the new plan, we were to proceed to the Consolidated Aircraft factory in San Diego to pick up brand new airplanes. There, we had three days to test fly the planes, identify and get any last minute squawks repaired. Our crews would join us on the morning of the fourth day and the bombers, twenty in all, would strike out over the Pacific bound for Hickam field in Hawaii. The thought of 2560 miles of nothing but the waters of the ocean below us was a bit unnerving both for novice aircrews and our leaders alike. The Army wisely decided to retain the ferry pilots experienced in transoceanic flight. Putting their experience to work, those pilots would accompany formations of twenty bombers each, thus increasing the ratio of ferry pilots to delivered aircraft from 1:1 to 1:20, while at the same time increasing the likelihood that all twenty bombers and crews would successfully reach their intended destination. The lead pilot would fly not a bomber, but a PBY Catalina amphibious aircraft to allow a sea landing and rescue should there be any mishap. Supply and transit ships departed the continent bound for Hawaii distribution centers almost hourly meaning we should never be more than a hundred miles or so from a friendly vessel should we need rescuing from the drink. The new plan made an amazing amount of sense, which was a bit disconcerting given the usual lack of reason we had grown accustomed to regarding anything military.

The train ride down the coast was beautiful, revealing vast ocean vistas difficult to access by any other means. Seeing these stretches of uninhabited coast, it was easy to understand the growing paranoia among Americans living along the Pacific shore. The western coast represented a blind spot requiring defense from the Japanese invasion that many, if not most, feared imminent. In the days before airplanes, a huge army of enemy forces could potentially have landed, penetrating the American mainland by hundreds of miles, remaining completely unchallenged for days. It simply was not possible to guard the entire coastline with a large contingent of soldiers, but thanks to those wonderful Wright boys, the coast could be monitored Canada to Mexico from a vantage point above, preventing the surprise landing of an enemy force of any significant size. To that end, I counted no fewer than twenty aircraft circuitously patrolling the westernmost perimeter, ever vigilant for ships or submarines. It gave me a sense of comfort thinking Mary would be well guarded from the sneaky little Jap bastards. We would be ready and waiting for them this time.

San Diego was already prepared for an invasion; the entire Consolidated Aircraft factory at Lindbergh Field had been hidden beneath an enormous camouflage net. From above, the massive assembly facility was completely concealed, successfully disguised as rolling California countryside and private dwellings. At 20,000 feet the illusion was complete, protecting the sensitive military target from the waves of anticipated enemy bombers.

The factory was an around-the-clock beehive of activity producing bombers in ever-increasing quantities. The number of completed bombers awaiting us there under the netting was awe-inspiring. There were easily a hundred or more brand new B-24s lined up in rows of five. The smell of fresh paint and engine oil permeated the air, the scent of newness, of machinery, of power. I sometimes awaken from sleep at night with that intoxicating aroma as fresh in my mind as it was that summer morning.

In much the same way we had been issued uniforms on our first day of enlistment, we lined up to sign for the receipt of one Consolidated B-24 bomber. My aircraft was serial number was 42-41808. The sargent at the desk admonished, "The aircraft is not yours to keep. It's to be signed over to your crew chief on arrival at your final destination. It's *his* aircraft," quick to educate us of a time-honored military tradition as well as put a couple of wet-behind-the-ears officers in their place. Ignoring the jab, Jack and I were the first of the group to sign then wander through the rows of awaiting aircraft to find our ship. Finally, there she was, sitting expectantly awaiting us, radiant in her newborn glory. She knew we were coming. We both walked around her like a couple of kids gawking at a newly acquired bicycle. She was something to behold. Disconcerting at some level, the airplane was a truly beautiful mechanical work of art, while at the same time the most powerful weapon on the planet, an aesthetic disconnect, yet compelling just the same. The hatch down, we climbed aboard, finding her just as amazing inside as out. New instruments, new radios, new guns, new everything, a feast for any technophile and most American men of the day were technophiles. The mix of emotions struck me as odd, kind of like a kid at Christmas. Excited about the presents under the tree including everything he had asked Santa for and more, but who knew that later Christmas day his house would burn down and maybe, quite possibly, kill everyone inside. A strange metaphor, I know, but the only way I can think of to describe how I truly felt. Maybe better would be wonder, awe, and fear all rolled into one big juicy package.

After all twenty pilots in our group had signed and completed the necessary paperwork, the aircraft were individually attached to tugs and pulled from the confines of the camouflaged enclosure onto an expansive concrete ramp, baking in the Southern California sunlight. Jack and I sat at the controls, along for the ride as the tug pulled us out. The aircraft was fueled as we did a thorough walk-around inspection. Soon, an engineer from Consolidated assigned to walk us through the checkout procedure joined us on the flight deck. Systematically, he instructed Jack and I to start each of the four big radial engines, monitoring various mechanical parameters, assuring each was performing as designed. With very little tweaking of the controls, the new engines ran flawlessly. Satisfied, the engineer invited us to "Take her up." We pulled out to the runway and once cleared, gave her the gas.

"Head east over the desert and I'll have you put her through her paces." I nodded agreement and turned to a 090 degree heading. Climbing to 10,000 feet, we began testing various mechanical controls, opening and closing the bomb bay doors, lowering and retracting the landing gear and flaps several times, everything performing flawlessly. She felt great, at least she felt like every other B-24 I had ever flown, heavy on the controls but consistently so.

Once the testing completed to the engineer's satisfaction, he directed us home. As "home" was concealed by camouflage this was no simple task. I have to admit, from altitude, the illusion of uninterrupted, rolling countryside was quite convincing. Upon landing, the engineer signed the officially completed bomber over to the United States Army with Jack and I acting as Uncle Sam's proxy, making the big ugly bitch officially our charge. After shaking hands with the engineer, Jack and I went for a beer at the officers' club.

The following morning, we were reunited with the remainder of our crew upon their arrival in San Diego. I watched as they excitedly scampered around the B-24 like kids on a playground. By noon the armorers had finished, and with our guns loaded and ready, we took our first flight together as a crew, flying high over the California desert to check out the guns and equipment. I flew circles for two hours, getting a feel for my new toy before returning to San Diego. Completing our checkout a day earlier than scheduled, I obtained passes for my men, turning them loose for one last fling Stateside before we headed out, bound for the great unknown. I use *unknown* poetically as I was pretty sure of the misery that awaited us in the jungles and waters and skies of the South Pacific.

CHAPTER 11

Our briefing began precisely at 0700 led by Captain John Davis, former ferry pilot now come expedition leader. John had made the round trip to Hawaii and beyond more than forty times for the Army, and more than a hundred times if you counted his five years experience prior to the war flying a similar route for Pan Am in their giant flying boat the *China Clipper*. He said flying the bombers had at first been a bit unnerving, alone over an endless expanse of water, unable to land should he develop an immediate need to. In almost the same breath he reported never in his career having developed that need, even including the time when he lost two of four engines. The inappropriateness of using the word *land* as a verb had never struck me before as it seemed a bit odd to describe an airplanes descent onto water a *landing*. He told us of flying around giant storms at sea and of mechanical mishaps, all of which he had successfully dealt with, allowing him to reach his intended destination unscathed. That the Army had a man of such experience leading this first large expedition was consoling. All of us feared the endless *what ifs*. Here before us was a man who had experienced the *what ifs* first hand and not only lived to tell about it, but was prepared to lead us through it.

As he spoke, our aircraft were being prepared, loaded with both fuel and ammo. The decision had been made for us to carry not only ammunition, but a full load of bombs as well. The military did not know the location of the Japanese fleet and it would have been unforgivable to stumble upon such a prize during this crossing and have nothing to drop on them but spit. This would be the first fully loaded takeoff and landing many of us had ever made. Given the long distance the extra weight was of concern, but I understood and liked their reasoning. It was worth the extra risk to be prepared for such a chance encounter. This was war, and waging war is not without risk. We could only pray to be lucky enough to discover the Japanese fleet between the mainland and Hawaii.

Our navigators were to use this experience as real-world training, ordered to give the pilots a position report every thirty minutes. As this should be an eleven-hour flight, I should receive twenty-two reports from CJ, giving me a real good idea of just how proficient a navigator he was.

The radio operators were encouraged to chatter endlessly. While radio silence was usually the order, we knew the Japs would be listening. The brass wanted us to appear to be a huge flight of bombers, hoping to fool the Japanese into overestimating our size. To that end, each ship would be given three different identifiers to be brandished about on the radio giving the illusion of our being a contingent of sixty or more bombers. The message? "Get scared you fucking little Nips, 'cause Uncle Sam is coming to get you!" And the ruse was true; we were in fact coming to get them, just not as quickly as any of us wanted. Until the day we were ready to deliver a punishing physical retribution to their doorsteps we had to be satisfied with merely delivering psychological retribution. A pathetic little game for the moment, but our day was coming and coming soon. In the meantime just let them simmer in the juices of their own fear.

We were to take off in groups of four and form up over San Diego before heading out to sea. After a few last minute questions we were dismissed to our airplane and crews.

"I guess this is really it, Jack. Here we go!"

"Yep!"

I would have loved to call Mary to hear her sweet voice before we were off, but that would have been a breach of security, an offense for which I could rightly be court- martialed. The last thing I wanted was for the Japs to be ready and waiting for us between here and Hawaii, bombs or no bombs. I quickly gave up the notion.

The crew was waiting for us under the wing, smoking, trying hard to appear nonchalant, but their anxiety was palpable.

"Here we go boys. Better kiss American terra firma goodbye. Hope you've all hit the head."

"I'm savin' mine to piss on the Japs," CJ said, his first of many quips on this voyage.

"It's up to you, but you'd better have a pretty big bladder."

"A big bladder goes along with a big dick," he said, not missing a beat. As the remainder of the crew chided CJ for his delusions of grandeur, Bledsoe got on his knees and kissed the ground before climbing through the hatch.

"I was kidding, Bledsoe."

"I wasn't," he stated, matter-of-factly.

There was a crisp excitement in the morning air and the crew had all inhaled of it deeply. Everyone was animated, which only added to the hilarity when an unusual B-24, painted red and white like a giant candy cane, taxied by.

"What the hell is that?" Lenny asked.

"That is our *Judas Goat*," I replied.

"Our what?"

"Our *Judas Goat*. It's our formation ship. It's all painted up like that so it stands out from the rest of the ships. I can identify her easily and fall into formation behind."

"It looks like a giant clown car," he said, laughing.

"I hope it's not sheep to the slaughter," Jack said dryly.

"Keep that thought to yourself please."

"Yep," he said, disappearing through the hatch.

I climbed through, following him across the catwalk. Looking down and seeing a full load of live bombs I thought, "I guess I'd better grease this next landing." Climbing into the left seat, I began going through the preflight checklist, calling off items one by one, to which Jack responded, "Check." When completed, I grinned at Jack and said, "Let's fire this bitch up!"

"Aye, sir." Sliding back the cockpit window, I signaled the waiting lineman by swirling my finger in the air. He responded with an affirming salute and pointed to the outboard left engine. Swirling his right hand in the air, he signaled that I was clear to start this engine. Jack obliged, priming the engine with fuel then hitting the starter. The big engine caught immediately and Jack quickly responded, moving the mixture from idle/cut off to full rich. Satisfied the big power plant was churning smoothly, he repeated the process with the next, then the next, and then the next. The lineman, satisfied as well, saluted again, then began gesturing with his right arm to proceed to the runway. We were second in line to take off. As soon as the first ship began to roll down the runway I taxied out to do the same. Advancing the throttles I said over the intercom, "Here we go, boys!"

Soon airborne, we followed the first bomber into the awaiting blue. Once at 10,000 feet I quickly spotted the goat and formed up behind it as planned. We made four large circuits over San Diego, waiting for the entire contingent to fall, first into groups of four, then into a line of groups of four stretching out behind the goat five miles. A loose formation, but close enough for comfort among a group of novices. The formation complete, the goat pulled away to be replaced by John Davis and crew in the *Catalina*. Turning ninety degrees we were now heading for the coast.

The entire contingent was strangely silent as we droned over the shoreline departing the mainland. Looking down I could see the white of breaker waves rhythmically meeting the beach. I saw no human forms and thought "What a shame to waste such a golden morning anywhere than the beach." Jack must have read my mind because after looking back at the shoreline he said, "Yep" in his usual terse fashion. I nodded acknowledgement and stared at the featureless horizon awaiting. After twenty minutes Bill reported from the back, "The coastline just slid out of view, Captain."

"Thanks, Bill. Hey CJ, isn't it time for a position report?"

"Aye Cap'n, it be," he said in his best pirate diction. "At present we be at 30.32.36 N latitude by 122.26.35 W longitude. That bein 'bout seventy miles west south west of San Diego. Hawaii lies 2410 miles on a heading of 220."

"You're not doing the pirate thing all the way to Hawaii," I laughed.

"Aye Cap'n, I be. Gonna be gettin me a parrot."

"Can one of you guys back there throw him overboard?"

The radio cracked, "This is lead one. I'd like all sixty ships to report in hourly beginning now."

"Roger that, this is…" It took five minutes for each crew to report three times each.

"Bledsoe, keep the chatter going. Make it sound real. Let's hope Tojo is listening."

"Will do, Captain. I'll even change my voice around if you'd like. I do a mean Clark Gable."

"You do that Bledsoe. Whatever keeps you entertained. Just keep it going." That started the ball rolling. Bledsoe took the task to heart and gave false position reports every five minutes under the guise of several different voices for the remainder of the trip. CJ began whining, "If Bledsoe gets to use a funny voice why can't I?"

"Because the brass wants us to sound like a much larger force." There was no immediate response, but the next real position report from CJ was issued in falsetto. If the Japanese were indeed listening I'm sure they thought we were a very large contingent of undisciplined fools or clowns.

After five hours the crew began getting restless, the conversations deteriorating much like a long car ride with bored school children in the backseat. I decided to give the group a little focus and asked if anyone had come up with a name for our ship.

"How 'bout the Queen of Hearts?" Joe asked.

"That's a good name, but I'm positive it's been used."

"Queen of Spades…Diamonds… Hearts?"

"Keep thinking."

Bledsoe jumped in, "How about *Magnificent Takeoff?* We could have a doll takin' off her top." Two or three of the guys liked that suggestion.

"I've already seen that one, too. I like your thinking though, Bledsoe. A double entendre is always a good pun."

"A double what?" CJ asked.

"A double entendre, a phrase that has two meanings," Bledsoe offered up in explanation.

"You're a smart one, Captain. I s'pose that's why you're the captain."

"Hey Cap'n, what's your wife's name?"

"Hey Bledsoe, what's your mama's name?"

"Don't you be startin' with my mama. I'll be back there and a-whoopin' your ass," Bledsoe shouted, his voice belying a sudden fiery anger.

"*Bledsoe's Mama*! That got a ring to it," Joe said, quick to join the row. "We can paint her up with big titties flappin' in the breeze."

"Big black titties," CJ added. The guys all laughed, all except Bledsoe who was now quite serious about defending his mother's honor. We had no idea how seriously Bledsoe would take our chiding, but CJ's ignorant joke inadvertently struck him very close to home, closer than any of us could have imagined.

Oddly enough, "Black titties" was a sexual term, arousing a group of white men regardless of the denoted race. I guarantee the first bare breast ever seen by any man aboard this ship had been black, secretive glances stolen in grade school, images of native African women, captured on the pages of the *National Geographic Magazine*. I considered giving the boys a lecture on the subject, but decided better of it. CJ meant it as a joke and nothing more. I opted instead to change the subject, "Simmer down boys. Bledsoe, my wife's name is Mary, but I don't like the idea of some Nip shooting at her and I sure as hell don't want her titties flappin' in the breeze for anybody but me."

CJ was quick to say again "Black titties," followed by a tense silence. From the corner of my eye I could see Jack stifle a chuckle. Pretty soon everyone was laughing, me included.

When we finally stopped laughing, and it took a few minutes because all were infected with what some term *church laughter*, the uncontrollable urge to laugh in a setting where laughter is inappropriate, a setting like the quietness of a church sanctuary, we all started howling again. It begins as a concealed chuckle, but quickly escalates to silent fits of upper body contractures soon followed by uncontrollable, teary-eyed laughs of loud, can't-catch-your-breath heaving. It usually tapers off before erupting again, repeating the bleary-eyed cycle until your face hurts from an exaggerated smile.

Bledsoe said, "We could…" and we started laughing again.

When all was at last quiet, Jordan suggested, "How about *China Doll*?"

After thinking about it, I warmed to the idea. "Great suggestion, I like it! Anyone else?"

Bledsoe added, "Yeah, and we can paint up this doll with her titties flappin' in…"

Before he could complete his sentence, Jack added, "Black titties." The unexpected source got us laughing all over again, including Bledsoe. Finally I said, "No titties, Bledsoe, black or otherwise." The crew groaned en masse.

"That doesn't mean we can't have a doll on the side. In fact we have to if we're gonna call her *China Doll*. Just no bare breast, we're better men than that. All in favor signify by saying aye."

Multiple voices rang out "Aye" in unison over the intercom.

"Any opposed?"

It was unanimous; our ship was henceforth dubbed the *China Doll*.

At six hours my back and legs were getting pretty sore in spite of the fact that Jack was spelling me every hour or so. I was getting pretty hungry as well and announced it as a question. I had thought to bring a couple of candy bars, but they were long gone. The thought of breaking open K-rations, leftovers of the last war thoughtfully provided by Uncle Sam as our inflight meal, was anything but appealing. The next thing I knew, I was being handed a fried chicken breast and a bottle of Coca-Cola.

"Where'd this come from?"

"Bledsoe thought of it. He stopped by the mess hall this morning and sweet-talked his girlfriend out of a basket of fried chicken. CJ nabbed the Cokes from the officers club. There's some potato salad too if you want some," Jack offered.

Over the intercom Bledsoe said, "Hey Cap'n, I didn't think to nab any forks, but a Dzus tool works pretty good."

"That sounds like a Godsend. Good thinking, guys!"

"I'll take it for a while. You go ahead and eat, then walk to the back and stretch your legs."

"I think I will, Jack. Thanks." That chicken tasted mighty good and Bledsoe was right, the Dzus tool did make an exceptionally fine utensil in a pinch. Finishing the unexpected feast, I took Jack's advice and walked back through the cabin.

Bledsoe and CJ were both at their stations just aft of the flight deck, Bledsoe talking on the radio, giving yet another fictitious position report from a fictitious aircraft, while CJ was shooting the sun's position with a sextant, preparing my next real position report.

"Nice work on the food, boys. I think I may assign you the task of feeding us on missions, Bledsoe."

"I'll be happy to work on it, Cap'n, but it's a lot easier if I've got a sweetheart in the kitchen."

"The cook in San Diego was your sweetheart?"

"No sir, not really, but she sure was nice to me the night before," he grinned.

"I see...," I said, pausing to return his grin. He went back to his broadcasting. Bledsoe was a charming man. He wasn't the most handsome man in my crew, but growing up as he did, continually in the company of pretty women, made him more comfortable around women than men. He parlayed that ease into a charming affect, affording him a success with the ladies most men could only dream of. CJ on the other hand was more of a man's man. His quickness with a lewd joke made him immensely popular with the boys but masked a timid lack of confidence with the fairer sex. Determined not to disturb CJ's work and even more determined not to start him telling an endless stream of jokes, I moved on. My legs were stiff after sitting for six hours, continually man-handling this beast of an aircraft into submission. They felt weak and shaky, making me a little nervous to walk across the catwalk. Looking down at that payload once again got me to thinking. I could envision dropping the load on an unwary Japanese carrier. Finding the fleet unprepared could end the war. I chuckled to myself, "What are the odds of stumbling across a single Japanese ship in the vast expanse of the Pacific Ocean? About the same as pigs sprouting wings and flying I suppose," a dose of reality quickly ending my Walter Mitty-esque fantasy.

The boys in the back had mixed it up a little, trading places out of boredom. Jordan was back in the tail while the other three sat talking. Joe was eating potato salad with a Dzus tool as I had.

"You boys doing okay back here?" I asked, shouting. The open side ports made the compartment windy, loud, and cold.

"You betcha, Cap'n. Say, we were wondering how long we'd be in Hawaii?"

"I think the plan is for us to be out of Hawaii day after tomorrow, depending on the weather, and since the weather is forecast to be perfect, I think it's a pretty sure bet."

"Any idea where we're headed after that?"

"You'll know when I know, boys. I guess the brass doesn't want any chance for leaks."

"Who we gonna tell up here?" Lenny asked.

"Truth is, Lenny, the brass may not have decided where we're going yet. Word is we're getting our asses kicked all across the Pacific, so *where* to send reinforcements probably changes every day, if not every hour."

"Were really gettin' our asses kicked by a bunch of little Nips?" Joe asked.

"What's size got to do with it?" Lenny asked, his back up at the slightest provocation.

"Size has nothing to do with it, Lenny. We just got caught with our pants down around our ankles. It's taken some time to pull 'em up, but we're getting there. You guys are just the beginning of a tidal wave that's gonna drown every last Nip in the Pacific, you'll see."

"Hey Cap'n, you think there's a chance we can get off the base in Hawaii? I heard it's beautiful."

"I can't promise Joe because I just don't know. I will ask, though. I'd kinda like to see it myself."

"My bet is we're gonna be sick of tropical islands before this is all over with. My old man says this war could take ten years," Jordy shouted from the tail gun.

"I doubt it'll be that long, but you never know. I've heard the other extreme, too, from folks who say we'll beat their asses and be home by Christmas. I don't believe either."

"We ARE gonna win though, right Cap'n?"

"Yeah guys, we're gonna win. Just not today or tomorrow," I said matter-of-factly.

"Hey Cap'n, Lieutenant Jack wants you back up front. He says something about some ships on the horizon." Turning quickly to answer Jack's request I thought better of it and turned back to reaffirm, "Don't worry, boys. We're gonna win this thing!"

Again in the left seat, I was soon piloting the bomber as Jack pointed out three ships he had spotted about twenty miles to the right of our course.

"You think they're Japs?" Jack asked.

"I don't know. Have any of the others reported spotting them?"

"Not that I've heard."

"I think we're obligated to let Davis know," I said. "Hey CJ, See if you can patch me through to Captain Davis."

"Roger Cap'n."

Ten seconds later I was talking to John Davis.

"Are you seeing what I'm seeing at our three o'clock?"

"I didn't, but I am now. Break from the group and head that direction. See if you can get a positive ID. We'll make a big circle and wait for you.

"Roger that."

Breaking right, we began a steep descent, our pulses quickening. I decided to approach the ships from as close to the deck as I dared, hoping against hope that we had remained unspotted. This could be our first taste of combat. Ordering my crew to their respective positions, we closed on the ships, skimming the ocean at ten feet above the surface. At this low altitude the waist gunners were getting soaked with salt water, a saturating spray whipped up by the prop blast. At a mile out there was no indication we had been detected as of yet. I open the bomb bay, preparing for the lowest drop I'd ever made.

"Everyone keep their eyes open for any flags. Jimmy, can you pull this off?"

"Yes, Captain, but I won't release till you command." So it was up to me. I'd sure hate to sink one of our own on my first run. From 500 yards I pull up hard as Jack yelled, "Abort, Abort! It's flying American colors." I began shouting over the intercom as well, "Abort, Jimmy, Abort!

"Not to worry Captain, I saw the flag just as you pulled up."

The Gs and the adrenalin rush were, in a word, exhilarating. I was just thankful we didn't sink a friendly vessel.

"Whew, that was fun. Let's do that again," came a lone voice over the shouting.

"That was amazing flying, Cap'n. Well done!"

"Hey, Cap'n, there's some guys on the deck back there giving you a one finger salute," Bill reported from the tail laughing.

"I'll bet they dropped a load…in their pants!" CJ said.

"We're soakin' wet back here, but it was totally worth it Captain."

"Yeah," Jordan agreed.

"*China Doll* to lead one. Vessels were friendlies. Three merchant ships flying American colors. We see you in the distance and will rejoin formation in the same position."

"Roger that….*China Doll?*"

"Yes sir, we just named her."

"We watched your run, *China Doll*. Well done!"

"Thank you, sir," I said. "We'll rejoin with the flight in about twenty, approaching from your five o'clock."

"Roger that."

"Good eyes, Jack. Too bad it wasn't Japs or we'd-a had 'em."

"Yep, too bad."

The encounter left me feeling pretty good, certain that had the vessel been an enemy, it would now reside on the bottom of the ocean. I assume the ship's captain was either unaware of our approach or he had seen us and recognized us as a friendly. In either case, we were not fired upon, leaving me to wonder. I still did not get to test my mettle under fire. Would it have made a difference if they had been shooting at us? I'd like to think not, but I still didn't know for sure. What is sure? I had just executed a textbook attack against a vessel at sea, earning a measure of respect from both my new crew and the others in the group who had watched from a vantage point 10,000 feet above.

Flying west we chased the sun, gaining three hours on our watches before the Hawaiian Islands first appeared on the distant horizon. The islands sure looked beautiful, glistening jewels atop an azure ocean; a welcome sight as finding them meant redemption. This crossing validated my apprehension, seeing how easy it might have been to get lost. The slightest miscalculation by the pilot or navigator, erring just a degree or two off course for only a limited length of time, could ultimately result in disaster. We easily could have missed the islands completely, run out of fuel in the middle of the Pacific, and never been found. In many situations the navigator could prove the most important guy on the ship. I made up my mind then and there to learn his job backward and forward. That's not to say that the other crew positions were not important, quite the contrary. For example, I'm confident had we found ourselves under attack from behind our hero would be the tail gunner. Each crewmember has a job to perform, some glamorous, others mundane, but all vital and valuable nonetheless. Take Bledsoe, who had been assigned the task of subterfuge, deceiving the Japs into believing we were part of a much larger force of aircraft. Was the ruse successful? I'll probably never know. Bledsoe had taken the task to heart, talking almost nonstop, portraying at least a dozen characters. It was comical to listen to his banter. Radio operators in the other aircraft travelling with us had long ago given up trying to get a word in edgewise. Bledsoe was doing such a good job it just wasn't necessary to add anything. I sure hope the Japs had been listening in. The guy deserved a medal.

The remainder of the flight was uneventful, but still memorable. From the air the islands of Hawaii appeared to be the most lushly beautiful spot on earth. Approaching from the northeast, we descended to 2000 feet before breaking formation, forming a single- file column north of Molokai. Proceeding to Hickam on Oahu, the *China Doll* was third in line to land. Apprehensive of my tenuous, highly explosive cargo, I greased the landing. It would have been a real shame to come all this way only to kill my crew and myself by botching a landing with a full load of bombs. I discovered later we would be the only group to make the crossing so encumbered. All future groups would only be required to carry two 500 pounders.

Arriving late in the afternoon, the bars of Honolulu beckoned. As Hawaii was under both a curfew and a nightly blackout, we decided to make haste, the officers heading to one club, the enlisted men to another. Before parting I slipped Bledsoe a couple bucks instructing him to buy a round for the guys on me.

CHAPTER 12

Our "One day, two at the most" layover in Hawaii slowly turned into an agonizing three-month layover. Not that I was complaining, mind you, but even paradise has its limits for a group of men primed, ready, and anxious for action. I suppose I would have felt differently had Mary been here with me. I could easily envision a Robinson Crusoe-like existence with Mary as my only companion, surviving alone in the lush tropical jungle. There were lots of things I dreamed about doing with Mary, or to her, on a secluded beach. If there had not been a war going on I would have sent for her, but an island in the mid-Pacific, a location that had already been caught off guard by an enemy attack, was just too close to the front for comfort. Instead I consoled myself with nightly dreams of her, passionate dreams that left me spent upon awakening.

On the second day at Hickam I received orders assigning the *China Doll* and crew to service with the Thirteenth Air Force, 384th Bomber Group with the suggestion that further orders were soon to follow. The brass still had no clue what to do with us so we would have to endure merely playing soldier until we were needed somewhere.

Early in our stay at Hickam the *China Doll* was truly born. Jim frequently claimed to be quite the artist so I gave him the chance to prove it, rendering our ship with a mascot. I wanted a redhead, but he suggested a blond instead, claiming "artistic license." Truth is, he was smitten by the image of a lovely, scantily clad vixen painted by Alberto Vargas for the December 1942 *Esquire* calendar. When he showed me the calendar, I had to agree, she was sexy and stunning, "But what has she got to do with a china doll?"

"Just trust me, you'll see," is all he would say. I remained skeptical, but I had to admit we couldn't go too far wrong with a Vargas girl. In the earliest days of the war, Mr. Vargas' work became quite popular among female-deprived American soldiers the world over; his idealized feminine images gracing scads of military aircraft, ships, and barrack walls. It took Jim almost a week, but when completed, his reproduction of that calendar gatefold looked almost life-like. Addressing my concern about making the image fit the name, he had added a touch of his own to Vargas' original. In her lap our blonde babe clutched a small toy china doll, hiding, but just barely, her beautiful breast. I couldn't have been more pleased. My boys liked her too! Lenny even climbed a ladder to kiss her on the lips. Below her, Jim painted the words "China Doll" in six-inch letters, red script, lined in yellow. Jim did a stunning job, so good in fact he soon found a booming business, hired to paint naked ladies on any number of airplanes at Hickam. I didn't mind his new venture as long as he showed up for duty on time and promised not to do as good a job for anyone else.

The following week we were assigned duty patrolling a 150-mile circuit around the Hawaiian archipelago. The *China Doll* along with three other *Liberators* would take off, one ship every twenty minutes; a schedule staggering loaded bombers strategically into a large defensive shield encircling the islands. There were four or five fighters, F-4 *Wildcats* that regularly made the circuit with us. The *Wildcats* were so much faster than the Liberators they could make two complete orbits in little more than the time it took us to make one. In sharp contrast to most American soldiers, we were lucky, privileged to fly in the skies of paradise every day with the added luxury of having no one shooting at us. We slept in the comfort of real beds, ate real food, and drank real beer all the while hearing tales of the men who were fighting and dying on a small island called Guadalcanal. We hoped soon to be assigned to Henderson Field, the English name given the Japanese base the Americans were at that very moment forfeiting their lives to capture and defend. It made us feel cheap and dirty, if not down right un-manly to continue our safe little vacation rather than be sharing in their misery. It's hard on a man's psyche to just sit by letting someone else take all the risks, do all the work, let all the blood. In comparison to those Marines on Guadalcanal, we were living risk-free in the lap of luxury. Our collective guilt at this disparity made us all miserable as hell. We wanted to go, begged the CO daily to find a way for us to make a real, fitting contribution to the war effort. Instead we played ring around the rosy with a bunch of fighter pilots, defending a group of islands that in all likelihood would never again in our lives see military action, even if we lived to be a hundred.

We fell early into a routine. Breakfast at the mess hall; a daily briefing on the locations of possible sub sightings within a two-hundred mile radius of Hawaii, the scheduled friendly shipping traffic as well as the official line on what was happening over on Guadalcanal; a daily briefing with my crew; eight hours of flying around the islands; debriefing the flight; hit the bars; write to Mary; go to bed to get up early the next morning to do the whole routine over again. Every third week we changed it up a little, assigned to fly the same patrol, only at night. The rotating schedule helped break up the monotony. With all the flying, I got pretty proficient at landing a *Liberator* night or day with an unspent load of hot munitions. I liked the night duty best when the moon was full; the soft light on the ocean, the glow of the mist enshrouding the rain forest all incredibly striking. Beginning our fourth week, we were awarded a day off every weekend, a day I personally spent lying on the beach or sleeping. The other guys were unmarried, and being spirited twenty-year-old men naturally had other pursuits. They were always inviting me to tag along to catch a glimpse of the latest hot doll waitress or barmaid or nurse, but I was crazy in love with my wife and figured no good could come of it, so I spent my days off in solitude. On occasion I would borrow a jeep, a perk of being an officer, and drive around the island, taking in the concoction of architecture that was uniquely Hawaiian. On one of these sojourns I discovered Honolulu had a very nice public library. I now finally found the time to do a little reading, a longtime passion of mine, which, due to my recent state of activity had been largely forsaken. I'd always had an affinity for the newer fiction from writers like Fitzgerald, Hemmingway, or Faulkner, and the library had all of their works on the shelves. I also looked for James Joyce in that same collection but couldn't find any. "I guess Joyce is banned in paradise too." This was quite discouraging, as I'd long intended to read him but never quit gotten around to it because it took such a Herculean effort to attain a copy. The book had been banned in my hometown of Valdosta and apparently in Honolulu as well, a fact that as a young man piqued my curiosity. I finally acquired a second hand copy of *Ulysses* purchased in a small bookstore and began reading, determined to see what all the fuss was about. What word or thought or deed in written form could possibly be so horrific as to deserve to be banned by a civilized society? I had to know and now was the time, a guilty pleasure I had to explain to no one but God and I didn't figure he really cared having given us free wills and all as he did. I read the book, pondered it, then read it again, finding it too intriguing to put down. Joyce certainly had a way with words, more I thought, than any other writer of his generation.

Feeling cerebral, I, of purpose, began acquiring tastes and habits I thought best reflected my new mindset. Subconsciously, I suppose, the new persona I was cultivating was a recreation of my granddaddy, a highly educated Southern gentleman, always wise and kind to a fault. A bon vivant and true eclectic, he had a passion for the finer things in life. Around that time, I took to drinking aged, single malt scotch after being introduced to it by a Navy admiral I had befriended. He had discovered the subtleties of scotch as a young man serving in the last Great War. A submariner, he commanded a ship that berthed regularly in the Firth of Forth in Scotland. It was there in the bars of Edinburgh he had been introduced to the "magic elixir" as he called it. I met him, oddly enough, sitting on a park bench in Honolulu reading, of all things, *Ulysses*. He was not in uniform so the intimidation I might have felt by his superior rank didn't come into play. Quite by serendipity I sat down next to an elderly man (all of sixty years of age) and seeing what he was reading, I turned to him and asked what he thought of Leopold Bloom.

"I like Stephen Dedalus better. I guess after the first book I feel like I've known him since he was a child," he said, without looking up.

"First book?" I asked, seeing how quickly my foray into intellectual snobbery had gotten me into embarrassment. Gracious, he let me off the hook saying, "You remember, in *Portrait of the Artist as a Young Man*. It's the same Stephen Dedalus."

At this point I could lie and say something vague like, "Of course," but fearing this deception would just lead me down the road to even greater embarrassment, I decided to fess up.

"No sir, I've heard of it, but I guess I just never got around to reading it yet. If it's half as good as *Ulysses*, I will love it."

He turned and pulled his glasses down, peering over the top to consider me, a thin young pilot with a distinctly Southern accent and a penchant for literature, and not just any literature, but James Joyce nonetheless. Not exactly an everyday find in Honolulu.

"Where are you from, son?"

"Valdosta, Georgia, sir."

"They must teach young people well in Valdosta."

Seeing the compliment I said, "Thank you, sir. I suppose they do ok, but most of my education was at the hands of my granddaddy. He was the town doctor, Harvard educated, fascinated by everything. He instilled in me that same fascination."

"Harvard, huh?" he said smiling. "I'm a Princeton man myself."

"Really? Me, too!" I said, feeling a sudden rush of kinship, then again embarrassment.

"Well, sort of. I was a freshman when the Japs attacked…I signed up the next day."

"This war has set many of us on a detour. I'm sure you'll go back after we finish this thing."

"Yes sir, I plan to."

"I see you're married?"

"Yes sir, to the prettiest girl in the world. We probably would have waited till after we graduated, but like you said, a detour."

"I see. What was your intended field of study, literature?"

"No sir, architecture. I had both an athletic and an academic scholarship," I said, hoping my brag might redeem me a bit in his eyes. I don't know why I cared what he, a complete stranger thought of me, but I did. I even noticed I was careful of my diction, afraid my Southern twang might make me appear stupid or at least less cultured.

"You must be a bright lad. And now you fly?" he asked. He must have noticed my wings.

"Yes sir, I fly bombers."

"Liberators?"

"Yes sir," I said, surprised at his insight. "And what is it that you do?"

"Oh, I'm with the Navy," he said nonchalantly. Given his garb I assumed he was a civilian contractor and left it at that. If he wanted to tell me more he would. Perhaps he wasn't at liberty to reveal his occupation, given security concerns and the war effort.

"So you're on a bit of a detour, too?"

"You might say that. Do you play chess?"

"Yes sir, my granddaddy taught me that too."

"Fancy a match?"

"Sure! When?"

"How about now?" he asked, producing a set. He seemed excited to find someone else who knew the game.

"Now would be fine I suppose."

He set the board between us and assembled the players, each to their assigned positions as he said, "Fantastic! I've not had a good game in months."

"You're guessing I'm gonna give you a good match?"

"I can tell that you're a plenty smart lad, I'm betting you will. I'll give you white since you're the guest."

I moved, quickly followed by him. Within three moves I recognized the pattern.

"You're surely not trying the *fool's gambit* out on me, are you sir?"

He smiled, "I knew you were a smart lad. Just wanted to see how smart. So you've studied the game have you?"

"I wouldn't exactly say studied, but I did play with my granddaddy quite a bit. Every day, in fact. The very first thing he taught me about chess was the *fool's gambit,* but only after beating me several times, enough times to make me mad enough to want to learn the game, but not so many as to discourage me."

"He sounds like a wise man."

"He is! The wisest I know anyway. He taught both my brother Davey and me to play. He never let either of us just win, so it was a happy day when I finally beat him. He was proud as punch. It kind of established a pecking order, too, 'cause Davey beat him before I did."

"I see, and Davey is…?"

"Younger than me by two years."

"Ouch, how'd you do with that?"

"Not too good at first. Granddaddy just said to work harder. He liked the competition it fostered between us."

"And you?"

"Not so much," I smiled weakly, "But I did learn to play…Check!"

"I'd say you did!" He studied the board for five minutes without saying a word.

"Check mate!" I proclaimed three moves later, careful not to be too boastful… just boastful enough.

"Bravo! Well done, young man. That's the best match I've had in years. The people I play with now are all afraid not to let me win."

"And why is that?"

"I suppose it's because I'm their boss. Maybe I'm just too intense about the game, I don't know. Shall we go again? You have to let me redeem myself."

"I'm really sorry, sir, I can't right now. I've got to report in an hour, but I promise you'll get your chance at revenge. Believe me, I've lost enough to know how you feel."

"Very well, then. Next week, same time, the loser buys the scotch?"

"You're on!" I said, shaking his hand. "You bring the board as I don't have one."

"Very good! Until then," he said cheerfully as I walked away.

The following week I found him there sitting on that same park bench, dressed in the same attire.

"Good morning!" he said, handing me a book, old, dog-eared and obviously well read. "This is my only copy. I'd very much like it back when you're done as we're old friends." I'd never before heard a book referred to as an *old friend*, but I immediately understood his sentiment. Holding it, I read the title aloud, "*Portrait of the Artist as a Young Man* by James Joyce. Thank you, sir. I'll take extra special care with your friend here."

"I knew you would or I wouldn't loan it to you. Shall we?" he said, gesturing to the board he had already prepared. "You won last time as I recall, which color would you choose?"

"You take white today, sir." Without a word he turned the board and made his first move.

Forty-three moves later I again announced, "Check mate!"

"Damn it! You're beating an old dog at his own game."

"Just lucky, sir."

"Don't be falsely modest. You won fair and square, playing a skillful game. Do you fly as well as you play chess?"

"I think so, sir. They tell me I do anyway. Uncle Sam wanted me to stay Stateside and teach other cadets how to fly, but I just couldn't do it."

"Your wife?"

"Was very unhappy about the whole affair, but I guess ultimately understood."

"A man's got to do what a man's got to do!"

"Yes sir, something like that."

"Well done! I had the same conversation with my mother before I joined the Navy back in '16. My son gave me the speech when he signed on last December. It felt a little different on the receiving end, but I understood."

"Where is he now?"

"On the *USS Hornet*, somewhere in the Pacific. He was the last person to beat me in a match, by the way."

"He must be pretty good then," I said by the way a compliment.

"He is, but I dare say you could take him. I believe I owe you a scotch," he said, giving me a congratulatory pat on the back.

"Yes, sir, and I'll be happy to collect. There's a little bar I know around the corner."

Gathering up the chessmen he said, "If you don't mind, I'd prefer the officers club where I've got a tab."

"You failed to mention you were an officer," I said, looking sheepish.

"You failed to ask, but that's okay, you might have been tempted to let me win," he chuckled.

Entering the club he was saluted by two Navy captains.

"Alright, now I'm afraid to ask. Exactly what do you do?"

"As I told you, I'm with the Navy."

Before I could ask the next obvious question a petty officer saluted, then opened the door saying, "Good afternoon, Admiral. Good to see you again."

"Admiral? Not fair!"

"What's not fair? That I'm an admiral and you're not, or that I didn't tell you I was an admiral?"

"Well, the way you play chess, I'd have to say both," I laughed.

"*Touché*! Now about that scotch. Seems I now owe you two."

"Yes, sir, but who's counting?"

"Well, I am, of course, but next week I'll be on the receiving end."

"We'll see about that. Barkeep, scotch on the rocks, please."

"Son, didn't your granddaddy ever teach you how to drink scotch?"

"Well, uh, no sir."

"Something you don't know? Let me educate you. John, scratch that 'on the rocks' nonsense and give me two of my usual. This young whippersnapper here won the prize…. today, that is."

"Comin' right up, Admiral!" John quickly complied and set two small glasses of scotch on the bar along with a small pitcher of water.

"In Scotland where my people are from every little town and borough has a distillery and each produces it's own version of the same commodity, single malt scotch."

"Single malt?"

"Different grains can 'malt' or germinate when water is added. Rye, wheat, and barley can all be malted. Single malt scotch is made from barley and only barley. It's distilled in a copper still, then aged for at least three years in oak casks. The longer scotch is aged, the more of the character of the cask it absorbs. The history of the cask is important. Some are secondhand, used first to age wine for several years. Some are burned or charred to give the scotch a smoky flavor. Nothing in the process is left to chance. Each distillery has its own recipe or process, secrets that have been handed down from generation to generation, secrets prescribing codes of conduct for entire communities. Revealing those secrets to outsiders was once upon a time punishable by death. The Scots take their namesake beverage very seriously. If it's not made in Scotland don't dare call it scotch, it's only whiskey. Say otherwise and you could very quickly find yourself in a fistfight."

"I see, go on…"

"The water is important too."

"Water?"

"Yes. Think about it. Every single one of those little boroughs has it's own source of water. Water is a universal human need. Towns in antiquity sprang up around streams or fresh water springs which easily supplied that need. It's subtle, but each of those water sources is unique, has its own unique taste and smell. I'll wager the water here in Hawaii tastes different than the water back home in Valdosta, right?"

"Um? Right, now that you mention it."

"Our water supply falls from the sky as rain and gets soaked into the ground. It's dispersed through an aquifer, the underground rocks and soil acting as a filter, before ending up in wells or springs or streams. Rock and soil, not to mention the plants that grow in that rock and soil are different all over the planet, producing distinctly unique-tasting water in different locations."

"You've thought about this a lot, haven't you professor?" I laughed.

"Didn't your granddaddy teach you about interrupting?"

"He did, sorry. Please go on or I'll never get this scotch," I said, mockingly rolling my eyes.

"Patience, lad. What was I was saying? Oh yes, the water is unique in each of these little towns. Did it run through fields of heather or peat or grass? You get the idea. Well in a very real sense scotch tastes like Scotland, different than anywhere else in the world."

"Okay, I'll buy that, but what about pouring it over ice?"

"I'm getting to that. In Scotland there is a prescribed way to drink scotch. It's always served in a clear glass accompanied by a small pitcher of water. Now let me demonstrate, take a drink of this," he said handing me the shot glass.

"Wow! Strong stuff," I said, stifling a cough after swallowing.

"Burns all the way down, doesn't it? Could you taste anything like heather or peat moss? No, all you taste is the ethanol." He then put a drop or two of room temperature water in the next glass. "Now try this…"

Taking a sip, I gave it careful consideration. "That's amazing! I really can taste the difference."

"Try to analyze it. What do you think you taste?"

Closing my eyes to eliminate distractions I took another sip. "I taste some kind of flower, but I don't know what kind, and something mossy like dark, dank earth."

"Smart lad. This is Glenlivet made in Ballindalloch by the same family since 1824. It was aged in a sherry cask for twenty-five years. The flowers you taste are heather and daises, alive at a time before the last Great War, probably before you were born. The earth you taste is peat, a type of soil rich in ancient, decayed vegetable matter, millions of years old. Peat can be burned and, in fact, was burned to fire the copper still, a copper still over a hundred years old, a still that continues to be used to this day. The distillery is set twenty feet from the river Spey and a spring called Josie's well, its source of water, the water used in the malting process that allowed the barley to germinate, then collected and distilled. The barley came from a specific farm in Portgordon, the same farm that has grown barley for the Glenlivet all these years."

"You know all of that from a single taste?' I asked, half mockingly.

"I know all that because I took the time to look. Scotch is about history and every brand is unique. Now that you know a little more, lets try some different brands and see what you like. John, bring us each a glass of Glenfiddich."

"Yes, sir, Admiral."

"Now this is not as old and won't have all the character of the last, but you should be able to discern between them."

John set the newly poured bronze liquid on the bar in front of us and I prepared them exactly as the Admiral had shown me. He took a sip, and then watched my face as I did as well.

"Smoky," I said as my first adjective. "Maybe a bit woody?"

He tipped his glass back awaiting the last rich drop to fall upon his tongue then said, "Smart lad! Now you know how to drink scotch. Next week, same time, same wager?"

"Yes sir. Thank you, Admiral. I'll see you then."

"See you later, John. Just put that on my tab."

"Thank you, Admiral, see you soon."

I sat at the bar and watched the Admiral exit before John asked, "How long have you known the old man?"

"Just a couple of weeks. I met him in the park and we played chess and talked literature. Hell, I didn't even know he was an admiral till thirty minutes ago."

"He's in charge of Naval Intelligence. Word is he's fucking brilliant. He issued a report warning the military that the Japs were planning something, sooner rather than later. Admiral Kimmel was the Commandeer in Chief of the US Pacific fleet at the time. Kimmel, or his staff, chose to ignore the report and look what happened. After Pearl, Kimmel was demoted and Nimitz became the new boss. Nimitz gave your man his fourth star. I heard him say you won a bet with him?"

"Sort of. I beat him at a game of chess. Well, two actually," I said, pondering the strangeness of the chance encounter.

"Holy shit!"

"Yep, that's what I say. Holy shit."

The following week I found the Admiral at the same bench, the board prepared at his right hand. Taking in the morning sun, he read as he awaited my arrival.

"Good morning, Admiral. Whatch ya reading?"

Without looking up he said, "Carson McCullers. Supposed to be the next great literary genius."

"Well?"

"Interesting read I suppose, but nothing earth-shattering. Did you finish the Joyce?"

"Yes sir. Couldn't put it down. Quite amazing! Here, I brought your friend back."

"Already? Good. Then I shall exchange it for this" he said, handing me another tome.

"*Finnegan's Wake?*"

"Another Joyce novel. His last."

"Last?"

"He died in Zurich back in January."

"I didn't know. What a loss," I shook my head.

"A world in turmoil hardly noticed. I read his obituary in the *Times*."

"So, Naval Intelligence?" I asked, not too subtly slipping the point into conversation.

"Yes! Sort of an oxymoron if you ask me," he said cynically, chuckling at his own irony.

"Sounds to me like you've got plenty of reason to be bitter. I'd sure have one hell of a chip on my shoulder if I were you."

"Because you beat me at chess?" he laughed, knowing already the answer to his question and which turn the conversation would now take.

"Because you warned the brass and they didn't listen to you."

"And you know that how? You don't have to answer that. I'd be deluding myself if I thought that rumors were *not* running rampant."

"I only heard it from one source, so I wouldn't say *rampant* exactly."

"If I'm bitter it's because I failed."

"Failed? You were right in your predictions. How is that a failure?"

"I failed because I couldn't make anyone else listen. You could call it the boy- who-cried-wolf phenomenon. We knew, I knew, an attack by the Japanese was inevitable. It was not a matter of *if*, but *when*. I guess we warned of it so often it began to fall on deaf ears…and here we are," he gestured with his hand. "Your move."

I complied, saying, "You can't help it if you were right and no one would listen."

"Tell that to the men entombed at the bottom of the harbor. Tell that to their wives, and children, and parents." He grew silent and studied the board before finally moving.

A flight of five *Wildcats* off of Hickam flew low over our heads, disturbing a flock of gulls into reluctant flight, their high-pitched squeals cursing the un-natural invaders daring to traverse their domain. Considering them, I turned my attention to the game at hand before countering the Admiral's last move.

"Begging the Admiral's pardon, but I think you're wrong, sir. You're taking the blame for what the Jap bastards did, an evil, misguided act that you rightly predicted. History, which you are so fond of, will remember you as a hero."

"You are too kind. Too bad for you I'm gonna win today," he said, not too subtly trying to change the subject.

"Don't get too cocky, Admiral. I'm looking forward to trying a new scotch with the added pleasure of you paying for it." I won in eight moves.

"Damn it boy, how do you do that?"

"I honestly don't know, sir. Partly pattern recognition I guess, and partly intuition. I try to figure your most logical moves then figure mine three in advance for each of yours. You play very logically, so you're easier to predict. Does that make any sense?"

"So if I played erratically, made crazy, illogical moves I might beat you?"

"I think the unexpected throws people for a loop. If you *zig* when a reasonable person would *zag* and do it at just the precise moment, it throws the competition off their game."

"That makes some sense. I'll have to think about that strategy for a while. In the meantime, it looks like I owe you yet another drink. Are you sure you want scotch? You don't have to drink it just because I do."

"Sure I do. I'm developing a new appreciation for history and culture one sip at a time." My answer must have validated his interest in me as he smiled broadly in response.

The daily missions were more and evermore mundane with only one success to show for two months worth of effort. On September 29th one of our *Liberators* got a Japanese sub only a mile off the southern coast of Molokai. The brazen little Nips were trying to navigate the straits between the islands when they were spotted by a flight of two *Wildcats* off the deck of the USS *Wasp*. A call to Hickam and a *Liberator* was dispatched. From only a thousand feet, they dropped a full load on the sneaky bastards. Within minutes of the attack, the kill was confirmed by the oil and debris that floated to the surface. This inspired us for a day or two, each hoping we could make a similar score and redeem our tarnished manhood. With renewed vigor, we diligently searched for subs or ships. Any Japanese target would suffice, but with each US victory in the Pacific the probability of encountering such a target venturing this close to Hawaii diminished by the day.

In May of '42 the U.S. Navy had fought the Japs to a draw in the Battle of the Coral Sea. They clashed again a month later in what was being called the Battle of Midway, giving our team a decisive victory. The hard-won fight proved an epiphany, a realization by both sides that Japan was not invincible. Before our first taste of success we all had unspoken fears, but with this victory the psychological tide of war began to shift. After Midway, the Japanese switched from a posture of aggressive expansion to one of defense. Being thousands of miles removed from the action, we began to fear the war would be over before we had our chance to make a meaningful contribution. The Admiral admonished me to not naively believe everything I read in the press, whose job it was to instill hope, patriotism, and pride of place in the dark days at hand. "While the victories are compelling, there will still be plenty of war left over for you." I knew the Admiral was in a position to truly know what was going on in spite of the fog of war, but buzzing around Hawaii, day after uneventful day, I grew increasingly more skeptical of the good admiral's advice. Every day our task was becoming increasingly more futile and frustrating and castrating. I could hardly bring myself to write the truth to Mary: that she and I endured this unhappy separation so I could fly around paradise looking for Japanese submarines, targets that in all probability would never materialize. The real truth is the mundane nature of my present situation would make her happy, as it implied I was not in harm's way. Why then did I feel like less of a man writing something home to her that would give her some comfort? I finally decided the manly thing to do was to protect Mary, the love of my life, at every opportunity given me. If I could give her peace of mind by telling her I was playing pilot somewhere in the Pacific without the slightest chance of being harmed, then I should do so. What do you suppose the men on Guadalcanal were writing home to their loved ones? True tales of horror and fear and death, or notes filed with the kindest of half-truths and mistruths, consoling messages of happiness and safety? I kept my frustrations to myself.

Most of my crew was doing the same as me, frustrated as hell, but putting on a good face for folks back home whose only knowledge of our whereabouts was we were stationed somewhere in the Pacific. I say *most* of my crew because the remainder was having the time of their lives. Bledsoe wasted no time upon arrival here before he had not one, but two lovely girlfriends or *ipo*, the Hawaiian word for lover. We all scratched our heads in amazement. Lenny said the only way he could figure it was that Bledsoe must be "hung like a horse." We all took to calling him "Whirlaway" after the Kentucky Derby winner. To this day I don't understand his success with women.

Jordan Fouts had found a young lady as well. It was an intense, but I'm sure asexual romance, which left Jordan, ever the good Baptist, wanting for more. He proposed to the young lady, but her parents forbade the union, as the mixing of Polynesian and white blood was taboo. The rejection devastated Jordan, being forbidden his first real love. Lenny tried to fix the situation by getting him drunk. Drinking alcohol was completely out of character for Jordan, but completely despondent and unwilling to argue, he went drinking with Joe and Lenny. As you can imagine, it didn't require much to get him totally inebriated. Though he spent most of the following day hugging a toilet bowl, Jordan took a liking to the amnestic qualities of beer, finding it helped deaden the pain of his loss. Jordan, Joe and Lenny became constant companions, comrades in arms. I couldn't think of three more incompatible guys, but here they were, thick as thieves. The Admiral said such was true of the nature of war, and of man since first he waged war on his fellow man. The intensity of emotions while embroiled in mortal conflict, the passion with which a man loves or hates makes him more alive than he ever has been or ever will be again. While it was indeed true there were no atheists in foxholes, there also were no teetotalers.

The Admiral was quite a man. Time spent with him was the bright spot of my time in Hawaii. In the process of becoming a good friend he taught me a lot on a multitude of subjects, but mostly, I suppose, he schooled me on the frailty and nobility of the human condition. My granddaddy was the wisest man I've ever known, but the Admiral was a close second. We continued meeting weekly in the park, clad as civilians, free of military trappings and conventions, to play chess, and more importantly, to discuss life. By mid-October he finally bested me at chess fair and square. I've never been so happy to lose anything in my entire life. He enjoyed his winnings so much that I bought him a second round as well. After the third Glenlivet his hardened exterior began to reveal cracks, tiny flaws violating thick armor through which his humanity began to seep. He got tears in his eyes when he told me of his wife leaving him for another man. His profession had been his mistress and this infidelity had cost him a hefty price. His son naturally stayed with his ex-wife and her new husband, a shopkeeper whose lack of both passion and a Navy career was seen as stability, something a submariner could never offer her. His last conversation with her had been over the telephone when she had called to curse him after their son announced he was joining the Navy. The Admiral laughed confessing that had been his finest day. His boy was a bright lad and the Admiral, though not an admiral at the time, had managed to acquire for his him an appointment to the Naval Academy in Annapolis. He graduated at the top of his class and began his career as a junior officer aboard the *USS Hornet*. Despite exclusion from his son's life for the last ten years, the boy idolized his father. The reciprocal was true as well, the boy undeniably the old man's pride and joy. Seeing the Admiral's face light up when speaking of his son made me think I too would someday like to be a father. God must have thought this fleeting desire for paternity a prayer because the following day, Oct 25, 1942, I received a letter from Mary.

Dearest,

I miss you so much. I hope this finds you safe and well. I've put off telling you as long as I dared, I know how you worry about me, but I've got amazing news. YOU'RE GOING TO BE A FATHER! I only wish I could be there to see your face. I know you will be as excited at the news as I am. The doctor says I'm fine and should have the baby in the spring. Please don't worry about me. I plan to go live with Mommy and Papa after Christmas. I'm praying the war will be over and you can be home for the birth of your little boy. I know it could be a little girl, but somehow I just know it's a boy. He'll grow up strong and handsome and smart just like his daddy. Please, darling, take care of yourself and hurry home soon.

I love you,

Mary

P.S. The Cardinals beat the Yankees in the series, 5 games to 1.

I listened to every game for you.

I read and reread the letter at least a dozen times to be sure I wasn't dreaming. Me! A father? It was just too good to be true. I wanted to celebrate! Announce my joy to the world, a world that today felt new and beautiful and different. We flew our daily mission around the islands smoking fat stogies I'd purchased to hand out to friends in celebration. The *China Doll* purred along like a kitten. What a great airplane! I'd buy all the guys beer tonight till they puked, but for right now we had to be satisfied with cigars. I realized that day there was something I desired more than vengeance; I wanted to live to see my wife and child. The very thought of being a father changed my perspective on everything. What had we been complaining about? We were a good thousand miles from any real action. Maybe Uncle Sam would decide he had enough help after all and send us home. Hell, after my news, I believed anything was possible.

"Hey guys, anyone here ever do a barrel roll?" Before I got an answer I ordered, "Everyone strap in. I'm gonna try something."

"You know this is against regulations, right?" Jack asked, drolly smiling.

I pushed the *Doll's* nose over to pick up speed before pulling back. At thirty degrees above the horizon I rolled the yoke as far left as it would go. The *Doll* sluggishly rolled inverted where it took all my strength pushing to keep her nose from falling through the horizon. She shuddered, but the roll kept coming. I knew she could do it, at least theoretically. It's only a one-G maneuver, but it sure surprised me just how much a physical workout a simple barrel roll gave me.

"You're fucking crazy, but I'd fly with you anywhere," Jack said over the din of the cheers and catcalls coming from the back.

CJ yelled, "Hey, Cap'n, is that how you got her pregnant, rolling her over?"

"Hey, that's the mother of my child you're talking about!" Laughter erupted from all sides.

"That was fun, Cap'n, but you just about lost Lenny through the waist port. The little bastard wasn't belted in," Joe said, laughing hysterically. Lenny was not amused. He was on his way forward to voice his complaints when I said, "Lenny didn't like that? Let's do it again!" I pushed the *Doll's* nose over as if I was going to repeat the roll. Lenny quickly grabbed a seat and buckled in before I leveled off. The guys really liked that.

The remainder of the flight was pretty much a carnival. When we landed I said, "Gentlemen, I think beer is in order."

"You gonna fraternize with us mere mortals, Cap'n?"

"I've already broken several regs today. What's one more?"

"I think the term is court-martial, Cap'n," Jack said, tongue-in-cheek.

We couldn't go to the officers club, so I suggested everyone change into *civvies* and meet at the Beach Comber Bar on Haniakala Street at 2000 hours.

"Aye aye, Cap'n," they replied in mass before disbursing.

I had one stop to make before heading back to quarters to change. I wanted to buy the Admiral a bottle of scotch, a present before our appointment tomorrow. I picked up two bottles, twenty-year-old Glenfarclas, another Speyside single malt, one for him, one for me before hurrying back. Jack met me at the door with a dour look. "I think you should see this," he said handing me an official looking, burnt umber colored envelope. It had been opened.

Skimming through its contents quickly I announced, "It's our marching orders. Looks like we're off to the real war on Monday."

"Yep."

"Wow, I don't know whether to laugh or cry. I guess this proves the adage *be careful what you wish for*," I said sarcastically. We've been waiting for this so long, but after my other news this morning I don't know what to think."

"Don't think anything. Let's get drunk tonight. Worry about tomorrow tomorrow. One day at a time is how we're gonna get through this. The good news is now you have two great reasons to look forward to going home."

"Jack, that's the longest string of words I've ever heard you put together," I laughed. "I suppose you're right. I'd give anything to go home, but it doesn't make a lot of sense to leave before the job is done. If we don't beat the bastards now there will never be any peace. I can't leave a job like that for my son, so let's go get it done."

"Yep!"

"Now there's the Jack I know." He rolled his eyes at me.

Changing into civilian disguise, we met the guys at the Beachcomber.

"Boys, I've got news. We've got orders. I'll tell you where we're going when we're loaded and ready to go Monday morning. Suffice it to say, we're gonna be a lot closer to the action and a lot further from anything like home, so drink up. Tonight's on me." That was met by a combination of cheers and orders shouted at the barkeep for beer. Lenny stood alone in his silence. "You're really not gonna tell us?"

"C'mon Lenny, you know I can't."

"Can't or won't?"

"Both. We've got thousands of miles of open ocean to cross before we get there. One slip of the tongue and we could have Japs waiting in ambush. It's a security issue Lenny, not to mention a direct order not to reveal. It's nothing personal. Drink up! You'll know soon enough. It's not going to change anything knowing today or knowing Monday."

"I know, Cap'n. It just seems unfair, that's all."

"Nothing about war is fair, Lenny. Have a beer and forget it. Look, Jordan the teetotaler has a head start on you." Placated, or at least satisfied I wasn't withholding information just to be an asshole, Lenny turned his attention back to the party at hand, "I'll be damned if you ain't right, Cap'n. I think we've corrupted the boy. Hey Bledsoe, order me one up."

Jack and I both got a beer and found a table in the corner from where we could watch the revelry. There were crews of at least five other ships here all doing the same thing, not a single uniform to be seen. Jack and I soon found our table joined by the pilots of those other ships. I thought it funny how the segregation of officers and enlisted men seemed to occur along natural lines even when we had taken specific steps to violate the no-fraternization rules. Would this unseen barrier always exist? I certainly hoped not. This, too, seemed another injustice of war. Not that I didn't understand the need for such rules, as familiarity always breeds contempt. In combat someone had to call the shots, otherwise chaos would ensue. Authority must be respected or enlisted men and officers alike could be hurt or killed. I found that I liked these men and hoped in our short time together I had conveyed my respect for them and in the process had perhaps earned their respect as well. Only time would tell.

The party raged on until the wee hours of Saturday morning when the bar was required to close. True to my oath I'd had only two beers, but the other boys had no self-prescribed limits and so were pretty drunk. I corralled my men, making sure they made it safely back to the barracks and to bed before turning in myself.

The following morning I was in the park at the assigned bench at 1000 hours, but contrary to his habit, the Admiral was not sitting there waiting. I waited half an hour before walking to a newsstand for the morning paper, then returned and waited some more. After another two hours I had finished reading the news of the war and still no sign of the Admiral. Concerned, I thought perhaps I should go to his home to check on him when it dawned on me that I had no idea where he lived. Instead I ambled down the street and into the officers' club and took a stool at the bar. John was there and after he'd waited on a couple of other customers, I called him over and in hushed tones asked, "Hey, John, have you seen the old man this morning?" He looked concerned and nodded toward the door as if to say, "Let's talk outside." Stepping into the bright sunlight John withdrew and lit a cigarette, inhaling deeply before saying, "I'm not supposed to know this, but I overheard a couple of officers talking about it this morning."

"It?" I enquired.

"*The Hornet*, sir. She went down this morning."

I stood, mouth agape letting the news sink in. The Admiral's son was an officer on that carrier.

"I don't suppose there's any word of survivors?"

"Too early, but you know that's where he has to be…Trying to get some word about his boy."

I didn't know the son except for what the Admiral told me of him. News of his loss, or potential loss, I should say, as we did not yet know if he numbered among those who had surely succumbed, was as painful as if someone had slugged me in the gut. I could only begin to imagine what The Admiral must be going through.

"John, I'm out of here tomorrow morning, probably for the duration. I doubt I'll get to say good-bye. Would you mind holding something for the old man from me?" I said, handing him the bottle of scotch.

"Sure, Captain, I'll be sure that he gets it. Any message?"

"Just tell him thanks and that I'll be looking for him when this is all over."

"You've got it, sir."

CHAPTER 13

There were fifty-two ships in the armada assembled to depart from Hickam on the morning of October 26, 1942. We were up before sunrise, personally loading our own bags and gear as fuel, bombs, and ammunition were being loaded for us. After our conversation the day before John had "procured" for me a case of scotch. I decided it best not to ask too many questions and just said, "thank you."

"I figure Uncle Sam owes you a whole lot more than a case of booze." I saluted him before taking the box from his hands and instructed Bledsoe to stow it in the front compartment under the life raft. Contraband was the order of the day and every crew departing had some personal luxury or marketable commodity hidden, stowed aboard in preparation for a long siege. At the front, cash wasn't worth the paper it was printed on, but cigarettes, liquor, or real toilet paper (not the waxy stuff Uncle Sam provided us with, but real, civilian toilet paper) could be bartered for just about anything, including sex.

I half hoped the Admiral might show up to say good-bye, but it just wasn't to be. Not wishing to abuse his position of rank to acquire information, the same information other parents back in the States had to anxiously await for months, he was to spend two agonizing weeks awaiting word of his son. He poured himself into his work with new vigor, helping him cope as he waited. Jim, his son, did indeed survive the sinking of *The Hornet* unscathed. He was one of the last three men to leave the ship before it was scuttled, sending it to the bottom of the Pacific. *The Hornet* had been crippled in battle beyond repair, so the decision had been made to abandon ship, sinking it of our own volition rather than taking the chance of it falling into Japanese hands. Following the heroic loss of his first berth, Jim was awarded command of a Navy cruiser, the *USS Nashville* (CL-43), from which he served throughout the remainder of the war.

Our flight that day was the largest formation I had or would ever again be a part of. The *Doll* was in the second group of four to take off. Forming up on the *Judas Goat*, we flew counterclockwise around the island of Oahu before departing to the southwest.

"I can tell you now, boys. We're going to New Caledonia."

"New Caledonia? Where the hell is that?" asked Joe.

Bledsoe added, "Nouvelle Caledonie. It was a French penal colony in the eighteen hundreds."

"Damn you, Bledsoe, how do you know all the shit you do?"

"Books I guess. I don't know, I just do."

"Don't feel too bad, Joe. I didn't know either, so I looked it up. It's a little chunk of rock in the ocean due east of Australia. We just took it back from the Japs. We'll be flying out of there for a month or two, then I suspect we'll follow our troops as they advance toward Japan. Any questions?" There were none, the crew silent, pondering the news. What awaited us in New Caledonia was largely an unknown, a nidus from which unspoken fear would surely grow, so I added, "The Japs have been very hard on the locals. We will be viewed as a liberating force, and that's a good thing." Still no response, I turned my attention to the task at hand.

The summer sun was just appearing, a glowing half orb over my left shoulder as the Hawaiian Islands disappeared, slipping into the past. It was a beautiful sight, one I doubted I would ever forget. Beauty tends to be overlooked during times of crisis, one of the great tragedies of human conflict. The Admiral had pointed this out to me while playing chess one day. I'd already determined to purchase a camera to record my exploits. I probably would have been content with a simple Kodak, having never experienced better, but The Admiral insisted I look at a Rolleiflex. "It might be considered treasonous since they're manufactured in Germany, but they really are the best you can buy." On his recommendation I found a camera shop in Honolulu that still had a camera in stock. The price was over a month's pay, which really made me sweat. I left the shop and thought about it for a week. Had I known Mary was pregnant at the time, I wouldn't have been holding the beautiful camera, memorializing for her the sunrise from 20,000 feet over the Pacific. I wanted a permanent reminder, something I could take home after the war perhaps to share some of the beautiful things I got to see. I exposed several rolls of film in Hawaii, but with this shot, if it turned out as good as I thought, the price of the camera had been justified. I was forced to be judicious in what I photographed, as I'd only been able to acquire ten rolls of film with twenty shots each. There probably would be no way to have it developed in the South Pacific and, I'm sure, mailing it home undeveloped would give the censors fits, so I had to be satisfied with delayed gratification. I was making, in effect, a time capsule, images and memories to be opened and shared with Mary and the baby when I got home…someday.

The flight was long and monotonous, but this time we knew better what to expect and were smart enough to bring along real food. Bledsoe had once again charmed some little girl out of a basket of fried chicken, potato salad, watermelon and pineapple, deviled eggs, pickles, and two pies. I'd never before had pineapple cream, but it sure sounded good and I was anxious to try it. When we finally broke out the food there were cheers all around for "Whirlaway." With strict orders to maintain radio silence, Bledsoe had little to do while CJ, on the other hand, was constantly occupied as Jack and I wanted position reports every thirty minutes. It was good practice for CJ and, because I was paranoid, I wanted nothing left to chance. If we got off course even a little we could all end up wet or worse. Keeping CJ occupied was a good thing for the remainder of the crew since he had taken on a new persona in Hawaii, that of prankster. No one, officer or enlisted man, had been spared falling prey to one of his practical jokes. I have to admit he was both funny and talented, but his hijinks became more and more complicated, not to mention dangerous. To get me, he tied a series of ropes around the bomber that allowed him to climb out the waist gun window and atop the plane while we were in flight. Imagine my startle when I saw him peering back making monkey faces at me through the front glass while at 10,000 feet above Hawaii.

"Shit, CJ! Are you out of your fucking mind? Get back in this plane," I yelled. There's no way he could have heard me but he must have read my lips because he saluted and complied. The boys in the back were in on the gag and were rolling on the floor laughing. While I had to admire the lengths he went to just to get me, I told him, "If you ever do that again, I will have you court-martialed."

His response? "Aw c'mon, Cap'n, I had a parachute."

"CJ, you're an idiot. A brave idiot, but an idiot nonetheless." The rest of the crew listened as I dressed him down. They were lucky they didn't develop hernias the way they were holding in their laughter. I did have to admit his pranks were funny. I guess secretly I was glad we were laughing as I suspected an equal amount of crying soon awaited us.

It was only a matter of time before he struck again. I swore I'd get him back before the war was over. Trouble was, I was neither as clever nor as devious as CJ. Mischief and practical jokes are the byproducts of an idle man's brain. Add an element of danger, either physical or the threat of being caught and reprimanded, and the compulsion becomes almost irresistible. It can manifest itself in many forms. For example, the boys in the back, especially Lenny, wanted to try out their guns, but I thought better of it given our proximity to friendly aircraft. I'm thankful they at least asked me for permission because I would have been the person reprimanded for their actions, an event that then would have resulted in them catching hell from me. As they say, "Shit rolls down hill."

The crew of *Hard Hearted Hannah*, as the Liberator to our left was known, was obviously falling prey to the compulsion. From the back Joe said, "Hey, Cap'n, look at your nine o'clock." *Hannah* had pulled forward and was passing me in formation. I could see the co-pilot, Phil Resnicki, laughing. *Hannah's* crew had their bare asses hanging out the waist window, aimed at us like weapons. I grabbed my new camera and snapped a quick shot. I figured no one would believe me if I just told them the story.

"Hey, Cap'n, you see those assholes?"

"Yes... literally."

"Can we return fire?" Lenny asked, his pants already around his ankles.

"Hold your fire, boys. We'll get 'em, but we've got to do better than that. Hey CJ, you got any ideas?" my question acknowledging him as the master. I don't think he could have been more proud.

"Let me give it some thought, Cap'n. It's gotta be a doozy." The rest of the crew got in on the act making suggestions, some outlandish, some lame. Lenny wanted CJ to crawl back outside the airplane, but I flatly refused.

"Simmer down, boys, it doesn't have to be today. In fact, it's probably better if it's not. They're expecting us to respond. Be patient. We'll get 'em, I promise. Right CJ?"

"Aye, Cap'n, we'll get 'em."

The remainder of the flight to New Caledonia was uneventful save crossing the equator. CJ gave us a countdown starting fifteen minutes before we crossed, and let out a war whoop at the exact moment announcing, "On October 28th at exactly 1237 GMT, the good ship *China Doll* traversed the equator," to which cheering all around ensued. The Navy has some traditions to commemorate a sailor's first equatorial crossing, involving both liquor and hazing. Novices were called *Polliwogs* while seasoned veterans were *Shellbacks*. To my knowledge the Army has no such induction ceremony or tradition. I considered suggesting something, but thought better of it after pondering what sadistic devices these boys might come up with. CJ added, "At the present rate, in one hour and eighteen minutes it will be tomorrow," hoping his words a clever riddle. Bledsoe quickly stole his thunder by asking, "International Date Line?"

"Bledsoe, you're a killjoy!" CJ pouted. Still, his proclamation gave us another event to punctuate the boredom.

Upon crossing the date line we repeated the same hoopla that served us crossing the equator, then everyone grew quiet, the weariness of the long flight taking its toll. The boys in the back were soon snoozing. I considered waking them up doing another barrel roll, but considering we were in formation with fifty-one other bombers decided against it reasoning it might be difficult to explain losing sleeping crewmembers over the Pacific Ocean. After inquiring of me the rules, Bledsoe borrowed my chess set. He and Joe put it to use trying their hand at a game neither had ever played. Jack took the reins for a while as I gave the boys a short tutorial. Bledsoe was a pretty quick study while Joe should probably just stick to playing checkers.

It certainly felt like tomorrow when we finally arrived over New Caledonia. After thirteen hours of flying non-stop I was ready to be on the ground, exceedingly happy to have found our destination especially since the *Doll* had less than one hour of fuel remaining. It took a while for me to recognize the runway, newly cut out of dense jungle vegetation. The Sea Bees had worked their magic, assembling an airport where two weeks ago there was none. The runway was constructed of *Marsden Matting;* perforated steel planking that locked together to quickly create a surface that was, in theory at least, capable of supporting the weight of my massive bomber. I say that cynically because until I observed the first of our group land on it I had grave doubts. Seeing their uneventful landing quickly followed by three more gave me a bit of confidence before it was the *Doll's* turn. I still held my breath and planted the wheels as gently as possible. I was surprised to find that though not as smooth as the concrete surfaces I was accustomed to, it still felt solid.

Pulling off the runway we were met by a sergeant frantically waving me to taxi as quickly and as far from the runway as possible. It seems the geniuses planning this expedition of fifty-two bombers had failed to take into consideration the limited ramp parking area of the new base. We now had a brewing crisis with more than forty bombers circling above, all with limited fuel remaining after a transoceanic flight. Parking large aircraft impossibly tight took time, precious time to the last few guys out there hoping to stay aloft on fumes, required to wait for access to an airbase that lacked sufficient space to hold them. Miraculously, all but the last three made it in successfully. Of the final three, the first attempted to land on the beach, the only patch of semi-cleared land he could find. On touchdown the volcanic sand gave way under the weight and the aircraft was destroyed. The other two pilots witnessed this and opted instead to ditch their aircraft in the harbor. Luckily, the crews of all three survived with only minor injuries. I was happy to have been already on the ground rather than a victim of someone else's tactical blunder. General Hale, the commander of the Fifth Air Force at the time, requested the idiots responsible for planning the operation be court-martialed. Watching the circus unfold, I whole-heartedly agreed. Though armadas of this size were a daily occurrence in the ETO, this was the first and last time such a large assembly of bombers traveled together in the Pacific theater.

Not only was there inadequate space for the number of aircraft, there were inadequate quarters for the number of airmen, the accommodations being tents and cots, and not enough of either. A near riot ensued the first night among the enlisted men, who found themselves too far back in line to get either shelter or bedding. A lot of men took refuge on the hard floor of their aircraft. Some had opened their parachutes and were trying to make hammocks of the canopy, ingenious today, but incredibly stupid for tomorrow. A general order went out forbidding any further parachute modifications. The guys who didn't get shelter at least got to be first in line for supper in the chow tent, a good thing since there was also not enough food to be served and guys in the back of the line got K-rations. Being an officer, I was spared most of this misery as officers were always allowed to be first in line. Although I was lucky enough to be given quarters and a cot, it was hardly the

Ritz; a large open-sided tent that would keep you dry only if it didn't leak, which it did, and only if you were under the center, which I wasn't. The tent did even less to provide sanctuary from ubiquitous mosquitoes the size of songbirds. If it rained, and I anticipated it would, I made the decision I'd sleep in the cockpit of the *Doll*. Regarding the latrines, all men were created equal; a trench is a trench is a trench, though with this number of men, a few more trenches would of necessity be dug tomorrow. I confess to being soft because I found the stench overpowering to the point of nausea.

They call this island paradise on earth, but I've discovered the best way to spoil paradise is to add a little humanity. Not exactly an original thought, as God found the same thing thousands, if not millions of years ago when he added man to his garden. Here we are today, still screwing it up.

The number of aircraft on the ground made routine operations impossible, not to mention a very tempting target for the Japanese. As an afterthought it was decided to split the group presently shoehorned into the small airport into three units, parceling the aircraft and crews out to three bases that had recently been hastily established. For ease and practicality, something unexpected from Army brass, the twenty aircraft sitting closest to the runway would henceforth be combined as a combat unit and be dispatched to Port Moresby in the morning. A second group selected by using the same criteria, that of runway proximity, would leave for Java tomorrow afternoon. The remainder, a smaller group of seventeen Liberators including the *Doll* would be based here on New Caledonia for the foreseeable future. We were to be designated the 6th Bombardment Group and fly sorties in groups of six aircraft, three bombers, and three fighters. Our principal target was to be Japanese shipping. As Japan rapidly and ruthlessly extended its reach into the South Pacific, their supply chains necessary to support their troops extended. I liked the mission, as every ship I sank would result in a Nip that would soon be running low on food or ammunition or both. Our first sortie would be launched just as soon as the boys headed for Java were airborne and our ships readied.

I was dead dog tired after our flight, but I still couldn't sleep that first night. Not only were the mosquitoes unrelenting, I was just too wired anticipating our first taste of combat. The rest of my guys were in the same tizzy save for Bledsoe who, I was soon to learn, could sleep any time, anywhere. All of us were up before sunrise, surprised to find the others checking on the *Doll*. I suppose this was a method of expending nervous energy. I've always found that doing something was better or at least easier than doing nothing at all. CJ had found other means of expending energy. He and Jim busied themselves repaying the crew of *Hard Hearted Hannah,* playing a practical joke before she left for Java. I had challenged CJ on the flight over to avenge our honor, our eyes sullied as they were by their bare asses. With *Hannah* and crew leaving, he had little time to either prepare or strike, but he rose to the occasion with great aplomb. Jim Hawthorn and Phil Resnicki had paid a fortune to have a beautiful naked babe painted on *Hannah's* nose, said to resemble Jim's girlfriend Hannah. They were quite proud of the image having it painted on their jackets as well. Somehow, CJ got hold of a photo of the real life Hannah, and discovered that though she was indeed quite attractive, she was several years older than Jim Hawthorn. That got CJ's wheels turning. Sometime in the night he and Jim took it upon themselves to repaint their mascot to what CJ described as, "More age appropriate," transforming the voluptuous, beautiful babe into a skinny, naked ninety-year-old women, her bare breast, looking more like two baseballs suspended in a pair of socks, hanging over her crossed arms to her knees. They renamed *Hannah* "the *Persistence of Mammories* after the famous Dali painting, a stroke of pure mischievous genius. Picking myself off the ground where I had fallen laughing, I ran to get my camera. When I returned, Jim, Phil and crew had arrived to discover the new art. They were mad as hell, threatening to kill whoever dared desecrate their icon. Failing to find the culprit or culprits before they left for Java, their new mascot's fresh paint glistening in the sun. I later heard through the grapevine that Jim painted over the granny, replacing her with his beloved, but he kept the name. His ship served throughout the remainder of the war known as *Mammories*.

Our flight of six was to fly a large geographic triangle, three hundred miles per side and 10,000 feet above the ocean, looking for any ship or vessel not registered to the Allies. All my boys had field glasses with which they were to scan the approaching horizon for ships or airplanes or anything else that might prove an enemy target. The larger Japanese convoys were usually escorted by carrier-based aircraft and battle ships, so attacking them with a large, slow aircraft would not be without significant risk. For daylight operations the prescribed technique was, after visual contact was made, to drop to the deck and approach from as low over the water possible with the purpose of avoiding detection. Surprising them was both the best and safest strategy. The fighters assigned us would remain high, providing cover if Jap fighters attacked us. While our little friends, as we were to call them, provided a great source of comfort, they could do little to protect us from antiaircraft guns firing at us from ship decks below. We were packing heavy; each bomber carrying eight 500 pounders, all with timed fuses, the idea being for us to lay them on the deck from low altitude and fly clear before each detonated. I was happy to be packing a punch, but must confess this ordinance scared the bejesus out of me. Opening the bomb bay doors to pass just a few hundred feet over the heads of angry Japs shooting at me was like a fighter exposing his soft belly to the punches of an adrenalin-crazed opponent. Bledsoe said, "The good thing is it'd be over for us really fast if one of those 500 pounders takes a hit." He was right; we'd be vaporized in an instant. I wondered if it would hurt or if we'd have time to know or think even a fraction of a last thought. I knew for certain that I had no desire to find out. I had my Mary and a baby soon coming to get home to.

With the second group off for Java we were soon loaded and ready to go. Before we rolled, Jordan asked if he might say a few words to the Lord on our behalf.

"I think that might be a good idea, Jordy. We can use all the help we can get." As soon as he finished and we all added "Amen," I advanced the throttles and we were off for war. It was strangely exhilarating, an electricity in the air that afternoon, each of us sharing its paresthetic tingling.

Flying north, expecting to encounter the enemy at any moment, all eyes aboard were alert; all but mine had binocular field glasses scanning the horizon. But hour after hour, all that met our eyes was the horizon, a subtle boundary separating vast sea and eternal sky. The only thing saving us from the hypnotic lull of sleep was frustration. No Japs, no targets, only ocean. Varying only the time and subtle trajectory changes, we flew essentially the same mission every day for three and a half weeks, each ending uneventfully the same. I can recount to you things that few men in the history of the world have witnessed; the subtle color variations of clouds over the uninhabited South Pacific Ocean in November as opposed to December; the way sunlight dances upon the afternoon water, forcing the vaporous formation of towering cumulonimbus; sea birds encountered hundreds of miles from any semblance of a respite. Of all this I could regale you with in the greatest of detail, but I could not describe the thrill of sighting an enemy vessel, my entire raison de vivre here, south of the equator. To say I was frustrated just does not quite capture the raw, gnawing emotion churning in my gut. Being away from Mary, especially now, had to have some meaning, some grand purpose, or all of it was in vain. I just could not, would not go home without accomplishing something of true and lasting value. This mission was costing me dearly as I now was forfeiting not only time with Mary, but the privilege of witnessing the birth of our first child as well. Weekly I marched into the commander's office to request, sometimes respectfully, sometimes not, a change that would put my crew and I into the fray. The commander was a full bird colonel, a large man of Polish extraction by way of Chicago named Wisnicki. Like my granddaddy, Colonel Wisnicki had enormous hands. With fists the size of hams, it was hard to imagine he could be anything but clumsy, but then I remembered what my granddaddy could do with a scalpel. Apparently the colonel had the same deceptive façade as he'd proven himself a talented pilot, rising through the ranks in the 1930s. He flew open-cockpit P-26 *Peashooters,* although I can't begin to imagine how he shoehorned his hulking frame into such a small aircraft. Like most longsuffering Catholic Poles, he proved infinitely patient as he heard the same speech from every ship captain on at least a weekly basis. Olexander Wisnicki would respond in the same manner he had been approached, sometimes respectfully, sometimes not, that he too had orders from superiors that must be obeyed. He was merely a conduit, a soldier who received orders from his superiors and carried out those orders to the very best of his ability. "Ours is not to question why, ours is but to do and die," was the mantra he would repeat in a singsong fashion every time I invaded his office.

"But couldn't we extend just a little further to the west? We might actually catch a fish or two," I said, exasperated.

"You could, but you won't. That is an order, Captain."

Sensing the limited extent of my license with this man I said, "Yes, sir," and saluted sharply before retreating. He was such a nice guy no one wanted to go above his head, even if it would help end our frustration. I did, however, mention our situation to The Admiral in a letter, asking if he might be able to discretely help get us into the war.

My crew always waited, expecting, hoping for a different answer. After the fourth such chat with the commander, all I had to do was shake my head and they understood, upon which we would retreat to the club, a makeshift bar that served officers and enlisted men alike. After another week of coming home empty handed, followed shortly thereafter by my usual chat with Olexander, I had a private conversation with CJ.

"If a fellow was to accidently set his compass off by, say, fifteen degrees or so, could he still find his way home?"

"Why yes, Cap'n, I believe that he could as long as he didn't change any other variable. 'Course that might just be a little difficult considerin' he was trav'lin' along with five other airplanes. They all would have to make that same mistake."

"I see...too bad. We can't be breaking orders, but it sure might be interesting to find out what's happening just a little over the western horizon." I searched CJ's beer-saturated eyes seeking some signal of accomplice, of gentlemanly, albeit complicit understanding of what I was hinting.

"Course I'm a believer in the power of mass hypnosis," he said with a wink. Nothing more was ever said about this conversation. To this day I don't know if we were on the prescribed course or not, I never asked and he never told. I do know that the following day, December 12, 1942, we had our first encounter with the enemy.

There were four flight teams out of New Caledonia daily, each charged with the mission of search and destroy. The teams were labeled primary colors; red, blue, green, and yellow. As officer of the day, I was in command of the team monikered Red Flight with the *Doll* being Red Flight One. We were six in all, having been joined at a rendezvous coordinate over the South Pacific by three FU4 *Wildcats* of the First Fighter Squadron. The Wildcats flew from a base on a neighboring island and were a welcome sight over the rendezvous point each day. Brave men all, I was to know none of their names until well after the war. The bombers of Red Flight were from our group on New Caledonia, with Jim Wright's ship *The Ace of Spades* and David Caldwell's *Daring Donna* at my four o'clock and six o'clock respectively.

Jack saw the Japs first, "Hey, Captain, we've got a ship...make that three ships on the horizon at eleven o'clock."

Taking his binoculars, I quickly found the potential targets.

"Bledsoe, report the sighting to center. Bombers, down to the deck."

"Yes, Cap'n."

With that we began a rapid, almost diving descent, leveling out mere feet above the waves. From up top the fighters confirmed that the ships, a destroyer and two cargo vessels were flying Japanese colors, heading due south at 180 degrees. There were no escort aircraft sighted, so I thought it safe to split the group. I instructed the *Wildcats* to circle wide and give us time to get into position. "Attack head-on from altitude and we'll sneak in their back door."

"Roger that," the radio cracked before the three banked steeply away.

It took us twenty minutes to get into a position trailing the ships by five miles. Approaching low over the ocean, there was no indication that our presence had yet been detected. From their vantage point aloft, the *Wildcats* gave us vectors to get into position as we had lost sight of the targets in our descent. From five miles in trail at ten feet above the water, I could just make out the narrow ship profiles on the horizon. The destroyer was forward and to the left of the pack. The Jap ships were separated by what I approximated to be about two miles, so our flight of three bombers separated by the same to allow for simultaneous attacks. The *Doll* would hit the destroyer while *Ace of Spades* and *Daring Donna* each targeted an individual container ship. From four miles out I saw the *Wildcats* diving, beginning their strafing runs, all concentrating their efforts on the destroyer. The Japs began returning fire almost simultaneously, a thick barrage of antiaircraft trained on the three little fighters.

"Lock and load boys, here we go," I said to a crew who had already steeled themselves for a fight. Advancing the throttles to full, I remember my palms sweating, my heart racing like a kid at his first school dance. We passed the first container about two miles to starboard below deck level with no fire aimed at us. Passing the second ship I said to Jack, "We just might pull this off." No such luck. I saw tracers whiz past the front glass followed by the THWAK THWAK THWAK of shells marching down the *Doll's* length. All of my gunners began firing, returning shell-for-shell, giving as good as they were taking. The bomb bay doors opened as I yelled at Jim, "You get one pass, give 'em all eight and make 'em count." I felt the *Doll* shudder as shells exploded in the air around her. The air was thick with the smell of cordite and sea spray and blood, no time now to figure out whose. The rear gunners of the destroyer, now wary, began shooting down at us. The first two *Wildcats* whipped past us overhead at lightning speed, then banked hard right to make a second pass. The third dropped a single hundred pounder that skidded harmlessly over the deck before sliding into the ocean portside. The *Wildcat* exploded into a hurtling mass of burning debris that spun into the waiting water, the pilot's life and munitions apparently spent in vain. I saw it meet the water with boiling fury as I yanked back on the yoke with all my strength.

"Bombs away," Jim announced as the *Doll* shuddered at stall's edge. Instantly 4000 pounds lighter, she began flying again as I banked hard left to miss the ship's stacks. I could see the eyes of the men on the deck below, men now returning small arms fire, bullets bouncing off the *Doll* with a ping, ping, men who were dead, but not yet aware of it. One of the *Wildcats* passed only feet to our right, heading back at the angry mass for another run. I held my breath mentally counting "one, one thousand, two, one thousand…" An eternity of five seconds later our delivered payload blew mid-deck, the concussive blast pitched the *Doll* tail up and rolling left. It took every ounce of both Jack's and my strength to keep the airplane from tumbling into the ocean, our prop tips striking, flinging saltwater before we completely recovered.

Jordy began yelling "We got 'em, we got 'em we got 'em!" from the tail just as I looked back to see the mid-ship boiling with fire and metal and men. I saw men jumping overboard, some aflame, as our friend the *Wildcat* appeared emerging from the fray, climbing away from the firestorm separating us. We all began cheering both our victory and our survival, but the sound of those cheers was soon pierced by a shrieking wail, that of Joe crying, "Oh God, Oh God, Oh Jesus!" with everyone else shouting "What? What is it?"

"It's Lenny! Oh God, he's missing half his head," Joe said, both crying and puking in the same instant, his pitiful sound sending a palpable shock wave through the crew, all falling silent. I started to ask if he was dead, but knew already the obvious answer and so held my tongue.

"I'm gonna climb back up and take a look see, why don't you go back and check on the boys, Jack?" He was looking at me, but appeared pale and dazed.

"You've been hit," he said.

"What? Where?"

"You're face is splattered with blood."

Quickly feeling, I did indeed have blood on my face, but I had no pain. Finding no injury, I returned Jack's puzzled look, before discovering the source of bleeding.

"Good God, Jack. It's your blood." Seeing the question in his eyes I said, "Your shoulder?" Reaching to examine his right shoulder he finally said, "Yep."

"How bad is it?"

"I didn't even feel it. Can't be too bad."

"Bledsoe! Get up here and check Jack out. Anyone else hurt?" Joe was still whimpering in the back, his soul broken, but no one else fessed up.

At 10,000 feet we passed again over the target.

"Red Flight One requesting damage reports." I already knew the fate suffered by one of the three *Wildcats*. That turned out to be Red Five, as Red Four and Six both responded no damage. Jim Wright in *Ace of Spades* reported as Red Flight Three, "Heavy damage, but no casualties." David Caldwell in *Daring Donna* did not respond, leaving me to assume the worst. I requested the fighters make a low pass to look for possible survivors, but without seeing anything from 10,000 feet I held out little hope. The dense smoke from the blaze consuming the destroyer continued to rise into the atmosphere, ascending several thousand feet above us, casting an enormous shadow over the ocean waters below. The billowing was fierce but stopped abruptly when the big ship finally slipped beneath the waves. One of the container vessels had already disappeared into the deep while the other, still afloat, smoldered on. It was dead in the water and from the flurry of activity on deck appeared to be taking on survivors. I could only hope that David and his crew were not among their numbers, knowing for certain they would not long fare well.

This injured, yet still afloat ship of pitiful survivors would have proven quite the moral dilemma had we more bombs to expend. Luckily for them, the conundrum was answered by a function of payload. I know at that moment my anger and hatred would have driven me to make the last of the bastards pay for Lenny and the others lost here today.

"Red Flight, this is Red Flight one. Let's head home." The flight home was intensely schizophrenic, the elation of victory jousting with the agony of our losses. I guess we got exactly what we had been begging for, a taste of the real war, a taste now savored more bitter than sweet. The entire attack had taken less than five minutes, and while those five minutes proved the most intensely alive I've ever felt in my time on this earth, what had been the true cost? We had lost twelve good young men including a valued friend and crewmember; the Japanese had lost perhaps hundreds of good young men. In the economies of war the encounter was a fabulously good trade if you were a general in an ivory tower, a not-so-good trade if you could personally put a name and a face upon any of the lost. We licked our wounds, silently ruminating philosophically.

Bledsoe bandaged up Jack's wound, pointing out how lucky we had just been. A shell had penetrated the right window, traversed his shoulder and the cabin then splattered me with Jack's blood before exiting my window. Bledsoe deduced the shells trajectory by connecting the dots. "You just missed getting a *Purple Heart* like Lieutenant Jack here. Hell, both of you missed being dead by only fractions of an inch." I shuddered at the thought. Bledsoe was right. That shell easily could have taken both Jack and I out, leaving the airplane pilotless and killing the crew in the process. I was speechless.

What an emotional roller coaster, from elation to despondence to regret to thankfulness, all within a span of but a few minutes, a ride once begun I was powerless to stop. All I could do was hold on and pray the speeding car didn't leave the track. Our wild ride was just about to take one more turn.

Still fifty miles from home and no land yet visible, CJ popped his head into the cabin and handed me his binoculars saying, "Hey Cap'n, I think you need to see this."

"Oh God, not another Jap ship. All we got left is spit."

"Not a Jap ship," he said grinning ear to ear. "Look down at the ocean at your seven o'clock."

Puzzled, I scanned where CJ suggested. "Well I'll be damned. Jack, I'm taking her down there. Red Flight One to Red Flight. Follow me down, I've got a surprise for you." I circled the *Doll* back descending rapidly from 10,000 to come up along side a friend feared lost, *Daring Donna* and her crew. My guys began cheering and waving. The *Donna* was responsible for attacking the container ship that had somehow managed to survive. She'd delivered a crippling blow, but got herself smacked in the process and now was struggling to survive. *Donna* was flying crab-like, her two right engines feathered and motionless, her two left engines taking her home, but just barely. There was evidence of fire damage and soot on the right wing, but no active fire or smoking. Bledsoe tried several tricks to raise them on the wireless, but to no avail. "Her radio must be gone too, Cap'n." I could see Captain Caldwell sweating in the left seat. He looked over and smiled at us, but couldn't take his hands off the controls. Remembering the effort it took to keep a *Liberator* in the air with just two engines, all I had to offer was commiseration.

"Well, let's slow down and follow her home. Those boys are damned lucky to be alive from the looks of things." Decelerating, we followed her all the way back to New Caledonia, the *Doll* at her seven and *The Ace of Spades* at her four.

News of our actions had already spread over the base and even Colonel Wisnicki was out to meet us when we taxied to a stop. Before anyone else got out, two medical corpsmen came aboard to remove Lenny's lifeless body from the ball turret. They covered him with a shroud, but it was impossible to move a body on a stretcher out of the hatch, so we had to lift him down like a sack of loose potatoes. There were no dry eyes. The turret ball was full of blood and gray matter that I assumed were brains, a large gaping hole, evidence of the shell that took his life. "The poor little guy didn't have a chance," Joe said. We all shook our heads in silent agreement. Emerging last, Colonel Wisnicki was there to greet me. In wisdom he refrained from appearing too elated at our victory saying only, "I want you in my office in two hours." Nodding acquiescence, I followed my crew along with the corpsmen who were taking Lenny. He saluted as our group walked silently away. We were not exactly sure of where it was we were going, but somehow we all shared the same compulsion to follow.

At 1900 hours we briefed Colonel Wisnicki on our mission. He began the meeting by offering his condolences for our loss. Lenny Markowitz from the *Doll* and the *Wildcat* pilot, whom the colonel informed us was Lieutenant Bill Bates of Tacoma, Washington, were the only American casualties. Three other guys including Jack had shrapnel injuries and/or burns, none life-threatening. The aircraft had taken quite a beating. *Daring Donna* lost both right engines, victims of fuel starvation after a single shell severed both fuel lines. "You boys all have lots of small holes as evidence you were in close quarters with the enemy. He then congratulated us for denying or delaying Tojo's invasion of Wilkes Island for weeks, if not months.

"You will be happy to know that the Navy has completed the job. Using coordinates supplied us by Lieutenant Murphy, the Navy dispatched a submarine operating in that area to send the last ship to the bottom. Right or wrong, it was sunk after allowing survivors to abandon ship.

"I find it interesting, gentlemen, that your actions occurred more than fifty miles west of your assigned territory. Anyone have any idea how all six aircraft could make the same mistake?" He looked about the room with a knowing, jaundiced eye, but no one fessed up. "No matter. You did a good job for our side today and I intend to see you all receive commendations. The loss of Corporal Markowitz has convinced me of another change. I don't think the ball turrets are as valuable here in the South Pacific as they seem to be in the ETO. I'm ordering their removal from all of the aircraft under my command. MacArthur can kiss my Polish ass. The change will take a little time so you boys take the opportunity to rest up. You've earned it!"

Dear Mr and Mrs Markowitz,

I know that by the time you receive this, the Army will have notified you of the loss of your son Lenny. If it's of any comfort to you, I want you to know that he did not long suffer, but died instantly.

As his captain I can assure you that Lenny was a brave man and a good soldier. His life was a credit to the way you raised him. You should feel both pride in him and in yourselves.

I'm just so sorry for your loss. Lenny was a fine young man and I was happy to have called him my friend.

I read and reread the letter several times. It sounded so insincere and trite. How do you convey the depths of your sadness and empathy to a couple of parents, dripping wet from the fresh news of the loss of their son? The death of a child had to be the worst thing any human could be asked to endure. Mine was not yet born and already I feared losing him or her. How do I say this? What words of comfort could I possibly offer? I read the letter again, then in frustration and defeat, crumpled it into a ball.

CHAPTER 14

The *Doll* didn't fly again until Christmas Eve, 1942. Sergeant Mac Evans of Muncie, Indiana, was our new crew chief, and after our recent encounter on the high seas had his hands full repairing the damage done by the Japs and removing the ball turret assembly as ordered by Colonel Wisnicki. I really liked and respected Mac. He was not only an exceptional mechanic, more importantly, he had the gift of common sense as well. No one loved the *China Doll* more than Mac, and his obvious affection gave the crew and me a great deal of confidence. We knew every time we left terra firma in the *Doll* nothing would be left to chance regarding her maintenance. Mac and his boys took great pride in keeping her not only mechanically sound, but primped and cleaned as well. She was his baby and he treated her as such. Working almost around the clock, he had the *Doll* in tiptop fighting form by noon on December 20.

A lot had changed in the preceding two weeks. We buried Lenny in a small cemetery; a parcel of land set aside on base to inter Americans or Allied forces killed in action. There were already too many residents in the one-acre plot, a constant reminder of the cost of this war. You couldn't land or take off from New Caledonia without seeing the cemetery and remembering. As another tribute to Lenny, Mac had made for us a small memorial, a five-by-five inch aluminum box riveted to the wall near the hatch where we could see and touch it every time we got in the plane. It contained Lenny's dog tags and a lock of his hair so that Lenny, at least in spirit, would be with us on future missions. Morbid? Perhaps, but it meant something to my boys and me.

The where and how of the war had changed as well, with vicious, costly battles being waged on small islands all around us. Not since the Civil War had United States forces suffered such losses. The battle for Buna was proving more costly in human toll than the battle for Guadalcanal. Losses as a percentage of the expedition force size fighting there were higher by a ratio of three to one. The Japs were dug in deep, dug in to stay and willing to defend their position to the last man. Their tenacity required us to develop both new techniques and a new resolve to be victorious.

Our group's tactics changed in that we were no longer searching vast, open expanses of ocean for supply ships. Early in the war the Japanese had been able to keep their forces supplied clandestinely, using submarines to deliver goods to soldiers awaiting them on the beach under the cover of darkness. While that probably was still occurring to some degree, the size and ferocity of the battles being waged required supplies to be delivered in much more substantial quantities, certainly more than could reasonably be delivered via submarine and rafts. Large-scale ships were now required, necessitating harbors and docks. This made our lives easier in some respects, as we now had geographically defined targets, but while hunting was no longer an issue, defense was. The Japs no longer lightly defended their supply shipping as they had when they were relatively hidden in the "big ocean." They now defended their positions with tenacity, realizing their very survival depended upon it, and our losses went up accordingly.

We still flew in relatively small groups as compared to the mass armadas that were being dispatched over the Germans, individual bombers or flights of two or three being escorted by small contingents of fighters. The *Doll's* first such mission fell upon Christmas Eve, 1942, our assignment was to destroy or cripple the Japanese airfield at Gasmata on the island of New Britain. The Mitsubishi *Zero* fighters based there were charged with both protecting shipping convoys and flying close ground support coverage of Japanese troops engaging the Allies on Buna and Cape Gloucester. They would, of course, be defending themselves. This would be the first real test of my gunners' abilities to defend the *Doll* from attacking fighters. I wished I had Lenny and the ball turret back.

We took off at noon on Christmas Eve, promising my boys I'd have them home, if you could call New Caledonia home, for Christmas. A flight of only one, we rendezvoused with four fighters from the First Fighter Group at our assigned coordinate precisely on time. The Japs must have known we were coming as we were met by four *Zeros*, battle ready and waiting for us at altitude. Our escort went to work defending us, as did my gunners. Joe scored his first kill of a *Zero* only a minute before we did a strafing run at 1000 feet right down the center of the Jap runway. The antiaircraft fire became dense enough to walk upon after the *Zeros* were clear of the firing range. The *Doll* shook with a vengeance, taking several direct hits before we cleared the area, leaving behind a sizable crater almost perfectly mid-field. This stopped the launch of more fighters coming to join the fight, but did nothing to dissuade the other three still in the air awaiting us. Lucky for us our fighters were still engaged, a heroic dogfight waged to defend us. We loved those guys. I have no doubts I survived that day only due to their exploits and the grace of God. At the end of the hour the score was Americans, two, Japs, zero (no pun intended). I questioned at the end of the day how long it would take the Japs to repair the damage to the runway? I suspected only hours, which begged the question, what was the risk-to-benefit ratio? Was disrupting the Japs' use of their runway for a couple of hours worth the lives of my crew? We'd know how much damage we had inflicted shortly, as the same mission would be assigned to someone from our group tomorrow, a perfect time for reconnaissance. If the Japs hadn't yet repaired the runway, perhaps the next guys, perhaps us, might have an easier time of it.

The *Doll* landed on New Caledonia at 1700 hours, first to the cheers, then the curses of Mac who was unhappy I'd dared return his baby with holes in her tail.

"After what we saw today, Mac, I have a feeling you'd better get used to fixing holes."

Christmas day had us strafing another Jap airfield, this time at Cape Gloucester. This mission was a little less nerve-wracking as we encountered no fighters, but the antiaircraft fire thrown at us by the Japs was still thick and furious. Our escort fighters went in first, firing upon the gunnery positions costing us one American compatriot, lost early to intense ground fire. The unfortunate pilot did not bail out, being struck at low altitude, leaving him no time to escape. Strafing our target from 100 feet off the deck, we discovered the mangled wreckage of his aircraft burning left of the runway when we went in. Too soon to tell whether or not he had survived, we opted to hold our load, making another pass. God forbid we injure or kill our own; the Japs were doing a fine job of it on their own. Bledsoe kept a close eye on the burning wreckage, and when he reported not seeing a survivor we began a second run, again from 100 feet off the deck. On this pass we lost our right outboard engine to fire just as we let fly our load. The damage slowed our ascent, and we took several more direct hits to our mid-section. Again blessed, no men were injured, and we limped back to the safety of New Caledonia and Mac's inevitable ire, convinced God had given us a second Christmas miracle.

When we landed that day I was given a stack of mail, a month's worth of letters from Mary. Though she diligently wrote me every day, the Army only managed to deliver her letters a collection at a time and only as frequent as a blue moon. It was feast or famine. To conserve precious space on cargo ships, the Army devised a system called V-Mail or Victory Mail, in which it received all letters addressed to soldiers abroad, censored them, then recorded them on microfilm, allowing 150,000 letters to be transported in a single mailbag. The prevailing joke was that it allowed the Army to lose 150,000 letters at a time. Once received overseas, the microfilm was expanded, printed onto a standardized V-mail letterform, and then delivered to individual soldiers. Six weeks had passed since I last received a stack of mail. The Christmas letters brought me current with life back home through mid-November.

The messages from Mary and Granddaddy were the best Christmas present I could have received. By Mary's account she was "Doing fine." The baby, she assured me, had to be a boy destined to be an all-star place kicker for Princeton, as he was daily practicing his burgeoning skills upon her liver. She enclosed a photo showing me her growing belly, which she insisted was enormous, though I couldn't see that anything had changed except for her breasts. Holy Cow, Mary looked great! She looked healthy and happy, which, I guess, was the best I could hope for at that moment. "Damn it, what a thing to miss," I said aloud. Our first child and here I sat on the other side of the world. The colossal unfairness of it made me more angry and bitter by the hour, but little things, mementos and memories, helped me keep my sanity intact. The stack of letters and the photo made me happy and miserable all at the same time. I desperately wanted, needed to go home to be with her, but I had a job to finish, and God only knew how much longer that was going to take. The only good thing about the intensity with which I engaged the world was that it provided me an occasional respite from thinking about being separated from Mary, always and forever Mary, and now the baby. I fell asleep re-reading her letter by flashlight, praying, "God, I've got to get home."

December 27 found a group of us bombing the runway at Finschhafen. A Zero scored against us before we reached the island, taking out the bomber *Bad Betty*. Struck from above, the *Liberator's* fuel tanks erupted into a ball of fire. Five of the crew escaped the flames by hitting the silk before *Betty* spiraled into the ocean. One of our *Wildcat* escorts stayed in the area to defend the boys helpless in the water. That same *Zero* returned, unsuccessfully strafing the survivors. The *Wildcat* got him on his second run before he could squeeze off another burst and the *Zero* spiraled into the sea. Returning the favor, the *Wildcat* circled back four times to fire upon the Jap wreckage, desiring to be absolutely certain he killed the bastard. Dishonorable Jap idiot! Swift justice had been dealt. A Navy PT boat fished four of our five airmen from the ocean within the hour. The fifth, badly injured and bleeding, was pulled under by a shark, snatched out of the hands of his horrified rescuers, a supreme irony that a boy from Kansas who two months ago had never laid eyes upon an ocean should become food for a shark. We remained oblivious to most of that drama as we continued onward, successfully completing our mission, inflicting damage to their runway for a brief, but hopefully gainful respite. We learned of the grim details of the shark attack at debriefing the following morning.

"What shitty luck, survive being blown out of the sky only to get eaten by a fucking shark," John Bolton, pilot of *Ambidextrous* said under his breath.

Colonel Wisnicki must have heard him because he stopped his report saying, "You're right, John. I guess the lesson to be learned here is if you find yourself injured in the water you've got to control any bleeding. Sharks apparently can smell blood from miles away. Use a belt or a parachute cord, anything you can get your hands on and make a tourniquet. Sharks in these waters are just a reality of life so we got to deal with them any way we can."

"Like the Japs aren't enough to worry about. Now we gotta worry about getting eaten by sharks." Wisnicki, realizing he had just lost control of every mind in the room wisely grew silent. He then dismissed us to our assignments saying, "Be careful out there today." Easier said than done.

Our target for the day, December 28, 1942 was one of three Japanese airfields on Rabaul, Gasmata, or Lae. Rabaul was reportedly the most heavily defended, and thus not a place any of us wanted to visit, so we drew straws to see who was assigned the mission. I won, or lost depending on how you looked at it, so the *Doll's* crew would be targeting Rabaul. The brass must have really anticipated the Japs putting up a fight because we were greeted at the rendezvous point by a larger contingent of fighters than expected, eight P-38s. Viewing them from the air, they had to be the prettiest aircraft ever produced. I'd heard all the scuttlebutt about the *Lightning*, super-turbo charged, counter-rotating props, lightning fast, and heavily armed, a fighter pilot's wet dream. I decided then and there that before the war was over I was going to fly one of those birds and see for myself if all the accolades were deserved. This was the first time we were to fly escorted by the *Lightning*, and though I liked them already, their presence at the rendezvous point was a surprise, both comforting and alarming. Was this an ominous portent of the fight that lay ahead? It was, as we were soon to discover.

There were three *Liberators* in our flight that day, the *China Doll*, the *Ace of Spades,* and a ship called *Carrot Top*, which sported a naked-to-the-world redhead on its nose. It made me think of my little redhead back home. I quietly wondered if our baby might also turn out to have red hair. I hoped I lived to find out.

It was beautifully clear that day, a refreshing change from the rain and storms we had contended with earlier in the week. Twenty miles out of Rabaul, we could see the Japs getting ready for our attack; the *Zeros* streamed out, clambering for a defensive position high above the airfield. They did not come out to play, but stayed whirling about the field like a swarm of angry hornets, ten fighters in all. This would be a gauntlet to run, but with their aircraft in the immediate vicinity it should limit fire from the ground, or, at least, so I thought. Our fighters went in first, engaging the defenders one on one. We followed close behind, diving steeply toward the runway. The *Doll* led the charge with the two other *Liberators* close in trail. I saw one of our *Lightnings* spin into the adjacent jungle, its pilot still swinging from his silk. I was happy he made it out alive, but didn't want to envision what the Jap bastards would do to him once they caught him. Our side had scored three *Zeros* before we made the runway. My theory about lesser antiaircraft fire was clearly remiss as the Japs opened up on us with a vengeance about a mile from the runway threshold. Once again, the *Doll* took tremendous punishment before we dropped our load, the crater we created completely severing the first third of the runway from the remainder. I loved the exhilarating lift the *Doll* gave us after we let our munitions fly, almost like she was saying to us, "Now I'll take you home." God, how I loved that airplane!

The *Ace of Spades* didn't fare as well, crashing into the dense jungle at the heart of the island. Her pilot, Jim Wright, survived the crash and ultimately the war, enduring years of punishment and near starvation at the hands of his captors. He would confess to me long after the war was over that he made the choice of turning inland rather than to the sea to crash that day, thinking his chances with the Japs would be preferable to getting eaten by sharks. He regretted making that decision. He learned later that his bombs destroyed five *Zeros* on the ground. "A pretty fair trade in retrospect," he said.

The tally for the end of our December 28 mission was the loss of one bomber and one Lightning fighter in exchange for four *Zeros* killed as well as denying the Japs use of their airfield for four days.

December 29, we got a little reprieve, as the weather was again bad. On the 30 the command got word the Japs were establishing a beachhead on the island of Wewak, and so we were dispatched there to bomb troops and vehicles. This was the first time we had been sent against a solely human target. It felt different, wrong somehow, and though I knew this was only a matter of semantics, I really didn't like the mission. We passed low enough to see the frightened faces of men running for any cover they could find, all hoping to escape the death and destruction our 500-pound bombs wrought. Our airplanes shuddered from the concussive wake as we flew away. I can only imagine what a blast of that magnitude would do to an exposed human being. I did not sleep well that night, recalling the actions of the day. They were Japs, and the enemy, and I hated them to my core, but somehow putting human skin on that enemy rather than killing them anonymously, as I had previously been required to do, disrupted my soul. I could not begin to imagine how the Marines fighting hand-to-hand, eye-to-eye, soul-to-soul must feel. Exchanging blow for blow at least seems chivalrous, if there is such a thing as chivalry anymore. Killing an exposed man, unable to defend himself, somehow lacked honor. Still, honor or not, it had to be done, as orders are orders and war is war. The more Japs I killed en masse translated into fewer Japs remaining, all honor-bound to kill my own brethren. Honor? What a conflicted concept, one man's honor, another man's crime.

No missions were flown on New Years Eve, not in deference to the holiday, but to the weather. The dense low cloud cover was unusual for this part of the world. Instead, we had a party to celebrate the demise of 1942, the shittiest year ever. Most of us got drunk, but not so drunk that we were defenseless. That sort of drunkenness on the battlefield was the gambit of either a fool or a truly brave man. I was neither.

1943 brought with it a feeling of hope. Perhaps this was the year we would defeat the Japs and go home. It would be the year of my firstborn's birth, with me or without me. Upon overhearing me bemoaning that fact CJ said, "At least you were there for the fun part." I laughed in agreement, but I was still sure I was missing everything truly important to a man.

Our target for New Years Day was again Rabaul, but this time we would be striking at Japanese shipping in the harbor instead of the airfield. The flight dubbed "Yellow Flight," consisted of three *Liberators* with an escort of four P-38s. This mission would be flown a little differently, as the *Lightnings* were carrying bombs as well. In addition to defending us from *Zeros*, they were to strafe enemy ships, delivering their loads of hundred-pounders from low level while the *Liberators* would stay up top, inaccurately dropping their loads from altitude. This technique was typical of that being practiced in the European theater on a daily basis. While it should be safer for the bombers, I was skeptical about how efficient or effective this new scheme would prove. I personally would rather fly in low and take the heat if it meant our efforts would be fruitful, a fair exchange for our greater risk. My crew all agreed as, "We're going to get shot at either way. Might as well make it mean something." I voiced those sentiments to Colonel Wisnicki at our briefing. He confided that while he agreed with us, there had been a "shake up" of the brass above him; new men with different ideas as to what might or might not work here in the Pacific. We were stuck with complying with their wishes, also known as orders, at least until we could prove them wrong. MacArthur was taking heat from the White House for what, now in retrospect, were being interpreted as tactical blunders. As a consequence, the command structure beneath MacArthur was thought to be at fault and therefore had to change. New commanders including many who had previously been serving in Europe had been quickly appointed. These ETO veterans came with preconceived ideas as to how best use aircraft in battle, requiring us to contend with their operational biases. So, bombing the harbor from 20,000 feet would be the mission for the day and the foreseeable future until we convinced our new leaders otherwise.

Flying the mission as ordered, at the end of the day we had little to show for it. We met little resistance, and not a single bomb dropped from altitude found its mark, but every *Liberator* came home sans bullet holes so the operation was considered a success. MacArthur's new cronies later blamed the mission's inaccuracies upon inept bombardiers instead of the inept tacticians who had planned the mission, making the crews furious. I had a heated discussion with Colonel Wisnicki after the fact.

"If we continue to fight this way, the Japs are gonna win this war."

"Discipline wins wars, Captain."

"But we exposed ourselves and accomplished nothing to show for it, damn it!"

"Captain, may I remind you that you are addressing a superior officer?" I dropped my eyes complacently so he continued, "Look, I know you're frustrated, but you'll get your chance again as soon as they figure out that we're right."

"We, sir?"

"Yes, WE! I agree with you, but give them a little time to figure it out."

"And how long is a 'little time'?"

"Give it a few days. I promise I'll have a talk as soon as I have some proof of our hypothesis."

The only thing I liked about the new modus operandi was that the bombers were indeed safer, but at what cost safety?

On January 3 we repeated the same fiasco over Lae and Madang. I'm sure the Japanese thought we had lost heart. Our efforts were like a duck trying to peck a tiger to death. On the fourth our mission was thwarted from altitude by an intervening cloud layer. We couldn't bomb what we couldn't see. Heading homeward, I decided to duck under the clouds for a look-see. Breaking out, we found a schooner about three miles off shore at Gasmata flying Jap colors and therefore a legitimate target. There were no other ships or aircraft in sight so I decided to drop down to the deck for a little target practice. We dropped our load from no more than twenty feet above the topmast, met only by small arms fire. There were two Jap officers standing on the aft deck aiming at us with pistols. The schooner was vaporized; all evidence gone before we were back at 2000 feet, save for ripples on the ocean's surface spreading out radially from the blast.

Someone must have seen our exploits and reported back because upon landing back on New Caledonia, Wisnicki was waiting there on the ramp, ready to rip me a new one.

"Did I sink a Jap boat today?" Before he could answer I added, "Did anyone else? I thought the reason I was here away from my pregnant wife was to kick the Japs' asses and go home." Seeing his anger doubling, I added, "Sir."

"Damn it, we've had this discussion. Now I have to explain how or why one of my men ignored protocol. The only thing keeping you out of the brig is your target. Seems you managed to kill a couple of Jap officers and their dates. They had commandeered a private vessel from a wealthy merchant on Rabaul to show a couple of friendly local girls a good time, a pretty stupid thing to do in a war zone. Only thing stupider was you breaking my direct orders and sinking them." He softened and began to chuckle, "I'm so damned mad at you I can't see straight, but MacArthur may just pin a medal on your chest."

"Sorry, sir," I said, though not sincerely

"Just don't let it happen again."

"No, sir, I won't, sir." My crew was hanging out just within ear shot, listening as I got my ass chewed. When the colonel had gone, CJ fell out of the hatch, rolling on the ground laughing. The other guys followed suit.

On January 5 we bombed Lae and Rabaul, again from altitude, and again with little strategic impact. I followed orders and stayed at 20,000 feet, dropping our load and headed for home. On the sixth we were dispatched to destroy a Japanese convoy of thirty-three ships, heading southwest off the coast of New Britain. The convoy was heavily and ferociously defended. We hit them almost non-stop for four days, but in spite of our efforts and losses, the convoy successfully made it to harbor at Finchhafen, losing only two transports in the process.

"Surely the brass will see how futile this is and go back to low-level attacks," I said over a beer at the club that night. There were clearly two schools of thought around the bar; the play-it-safe crowd and the get-the-job-done crowd. I was firmly entrenched in the latter and everybody in the bar knew it. I thought about Lenny, who had paid the ultimate sacrifice. I was keenly aware exactly what he would say if he were still living. In my mind I could hear his voice saying, "Balls to the wall, Cap'n. Let's nail the little bastards." I also had no doubt upon which side Mary would fall in the discussion, and I can't say I'd blame her. She shouldn't have to raise our baby alone, the fate assigned her should I foolishly got myself killed. Playing it safe was the best option for Mary and the baby. I knew that, believed it strongly in my gut, yet the innate warrior in me, that thread woven into my soul, indeed into the soul of every man by their creator, the warrior me won out every time.

After all our futile and wasted effort over the last few days, January 12 found us again bombing Finchhafen and Madang from altitude. I could swear I heard the Nips laughing at us from below, at least the ones unaffected by our bombs, which was undoubtedly the majority. On the fifteenth the *Doll* was finally given a target that she was permitted to strike from low level, a newly constructed bridge on Wewak. It was not quite as simple as it sounded because the Japs defended each end of the bridge with large antiaircraft guns. The most certain way to destroy it would be to run down its length on centerline from about ten feet above letting the munitions fall on the middle. The flaw with this plan was that it required we pass about ten feet over the defending guns as well. I figured our best chance of surviving the day would be to approach the target from low enough over the jungle to catch them by surprise, so that's exactly what we did. I don't know how surprised they were, but we were moving as fast as the *Doll* could go, which didn't give the Japs very long to get a bead on us before we were atop the bridge dropping our load. The *Doll* suffered several rounds, but just like always, shook it off and flew us home after we'd successfully destroyed Wewak's vital bridge.

This was to be our last mission out of New Caledonia. Our proven success against maritime targets convinced the brass that we might indeed have some special kind of magic. On January 18 of 1943, I was invited to visit Colonel Wisnicki's office for what I assumed would be yet another dress down for an infraction, a violation real or imagined, but for the life of me I couldn't figure out what I had done wrong. The crew assumed likewise and came along for moral support. The commander's secretary, a physically slight corporal, didn't bother to acknowledge our entrance by looking up from his book, but said, "Go right in Captain, the colonel wants to see you right away. The rest of you wait here." I entered with more than a little fear and trepidation, as I had no idea how I'd screwed up or what aggravation awaited me inside. Opening the door for me, the colonel greeted, "Hello Captain, come in, come in," in a tone sounding like I was an old friend he was pleasantly surprised to see. "Let me introduce you to General Twining of the Thirteenth."

"General," I said, saluting. He returned my salute then offered a firm handshake.

"And this is Colonel Stewart Wright."

"Colonel," I said, also saluting and shaking his hand.

The general began, "Son, I'll come right to the point. We're forming a new group, a bomber command outfitted with *Liberators* retooled to support some new, top-secret equipment that Colonel Wright here has developed. He's been working in conjunction with the Radiation Laboratory of the National Defense Research Council and MIT. Colonel Wisnicki here has been telling me of your exploits and I think you may be just the man we need to head up this group, that is if you're interested."

"I'm listening, sir. Don't know if I'm interested until I know a bit more."

"General Hap Arnold has ordered the formation of this group, or two groups actually. One will be based on Guadalcanal and the other on Espiritu Santo. We'll be targeting Japanese shipping. Right now you seem to be our expert with two kills to your credit."

"I think I know how to get the job done, at least when I'm allowed to do my job," I said wryly. Colonel Wisnicki shifted in his seat and coughed.

"The good colonel has told me that you've been frustrated by operational procedures. What if I told you that you would be attacking the shipping at night?" My puzzled look a question, he continued. "Your ships will be painted black and outfitted with a new device called radar. This radar will allow you to find the ships at night even without seeing them." He paused and awaited my response.

"That's a fascinating proposition, General. Does it work?"

"I'm told it works very well."

"Okay, so how do my crew and I fit into this picture?"

"This is a new concept. What I'm looking for is someone who's been successful with the old ways, but bold enough to experiment with something new. I've reviewed your performance since you've been in the Pacific theater. It was clear even back in training you were a natural pilot and destined to do great things."

"I don't suppose the Admiral had anything to do with this?" I asked already knowing the answer.

"He brought you to my attention. Bill and I have been friends for years. In all that time I've never beaten him at his game of chess. He tells me that you took him to school, like it was effortless." I smiled and felt my face redden.

"That impressed me, enough so that I looked into your record. At present you're the only man in the Air Corps who can claim two kills of heavy vessels, both within a month. You sunk a destroyer on your first combat mission. Was that luck or skill?"

"A little of both I suppose. Of course it was a team effort. I only flew the airplane."

"False modesty does not become a soldier. Can you do it again?"

You want bravado? Fine, I'll give you bravado, "Yes sir. In my sleep!" It wasn't a brag.

"Good, I thought so. Are you interested?"

"I'm interested if it's a flying job you're offering me. I'm not much on paperwork and I have no desire for a desk job."

"And I have no desire to waste your time or talents flying a desk. Colonel Wright here is our idea man and our administrator and damned good at both. We both agree what we need to make this mission a success is a hands-on kind of guy with proven combat skills. We believe now, after reviewing your record and talking to you that you're the man we want. Do we have a deal?" Wright was a lab rat, brilliant, but a lab rat none the less, while Twinning was a no-nonsense, get-the-job-done-whatever-the-cost kind of guy. Finding I liked them both, I thoughtfully considered their offer for all of two seconds before extending the general a handshake of acceptance.

"Good. You'll become part of the Thirteenth. There will be ten aircraft to start with. You're to be the CO of the squadron on Espiritu Santo and answer directly to me. Colonel Wright here will command the squadron on Guadalcanal. Guadalcanal is still a hot zone, so your boys will get a bit of a head start and prove the concept. This job comes with a promotion, Major."

"Thank you, sir. Begging the General's pardon, will my crew chief be reassigned along with us?"

"That's not the usual practice, Major." I liked the ring of that title.

"I know sir, that's why I ask. I'd very much like to keep my team together. We trust Mac, Sergeant Mac Evans, to take care of the Doll. I just don't know we would feel as comfortable with anyone else."

"I see. Well, if it's that important to you…"

"It is, sir."

"If it's that important to you I'll see that it's done. Any other questions?"

"No, sir."

"Well that was easy. Good!" he said looking at me as though trying to read my response. "Plan to fly your ship to Espiritu Santo Island in the New Hebrides tomorrow. What do you call her?"

"The *China Doll,* sir."

"Well, the *China Doll* will be the first ship painted black and fitted with Radar."

"We'll be there. Thank you, sir."

"Don't thank me, your admiral friend is the one you should thank," he smiled.

"Yes, sir, I will, sir."

Closing the door behind me I said aloud, "Well I'll be damned! Boys, pack your stuff. We're moving to Espiritu Santo."

"Moved by the spirit?" Bledsoe quipped. I was the only one who laughed.

Espiritu Santo was a beehive of activity in January of 1943. There were men and ships and airplanes all over every habitable site on the island. The westernmost side of the island is mountainous with peaks extending 5500 feet above sea level, a range extending the length of the island like a backbone, covered completely by dense jungle foliage. From altitude, four runways were visible scattered around the islands major town of Luganville, with a fifth being rapidly constructed. CJ had not done enough homework to know which of the fields was expecting us. I could have cursed CJ, but I held my tongue. Being pilot in command I had the ultimate responsibility of knowing where I was supposed to land, not CJ.

"Which of those fields down there do you think is ours?"

Jack thought about it for a moment then said, "Only a guess, but I suspect the Navy would claim the runway closest to the beach. That longest one out there west of town would be my choice."

"That's what I was thinking as well," I lied and Jack laughed, knowing. I racked the big bomber around and entered the pattern for the selected runway, putting the *Doll* down squarely on the numbers. Before we could shut down we were greeted by a corporal in a jeep who redirected us to Bomber One, which proved to be the shorter runway two miles to the east. Egg on my face, I repositioned the *Doll* to Bomber One and acted as though it was the most natural thing in the world. Landing, we were met by a jeep with a "Follow Me" placard on the back and so followed him to a hanger on the west side of the runway, opposite where most of the bombers were parked. The hanger was of Quonset-style corrugated steel, partially buried in an excavated hillside. The entire facility looked and smelled as if freshly cut from an ancient jungle garden, the earthy, primordial scent of continually rain-dampened soil and vegetation and invisible creatures all entwined, undisturbed since the world began.

The driver of the jeep greeted me as soon as I climbed from the hatch, my B4 bag in hand.

"Major, I'm Lieutenant Dan Richards and this is Sergeant Michael O'Malley. General Twining has instructed us to see that you're properly settled and briefed on your new command. I'm to see that you have everything you need, sir."

"How about a nice scotch and a night with my wife?" I joked, saluting the lieutenant and sergeant, before shaking their hands.

"I can help with the scotch, sir, but as to your love life I…"

"Just joking, lieutenant. Where are we to bunk down?"

"You and your men will have quarters on this side of the field. Your men will be in tents for the time being, until construction of more permanent quarters is completed. You have an office and quarters in the hanger behind me. The other side of the field is the 307th Bomber Group. Your mission remains a secret; the men across the field know nothing about you. General Twining requests that you keep it that way."

"I understand. Any idea when…" my question interrupted by Mac who'd come trotting from the front of the aircraft, clearly mad as a hornet. The *Doll* was already being attached to a tug to be pulled inside the hanger.

"What the hell do they mean the *Doll* is getting modified? They ain't touchin' her without my permission!"

"Simmer down Mac. Step over here and I'll fill you in." We walked away from any overhearing ear and I explained to him what I presently knew of the proposed modifications. "You're to oversee those changes and make sure they make sense. Most importantly Mac, no one else can know about this until its time, understand?"

"Yes sir, I'll get right on it." He then began barking orders to the privates on the tug as to the proper procedure for moving *his* aircraft. Mac reported to me later that it would take two weeks to accomplish the painting and retrofit. As the first official order issued in my new command, I put Mac in charge of overseeing the modifications, not just of the *Doll*, but of all ten of the *Liberators* in the new group.

Befitting the mission, the new group would be called *The Snoopers*, a name chosen by General Twining. We were to fly alone at night, targeting Japanese shipping which we would find allegedly with the aid of a new forward-looking radar system. Specially trained radar operators, men who had yet to join us here in the South Pacific, would be added to each of the crews. I would be increasingly anxious for the group to arrive here on Espiritu Santo so I could try my hand at this new venture. New, specialized techniques of engaging the enemy would of necessity need to be developed, and I wanted to be intimately involved in their creation, beginning sooner rather than later. Five bombers and crew would be joining us from the 307th across the field. Four others were to arrive within a day or two, chosen from other outfits presently designated as the Fifth Air Force, just as the *Doll* had been. I assumed the garnering of crews in equal numbers from both the Fifth and Thirteenth Air Forces had some political motivation. I was just happy to be included in the group, let alone be its commander.

I wrote Mary of my promotion, but couldn't divulge any more detail. I hinted at the fact that I should be a little safer in my new position, a notion I really believed as I figured the nature of attacking the enemy at night would be met differently, not by enemy fighters as in the light of day, but by reactive rather than proactive antiaircraft fire. I'd much prefer taking those chances to what I'd been doing of late. I worried more about the feasibility of the mission than of its danger. I'd never seen a radar system work and had no idea how successful it would realistically prove to be. At the moment all I could do was wait. Waiting was probably the most damning aspect about being in the tropics. The weather was atrocious. It rained without fail some part of every day, and the moisture combined with incessant heat made the humid air thick enough to drown in. We un-acclimatized humans hated it, but the malaria-carrying mosquitoes thrived in it, as did the bats that ate those mosquitoes. I came to the South Pacific expecting an exotic paradise, but I could not have been more wrong. Regardless of how inhospitable the climate, the real killer of men's souls here in the South Pacific was boredom. The incessant passage of seconds become minutes, become hours, become days, all without any punctuation to make them pleasurable or at least memorable, something more than sheer, maddening monotony, a hellacious boredom encased within the stark visual beauty of the islands. Plato said, "Anything that deceives can be said to enchant." The tropics are in fact enchanting, the guise of paradise, the torturous sameness of hell. Just anticipating the boredom of two weeks without a mission was enough to make me crazy.

Mac was anything but bored getting the *Doll* painted and fit up with radar. He masked off our Vargas babe on the *Doll's* nose before covering the remainder of the ship in pitch black. She was the heart and soul of the airplane and we agreed had to be preserved at all cost. When we finished painting, the *Doll* never looked better. The crew and I had decided to fight boredom by working for Mac. Resistant at first, he finally relented saying, "Hell, I guess anyone can swing a paint brush, but if you get even one drop out of place it won't be the Japs you gotta worry about." He was quite serious. I think we were probably more in his way than helping, but the task kept us from lunacy. While we helped or hindered in the paint job, the radar installation was quite another matter. This was top-secret stuff, technology that, if it fell into the wrong hands, could very well lose the war for us. If we were to crash or be forced to abandon the aircraft for any reason we were ordered to destroy the radar units, even at the cost of our lives. A hand grenade was permanently mounted to the unit for that express purpose. Even more so than the infamous Norden bombsight, knowledge of the radar's very existence was highly classified. The development of radar, an acronym for Radio Detection and Ranging had been rumored, spoken of only in hushed tones since before the war. The first equipment was gargantuan and notoriously imprecise, but scientists at MIT worked feverishly to rectify both drawbacks. The devise being installed in the *Doll* relied not on radio waves, but upon a cousin in the electromagnetic spectrum called microwaves. Two civilian engineer types from MIT worked with Mac on retrofitting the *Doll,* accomplishing installation of the radar inside a locked, sentry-guarded hanger. We called those two guys the *spooks.* They were forced to remain aloof to safeguard the nature of their mission. As squadron commander, the *spooks* answered to me, but answering to Mac was more important and I let them know that day one. The crew was not allowed to help with this part of the project. While I could not imagine Mac would be able to repair the circuitry in the radar units themselves, I did hope he would be able to learn and manage any field maintenance issues. Our very *raison d'etre* as a squadron would depend upon the continued reliability of the radar units. Without them we had little hope of success, forcing Mac to learn as much as he could about the magic in the boxes. I had complete confidence, believing if anyone could make the new system work with the old, it was Mac. It took a week longer than promised, but finally on February 20, 1943, the *Doll* emerged, equipped with an SRC-717-B search and navigation radar and an AN/APQ-5 LABS bombing radar, both operational and ready for our first trials.

We took the *Doll* out that very same evening for her first test flight. Our promised radar officers had yet to arrive from training in the States, we took the *spooks* along for the ride, observing firsthand the fruits of their labors. Civilians were forbidden to fly combat missions so our test runs had to be staged using known friendly targets rather than enemy targets, not that I would have passed up an opportunity to sink anything flying Jap colors. The moon was bright and almost full so I had very little hope of reviewing the radar's prowess over and above what our own eyes could detect. I was pleasantly surprised at being proved wrong. From 10,000 feet, the horizon was visible only as a faint crescent line, devoid of any detail. We flew east fifty miles before turning to a bearing along which we knew our own shipping would lie. To my great surprise and relief the radar detected the presence of something, however nondescript, on the horizon, something yet invisible to either the naked or aided human eye. The device indicated range to the object was forty-seven nautical miles on a bearing of 270. The target detected was in motion, necessitating small course changes if we were to eventually rendezvous with it. CJ fed me minute-by-minute heading changes and constantly updated me on the calculated range using airspeed and time as variables. Flying directly toward the target we were soon rewarded with sighting a United States battleship steaming southward, alone in the moonlit night.

The radar proved to be amazingly sensitive and accurate in both finding and tracking a target. It was not, however, very good at segregating targets into friend or foe. We needed, over the coming weeks and months, to devise a system that would allow us to differentiate friendly from enemy vessels or risk sending our own down into the depths.

Sharing my concerns with one of the *spooks* he said, "Very astute question, Major. We've developed a system at MIT called IFF or Information Friend or Foe. Friendly ships or airplanes will have a box that attaches a signal to the radar beam of the object being targeted. The good guys will have the box, the bad guys won't."

"I know the military," I said facetiously. "How long will it take to build and distribute this IFF box to protect our side? That includes our allies, by the way."

"Realistically? A year or more."

"We don't have a year or more. Like I said, we'll have to develop a way of identifying the targets before we strike."

"Since your target is Japanese shipping I suspect you'll have to work pretty close with the Navy on shipping schedules and ship recognition."

"Clearly ship recognition is going to play a role. That's going to be kind of difficult on a moonless night on the open sea. I'll have to give this very careful consideration."

We successfully sought out three other known targets before returning to Bomber One. I landed that night having gained confidence in radar's capabilities. Clearly I had my work cut out for me as how to best deploy this technology. Killing Japs was one thing, killing our own by mistake was another matter entirely.

Learning General Twining was back on Espiritu Santo, I met with him the following morning to discuss my concerns, and offer some suggestions as to how I intended to overcome the present limitations. I asked permission to fly to Hawaii, hoping to meet with the Admiral and cement a relationship between the Army Air Corps and the Navy, a relationship that had historically been somewhat tempestuous. I desired also to pick his brain, as he was a brilliant tactician. The general encouraged me to go before chastising me for asking. "You are the commander of this outfit. You make the decisions. You come and go as you see fit. Do anything and everything you need to make your unit successful," then he added with a half smile, "And I'll take all the credit."

"Then I'll be on a flight tomorrow."

"Why wait? There's a plane leaving in half an hour."

"Thank you, sir. I think I will." I saluted then took off in a run to grab some fresh clothes. I stuffed them and my dopp kit into my B4, and then ran to catch the transport plane.

"Jack, I'm heading to Hawaii for a couple of days. You're in charge here.

Keep things moving forward and don't let the boys get into any trouble in Luganville. I'll be back soon as I can."

He took his pipe out of his mouth just long enough to say, "Yep." I loved Jack. With one syllable, a sound that's probably not even a real word, he took charge. Best of all, I knew he really would do all his "yep" implied.

I caught the C-47 just as they were closing the hatch. This airplane had been configured much as a civilian airliner would be, with rows of padded seats purposed to transport large groups of men in relative comfort. I was surprised to discover a pair of Negro stewards, both enlisted men sporting white waistcoats, aboard to serve, at our beck and call, food and drinks or anything else we could want for, mimicking the finest of luxury establishments. This is war? I was frankly offended at the opulence, a stark contrast to the foxholes many American soldiers would be sleeping in tonight. This airplane was making the trip to Hickam on an every-other-day basis, transporting officers and VIPs in and out of the Pacific Theater of Operation. Its very existence seemed patently unfair, an affront to the sacrifices being made by the average Joe. In spite of the padded seats and servants I probably would have been more comfortable flying the *Doll*. At least in the *Doll* I had some sense of being able to defend myself. Chance enough being alone over a vast expanse of ocean, I knew this unarmed and unescorted C-47 loaded with American and British officers would to be an irresistible target to any enemy aircraft lucky enough to stumble upon us.

I decided to sleep or rather was overcome by sleep almost the minute the wheels left the ground. I suppose I didn't know how exhausted I really was, because I slept the duration of the flight, including a stop for refueling, all without awakening. It was 0330 at Hickam when we landed. One of the stewards was kind enough to offer me a warmed, moistened towel as I'd managed to drool all over myself in my sleep.

"Good morning, sir. Welcome to Hawaii," he said cheerfully. His was not Gullah, the Southern Pidgin English of the Negroes I had encountered in my youth, but clean and crisp and decidedly proper. I felt sorry for the obviously bright young man, relegated to menial servitude solely because of how black men were regarded by their fellow white men. I use the term fellow loosely, as nothing resembling fellowship existed between the two groups, separated as my granddaddy had said by "a wide gulf of hatred and ignorance." In my own ignorant, insensitive act I offered him a tip which he politely declined saying, "Oh no, sir. I'm just doing my part, just like you."

"Thank you," I said feeling at a loss for appropriate words.

Awake and refreshed, I decided to have an early breakfast. The mess hall opened at 0400. After consuming more than my fair share of steak and eggs, I realized that, having crossed the date line in the middle of my slumber, it was again Sunday morning. The Admiral would undoubtedly be at the park on his usual bench in a few hours, enough time for me to come up with a present for the old man. I wanted to show him my appreciation, as I had him to thank for my new position. I was at a loss as to what to get him or where to get it on a Sunday when I said aloud to nobody listening, "Scotch, of course." The officers' club was just closing, but I brow beat my way through the door saying, "I need a bottle of your best scotch."

"We don't sell scotch by the bottle, sir," said the tired barkeep.

"Look, it's for Admiral McCallister," I said offering him a ten dollar bill. "You can keep the change." His demeanor changed almost immediately.

"Yes, sir!" He hurried away returning soon with an unopened bottle of twenty-two year-old Glenlivet.

"Perfect, thanks."

Gift in hand, I purchased the Sunday newspaper and parked myself to wait on the Admiral's bench.

At exactly 0830, predictable as the sunrise, the Admiral walked up saying, "Good morning, Major. How was your flight?"

"You already knew? Of course you did. How foolish of me. Here's a little token of my esteem. I understand I have you to thank for my new job."

"I just suggested that you were a talented young man, nothing more."

"Well, whatever you said, it worked. Thank you!"

"You're welcome. Chess?" he said producing the board.

I laughed, "But of course."

We played as I explained my thoughts about the new mission. He had already anticipated most of my questions and given them considerable thought.

"The Navy has already ordered a thousand SCR-729 IFF units from Sperry, but the delivery time won't be till mid-summer. After that, your life should get a bit easier. You'll still need to have each of your bombardiers trained to identify silhouettes of Japanese or German ships. I suggest you do your hunting from low altitude along known Japanese shipping corridors. They won't, they can't, stray too far from those corridors. As for us, the Navy will supply you weekly with schedules and coordinates. If you section off your target area into various sectors it should be pretty easy to know who should and should not be in a given sector on any given day. My boys will be ordered not to fire upon anything resembling a *Liberator*. If you find yourself taking fire, it shouldn't be from friendly shipping and be yet another confirmation the target is an enemy vessel."

"That all sounds great, but you know mistakes will be made and I…."

"We're humans. Mistakes are an inevitable part of life and death and war. Just do your best and err on the side of caution. If the vessel can't be positively identified as hostile, hold your fire and move on. There will be other targets."

As always, his advice was flawless, leaving me an overwhelming sense of gratitude. I still won the chess match, to which he smiled and said, "One other thing, Johnny." He never called me Johnny unless he wanted to play up the father-son theme, "I need a favor from you." Oh oh, here it comes, I thought. "I want you to do a little babysitting."

"Babysitting?" I asked incredulously.

"The president has a friend whose son is an Army officer. He's a pilot who will soon be assigned to the Snoopers."

"I see…"

"No, you don't see. He's a terrible officer, the kind that gets men killed. Because of his connections he was headed for the Pentagon. No telling how many men he could have killed if left in charge. I want you to take care of him. Be sure he survives the war if you can. Just don't put him in a position of leadership or we all will regret it. You'd be doing me and your country a great service, understand?"

"Yes, sir, it would be an honor."

"Oh I doubt that very much," he laughed. "You'll see."

We had lunch and I caught the very same C-47 returning to Espiritu Santo before it departed late afternoon. In hand, I carried with me the Navy's top-secret documentation of known silhouettes of Japanese and German ships. We had a lot of homework to do before beginning operations as the *Snoopers*. I wrote to Mary, first things first, then began studying the literature supplied me by the Admiral before again being overcome by sleep. The same steward offered me yet another towel awakened me upon landing at Bomber One. He must have felt comfortable with me because he asked, "Do all you white folks sleep this much?" I chuckled replying, "No, just me."

At the present rate of retrofitting one *Liberator*, newly painted and equipped with radar every three weeks, it would be mid-August before the *Snoopers* could become fully operational. I convinced both General Twining and Colonel Wright to allow me to begin immediately flying radar missions under the guise of developing operational techniques and protocols before the *Snoopers* officially opened for business. While waiting for the remainder of the ships to get changed over, Mac and I created a schedule allowing the Liberators presently flying missions to continue in their present capacities as long as possible prior to commencement of operations as a squadron on August 15, 1943. This schedule allowed those crews to continue their usefulness in the war effort while honing their combat skills. Unfortunately, in mid-July one of the crews awaiting transition was lost in combat, the victims of a deft *Zero* pilot over Rabaul. They were to be one of the units assigned to

Colonel Wright at Guadalcanal, so the job of picking a replacement fell to him.

Being unit commander had its perks, the best of which was getting first pick of any new candidates for flight crewmember. In addition to new equipment and airframe modifications, each of our aircraft would soon be assigned a radar operator, a new flight officer prepared with six months of intensive, specialized training by a top-secret military school. Like pilot training, only men with college education were allowed to apply for this special program. Initially limited to a class of only forty, these radar boys belonged to a group significantly more exclusive than the pilot corps. Our quiet little initiative here in the South Pacific must be on General Hap Arnold's front burner because he arranged for half of the very first graduating class to be assigned to the Snoopers. Of that group I selfishly picked the cream of the crop, Captain Bill Johnson of Missoula, Montana, to join the *Doll's* crew. Already having a *Bill* in the crew, we all took to calling him Doc to avoid any confusion. Before the war, Doc had been a medical student. In the last war, Doc's daddy had been a doctor as well, assigned to a French field hospital. He had cautioned his son about the futility of such service, the numbing indifference a military doctor inevitably develops in response to an endless parade of carnage and misery. This was not a recipe for the compassionate physician he dreamed of his son becoming. Bill knew within days of graduating from medical school he would be pressed into military service and offered no choice but to be a field doctor. Heeding his father's advice, reasoning that he would have the remainder of his life to practice medicine, Doc dropped out of school six months prior to graduation and enlisted on December 8, 1941. He offered his service to Uncle Sam without breathing a word about his medical school experience. A college graduate, he was quickly whisked off to officer candidate school, and upon finishing at the top of his class, was offered a slot in the soon-to-be-created radar officer technical school. A smart, humble, funny guy, Doc fit into our crew with grace and ease, quickly became indispensable. My boys all loved him from the start.

We began taking nightly excursions along the *Tokyo Express,* the name given the Japanese supply shipping route. Checking and double-checking the Navy's schedule, I confirmed the only American vessels scheduled to be in the area were submarines. We struck pay dirt our third night out, coming across a Japanese merchant vessel enroute to Rabaul. Doc, replacing Bledsoe who had functioned as our temporary radar operator, reported the target at fifty-two miles range. We had been flying at 1500 feet above the surface, but were able to drop to only twenty feet altitude without losing radar bearings to the target. I got as close as twenty miles broadside to allow Jim to verify the silhouette before beginning our initial run. Continuing to stalk our prey, we swung wide before attacking from the rear. They never knew what hit them until it was too late, not a single shot fired in their defense. The kill was almost too easy. While we celebrated the victory I couldn't help but feel like we had been the guys in the Western movies who wore the black hats, bringing themselves dishonor by shooting their opponents in the back. Five minutes after we flew from the scene, the entire ship blew skyward with such violence there could be little doubt their cargo was explosives, ammunition to be delivered to awaiting Jap troops. That those troops would now thus be denied made me feel like the good guy wearing the white hat again. Funny how we carry around little moral lessons like that, learned in childhood, still found buried deep in the recesses of our souls. Being responsible for the death of another human, enemy or not, always made me dig out these nuggets from within and consider. Play with them. Roll them in my fingers. Smell them. Listen to them whisper of their secrets, the embedded knowledge of right and wrong, before weighing them against my actions to see if I came up worthy or wanting. Do all men struggle thusly in war, or am I the only sap? From what little I'd observed I think most men do wrestle as I, they just don't speak of it, certainly not in the company of other men, if ever at all. The very nature of being a warrior is to shun weakness or anything even hinting of weakness. The discussion of one's feelings is viewed in the camps of men as a women-like frailty. Humans are pack animals just like wolves. The weakest among the pack finding them selves relegated to the altar, a sacrifice to strength. Strength and weakness are, in truth, relative terms. The strongest man is weaker than an almighty God. It requires knowledge of weakness to be able to discern strength, just like it requires knowledge of illness to discern health, or evil to discern good. I think too much… a habit that will lead me either to madness or nirvana.

The *Doll* flew missions alone throughout the summer of '43, waiting the refurbishing of the other ships and the training of their crews before we would fly as a squadron. We had a modicum of success, sinking eight different Japanese freighters, accounting for over 20,000 tons of cargo, supplies and munitions, now denied to Japanese soldiers in the field. In doing so, we developed techniques by trial and error, learning as had mankind from time immemorial what technique worked and what did not.

CHAPTER 15

I had a real conundrum on my hands about how to deal with Captain Skip Johnson, the new charge assigned me by my friend, Admiral Bill McAllister, *assigned me* a euphemism for a favor, not an order. An order would have been easier to overlook or ignore in totality, instructions abandoned, lost somehow in the fog of war. Owing the Admiral a great debt of gratitude, I became honor-bound to find Skip a position where he would be safe, yet could not compromise the safety of men in his charge. That the Army in its infinite wisdom had awarded Skip an officer's commission, based not upon skill or intelligence or even education, but upon pedigree, compounded my task. True enough, he enlisted just as had I, a college student having yet to complete a degree or course of study. Somehow, miraculously perhaps, he also survived pilot training and now wore the same silver wings pinned to his chest as did I. The Admiral felt both titles were more window dressing than actual positions, but confessing that reality to anyone who had signed on and was willing to risk his life in the service of his country was no easy matter. "You're an officer and a pilot, but we don't really want you to be either," spoke the truth of the matter, but was impossible to say and probably illegal to enact. This situation had to be dealt with using finesse, the most adroit of maneuvering. I struggled for days about how best to accomplish it until Jack finally said, "Giving him his own ship would be foolhardy. I've always wanted my own ship. Seems to me you have your answer."

"Jack, I could kiss you!"

"Nope!"

The following day, Jack was at long last awarded a ship and crew and Skip Johnson became my co-pilot, a perfect solution thanks to Jack's suggestion. Best of all, Jack and I both got exactly what we wanted, or at least so I thought. Out of pure selfishness if not inertia, I had previously kept Jack at my side, my trusted advisor and confidant far too long. He was every bit as competent and capable a pilot as I and deserved a chance to shine.

It seemed the perfect tactical solution, and I was quite happy with it until the day of our first mission sans Jack. With fear and trepidation I approached the mission, as I was confident Skip would not assimilate into our crew with the same poise Doc had demonstrated. We had been very successful with Jack occupying the very same seat and now here sat this upstart, this unproven and apparently untrusted commodity staring back at me. Skip was an amiable enough guy, the kind of guy from whom I would have little problem purchasing life insurance, or a new car, or a widget. He was a natural salesman, friendly and handsome, charming to the point of incredulity. Oozing insincerity through a chiseled smile, Skip was a slimy politico, more suited to becoming a senator than any guy you would EVER let call upon your daughter.

It was amazing how much of my thought now centered around children, sons and daughters or someday hopefully both; some day, but when? Our first should have arrived days ago, but how would I know? "My God, has our baby been born?" Mary was a great gal, always faithful to write me every day, but to actually receive one of those letters, delivered intact in sequence to me, the intended recipient in the South Pacific, was more mythical than fact. A letter could be delayed by as much as six weeks. It might as well have been a million years; six weeks being equivalent to an eternity as the end of Mary's pregnancy approached. I'd received her last letter three weeks ago, and Mary's due date had now long since come and gone, just as had my ability to focus upon anything else. At best, I was at present the proud papa of a son or daughter, a daughter who would never date the likes of Skip, money or not. At worst, I was a widower. My God, had Mary been right? Had I forfeited the last nine months of contentment with Mary, the only happiness I could ever know in this life all for the sake of killing men I had never known and who had never known me? War on the scale we were waging was sheer madness. Why did I feel it so necessary to be a part of the maelstrom? If I had squandered her last days, selfishly being true to myself, playing the warrior to fulfill some misguided internal instinct, the penchant of the male of our species…. I could hardly bear to think such thoughts, let alone live with them the remainder of my life, awash in a vast sea of remorse, regret, and worst of all, guilt.

To say I was distracted and conflicted to the point of irritability was an understatement. The huge unknown about Mary and the baby was killing me. And tormenting me further, rubbing salt into open wounds was this grinning, pompous idiot, schmoozing up to me because I was his boss. This guy actually thinks he can replace Jack? Blatantly obsequious, Skip chattered endlessly. We had been together only half an hour and already I wanted to kill him. I had to keep reminding myself exchanging Jack for Skip was 'my' decision, my solution to the Admiral's request, not his, so I shouldn't take my frustration out on him, but the Admiral? I had owed him a debt for getting me promoted to my present position, but the pendulum had swung the other direction. He now owed me big.

My boys were apprehensive about flying a mission without Jack as well. Not that they doubted my abilities in the absence of Jack, or Skip's abilities either, at least according to Bledsoe, but as a crew we had, up to this point, been very lucky. It was easy, immersed in the stress of these unfamiliar and unprecedented times, for men to become quite superstitious, ascribing to voodoo and magic the primitive notion that chance was not merely a mathematical construct, but a living, breathing being, a fate that could be wooed with the proper talisman. Many reasonable, devoutly God-fearing men, men who should know better, would know better in less trying times, had fallen prey to fallacious thinking, proved by their carrying good-luck charms. "I've carried this cigarette lighter with me on every mission and been lucky so far. I'm not gonna risk flying without it now," or so the reasoning went. There had to be some reason, some purpose as to why we aboard the *China Doll* had remained successful and unscathed while people around us, every bit as skilled and intelligent and brave, had not. Would changing co-pilots aggravate the fates, tempting them to deliver us our oft-anticipated and long overdue run of bad luck as a consequence? Was Jack our equivalent of a rabbit's foot, or four-leaf clover, our Luck incarnate? Would acquiescing to superstition alienate a loving God who had been our shield and protection? I thought of the words to a song I sang in church as a child, "A Mighty Fortress Is Our God." Could exchanging Jack for Skip end our good fortune, making null and void our contract with whatever forces governed such things? These questions loomed gigantic in the minds of my crew as we prepared for this mission, the first with Skip as our co-pilot. I must confess the notion crossed mine as well.

In preflight checks, Jack and I had long ago established a routine, dividing the labor and speeding the process. I trusted him to do his part and he trusted me to do mine. Tonight I performed all the checks myself with Skip in tow, showing him how I wanted and expected these inspections to be accomplished from here on out. He followed me around the *Doll* with the appearance of paying attention, but I noticed he was not writing anything down so I sent him for paper and pencil. "I don't trust my own memory and I sure as hell don't trust yours," I barked at him, a partial truth, because I really trusted my own.

The boys were all in their assigned positions, strapped in and waiting for Skip and I to finish our walk-around, each getting more anxious by the moment before at long last we boarded the *Doll*.

"Something wrong out there, Major?" CJ looked concerned. He knew there probably was nothing wrong , but wanted to hear me confirm his belief.

Skip answered before I could speak, "Not to worry, Lieutenant. The Army doesn't give these wings to just anybody," he said, pointing at his lapel.

Unseen by Skip, I subtly nodded my head to CJ, an almost telepathic message to "Drop it." Responding with only the hint of a smirk, CJ continued his preparations, making me proud of him for his restraint. Taming the tongue of a natural born smart ass is a difficult feat to accomplish, something I have wrestled with all my life. CJ is a bigger smart ass than me; if he could do it, I could do it, too.

With that in mind I did a pretty good job of controlling my venom in spite of the fact that virtually every word out of Skip's mouth irked me, irritating like an endless swarm of gnats. He talked incessantly while Jack could limit an entire flight's worth of conversation to grunts and nods. I just was not accustomed to such a constant need for interaction or validation. Did his daddy deprive him of *attaboys* growing up? I suppose what offended me most was that Skip wasn't Jack, never was, and never could be.

The flight was uneventful from a military standpoint; we came home from the hunt empty handed, but was still memorable for two reasons. First, even without Jack, our luck had not run afoul of the forces that control such things, and secondly was how the flight ended. Pulling to a stop on the tarmac and shutting down the engines, Skip read from our post-flight checklist as I performed the various attendant procedures. Before I got out of my seat, a young corporal boarded and worked his way up the catwalk to the cabin to hand me a stack of mail. Everyone in our squadron knew how anxious I was to receive word about Mary and the baby and assumed one of these letters just might bring the word I so desperately needed to hear. The corporal handed me the letters with a huge grin, saluted and departed as quickly as he had appeared. My crew got word of what was going on and worked their way forward, waiting just aft of the cabin, feigning nonchalance in hopes of seeing my reaction.

I later discovered the corporal was Bledsoe's friend, employed in the base post office. Bledsoe paid him five whole dollars to watch for letters addressed to me, and to personally deliver them at the earliest possible opportunity. My friends watched in silence as I sat with trembling hands, almost fearful of the news contained within the sealed envelopes. I screwed up my courage and chose the letter with the most recent postmark.

"Here goes nothing," I said, tearing through the paper.

Hello Daddy,

It's official, you're the father of a HEALTHY seven pound, ten ounce baby boy! Born March 23rd. My labor was twenty-three hours, but your granddaddy never once left my side. He was just so proud of you and our little Johnny. I so wish you could have been here. I'm so proud of you too. I'm fine; the baby is just so beautiful. I've never been happier, John. I can't wait till you can come home to meet your son. I love you and miss you so much. Try hard not to worry about us. Till then, darling.

Love,

Your Mary

"I've got a boy!" I shouted. The boys all cheered and congratulated me. Bledsoe broke open a box of cigars he'd smuggled aboard and passed them around.

"How in the world do you come up with stuff like this?" I asked him, truly impressed at his thoughtful gesture. Most guys wouldn't do something like that.

"I have my ways," is all he would say. We puffed on those stogies and told jokes and stories for almost an hour, the smoke creating a thick fog in the *Doll's* cabin, time well spent as we wound our workday down together. The news was a welcome relief; just knowing Mary and the baby were both alive and well was all I really needed in the world at that moment. I felt truly content, albeit anxious to see my new son and hold my wife. "All in due time," I consoled myself. I hit the sack that morning feeling like a blessed man; thankful God had shown me such favor.

The *Doll's* luck held firm throughout the remainder of 1943 and into '44 as we perfected night-time operations and the skill of finding and identifying enemy ships on the open ocean, the cover of darkness proving no match for our radar system. In 1944 alone the Snoopers dispatched over one million tons of shipping, supplies and munitions bound for an increasingly hungry enemy to the depths of the Pacific Ocean. Flying sorties nightly, we extended our range over suspected shipping lanes, venturing ever further north towards the shores of the Japanese homeland, continually on the hunt along the area we referred to as *The Slot.* Our missions grew in both distance and complexity, sometimes extending as far as 2500 miles round-trip and lasting ten hours or more. We returned from such missions fortunate the engines miraculously still turning with nothing more than fumes remaining in the fuel tanks. We accomplished all this with an incredibly low loss to tonnage ratio, one crew lost per 100,000 tons, a good number, but a gruesome number just the same if you or your crew were a victim of this statistic.

While the *Doll's* lucky streak continued in spite of Skip occupying the right seat, Jack's luck did not fare as well. Perhaps the *Doll* was 'his' talisman? Jack and his crew were incredibly successful at first. Flying a *Liberator* dubbed the *Shangri-La,* they accounted for sinking 55,000 tons of shipping in some thirty missions, a higher kill ratio than my own crew. His success continued until late November of 1944 when Jack and crew failed to return from a night raid 1000 miles north along *The Slot.* Rescue craft were dispatched along their proposed route within hours, but to no avail. After a week of intensive search with no wreckage sighted and no survivors recovered, all realistic hope of seeing our friend and his crew again in this lifetime was abandoned. I made sure that the Army posthumously promoted Jack to the rank of Major, then we had a memorial service to bid farewell to Major Jack Lafarge and the crew of the *Shangri-La.*

The Christmas of '44 was bleak indeed, and though it was widely speculated that the Allies were winning, there still remained no end in sight to this debacle. The weariness of war hung heavy over our collective psyches until mid-February, when a glimmer of hope began to shine through. As the Allies rapidly advanced upon Berlin, an end to the war in Europe seemed a distinct possibility; the total defeat of the Nazi regime could soon be within our grasp. The waking dream was to come about faster than I could have imagined. On May 7th the entire world celebrated VE or Victory in Europe day. Even the vanquished had cause to celebrate; at long last the nightmare of war was over. Now hopefully the Allies would turn their previously divided attention to the defeat of the Japanese empire and we could all go home.

"Soon, God, let it be soon!" was my prayer. Though we were clearly winning at this point, the Japanese retreat back to their home islands occurring at an ever accelerating pace, I remained fearful of the carnage, the unspeakable losses we would encounter, if we were forced to set foot upon Japanese soil. I'd witnessed the resolve of the Japanese enemy firsthand. They would not willingly surrender their nation to those they considered inferior, but instead would defend it down to the last peasant farmer. The worst was yet to come, God help us all.

CHAPTER 16

It began as do all endings born of complacency, oblivious to the knowledge that an end game would soon be required, an end game that, regardless of brilliant execution, would fail to prevent one from succumbing to the snarling black dog of fate, the beast anxiously awaiting every mortal at the precipice of time. Complacency is a sin that gets us greedily snatched from life while we heedlessly anticipate more and yet more of the same. The *Snoopers* had been phenomenally successful at our assignment. To date we had extracted 1,300,000 tons of shipping from the Japanese military, rendering them increasingly needful, sick, cold, wet, hungry, and most importantly, unarmed. By ignoring simple geography, the Japs had fallen prey to the same hubris-derived fate that so vexed Napoleon. Woefully overextending their reach in a desire to conquer a vast domain, their death-grip upon the conquered required a continuous, strong military presence. Maintaining that presence in turn required regular shipments of supplies, staples of life such as food, shelter, clothing, and, in some cases, even water. To continue dominance it also required ever more powerful munitions than those possessed by the dominated. In denying the Japs these necessities, we were forcing their retreat while the remainder of our brethren chased those retreating back to their home islands.

I was very proud to have been a part of this mission. The *Doll* and crew were responsible for over thirty percent of the total tonnage claimed, the lion's share of the kill, all without personally receiving so much as a scratch in retribution since beginning the new squadron. We'd just last night had a party to celebrate our successful completion of fifty missions, a number that did not include the pseudo-missions flown around Hawaii two summers ago. If those were included we had flown ninety-three missions with only one significant loss; Lenny.

I had become famous, or perhaps infamous is a better word, not among the Allies but among the Japanese. I discovered I had a price on my head, a bounty not unlike an outlaw in the Old West. The Japanese military wanted me dead and advertised the bounty over the airwaves. Out of sheer boredom, a number of our guys listened to Radio Tokyo and most especially to a show called Zero Hour featuring the enticing female voice of Iva Toguri, a Japanese American who'd found herself trapped in Japan at the outbreak of the war. Her on-air sobriquet was Orphan Ann, chosen presumably after the popular American cartoon character Orphan Annie, but we all called her Tokyo Rose. Thinly disguised psychological warfare designed to demoralize our troops, the show was broadcast in English and played contemporary American music, making the propaganda palatable if not downright entertaining. As the war progressed, the show got more intimate, reporting events at home and occasionally mentioning ships, airplanes, and sometimes even specific soldiers by name. Whether a lucky, chance encounter with specifics or true clairvoyance, hearing your own name on a Japanese radio was un-nerving to say the least. Tokyo Rose announced the bounty on my head in one of her infamous broadcasts. I was denounced as a murderer of unarmed men, responsible for sinking numerous Japanese merchant vessels and hospital ships transporting wounded and defenseless men. The government in Tokyo was offering a bounty of 10,000 American dollars to anyone responsible for my capture and "preferably horrendous" death. She further stated after the inevitable Japanese victory I would be found, tried, and most assuredly executed. The offer of cash was extended to Americans and Japanese alike. Most disconcerting of all, the broadcast concluded by congratulating me on the birth of my son and offered him and my wife condolences for the fatherless childhood that would be his fate. I turned the radio off asking, "How did the bitch know that?"

The guys all cheered, hooped, and hollered when they heard my name announced, but grew quiet when she congratulated me. I was unsure how to respond. On one hand, I'd be a liar if I said the broadcast didn't scare me a little. How did they know my name out of thousands of men fighting in the Pacific? How did they know about Mary and the baby? On the other hand, I was honored, as it meant the *Snoopers* were successfully rattling their cages. I decided laughing was the best and most reassuring response.

CJ quickly solved the unspoken riddle saying, "Look at it this way, Major, this means that Jack or some of his crew must still be alive and captured. How else could they know something like that?" I thought hard on his words.

"Alive, yes, but probably better off dead. Jack would never have told them anything other than name, rank, and serial number unless he broke under torture." CJ got tears in his eyes at the thought, knowing I was right, and in my correctness, all the dreadful implications for Jack.

"Bastards," was his single barely audible response.

General Twining called me into his office the following day to say, "Given the new developments, the time has come for you to stop flying and concentrate instead upon leading. You're too valuable to us now and the risk to you personally is too great if you were to be shot down and captured."

"I'm no more valuable than any of my men, and if I were lost today, the mission would continue. Besides, if we cower in fear we've given them exactly what they want. They win! We can't let that happen, General."

"I don't know....I've got to consider not only what's best for you, I've got to consider what's best for the squadron."

"Please, General, nothing's going to happen. I'm really good at what I do. That's why I haven't gotten so much as a scratch yet. I'm the best you've got and you know it!"

"Which is precisely why we can't afford to lose you."

"If you park me behind a desk, haven't you in effect lost me?"

"Yes, but…"

"Why change something we've had proven success with?"

"I don't know…"

"General, what would you do in my shoes?" Knowing his history, my question was a well-executed parry and thrust.

He smiled, knowing exactly what he would do. He already had. As a general he was deemed too valuable to fly combat missions, but that didn't stop him. Ignoring direct orders, he flew combat anyway, several missions in fact, before having the misfortune to be shot down over the ocean. He survived eight days in a raft before being spotted and picked up, during which time the Army and Navy spent an inordinate amount of time searching for him or his remains. Prior to this, he'd argued for rescue radios to be placed in the survival gear of each aircraft. The Pentagon said the radios would not be cost effective. After his rescue from eight days lost at sea, eight days that could have been significantly less, the radios previously deemed frivolous by the Pentagon magically appeared, but Twining never again flew combat. I suspect this was the trade they forced him to make to procure the rescue radios for his crews.

"Look, John, you know how I feel. Let me ponder on this a bit and get back to you."

"So I'm still free to fly as I see fit?"

"Until you hear otherwise from me, yes, you can fly."

"Thank you, sir. I'll be okay, I promise." Famous last words…

The *Doll* flew two more missions the week following my chat with General Twining, each time extending our search further north along *The Slot* than before, but we returned home from the hunt both times empty-handed. The frequency of our successes had slowly diminished over time, prompting our growing frustration, pushing us to fly ever further north along *The Slot*.

Throughout the second six months of 1944 and well into the spring of 1945, our primary target, large container vessels, became increasingly scarce as our tally against them continued to mount. We were not sure if this paucity was a reflection of our success with attrition of vessels from heavy losses, or were the Japs developing other ways to supply their far-flung troops? I strongly suspected both were the case. Necessity being the mother of invention, the Japanese command responded to the need we were creating for the average soldier with new, albeit inefficient, innovations. We knew for a fact they had stepped up their use of submarines. Just as they had been earlier in the war, subs maneuvering under the cover of darkness were being employed to supply some of their island outposts. Our radar was useless to detect those subs unless we were fortunate enough to encounter them cruising along the ocean surface. Save operating deeply submerged, subs could easily be spotted from the air in daylight, but cruising submerged at night, they were successfully eluding the *Snoopers'* search. In the past year we had scored only once against a Japanese sub, and that was probably a fortuitous accident, the hapless sub stumbled upon, stranded and vulnerable topside, crippled by a mechanical inability to dive. Though the subs were successfully avoiding us, we were not too concerned, as the typical submarine in the Japanese fleet had very limited cargo capacity, rendering this method of delivering supplies grossly inefficient. At best, the subs were able to provide only the most basic of human needs and even those in extremely small quantities.

Transport aircraft such as the Mitsubishi Ki-57 or the Kawasaki Ki-56 were also being increasingly used to supply Japanese soldiers in the field, but again the volume of freight per aircraft was a limiting factor, especially compared to the massive tonnage able to be transported in a large ship. Because of the *Snoopers'* success against conventional maritime shipping, the Japs were forced to sacrifice volume efficiencies for either stealth or frequency, or both. An airplane or submarine had to make multiple trips to even begin to equal the effectiveness of a container ship. The new delivery techniques represented an evolution of Japanese targets against which the Allies would need a new and concerted effort, but tempting as these new targets were, I was determined to remain true to the mission we were originally tasked with, maintaining the relentless pressure we exerted against conventional shipping. Not that the *Snoopers* would pass up a chance to strike against any enemy target we might stumble upon, targets of opportunity as they were called in the ETO, but the strategic hunt for these new targets would have to become someone else's mission. We wanted Ships.

April 15, 1945, began of the sameness enveloping any other day in the tropics. The cries of birds, those God-made clothed in feathers, and man-made clad in aluminum, awakened me from a deep sleep. This didn't make me happy; snatching me unfulfilled from a happy albeit erotic dream of Mary, the woman I love. Every morning I awoke to find the world shrouded in a transient jungle mist, a grey veil that inevitably would disappear, burning off as the day heated up before 10:00 a.m., lifting first off the ground then dissipating en masse to reveal the dense, lushly green foliage, pervasive upon the surrounding hills and mountains. A reverse phenomenon was true over the ocean where the air above was clear at daybreak, revealing upon the horizon a neighboring island, dominated by a stark volcanic mountain that towered over the water. As the day's temperature rose, a thin, almost invisible sea mist formed over the ocean's surface performing an amazing feat of magic, making that distant mountain vanish, disappearing as if into thin air.

The smells of salt air and of a myriad of blossoms, of constantly moistened mosses and ferns, the primordial incense of a land if ever known had long since been forgotten, only now to be rediscovered and spoiled, was now tainted with the man-made scents and stinks of engine exhaust, burnt metal, cordite, cigarette smoke, and coffee, always of coffee. Uncle Sam actually did a pretty good job of keeping us supplied with both coffee and cigarettes. This morning was for the most part beautiful, but invisible, cloaked in a shroud of sameness, nothing to punctuate my memory, to suggest this day would be different from all the others and should be inscribed upon my cerebral cortex as Holy, a Greek word used to describe an attribute of God, that of being set apart, different from anyone or anything.

On the previous evening Captain Donald Douglas and crew encountered two large merchant vessels traveling southward along *The Slot*. Their bombs hit their mark and dispatched one of the vessels to the deep. The other, it was assumed would still be there and vulnerable, awaiting all-the -while praying to be spared the deathblow the *Doll* would soon deliver. At long last, a target! We eagerly anticipated any morsel; an anxious wanting propelled by the famine of the previous three and a half weeks, but with tonight's hunt the promise of satiation, a feast of meat to quiet the gnawing hunger in our guts.

Taking off at dusk, we flew north along *The Slot* a full six hours without the Radar giving so much as a blip of foreplay.

CJ reported, "Major, we've got to make a decision here. We're approaching maximum range if we want to make it back to Bomber One without refueling somewhere else."

I knew he was right. CJ also knew how much I hated to land the *Doll* to take on fuel from another unit. Our success had made us prima donnas in the jealous eyes of those less successful, and we paid for the fuel we took by ignoring the chiding attitudes of our fellow countrymen. The Brits were even worse, but knowing that ship had to be somewhere out there unless she had been already claimed by one of our subs, and such an encounter had not been reported before we lifted from Espiritu Santo, I wanted to press on in the chance our luck might improve.

"Can we milk it for another fifteen minutes, CJ? That damned ship didn't just disappear."

"Fifteen puts you right at the edge of the envelope, Major. It'll be tight, but I think we can do it provided we don't have any other wrinkles."

"Roger that," I said, thinking I would split the difference and fly north another ten minutes before throwing in the towel. However, I burned up a full fifteen minutes thinking, "Just one more minute…just one more…just one more," before seeing my efforts were destined to remain unrewarded and turning the *Doll* homeward. Still, all was not lost as we might find the target on the return leg. To that end, I let our course creep ever more westerly, closer to the Asian continent. CJ saw what I was doing and, to his credit, didn't chastise me. He wanted another kill as much as I did and vividly remembered the gambit he and I had secretly played now over two years ago, a bet that rewarded us with our first kill. We both knew the risk we'd taken, but had never again spoken of it. Today we were again taking that risk.

After two more fruitless hours my two degrees of cheating had rendered us a full hundred miles off course. I finally surrendered to the notion of going home hungry.

"Okay, CJ. Give me some vectors."

"I thought you'd never ask, Major. Steer fifteen degree left to a heading of 178 degrees. That ought to do it."

Onward we droned for another hour before Doc said, "Well looky here, ain't you pretty. Major, I've got a target at sixty miles on a bearing of 220."

"Bingo! How about it CJ, can we make it?"

"We can, but forget making back to Espiritu tonight."

"You figure out the logistics. I'll even take fuel from the Brits if we have to. We're gonna get that ship!"

I turned the *Doll* towards the target, descending to twenty feet off the surface. In twenty minutes we could see her on the horizon steaming southward, fast as she could muster.

"Okay boys, you know the drill. Everyone to combat positions, bomb bay coming open." They were wary of our attack and began firing a pair of deck-mounted fifty calibers in our direction. Our top turret and nose gunner returned their fire, temporarily silencing the defense. I pulled the *Doll* up to clear the bow deck by mere feet and Jim let fly six 500 pounders with timed fuses. The bombs slid down the deck with a pair crashing through the front wall of the bridge. Clearing the prow of the ship, we were climbing when all six simultaneously blew. Again another munitions ship, the cargo igniting with a tremendous explosion viewed this time from a distance, wisdom gained from having done a few of these.

"Un-armed, my ass!" CJ said derisively.

After three wide circuits we watched the ship nose up, bob like a cork, then slide beneath the waves to find a resting place on the floor of the Pacific Ocean, leaving behind upon the surface a residue of scattered debris and two lifeboats, one of which was empty.

"Okay, Major. Turn to a heading of 165 degrees. We need to buy some gas from the Brits."

"It's worth it, don't you think?" Everyone agreed with me though we all hated dealing with the pompous bastards.

After the tension of the attack we all began to relax and joke as most men are want to do after successfully navigating a trying event. I let Charlie fly for a while and kicked back, propping my feet on the center control console.

"Hey Bledsoe, what'd you bring us for supper? I sure could use a beer," I joked.

"No beer, Major, but I've got some Pepsi if you like. I also swiped a pie."

"Damn it, Bledsoe, don't tell me you swiped something. I'm the boss, remember?"

"It's apple, sir," he said, ignoring my chiding, knowing apple pie was my favorite and swiping the boss's favorite for him will more than likely be forgiven.

"That sounds great, and a Pepsi, too? Bledsoe, you continue to amaze me. I'll take Pepsi over Coca-cola any day."

"I'll bring it right up, Major." Just as he made it into the cabin to deliver our grub we heard an explosive Wak! Wak! Wak!, the nauseating sound of large caliber shells striking the fuselage." I spun around to grab the controls just as Bill yelled, "Oh fuck, Major. We've got trouble."

"Did you see it?"

"It's a *Zero*, sir, and he's coming back."

"C'mon boys, time to earn your keep." I heard three of our gunners open fire then quickly stop as Bill yelled, "Does anyone see him?"

"Negative!" came multiple replies.

"Where'd this guy come from, Major?"

"They want us bad! I suspect he was shadowing the ship we just sank hoping he might score and get us. You guys focus! Don't panic and shoot wildly."

"Yes, sir," they replied as the sound of striking munitions again raked along the fuselage, rattling the ship".

"He's overhead, he's overhead! Three o'clock," CJ yelled. "I can't see him but I see the tracers."

"Follow the tracers back to him, just get the bastard!"

The Jap's shells marched down the center of the wing before finally finding their mark, the center tank erupted into flames that trailed back over the top of the *Doll*.

"Oh shit! We're on fire."

"Can anyone get an extinguisher on it?"

"No, sir, and here he comes again!"

This time I could see him, illuminated by the flames from the *Doll*'s wing.

"This guy doesn't give up, does he?"

"Hang on boys, we're gonna get wet." Both outboard engines were now trailing flames.

"Shut'em down, Skip!"

"Major, I can't swim," CJ shouted.

"Well now's one hell of a time to tell me."

"Should we bail, sir?"

"If we do we'll be scattered across the Pacific. Stay with the ship if you can."

"I don't want to burn up!" Skip cried, seeing the inboard engines were now blazing.

"Shut 'em down! Our decision is made. Boys, buckle in and be sure you've got your vests on."

The *Zero* made one final run at us, this time from below. The *Doll*, crippled and silent, the shells struck with a reverberating thud, thud, thud. CJ cried out, "Oh God, I'm hit."

"Forty degrees of flaps, Skip."

"No flaps, Major, no pressure."

It felt like attempting to fly a flaming rock. The only good thing about being on fire is it allowed me to see the ocean as the flames reflected back on us.

"C'mon baby, just hold together for a few more seconds." As soon as the word "Baby" came from my mouth I thought about Mary and my baby.... soon to be fatherless just as the Jap bitch had prophesized. The water was coming into view, rushing towards me much too quickly.

"Brace yourselves, boys." I said into the now dead intercom. The cabin was filling with smoke. Skip and I both began coughing and gasping. Don't give up now, John. Hold it off, hold it off, hold it off... The *Doll's* tail feathers caught the water with the roar of twisting metal and the cries of freshly broken men. The nose slammed down with a surreal, painful blinding flash followed by dead silence.

I awoke cold and wet and breathless, several feet under water, every fiber in my body alive with pain, but my mind strangely serene. Everything seemed to be passing in and through a slow, syrupy suspension of time. The *Doll* was still on the surface ablaze. I remember thinking, "That's odd! How did I get here? Mary was there, smiling invitingly and naked to the world. I saw sunlight playing, a glistening kaleidoscope of colors amid the tiny, imperceptible hairs on her skin.

"How did I get here?" I asked.

She said to me, "Silly boy, I brought you here."

"But where are we?" I asked.

"I told you, we're here." I wondered why Mary was here in this black-as-night water, yet drenched in sunlight, then wondered why I was here. Though confused I felt placid. So many incongruities puzzled me, but non-answers were answers all the same, and acceptable, and somehow…Perfect! I wondered how I could have been thrown clear of the aircraft, and then remembered, "Ah, I didn't put my seat harness back on after the *Zero* hit us on the first pass." Ironic, as I always harped on the men to wear their seat harnesses. Bledsoe would get a kick out of this when I told him what happened to me tomorrow. Then it struck me, there is no tomorrow. Suddenly awake, I thought, "The men! I've got to get the men out." The blazing wreckage lit my way to the surface, which was a good thing for without it I wouldn't have known which way was up. I broke water just in time to see Bill pull the tab on Jordy's vest and push him out the side hatch. Joe was already out and floating, his life vest suspending his unconscious head above the water. The world around me was confused and panicked and desperate. I shook my head trying to waken myself from the nightmare, but it was no bad dream, and I'd best quickly come to my senses or I was going to die today. As I was thinking this, my adrenal glands must have kicked into high gear, for I felt a sudden rush, a strength and clarity of mind such as is only vested upon the dying. I looked for Bill, but he had disappeared, going back into the flaming ship for more.

"Bill!" I shouted. "Bill, throw the raft out. She won't stay up long; we've got to get the others. I'm going to the cockpit!" But how? The *Doll's* midsection was now an inferno, steam from the superheated water hissing menacingly at its periphery. The *Doll* was sinking, soon to disappear into the depths long before she burned up completely. There had to be a gap in the side, how else could I have been thrown clear? I had to find it! Diving again, passing below the flaming wing, I swam under water till clear before surfacing at my side window and pulling myself up. Sure enough, there was a man-sized hole through the front windshield, jagged and hazardous, but passable; an exit I assume fate had just created, using my hurtling body as a battering ram. Salt water was pouring in, quickly filling the cabin. Skip was down the hatch, pushing Jim's limp body to the surface. I slipped through the hole to help him, gashing my arm and leg in the process. Together, we managed to push him up and through the hole, where he fell landing face down in the water.

"Go keep him up, I'll get the others." Just as I said that, Bledsoe popped to the surface holding CJ.

"I think he's dead, Major. Can you give me a hand?" Bledsoe shouted so as to be heard, but his voice was steady, exuding an amazing calm.

"Can you push him out?"

"Yes, sir, I think so." We both tugged CJ to my seat, then up through the window."

I pulled his vest tab, but nothing happened. The bullets that violated his chest and probably killed him clearly had not spared his vest.

"You go out first, Bledsoe, and I'll pass him to you." Bledsoe was deftly through the hole and treading water, waiting to keep CJ afloat. I then realized Doc was standing on the *Doll's* nose helping me to keep CJ from slipping unconscious into the water. Doc's face was a bloody mess, his nose splayed to one side like a boxer's after losing a prizefight. He had a dazed, otherworldly look in his eyes, incapable of clear thought. I reached through the broken windshield to pull the tab on his vest; it expanded with a *pop* before I pushed Doc off the nose into the swirling water.

"You got him?"

"Yes, sir," Bledsoe replied I let go of the grip I had on CJ's limp arm. Before leaving the ship, I quickly ran through the crew list in my head; Jim, CJ, Bledsoe, Skip, Bill, Jordy, Doc, and Joe. "That's eight! Damn, whom am I missing?" Then it hit me, it's me, MORON, I'm the ninth guy. Back through the hole, again cutting my ankle, I stood up on the nose then dove into the water. The *Doll* was sinking rapidly now, the air above her alive with fire and smoke and sound, the fury of escaping air, forced out by the replacing salt water. It was as though the *Doll* was sighing, reluctant even in death to leave us alone. Within fifteen seconds she was gone from the surface, the flames extinguished into sizzling steam, the red hot metal aglow, lighting her way as she receded into the depths of the Pacific and of eternity.

"Major, I need a hand here," Bledsoe called above the *Doll's* sizzling death cry. The other men were all shouting out. Bill had been successful in tossing out the raft and it inflated with a *FOP*. Scurrying quickly over the side, he reached out for the injured, pulling them out of the swirling, black, unforgiving waters and into a measure of salvation. I swam to Bledsoe and helped him keep CJ afloat. He stage whispered to me, "Major, we got to get him out of the water quick. Remember the sharks! We've had enough trouble for one night. No reason to add sharks into the equation. If they really are sensitive to blood in the water as the experts say, we may already be calling out to them."

"Oh yeah, you're right!" With CJ's arms draped limply over our shoulders, we swam with the utmost haste to the raft. Bill had already pulled Jordy and two others into the boat, but I couldn't make out who in the darkness. They continued calling to us, their cries a beacon towards the raft, at one moment visible, perched upon a wave, the next moment disappearing into the trough and into the darkness.

I could hear Skip swimming with Jim in tow several yards away, continually prodding his charge with words of encouragement, "Just a little further, Jim. Were going to make it. Stay with me, Jim, you can do it!" They reached the raft before Bledsoe and I with CJ, his body dangling from ours, slowing our progression like a water brake. After another two minutes of swimming hard, we at last arrived at raft's edge, and the three already aboard pulled CJ up and over the side. They next did the same for me and then for Bledsoe. We were both breathless, our energy spent saving CJ and ourselves.

Doc, his mind having rejoined the present, found a flashlight, and, beginning with CJ, systematically examined everyone's wounds.

"I think he's dead, Major." He felt for a pulse then put his ear to CJ's motionless chest, then shook his head to confirm. His intended efforts for

CJ deemed futile, Doc began looking each of us over, searching for anything needing immediate attention.

"Where do you hurt Major? You look like hell!"

"So do you," I said, trying to imagine how I could look any worse. "I got thrown through the windshield. Lucky for me, my head took the brunt of it," I laughed sarcastically. My head was really beginning to throb with pain.

"You've got a big gash on your forehead. Hurt anywhere else? He asked, beginning to wrap a turban-like dressing around my scalp.

"I'm pretty sure I've got cuts on my shoulder and thigh, but my head feels the worst of it. Go ahead and tend to the other guys. They need you more than I do."

"I know they're hurt, but you're the only one actively bleeding. There's not a lot more I can do for them." He leaned in and whispered in my ear, "CJ is dead, Jordy broke his back…He can't move or feel his legs."

"He's paralyzed?" I whispered back.

Doc nodded. "And I think both of Jim's shoulders are either broken or out of socket. He was in the tunnel when we hit the water and shot through it like a cannon. His head broke the front glass and his shoulders hit the frame on both sides or he would have been thrown out just like you."

"It's a wonder he didn't break his neck."

"He might have…He says it hurts like hell. I wrapped a dressing around it to keep him from turning or bending it."

"What good will that do?"

"It may keep him from pithing himself." I looked at Doc questioningly. "It means severing the spinal cord, in which case he'll die or become paralyzed from the neck down. Given our present circumstances, that would be a death sentence." I nodded understanding, "Don't let that happen, Doc." He smiled weakly.

Skip began to curse, "Where the fuck did that Jap come from, the worthless shit? I wish I could get my hands on 'em! We're in the middle of fucking nowhere with no Goddamned food."

"Skip!"

He continued his tirade.

"Skip?....CAPTAIN JOHNSON!" I shouted, hoping he might take the morale of his fellows into consideration, not that he was saying anything that we weren't already thinking. Regaining his composure, he slumped down into a despondent mass, huddled against the raft's wall. I looked at my watch and said, "It's 0330 boys. Might as well sleep if you can. It'll be morning soon and they'll figure out we haven't come back and start looking for us."

"So will the fucking Japs," Bill said under his breath as if no one else was listening, but I was listening, all the while Tokyo Rose's words reverberating in my memory.

CHAPTER 17

I awoke to the sun climbing above a featureless horizon, my head throbbing like the hangover from a week long drunk. The other guys were all sleeping, but their breathing and sighs betrayed the fitful nature of their brief repose, an amalgam of pain, fear, and anxiety depriving them of any real rest. I knew intimately of their journey, for I had just returned from that same world, awakening to find myself adrift in a canvas and rubber raft in the middle of the Pacific Ocean along with eight others still clinging to life and one who had lost the battle.

"Thank God for General Twining. His radio will probably save our lives," I thought, opening the raft's rescue package. The wax-wrapped package contained food rations, water, medical supplies, a flare gun and flares, a signal mirror, and the radio. Attaching the antennae, I flipped the switch, anticipating the radio's hum as it warmed to life, but it remained lifeless, dead in my hands. My pulse quickened as I waited, thinking, "Perhaps it just needs a little more time." After two minutes my panic reached a peak, and I could no longer remain patient. Shaking the radio, gently at first, my gyrations became more vigorous, all to no avail. My optimism dwindled when I noticed a small seam outlined by crystalline deposits. Prying off the back with my hunting knife, my fears were realized; the tropical sea air had done its damage despite the wax packaging. The batteries had leaked, corroded beyond usefulness, long ago devoid of even a meager electric charge. "Damn, we really are screwed," I think, news I'm not ready to share with the boys.

"How can anyone let this happen? I'm gonna have to chew Mac's ass for this one." Now our only chance was luck, the good fortune of being spotted by a friendly aircraft or ship. Checking my watch, it was 0630. They'd be launching a search-and-rescue mission soon when we'd not returned as scheduled. They'd send a PBY *Catalina* to look for us, retracing our presumed route. Only CJ and I could now know how incorrect that presumption would be. In my lust to make yet another score, I had of intent strayed from the prescribed course ever so slightly. A tiny enough deviation to be imperceptible to the others, but, like sin, even a minor sin perpetrated for a long enough period of time, my deviation could and probably would leave us far enough from the fold to be un-findable by mere mortals. I may confess this indiscretion to them someday, but now is not the time. Anything that diminished hope, as my confession surely would, also diminished the chance of surviving, or at least the chance of surviving sane.

If we were unlucky, or perhaps I should say unluckier, we would be found not by the Americans, but by the Japanese. Our last position was known precisely by only three men; CJ, now dead, the Japanese pilot who had dispatched us to this vulnerable place believing he had left us all dead, and me. Given the nature of the kill, that Jap pilot knew who he was attacking. He hadn't randomly discovered us at night over a vast ocean after having sunk yet another of their precious ships. This was planned, premeditated, and though they did not know it was *me*, they knew it was *us* they were attacking. That cargo ship was merely bait, a tasty morsel to lure us in. Foolishly, I'd taken the bait, hook, line, and sinker, leaving me to be the catch, flopping in the creel. It now was only a matter of time. They would come back, come looking for our radar, a prize too great to let sink into the ocean without attempting to snatch it.

That sooner or later the Japanese would develop their own version of radar was inevitable. In fact, utilizing their earliest attempts at airborne radar is probably how they had tracked the *Doll* through the darkness of night before attacking us. Thankfully for the Allies, Japanese attempts at radar remained rudimentary throughout the war, lacking the sophistication or sensitivity of ours, giving us a clear technological advantage. The Japs hoped to level the playing field by stealing our superior technology, and, in desperation, must have made the capture of one of our units a top priority. The chance of also capturing some of us alive, me in particular, a feat that would play very well in the press back in Japan, was merely icing on the cake. I had already been declared a prize in their press, at least in their broadcast news media and I assume in their written word as well. If they found us, the lone *Zero* pilot would be lauded as a hero while we would be tried, convicted and summarily executed, just as Tokyo Rose had promised.

If we were most unlucky, the sharks would find us. Could they, would they, attack us in a raft? I poked the raft's side and thought, "Teeth that could rip through flesh in one bite would have little trouble ripping through this." The question wasn't whether or not they would find us, they would, for God knows we had let enough blood to bait them, but would they try to get at us if we were not directly in the water? If they did, would a .45-caliber handgun be enough to deter them? I pulled the .45 Colt from the holster at my side to consider it, and then watched as salt water spilled from its barrel.

"That can't be good."

There was one other entity looking for us, although *looking* is a euphemism as death always knows exactly the location of every man, held at bay by time alone.

How long did we have if we remained unfound? We had rudimentary provisions, food enough for a day or two, fresh water for less than a day. How long could a man last without water, let alone a group of men, exposed as we were to the tropical heat. Searching the heavens, there was not a single cloud in the sky. If it did not rain, and I saw nothing that gave me hope of rain, we had maybe three days to a week before succumbing. Dying of thirst was not my first choice of endgames.

"And so the race begins," I thought. Who will be the first to get to us? I wasn't feeling so lucky anymore. I awarded the better odds to the Japanese or the sharks. One or both would come looking for us, for the radar, for me, for supper. Good thing the radar was now untouchable, safely resting with the *Doll* on the bottom.

The *China Doll*, I'd yet to mourn her loss. Can a man love a machine? Is it right or proper to do so? Right or wrong, I loved her. She had taken care of us, keeping us safe right up to the last second, finally offering herself up in sacrifice to light my way to the water. I heard her cry, heard her say good-bye to me, exhaling before slipping beneath the waves. To the day I die I will love that ship, sorry that I'll never again lay eyes upon her. Perhaps someday, in a million or billion years when the oceans dry up, someone will find her and sense, just as I did, she was something special.

"Good-bye, old girl!" I said aloud.

"Yeah, she was something else, wasn't she?" Bledsoe, now awake whispered in response. He didn't want to awaken anyone else. I smiled sadly and nodded. Seeing the disassembled radio in my hands he asked, "How long till you think they'll find us?"

"Soon," I said. He was smart enough to know the double entendre of my answer. Ever positive he said, "I love those *Catalinas*. Did you ever fly one, Major?"

"No, Bledsoe, I never did."

"I suppose they'll just land right here on the water."

"Yep! Right here on the water." As their leader it was my sacred calling, my duty to remain positive. God help me, because I felt anything but positive. The Bible says that God hates liars, but I suppose in this setting, where the greater sin would be to destroy hope in another, God forgives the liar he declares his hatred for. I certainly hoped so, as the wrath of the Japanese is about all I can bear to consider at the moment.

Soon after, every man aboard was awake and bristling with how and why, logical questions about an event that defied logic save for one word, War. There may be logical reasons why men fight men in the broadest sense of nation versus nation, but at the microcosm of man versus man, all reason dissolves. As their leader and their friend I had no answers for them. I didn't even have answers for myself.

The day was beginning to heat up and already there were requests for water. I allowed each of them a sip only. "Until it rains, this is all we've got." Seeing panic in Jim's eyes I said, "Don't worry Jim. Doesn't it rain here every day?" My words did little to console him.

Another two hours later it was getting really hot with no respite from the tropical sun to be had before nightfall. If only we had a canopy, something to offer us a little shade. Then I realized that Bledsoe had not cast off his parachute when swimming last night.

"Hey Bledsoe, pass me your chute." He looked puzzled at first, and then an A-ha look struck his face. We soon had the parachute open and the canopy draped over the raft to offer some semblance of shade. Our skin was already sunburned and if we're to be out here long the canopy could very well save our lives.

Soon all were again quiet, each receding into the sanctuary of his own mind, taking stock of misery. My head was really hurting; pounding, relentless, and unmerciful. I'm sure it was being compounded and magnified by my increasing dehydration. The only good thing about my headache was its intensity, as the pain was so encompassing I could think of little else. Certainly my other aches and pains were paltry in comparison and therefore ignored. I'm glad all I had to contend with was pain. Poor Jordy would probably never walk again. I think I'd rather be dead, but he seemed happy just to be alive. He'd face a trial of bitterness if we were lucky enough to survive this, but he was content, relieved I suppose was a better word to describe his mood. I should be so brave. I attributed his attitude to bravery, but it may be shock, both emotional and physiological, producing *la belle indifference* to the direness of his situation. I drifted off to sleep again in spite of the throbbing in my temples. Mary was there awaiting me in the bed at the Netherlands, always sweet and beckoning and naked. We lay together on crisp clean sheets and talked for hours before making love. She was so very beautiful I couldn't take my eyes off her. How could any man? She was mine, my prize she says for just being me. Damn, I'm a lucky guy.

When I awoke it was 1600 and I felt drier than ever before in my life. My tongue was sticking to the roof of my mouth. In a panic, I bolted upright, then remembered myself and regained my composure. No rain or water, but no sharks or Japanese either. Perhaps it wasn't all bad. We just had to hold on. I looked at CJ's stiffening corpse and thought, "At least I get the chance to hold on." CJ was a good guy. If we were not rescued soon we'd have to figure out what to do about CJ's body. As much as I hated the thought of tossing him overboard we had little other choice. It wasn't doing any of the rest of us any good seeing him that way. Bodies decompose pretty quickly in the heat. Seeing him, or worse yet, smelling him rot away would be a nightmare. He wouldn't want that for the rest of us. Neither would I.

Everything was drying up, my skin, my lips, my tongue. My throat felt as though I had swallowed a Brillo pad whole. We had only half a canteen of water remaining. No one was to receive another drop until tomorrow morning. All I could think about was water. Forget food, forget sex, man could live for a long time without either, but no water, how long could a man last even in less temperate climates? Two, three days? A week at the outside? I couldn't begin to imagine, didn't want to imagine, knowing how I felt, the last drop to moisten my tongue only fifteen hours ago. I looked at the extensive ocean around me and considered the irony. "Water, water everywhere, and all the boards did shrink; Water, water everywhere, nor any drop to drink," *The Rhyme of the Ancient Mariner* by Samuel Taylor Coleridge. Little did I know back in eighth grade the poem would be about me. Mrs. Nethery made us learn it, memorize it completely, a way to "exercise and expand" our young minds. I can still say it, I think; at least I can still remember the day I had to recite it before the whole class. We all had to. Stevie Wright hit me with a spitball about halfway through and Mrs. Nethery took him out into the hall and wore his ass out with a paddle, then came back and made me start all over again. "Completely unfair," I thought and said so, but she just said, "Life isn't always fair, Johnny, now continue…"

She was the toughest teacher I ever had so it seems odd now that I recall her with the most fondness. At the time I despised her for all the homework she gave us, "Busy work, assigned just to be cruel." She also made us memorize Lincoln's *Gettysburg Address*, Tennyson's '*The Charge of the Light Brigade*', and Longfellow's '*A Psalm of Life*' and '*The Midnight Ride of Paul Revere*.' Even now as I lay here, probably dying, I can still hear her voice as she read to us, my favorite part of everyday in her classroom. She would make us put our heads down upon our desks and listen as she read poetry and history, Shakespeare, and Mark Twain. We all thought she was crazy, at least we said so to one another for making us, eighth graders no less, take naps like first graders. Lots of the guys did take naps, falling asleep as she read, but I never did. I clung to every word. Looking back on it now I think how noble, how grand. I still love to learn today, thanks to the enlightened tutelage of crazy old Mrs. Nethery. It seems now eons ago, and yet it was only just ten years past. I wonder what's become of her. Is she still among the living? She was ancient when I had her, approaching seventy years old, old enough to have taught my daddy when he was in second grade and he said she was old then. I'll have to remember to ask Granddaddy when I get home. I think he may have called upon her a time or two.

I was startled from my daydream by a rustling from the other side of the raft. Jordy was beginning to get delirious, murmuring strange sentences and talking to people who were not in the boat. He appears to be chilling as his agitation increases. I felt his forehead with the back of my hand, just as I saw my granddaddy do so many times when I would accompany him on his rounds. Jordy felt hot, but it was hard to tell given the ambient temperature under the makeshift canopy. Recalling seeing Aspirin in the survival pack, I opened mine and gave him a tablet and the canteen. Even in his delirium he gulped down the water desperately.

"Hey, no fair," Skip said like a three-year-old.

"He's hurt and gonna die if we don't get his fever down and get him some water," I said despite a mouth so dry my words came out glued together.

"We're all dying Major, what's your point?" So it had come to this "every man for himself" mentality already? Giving him my sternest look, I said, "We have a chance of surviving to get water. Jordy doesn't. Can't you see he's getting worse?" Skip backed down, acquiescing more to my rank than my demeanor, a slave still to the convention of authority. "But for how much longer a slave?" I wondered. The trappings of leadership, of authority, begin to fail as men get more and ever more desperate. That innate drive to survive, poured by God into every living creature, trumps any semblance of rank or privilege when the shit hits the fan. That so few men desert in the heat of conflict is a testament to the will of man over nature. While most men are willing to die a quick honorable death for something they believe in more dearly than life, add a component of time, of lingering and languishing to that equation and all bets are off. The law of the jungle will take precedent. In such situations men have more time to think, to weigh options, to talk themselves into abandoning honor for the sake of a little more life. Death is inevitable as it comes eventually to every man; the timing of that death is the issue. My job as leader is to maintain my position as the leader, not allowing my crew to fall prey to the chaos of a jungle mentality.

Immediate crisis averted, we all fell back into ourselves, into the silence and solace of contemplation. Most were soon asleep again, the respite of imprisoned men, and surely we were imprisoned, restrained within the confines of a canvas and rubber raft and the 200 quintillion gallons of salt water that is the Pacific Ocean. Prisoners on Alcatraz had more chance of escaping than we did from this boat. I drifted off again into a deep and dreamless sleep, no Mary to comfort me this time. I awoke just in time to see the sun disappear over the rim of the Pacific. I watched closely for the green flash that is said to occur at the exact moment the globe of the sun is no longer visible, but I saw nothing. I think such an occurrence must be a popularly circulated myth, but old sailors swore by it. I've looked for it in every sunset over the ocean I've ever witnessed, but have never been rewarded. Maybe it's like images of the Virgin Mary, only the purest of hearts can see. Or angels. Or ghosts. I've yet to encounter any of these phenomena either. Do they really exist? I'm guessing they do, as many sane and noble men have reported their experience with such beings of the spiritual realm. I've never seen God, yet I believe he exists. I suppose I believe he exists because my granddaddy was so convinced. I looked over at CJ's covered mortal remains and thought, "He knows now, if there's any knowing to be done." I've never really been a praying man, at least not of my own accord. Sure, Granddaddy always made Davey and me say grace at mealtime, but it was more of a social convention than any real offering of thanks. I suppose I always figured God was too busy running the universe to care about the likes of me, but my Granddaddy was a true believer who started and ended his day on his knees. I always thought it quaint and endearing, a quirky superstition engaged in by an otherwise reasonable and wise old man. Did he really know something that I didn't? I considered for a moment then decided there's never going to be a time better than the present, so here goes; God. If you're there and you're listening, we could sure use some help about now. Even a drop of water… Make that DRINKABLE water, would ease our pain a bit. I know I haven't looked for you, as I should have. I've just never had the time, but I'm here. Now. If you're ever going to make yourself known to me now might be a pretty good time. Thanks God.

Resting my back against the wall of the raft I pulled the parachute down so that my head stuck out and lay looking at more stars than I thought could possibly exist. I had done nothing more than sit in a boat all day sleeping and yet I was physically spent. My head hurt terribly, my throat hurt worse. My tongue was beginning to crack and though I couldn't see it, I was sure it was bleeding, for I tasted blood. My lips were swollen and felt like two pieces of sandpaper being rubbed together. What I wouldn't give for a cold glass of water? The list was a short one, my wife and child. Pretty much anything else I'd ever possessed or ever would possess I'd forfeit for a single glass of ice water, cold and refreshing, beaded sweat on the rim, moisture condensed out of the surrounding air. I was fantasizing about a glass of liquid like I did about naked women when I was fifteen. I'd read tales, some fiction, some actual accounts, of men who'd endured days without food or water. Intellectually I thought I understood what it was to be truly thirsty, but I was wrong. I couldn't know the pain involved, the incapacitating weakness suffered by not having water until I experienced it myself. I grimaced, thinking, "I'm only just approaching twenty-four hours of this hell." Knowing it would continue to get worse, though in my wildest imagination I couldn't fathom how, I again drifted off to sleep.

The morning brought with it new pain, new suffering, new longing, developing ever so slowly. Insidious is the word, a death that creeps up while we're lost in the morass of our suffering, metastasizing unnoticed, but unabated. Sometime in the night, masked by my sleeping, a new constellation of torture invaded. I awoke to pain in my chest, each breath inflicting a sharp searing pain as my trachea and bronchi, devoid of lubricating moisture, dried and cracked, fragmenting a bit more with each inhalation. A unique, exquisite pain, sharp as a razor, I began to feel short of breath, not because I couldn't breathe, but because it was torturous to do so. No one talked. It hurt too much to set one's thick-as-shoe-leather vocal cords into motion, let alone waste the breath to do so.

I spent more time peering into the soul of the others through the portal of their eyes than I had ever been bold enough to do. In polite society, gaze is averted after but briefly engaging, even if the voice continues to communicate. Talking is filtered, words and ideas conveyed, censored by one's conventions and sense of propriety. Not so looking into the eyes of another, subtle but revealed, nothing hidden, nothing filtered. After a while, people can communicate on a level not attainable by words or language alone. So it was in this, our raft prison. A *while* was all we had, all we shared. Being too much alone inside your mind can be a beautiful thing, but it can also be torturous, a maddening journey to parts of oneself previously unknown.

Our raft seemed to be slowly drifting westward toward the Asian mainland. At its present rate of travel I had little delusion any of us would survive long enough to see the coast of China. No Allies. No Japanese. No sharks. No death save for CJ, whose spirit, I prayed, had soared away, oblivious to the suffering of his friends, we the survivors of the crash more to be pitied. No one yet to snatch the golden ring and claim us, the prize, the reward of us to be captured or rescued, but released all the same, even if only the release of our spirits from the confines of our present hell. Perhaps that's it! I'd died and now was in hell, an eternity to spend in my present state. The thought truly frightened me. Even in the heat of the day I felt a cold chill transcend my body. What if this was all there was forever? There are things that are far worse than dying. Nothingness is better than this. Nothingness is what I sought in sleep. To that end, I drifted in and out of a dream world, more often unconscious than lucid, a world habited, to my delight, by my beloved Mary, but also by strange creatures. Flying sharks and ferocious black dogs, of colors that were palpable and sounds to be smelled. I was just telling Mary how I'd never noticed how wonderful and fulfilling Yellow felt when the real world rocked, returning me again to lucidity and pain.

Everyone had been awakened and was now silently questioning, "What the hell is going on?" Looking about, I saw no change. After a minute or two I relaxed my guard and began dozing when, startlingly, the raft rocked again, this time the entire side of the raft raised up free of the water only to fall again with a loud Fwap.

"Oh shit, they've found us! Sharks!" I tried to shout, my voice sounding more a raspy wind than an alarm. I drew my .45 from its holster, as did Skip, and waited for the next blow.

"Careful not to hit the raft or we're dead just the same," I said to him as we both stood to find our nemesis.

"You watch that side, I'll watch this one." Within seconds, the raft under my feet heaved violently, knocking me backward. I would have fallen over the side had Bledsoe not grabbed me. Skip opened fire, getting off five rounds. I saw the shark's eye, a glimpse into a soul of pure evil, if such characteristics can be ascribed to any creature other than man. I shuddered, having seen the heart of my enemy.

"Did you get him?"

"I tagged him at least once, but I don't know if that killed him. That's a big fuckin' fish." We again waited for another strike. Next time we saw him coming. He'd swung wide and was rapidly heading toward us like a torpedo; his dorsal fin belied a massive body skimming just below the surface. Skip and I both opened fire, which didn't seem to deter the beast in the least. As the massive shark rammed us, striking this time at the waterline rather than from below, the raft again pitched up with seismic force before slapping down. The tremendous blow knocked both of us to our knees, but the raft, thankfully appeared undamaged. I thought, "This thing is going to get us before we get him," then I noticed several trails of blood in the water. We'd hit our mark numerous times. The prehistoric predator just didn't know he was dead, his blood baiting all his shark brothers to come to the frenzy. The ocean boiled red as smaller sharks devoured the injured, there being as much honor among sharks as among men. Would they come again en masse to attack us, or would their feast satiate ravenous appetites? We watched in silence with renewed vigor, born of fear, for well over an hour, well after the last bloody vestiges of would-be attackers disappeared below the surface.

After the shark attack it was 3:00 p.m., the heat of the day. We retreated to the shade of our canopy and fell exhausted once again into the embrace of sleep.

I awoke several hours later to the voice of Jim, raspy and foreign saying, "Major... Major, wake up."

"What is it Jim?" I asked, not opening my eyes.

"It's just that, well...We've got to do something about CJ. He's really getting ripe."

"I know. I've been putting it off hoping we might get rescued. I suppose we need to go ahead. Everyone else agree?" While this was a dictatorship and

I its leader, I resorted to the rules of democracy in this case, offering each man a vote. It was important to have a consensus on whatever we decided to do in this situation, as the next person dead could easily be any one of us. It would be comforting to know whatever the survivors might do with my mortal remains, it would be done with respect. The other boys felt the same. The bounds of respect represent a social convention and thus need to be established democratically. Looking each man in the eye, I took tally, and soon was sure of everyone's opinion save for Jordy, whose febrile mind was devoid of rationality.

"Jordy? Jordy, do you have an opinion on what we do about CJ?" Jordy stared through me, his eyes not focusing upon me, but upon a distant realm known only to him.

"I think we have a consensus. We need something to weight him down, or his body will just float and drift along with us. Any ideas?"

"I've got the pack from my chute and the pressure bottle from the raft weighs about fifteen pounds if you think that's enough," Bledsoe was quick to offer. "I wish we had a sheet or something to wrap around him, but I don't think we dare use the canopy." We all agreed that CJ would not want us to risk exposing ourselves so that he could have a burial shroud.

"Good thinking, Bledsoe. The bag and bottle should do it if we soak the bag so it doesn't have any buoyancy itself." He hung the bag into the water as I asked, "Anyone have something to say? A prayer or psalm or something?"

"Jordy was our man of the cloth. Too bad he can't say something. CJ would have liked that." We all agreed.

"I know the Twenty-Third Psalm," Jim offered. Bledsoe affixed the weighted bag to CJ's boots as Jim recited the scripture he knew from Sunday school, "The Lord is my shepherd, I shall not want…." Deep from within the recesses of his brain, Jordy began to recite the same verses. There would have been no dry eyes in the boat if any of us had been hydrated enough to make tears. When we finished, Jordy went back to his delirious dream world. Bledsoe hoisted the bag over the side as Skip and I placed CJ's body up on the wall of the raft. As we were preparing to let him go, Bledsoe said, "Wait, get his tags."

"You're right!" I retrieved the dog tags from around CJ's unyielding neck. It seemed very eerie; I had never before touched a dead body in this stage of rigor mortis. I slipped the chain and tags around my own, more compliant neck and then together we hefted CJ over the side.

"Good-bye, my friend," I said saluting as CJ sank into the deep embrace of his watery resting place. The others saluted as well, save for Jordy who remained unaware and Jim, whose shoulders were both broken. It wasn't much of a ceremony, but it was meaningful and respectful just the same. While I'm sure each of us would like to have done more, given our circumstances it was the best we had to offer. We consoled ourselves with the notion that CJ would have been pleased, not necessarily with the lack of pomp, but with the attitudes of our hearts.

"Only thing else he would have wanted was a joke or two," Bledsoe said. We all laughed and agreed, then settled back into contemplative silence for the longest time before he slyly said, "Black titties," to which we broke into peals of hoarse laughter, save for Skip and Doc, who had not been party to CJ's joke. Joe then regaled us with every joke from CJ's ribald liturgy he could recall, each funnier than the last. We all laughed till we cried. CJ would have loved it.

Distraction from our physical misery even in the form of a shark attack and a funeral-come-comedy routine had been a good thing. The sun was still high in the western sky, and we endured the hottest part of the day with the canopy folded, allowing contemplation of the endless sky, watching its evolution in color from jewelesque blue to azure, warm yellow sunlight of evening adding hints of green before yielding to reds, pinks and purples. The first stars of evening finally began to appear along with Venus, one or two at first, but soon thousands, millions, even billions perhaps, illuminated the sky, certainly more than could be counted and named. At long last I again found sleep and Mary and little John. John had turned two years old in March, having never once laid eyes upon his erstwhile father. If it didn't rain soon, he probably never would. I could imagine him though, conjure up images in my mind of what he must look and sound like. I could only hope what we were doing here might save him from one day having to do the same. If that desire comes true, then all the pain and loss has been well spent, endured to purchase such a prize. A pipe dream, a delusion, I know, but having now witnessed firsthand the atrocities of which man is capable, a dream worthy of any loss. God had dreamed it, too, 'Peace on earth, good will toward men.' I have a new appreciation of that familiar scripture now. I slept soundly despite the pain, drifting as we were, slowly westward.

I was awakened by the wind the following morning, a gentle and wispy zephyr, feeling like a velvety balm, soothing my sunburned face. My skin felt thick, stiff like tanned leather, making it an effort to move even my hands, my toes, my face. Opening my eyes proved a new, deeper breath of pain. Without tears to lubricate them, my eyelids were stuck together, and to the globes beneath, now sunken within their orbits. In desperation, willing to try any remedy, I dipped my hand into the ocean and rubbed the salt water into the slits from which my eyes once peered. Anticipating pain, the salt water was actually quite soothing. After several minutes I was finally able to open them, albeit painfully, to the morning light. Everyone else was still asleep, I alone noticed as the wind had picked up a bit. There was a high overcast, a thin layer of clouds, higher than I could fly an airplane. In the distance, perhaps twenty miles or so to the west, I saw, to my amazement, our immediate salvation. "Perhaps God does care," I said aloud, awakening the other boys. "Look at this!" Scattered across the horizon we saw rain showers, fresh drinkable water falling from intermittent clouds. If only one of those showers would continue long enough to fall upon us we might survive for a while longer. The showers appeared to be moving slowly to the east. If we sat stationary, the closest shower would miss us, passing south of us by a mile or more. "We've got to row!" I shouted hoarsely. "Any man able, grab something, anything and start paddling." With the prize being water, everyone aboard except Jordy and Jim forgot their pain and began frantically paddling. Our pace was slow, but we were indeed moving southward over the water to where we could intercept the rain shower. It reminded me of a story Mrs. Nethery told us of a Greek named Tantalus. Good old Tantalus upset Zeus by stealing Ambrosia, the nectar of the gods, and giving it to mortals to drink. Enraged, Zeus cast Tantalus into Tartarus, the Greeks version of Hell to be uniquely tormented for all eternity. It seems Tantalus was bound, standing in water under a fruit tree. Whenever he reached for fruit, the limbs pulled back to withhold their prize just beyond his reach. Likewise, when he bent to get a drink from the pool in which he stood, the water would recede and dry up, leaving him to forever thirst. This tale from Greek mythology is the basis for the English word tantalize. Forevermore I would have a newly found appreciation for the word, to be so close yet be denied. "Oh God, be the God of the Jews and the Christians, not the ancient Greeks," I thought.

Non-stop we worked. Incredibly, miraculously we worked, given our injuries and health.

After an hour and a half we were there, waiting in the path of a summer shower and praying aloud, "Oh God, don't let it change directions or, worse yet, don't let it stop raining." Men aboard the rubber raft, men previously dead in anticipation of dying were now animated, frenetic in anticipation of living if but a little longer. We could smell it on the wind long before we could taste it, feel it as it fell, revel in it. And then it was there! I turned my face skyward, letting the cool rain pool into my mouth before swallowing, an orgasmic, overwhelming, release of pent up wanting, life giving, life sustaining, life altering. After drinking more than we should, three of us stood holding aloft the parachute canopy to catch and retain as much of the glorious liquid bounty as possible. We had only one canteen and nothing else in which to store the water collected. Thinking more quickly after a little hydration, I took my bowie knife and cut a wide piece of the silk. Taking that swath, I folded it to create a crude bag several layers thick. Seeing our creation would not long contain liquid, I took a tube of salve from the survival kit and covered the outer layer of the bag with the thick, viscous ointment. Eureka, it worked! We filled the bag with the water collected just as the saving rain slowed to a slight drizzle. By God's grace and our ingenuity, we now had almost two gallons of water to satisfy our needs. We could now survive for at least a couple more days, if we were judicious in its consumption. I gave Skip the job of guarding it with his life. "No one touches that bag without my permission, understand?" He clutched his holstered .45 and nodded to say "No one will get close to this bag without being shot." He meant it. So did I. However, the rainwater that had collected within the bottom of the raft remained fair game for all as long as it might last. "Drink that water up, boys. In this open raft it will only evaporate. Better in your bellies than in the air." The act of drinking from the bottom of a raft was interesting to watch. Like Gideon of old, I watched as some men bent down to lap up the water, as would a dog, while others scooped it to drink from cupped hands.

The line of showers continued their slow march to the east. The sky was our only point of reference, the cloud movement gave the false perception that our raft was drifting rapidly, ever westward. Soon the sky above was clear, gone was the shelter from the noonday sun and out again came our parachute canopy, a bit disfigured, but still functional for our present purposes. With new hope and moistened membranes, the men were chatty, quietly talking about our rescue, our future, our mission, our lives. Our minds were back from the dregs of death, full of questions, but strangely, given the events of the last three days, not *if* questions, but *when* questions, queries requiring answers that presupposed a future, resembling the future of our past and not necessarily the future of our present. How long would it take to get a new ship? Would we be given some time off, maybe even some time back in the States? How long till Jordy was better and walking again? Who would be the next women Bledsoe would nonchalantly bed? That was my favorite question as it had some brace of reality and set off a lively, albeit raucous rant of the type CJ often led. Bledsoe was ever the gentleman, even in this situation, oblivious as always to the jealousy of the mere mortal men around him.

Relaxed now, our immediate crises having been at least temporarily resolved, we talked for hours, speaking out of boredom as much as anything else. We talked of home and of life, childhood memories, school, and baseball. Oddly enough for a boat full of men being tested, stressed and stretched to the breaking point, our conversation remained light and casual, something to help us ignore the slow pace at which time seemed to be passing. Einstein was right, the passage of time is relative to the observer. The bias of our perceptions, real or imagined, was a double-edged sword. Knowing with each passing moment our chances of surviving waned, one would think it wise to desire time to pass more slowly, and yet boredom generated by that perception begs for the clock to turn as fast as a propeller. Regardless of our perceptions, time passes, marching on into eternity without fail. The sick and injured among us would be the first to go, one at a time, leaving the others to cast their remains into the sea. The last man living would be the only one deprived of final acts of human kinship, not mourned by anyone present, his prize for being the strongest being his remains left to drift in the life raft until, as one, they sank or washed unheeded ashore. At that point would it still be a *life* raft? I puzzled the ironic semantics alone, unshared with the others. Was I alone in my calculations of the end, an end, regardless of the means, which I thought was imminent? Surely not! I suspect we all had done the math alone in the solitude of our minds, grisly math, more daunting than any calculus or Boolean geometry theorems to be contemplated by greater minds than ours. There perhaps remain variables to be considered and tried, but the value of X will soon be determined. It was now just a matter of time before the great professor says, "Time's up, close your exam books and place your pencils on your desks."

I was just about to drift off to sleep when Bledsoe said, "Did anyone else hear that?"

"Hear what?"

"An airplane!" At Bledsoe's alarm we all again immediately bristled like a pack of hungry wolves, sensing prey, hyper alert. At first I heard nothing as I scanned the sky, hoping against hope, and then, there it was in the distance, a small single-engine aircraft. No, make that two…no, three!

"We're saved," Skip shouted, quickly pulling the flair gun from its container.

"No, not yet!" I shouted, but my words fell upon ears deafened by the prospect of being rescued. He aimed the gun skyward as in desperation I tackled him, both of us falling overboard, landing in the water.

"Damn it Skip, What if they're Japs?" I could tell by the look on his face he had not considered that possibility.

"Be still everyone! Don't move until we know." Skip and I treaded water, an anxious two minutes passing before we could make out the silhouettes. The three *Zeros* passed over us at, I'm guessing, 10,000 feet, thankfully without seeing us. Had they seen us, I know from firsthand reports they would have fired upon us.

"I'm sorry, Major. I just thought that…"

"No, Captain, that's the problem. You didn't think. If we're to survive you had better get your brain into the game," I said, not trying to hide my exasperation.

"Yes, sir," he snapped back coldly, before rolling over to swim to the raft.

"Thank you, Major," Bledsoe said as he pulled me back to the safety of the raft. As I dried in the late afternoon sun, I watched the sky almost continually. Before dusk we saw three more contingents of three *Zeros* each flying southward. Each squad oblivious to our presence, they flew over at roughly the same altitude as they continued to climb.

"Boys, I'm thinking we must be close to a Jap airfield, there must be an island just over the horizon. They all seem to be coming from that direction and climbing," I said, pointing in the direction my suspicions suggested, lying on the same westward heading we'd been drifting for two days now.

"What are we going to do, Major? Jim asked, the sincerity of his tone belaying his innocence.

"Yeah, Major, what are we gonna do?" Skip said, his tone betraying his heart as well.

"We seem to be on the flight path. I think that's a good thing, as they're probably too busy to notice us as they climb out. I guess the real question is whether or not we try to make for that island."

"Are you fucking nuts?" Skip spat back. I turned to wordlessly stare him down. After several seconds of mutual animosity I continued. "We're too close to the Japs for the good guys to come looking for us. That narrows down our options. If the Japs see us on the water we're dead. If we paddle away from the island and don't soon find another, we're dead." I looked around to see if my words were sinking in. "If we try to land on that island and we're captured, we're dead, but if we can land and stay hidden we just might have a chance."

"Fat chance," Skip said sarcastically.

"The way I do the math it's the only chance we've got." I waited for their consideration before saying, "I say we take it. What say you?" Bledsoe was the first to speak. "You've brought us this far, Major. I'd follow you anywhere!"

"Thanks Bledsoe, that means a lot." The others, save Jordy, who was not able to weigh in, quickly joined. Only Skip remained skeptical, his skepticism borne more of his dislike of me than of the soundness of the plan itself.

The existence of the island remained only theory, as it was not yet visible on the horizon. Our job was to stay undiscovered until we could find that island. Since the crash, we had not had the need to post a watch, but that now changed. Our survival would depend upon us knowing the whereabouts of the Japs before they could discover the same of us. Jim took the first watch saying, "My arms don't work so good, but there's nothing wrong with my eyes."

"Good man, who's next?" Bledsoe was quick to volunteer.

"Good. Jim you watch till 0130 then Bledsoe can take over. The rest of you boys get some shut-eye. I want you to conserve your strength. I have a feeling we may find ourselves very busy in the next twenty-four hours. With any luck we'll be on dry ground this time tomorrow.

At 0300 Bledsoe woke me up. "Major, Major, wake up. I see an island. I couldn't see it till the moon rose high enough." There it was, two, maybe three miles to the west, a single peak rising above a blanket of sea mist.

"Have you seen any activity?"

"No, sir. What's the plan?" Stripping off my boots and clothes down to my shorts I said, "I'm gonna go for a little swim. With a little luck I can pull us ashore before dawn. If not, we're sitting ducks. What are you doing?" I asked as he stripped down as well.

"Two of us swimming, we can make it for sure."

"Remember the sharks? I don't think you should."

"Sorry, Major, unless that's an order…Even if it is, I'm helping you," He said, undeterred. I nodded understanding, as I would have done the same.

"Thanks," I said and dove in, Bledsoe following suit. We each tied a bow rope over our shoulders and began swimming, hard at first, but after fifteen minutes I had to rest. Bledsoe humored me and did the same.

"I think we'd better pace ourselves if we're going to make it."

"Yeah, this boat is a lot of drag. I could have been there and back by now if it wasn't for the boat."

"I didn't know you were such a swimmer."

"When I was a kid we used to swim two miles across the Mississippi just for laughs."

"I guess that explains it, then," I said before renewing my efforts. We both began swimming, this time pacing ourselves. Pulling the raft was much like trying to pull a pickup truck uphill, the forward progress exceedingly slow. I was constantly expecting to be pulled under the water, entrapped within the massive jaws of a shark. After three hours Bledsoe and I were spent but satisfied, having reached the shore. Together we pulled the raft onto an uninhabited and apparently unsecured stretch of beach. We had made landfall half an hour before sunrise, the cover of darkness save for the light of a crescent moon, having hidden our arrival from enemy Asian eyes. Wading ashore, the earth felt weighty and substantial, solid under my feet after three days subject to the elastic surfaces of the raft. I collapsed, so breathless I could barely speak, all of my remaining energy spent getting my crew safely ashore. Bledsoe and I sat in the shallow water gathering our wits; our chests heaving, coughing up ingested salt water.

I smiled at him with eyes closed and nodded my head to say, "Well done." Finally able to talk I added, "I couldn't have done it without you."

"Do you think the Japs are on this island, Major?"

"I don't know. I'm going to assume yes, and insist everyone remain hidden until we can establish the fact."

He nodded before saying, "Then there is something I want from you Major."

I looked at him puzzled, "Go on…"

"I want your dog tags."

"And why, may I ask, do you want my dog tags?"

"Because the Japs want *you* specifically, Major. You've got CJ's tags around your neck. From this point on you're Captain Carl Jonathon Murphy," he said, lifting the tags from around my neck to read, "Serial number 47-2630. If we get caught the Japs won't know any different." He searched my eyes for some measure of understanding as I considered the wisdom of his words. Cunning and clever, he was exactly right. The Japs knew my name, but they didn't, I'm guessing, know my face. I would just be another American prisoner, not their prize.

"You know Bledsoe, you're a pretty smart fella."

"I like to think so," he laughed. "Go pick a tree on the shoreline and bury your tags under it. After we get rescued you can come back and dig 'em up." I did just as Bledsoe suggested, careful to remember the precise tree, then hurried back to help him get the men into the jungle. They had all slept as we swam, and were surprised to awaken ashore. Together, Bledsoe and I corralled the sleep-stunned men into the jungle to be hidden beneath dense undergrowth before the light of dawn betrayed our arrival. I was just about to relax when I remembered, "Damn it, the raft!" Seeing no Japanese, I ran back to the empty craft that had at once been both our prison and our salvation. Like the *China Doll*, it was a tool that had served us well. It hurt my heart, but I quickly punctured its side with my bowie knife, rapidly deflating it and dragged it into the jungle and out of sight. Dragging it over the path we had taken, I erased our footprints from the volcanic sand. I felt a bit like Hernando Cortez, who in 1519 prevented the retreat of his men from the mainland of the new world by burning his own ships, a fact I learned in eighth grade. Right or wrong, we were here to stay. I lay down on the hidden remains of the raft and thought, "Thank you, Mrs. Nethery, wherever you are."

CHAPTER 18

I slept my first real sleep in four days, deep and rejuvenating, hidden beneath the dangling roots of a banyan tree until awakened by the low pitched rumble of an idling marine motor. My subconscious incorporated the mechanical sound into a dream before I awoke, rejoining the real world with a start. Though disrupting my slumber, the engine noise had simultaneously sounded the alarm and answered Bledsoe's question; the Japs are here! The sound emanated from a heavily armed Japanese patrol boat making what I assumed was a daily, if not more frequent, inspection of the island's perimeter. I rolled onto my belly in the dense undergrowth, cautious not to be seen, to watch the enemy motor by, looking at, but not really seeing, the exact spot on the beach where we had landed. I looked at my wristwatch to note the time, 1510. If they noticed anything peculiar or suspicious they gave no indication, but continued cruising slowly south, following the island's contours about forty feet out from the shore. The craft moved slowly, the meandering pace of men who had performed the same task every day, day after day, month after month, without ever even once having been rewarded with the object of their search. The phenomenon observed was a product of human nature, regardless of race or culture. In the beginning I'm sure those patrols were dutifully performed by earnest, diligent men suspicious of an enemy around every bend, but after performing the monotonous task ad infinitum without reward, it was only a matter of time before the job was performed by the act of going through memorized motions, devoid of thought and the vigilance required to actually perform the task. Or, maybe we were just lucky and the island was patrolled by a group of Japanese buffoons, a scenario I highly doubted. In either case, the outcome was the same; our landing had gone thankfully unnoticed.

We all stayed hidden, separated by short distances. I knew the men had seen the patrol boat, for I could hear their anxious, then relieved whispers. After waiting several minutes to be sure the coast was clear, we met around the group of scrub bushes hiding Jordy, an impromptu congregation of primary concern. He looked bad, pitiful in the truest sense of the word, but still I sought confirmation from our medicine man.

"How is he?" I asked, already knowing the answer.

"He won't last out the day without some antibiotics. Probably wouldn't last even if we had some," Doc said solemnly. He wasn't predicting anything our non-medical eyes couldn't discern for themselves.

"Maybe we'll find some," I said hopefully.

"You mean steal some," Bledsoe added knowingly.

"Yeah. The Japs must have some. We've just got to figure out where."

"Better make it quick," Doc added.

"With all due respect, Major, this is a foolhardy notion. Are you willing to risk all your men for the sake of one who probably won't make it anyway?"

"You mean to offer me NO respect, Captain, but I'll put it to a vote. All in favor of stealing antibiotics from the Japs along anything else we can get our hands on say aye.

"Aye" was the response from everyone except Jordy and Skip. "I've got to try, Captain. I can't just let this kid lie here and die without putting up some kind of fight on his behalf. Besides, we have the advantage, the Japs don't know we're here."

"And if you fuck up they will."

"I don't like your tone, Captain."

"And I don't like your plan, Major. You have a responsibility to every man here, yet you're willing to put all of us at risk for a kid who's not gonna survive, regardless of what you do." Now I was mad, angry enough to punch his smug, condescending face into a bloody pulp. Bledsoe saw my stance, my hands tightening into fists and stepped between us.

"Don't do it, Major, he's not worth it." I shouted over Bledsoe's shoulder as he jockeyed to keep us separated, "I made a promise to every man in this crew long before you joined us that I would do everything in my power to see them home safe. I mean to do just that!" Skip glared at me, transmitting unadulterated hatred before retreating, knowing that in a fair fight I'd best him. Bledsoe Courage was right again; Skip wasn't worth busting up my hands over.

Regaining my composure a bit, I finally said, "Here's the plan. Jim, I'm appointing you quartermaster." He looked happy to be included. Even injured I knew he wanted to contribute, so I gave him a job his injuries shouldn't preclude. "Take stock of what provisions we have. Doc, you stay here with Jordy and keep him hidden. We know the Japs patrol the beach, so everyone stay in the bush, away from the shore. Bill, you start looking for fresh water. Food and shelter would be nice, but water first."

"Shelter, sir?"

"A cave perhaps, something hidden in the jungle. Keep in mind there is probably an airfield here, so being exposed to the sky is not a good thing. Bledsoe and I are going to the top of the mountain to get the lay of the land. From there we can hopefully see any Japanese encampments. If we have any chance of stealing from the Japs it will be tonight." Every face looked disappointed at my last statement, knowing that for Jordy time was of the essence. "We can't very well just go in guns ablaze and take it. We've got very limited ammo, even if we were stupid enough."

"Does that mean we're gonna just sit here and hide from the fuckers?"

"Choose your battle, Skip. Two minutes ago you wanted to stay hidden. Which one is it?"

He had no answer. He just wanted to be on whatever side I was not.

"First things first, gentlemen. Let's get settled in. We can plan our conquest of the Japanese mainland when we're ready. Skip, for now, go plant yourself somewhere you can see the shoreline. Was that patrol this morning a regularly scheduled event or was it a fluke?"

"Yes, sir," he said docilely, his attempt at trying to reestablish with me some semblance of military decorum. I'm sure he had sorted out where everyone's loyalty lay and decided he'd better behave himself. I appreciated the effort. I had enough enemies to fight on the island without having to worry about fighting my own men.

Bledsoe and I began our long trek through dense tropical vegetation. It was clear there had not been any creatures as large as humans pass this way in a very long time. It took us an hour to traverse only 300 yards and a gentle incline. We were perhaps ten feet higher in altitude than when started, but the walk from that point on became dramatically steeper. It soon became more of a climb than a walk. The vegetation that so hindered us at the beginning now provided us with handholds and leafy platforms on which to step. It would have been almost impossible to climb if the mountain had been devoid of plant life. Not only did it aid in our climbing, it hid our presence from the Japanese who surely would have seen us without its protection. We'd heard aircraft overhead a couple of times, but were unable to see them. It was a pretty safe assumption the reverse was true as well. After another hour we had reached a level just shy of a clearing in the canopy of trees and stopped to catch our breath. I was feeling powerful hunger pangs, having eaten nothing since we arrived on the island, and next to nothing since the crash.

"Sure wish you had some of that fried chicken, Bledsoe."

"Would you settle for some K-rations?" he asked, pulling two thin, worn tins from his pocket. "I don't have the whole meal, but I've got the cans if you'd like?"

"Hell yes, Bledsoe, you're the best!" We pried the tins open with our knives and devoured the contents, a viscous bullion paste tasting vaguely of chicken. As we sat eating I noticed for the first time the faint sound of rapidly running water. It sounded like a stream, two, maybe three hundred yards to the south.

"We'll look for the source of that tomorrow," I said, nodding in the direction of what I assumed was a mountain stream. The sound was consoling as it meant there was fresh water to be found on this side of the island. It had to end up somewhere, a pool or stream empting into the ocean.

We had landed on the eastern side of the island and by the time we had awakened and started our exploration, the sun had disappeared over the crest of the mountain. We climbed in the shade of that mountain, ever ascending toward the light awaiting us at the top, another 400 feet above our present position.

"How long you think, Major?" Bledsoe asked, gesturing at the top.

"Another hour or two. We'd better get moving if we want to see the sights before it gets dark." He nodded in agreement and wordlessly we both resumed our trudge.

I walked five feet behind Bledsoe Courage on our way to the top, pondering the inequities of military life made manifest before me. Bledsoe was bright and courageous, a natural leader. The most completely unflappable man in any situation I've ever met. Growing up poor and lacking for opportunities, Bledsoe had no college education, a deficit automatically relegating him to the duties of an underling. Meanwhile, men like Skip were automatically made officers, not based on their abilities but on the fact their daddies could afford to send them to a prestigious school. Skip wasn't stupid; he was just a guy with average intelligence and a family trust fund. Why did that justify giving him a position of leadership when he was so obviously suited for following? Maybe it's an unfair juxtaposition, because Bledsoe makes everyone else look bad in comparison. I just know I'd personally prefer to follow a man like Bledsoe into battle than lead a man like Skip to the market.

With much exertion as well as the scratches and bruises naturally acquired when trespassing inhospitable terrain intended by God to be passable only at great cost, we reached the crest of the mountain. I had hoped for a grand vista, but from the mountaintop the view was just more of the same jungle flora and fauna we had been looking at for the last several hours. At the ridgeline of the mountain grew a grove of coconut palms each fifty feet or more in height. Bledsoe studied the trees for a few minutes, then said, "Give me your belt, Major. I'll go scope out the situation." Puzzled, I took off my belt and gave it him as requested. He fastened his and my belts together around the tallest palm tree and his waist and began working his way up the tree.

"Bledsoe, you're a genius. Where'd you learn to do that?'

"I worked one summer as a lineman for the telephone company in New Orleans. The foreman always made the new guys go up the pole, so I got pretty good at it. It's a lot easier with ankle spikes, but this will work, too."

"Just be careful."

"Not to worry, Major. I could do this in my sleep." In next to no time Bledsoe was in the fronds atop a fifty-foot tree looking down, making mental notes about the geography of the island as well as any signs of civilization. Working his way back down he said, "Well, the Japs are sure here. The island's pretty small, shaped like a deep crescent around a shallow harbor, which opens to the northwest. Ten, maybe fifteen miles from tip to tip and no more than five miles wide at it's widest. The mountain we're on is about one third the way up from the bottom of the crescent. We're at the highest point, but it extends down the south east side of the island like a back bone." Finally back on the ground, he took his knife and with its tip, sketched out a map of what he had just told me. "There isn't any beach from here on around, the mountain falls straight down to the ocean, just a sheer cliff. The water we heard running spills over the side, a narrow waterfall right into ocean. The Japs have an airfield right here, 4500 feet max. I counted thirteen *Zeros*, a *Zeke*, and two *Bettys*. A fuel dump sits here between the end of the runway and the harbor. There was a submarine in the harbor, but way out at the mouth, tied up to a patrol boat like the one we saw this morning. The harbor is too shallow to let it come in. There were two other patrol boats and a dock at the eastern side of the harbor, and a bunch of little fishing boats tied up on the other side."

"Natives?"

"That'd be my guess. They were here by a small village. There looks to be a garrison of some sort here and an enclave of tents, maybe twenty or so right here."

"Any clue where an infirmary might be?"

"There was a tent with a red cross like a hospital here," he said pointing at his crude map with the tip of his knife.

"The jungle stops here, right by the tents. We can stay hidden in the jungle almost to the infirmary. We just have to make it past these three tents."

"Piece of cake," I said, trying to sound reassuring. "Let's get going."

"Wait, Major, there's more. There are antiaircraft guns here, here, and here. They're pretty much out in the open, but I think there may be some guns here, and here dug into the mountain to protect the harbor. This one here can't be more than a quarter mile away."

"Did you see anything on our side of the island?"

"No sir, but that doesn't mean there isn't"

"That explains the patrol boats. It gives them some sense of security. An attacker coming from the south east would have to go over the top of the mountain to get to them."

"We'd best be really careful going down that side of the hill. We could find ourselves in the midst of some Japs real quick." I nodded agreement.

"I'm thinking the best way back might just be around the island rather than trying to cross the ridge at night. Won't be much of a moon tonight. I'm thinking we just wait till after dark and walk right in and take what we need."

"That was pretty much my plan. I'm hoping it won't be too hard, as the security should be pretty lax. I don't recall this island on any of our charts.

They've been here probably the whole war without being noticed. This island hasn't been attacked because we didn't know it was here till now. I'm counting on the men here being complacent, their routine rarely, if ever, challenged. My bet is we won't see a soul tonight, except for a sentry or two who've watched so long without seeing anything they've become blind. The trick is not only not to get caught, but not to take so much of anything it gets noticed."

"You've given this a lot of thought, Major."

"That's my biggest fault. I overthink everything I do."

"Well, that's better than someone like Skip who doesn't appear to give any thought at all to anything he does."

"The men don't like him very much, do they?"

"I don't know if *like* is a good word. The men don't respect him much. I'd say they like him just fine."

"It's too bad he's not you."

"Excuse me, sir?"

"I was just thinking today what a fine officer you would make. A real credit to the Army."

"Well thank you, sir…I think?"

"Oh it's a compliment. It's just you're a natural leader, and you're smart. Men *do* respect you, Bledsoe. Me included." The man actually blushed at my compliment.

"Thank you, sir."

The trek down the mountain was easier when we first began the descent, but seemed to get more difficult the longer we walked, stressing and stretching muscles other than those used on the way up. We climbed down as fast as we could, seeing the daylight quickly waning, reaching the enclave of tents Bledsoe had described just before dusk. Concealed at the jungle's edge, we sat observing the rhythms of the comings and goings in the Japanese camp. Gone was the discipline borne of immediacy, replaced with a blasé indifference to what might happen, the spawn of monotony. The men relaxed as all soldiers do in the company of other men, only men, inventing ways to pleasantly pass the time. There was a card game in the nearest tent with men drinking and gambling, both unsanctioned and probably forbidden, but ignored just the same as superiors were engaged in the illicit activities as well as the enlisted. There were fifteen men in the tent at present, and no indication their evening's activities would soon dwindle. In the next tent were nine men lying in cots sleeping or reading, or writing to sweethearts or wives. In both tents, the activities so engrossed the inhabitants, I had little concern Bledsoe and I might not slip past in the dark unnoticed. The real gamble at present was choosing the location of the infirmary. We guessed it should be the third tent, a guess substantiated by the red cross painted on its top. The camp was dark, made darker by the moon rising on the other side of the mountain, the crest illuminated by a faint glow that seemed to suck the ambient light from everything below. There were two sentries patrolling the camp, a euphemism for their real activity, which seemed to be sitting by the harbor in a jeep-like vehicle, smoking cigarette after cigarette, the glowing orange embers the only light on that side of the camp. After an hour of observation little had changed other than the men in the second tent had finally surrendered to the darkness and were now snoring.

"Time to go," I whispered. Bledsoe silently nodded in agreement. Stealthily, we walked past the first gathering of men, cautious not to let our feet break a twig or emanate any sound that would be unanticipated in the night, then past the second group, all lost in sleep. Slipping into the third tent we stopped and looked and listened in the stillness for any signs of an inhabitant. The tent was indeed the infirmary, and thankfully empty of patients. There were six cots on the far wall, made up with sheets and pillows. In the center was an exam table, which, judging from the large unlit lamp, also doubled as an operating table. At the far end of the tent were three tall glass-enclosed cabinets. The first contained surgical instruments, the second gauze and bandages. The third held what we were seeking; at least we hoped that it held what we were seeking, as the bottles and packages contained within were all labeled in Japanese. "Fuck!" I mouthed silently. I had not anticipated this complication. How incredibly stupid could I be? My heart stopped yet again when I saw a keyhole on the handle. Slowly I turned the latch hoping I would not meet the resistance of a lock. Complacency won out again…the door popped open with a faint creak.

"Just take a little of everything and we'll figure it out later," Bledsoe whispered. I nodded agreement and began to fill both his and my pockets with the unknown substances. Surely to God one of these was an antibiotic. We took as much as we could carry, but not so much of any one thing as to bring attention to the theft. Having acquired at least one of every package and bottle, I silently closed the cabinet. On our way out of the tent Bledsoe noticed a pile of tin urinals. "Think they'd miss a couple?" he asked.

"Why do you want urinals?" I asked incredulously.

"Water!" Ah, of course. Bledsoe was a clever fellow. He took two and stuffed them into his shirt.

Pulling back the tent flap, we discovered the two sentries had moved and were now sitting, their jeep not more than fifteen feet away.

"What do we do now?" Bledsoe gestured with his hands. I pointed at the back wall and pantomimed lifting the tent wall and slipping under.

"I'll lift it up and you slip under, then you lift it up for me," I said barely audible. He nodded understanding. The tent side was a bit more taut than I anticipated and Bledsoe had to take the urinals from his shirt to slither under. He reached back under to retrieve them and I then got on my belly and waited for him to lift up the side for me. When after several seconds he still had not lifted the side I began to get anxious. I heard him tapping faintly on the tent canvas. Then I realized it was Morse code. .--- .- .--. .--. .. ..-. --.

J A P P I S S I N G. I stifled a laugh. Fifty feet from the back of the tent was an open trench latrine. Bledsoe had stuffed the urinals back into his shirt and was about to help me get under when he saw through the darkness a sleepy Jap soldier stumble from the second tent and to the latrine to relieve himself. Bledsoe stood motionless, pressed against the tent side, watching the unwary Jap stretch and yawn and scratch himself before voiding his bladder into the trench. I could hear the faint sound of urine splashing from my vantage point, a sound unmistakable to any man. I waited for what seemed several minutes before Bledsoe at last lifted up the wall to allow me to pass under.

We began walking northward at the jungle's edge, constantly vigilant before and behind, wary of any motion that might represent the enemy. After walking cautiously for several minutes we were several hundred yards away from the camp's unbounded perimeter. Stopping to look back one last time, we both began running, the urgency of our quest never quite forgotten, but now imminently recalled.

"That was almost too easy," I said as congratulatory.

"Do you think he'll still be alive?" Bledsoe asked in a loud whisper.

"I certainly hope so! Either way, we did what we had to do. I couldn't have lived in my own skin if we hadn't at least tried." We ran silently on, side by side. I knew Bledsoe felt the same.

Running at least three miles, we at last arrived at a point on the beach that looked vaguely familiar, so we stopped to catch our breath. After a bit we heard Skip call out, "Hey, over here." Bledsoe and I joined him in the undergrowth.

"Is he…?"

"Yes, but Doc says he won't be by morning. Did you have any trouble?"

"Piece of cake!" Bledsoe said quickly. Doc was anxious to see our haul saying, "What'd you get?"

"We don't know," I answered sheepishly.

"Don't know? If you didn't get some sulfa or penicillin this kid's gonna die!" I started emptying my pockets as Bledsoe did the same. Doc took the first packages then realized our conundrum. Giving me an exasperated look he said, "Shit!" Thinking for a few moments he said, "Maybe I can tell by the smell."

"Let's hope so," I said, as one by one we opened the queer little packages and passed them under Doc's nose.

"Don't know…don't know… Don't know… That one's morphine or some opiate… Don't know… Don't know…. That's it!" he said at last. "That's sulfa, I'm sure of it." The box contained a white granular powder that was presumably to be used topically, spreading the contents upon an open wound.

"Okay, how do we use this?"

Doc said, "Get the water. We'll mix the powder up like Kool-Aid and slowly pour it down his gullet."

"You can't inject it?"

"I could, but with what? No, this will have to do." Doc said, mixing up the malodorous potion. "We can't afford to waste any of this, so let's try to give him a little drink of water first." I held his nose and opened his jaw as Doc poured in an ounce or two of water. Jordy coughed and sputtered as I repeatedly said, "C'mon Jordy, drink." After the first mouthful, Jordy reflexively began to swallow.

"Keep giving him water for a bit. He's dry as a chip and the water may help him more than the sulfa." Eight ounces later Doc said, "Okay, let's give this a try." He put the concoction to Jordy's lips and slowly began to pour it into his open, but still unaware, mouth. Again, reflexively, Jordy swallowed and continued swallowing until the medicine was consumed.

"Now if he can just keep it down. We've done all we can do."

"Except pray," I was quick to add.

"Now that we have some morphine, I may be able to fix Jim's shoulders," Doc said, happy to have something positive to say. He had tried to put one of his shoulders back into socket on the first day we were in the raft, but with no pain medicine and lacking a rigid surface that would not give way when heavy forces were applied, he had been unsuccessful. Doc took the package he had identified as an opiate and mixed it with water giving it Jim to drink. Within thirty minutes Jim was sound asleep, his muscles flaccid. Doc took his shoes off as we all wondered just what the hell he was up to.

"A couple of you guys hold him down now and I'll get him fixed." Still wondering what was about to happen, Bledsoe and I complied with Doc's instructions and grabbed hold of Jim so he couldn't move. Doc then put his foot into Jim's armpit and grabbed his arm, pulling traction against his foot. Jim woke up and started swearing and trying to get away, but Bledsoe and I held him down. This continued for about thirty seconds before Jim's shoulder made a SHLUNK sound, at which point Jim again became quiet. Doc relaxed his grip and asked, "How's that feel?"

"That's better, Doc."

"Good, lets get the other one done, too." Jim groggily nodded. Doc switched sides, puting his foot in Jim's other armpit, repeating the procedure, complete with Jim again swearing. It took a bit longer this time, but Doc's efforts were eventually met with the same SHLUNK. Now Jim relaxed, completely oblivious to the world. Doc took each of his arms and moved them to emulate Jim touching his opposite shoulder. "That's good. You can't do that if the shoulders are dislocated. He's pretty sleepy and I have no idea how much medication I gave him. Major, if you'll take your knife and cut enough cloth out of the parachute to make a sling for both arms, I think we've got him fixed. We'll put him over by Jordy where I can keep an eye on both of them."

"You've got Jim fixed?' I asked.

"Yep! Both his shoulders were dislocated when he came through that window. I can't begin to imagine how much that hurt, but he should be fine now, just sore for a few days." That said, the long vigil began, each of us taking turns watching, except for Doc, who left their sides only to relieve himself. Jim's breathing got pretty shallow at times over the next several hours and Doc would slap him or pinch him, anything to stimulate Jim as a reminder to breath. After about six hours, he awakened, excited that he could move his arms without excruciating pain.

"Don't try to move them just yet. Your shoulder joints were dislocated for several days and need a chance to heal properly."

"You don't understand, Doc, I couldn't breathe without pain before you fixed me. Thank you! I feel better than I've ever felt in my life."

"I'm not a doctor, not yet anyway."

"You're the best damn doctor I ever saw," Jim said, his eyes teary and grateful.

"Thanks, Jim, that means a lot to me."

While Bledsoe and I were off scavenging, Bill had been successful in foraging food. First and foremost were coconuts. The tall, indigenous palms could be found all over the island and, like a Godsend, would assure no matter how long we were stranded on this little crescent of dry land we would not die of starvation. He had devised a way of cracking open the stubborn fruit by placing the coconut on a large stone with a cup-shaped indentation, then striking it with another large stone, crude but effective. After the first few, he became more and more adept at cracking the nuts without completely breaking them, thus retaining most if not all the sweet milk-like liquid each contained. We then pried them open the rest of the way and feasted upon the contents. Coconut was a luxury before the war and getting to eat my fill seemed positively decadent. I knew after the first few days the novelty would give way, first to indifference, then to disdain, but it sure seemed God was being extravagant in his providence early on.

Jordy didn't die within hours as we anticipated, but he didn't get a lot better either. He just seemed to linger, hovering somewhere between life and death. We began that first day giving him coconut milk diluted with water, hoping it might provide him a little nutrition, since he was unable to eat or drink on his own. Neither the coconut nor the antibiotics seemed to have a noticeable effect on his recovery, appearing only to lengthen his lingering in this world.

Bill was becoming quite the hunter-gatherer and had recruited Joe in his venture. Joe found red berries and deduced they could not be poisonous because the birds had been eating them. They were extremely tart, but palatable, and provided a nice addition to the coconuts that would become our staple. Bill also reported finding several large lizards that he described as "easy pickings" if he could but shoot them. I had ordered the men not to fire their side arms as we had limited ammo and more importantly the sound of gunfire could easily alert the Japs to our presence. "No, the .45s are to be used for defense only." Bill, not be denied his lizard meat, fashioned a spear of sorts, attaching his bowie knife to the end of a pole he'd whittled down from a larger tree branch. The lizards were pretty speedy over the ground and it took Bill a while to become proficient, but by the end of the third day he came back to camp with four large lizards, their tails tied together and slung over his shoulder. Hard to believe our writer wannabe was our hunter, the provider of protein and probably the most important man in our little society. We couldn't cook the meat since a fire or smoke may draw the Japanese, so we decided to dry it instead. After filleting it into strips and laying it out in the tropical sunlight after salting it with ocean brine, it quickly dried, becoming a lizard jerky worthy of the best of cowboys. We did the same with small fish that Bledsoe had caught in a mountain stream not too far from where we had decided to make camp. We continued residing close to where we had landed that first day. Fortuitously, the Japanese camp was on the other side of the mountain, their forays into our domain exclusively consisting of patrols conducted by the same crews in the same boat that had awakened us the first morning on the island. Those patrols occurred at the same times twice a day, making them easy to anticipate and therefore avoid.

Almost as if on a schedule, it rained every morning from 9:00 a.m. to about 10:30 a.m. After a couple of days of getting wet, we decided to begin construction of some type of thatched shelter, something both impervious to rain and invisible to wary Japanese eyes. Bamboo was plentiful, the indigenous plant found in four distinctive varieties on the island. The largest caliber bamboo was several inches in diameter and grew in height eighty to one hundred feet. Moving from the beach one hundred yards inland to the base of the mountain where the ground's gentle upward slope began a dramatic upswing, we built the first of three open-sided huts. We used bamboo to construct a framework, lashing the poles together first with parachute cord, then using the ubiquitous vines. The thatched roofs were made of multiple layers of spent, drying palm fronds topped with squares of moss and mud. Working non-stop, we had our first shelter completed in about sixteen hours, getting Jordy moved and settling in just before dusk of the third day.

Our ingenuity was quickly tested the following morning as, right on schedule, the rains came. The roof leaked a little, but kept us comparatively dry, certainly drier than the canopy of jungle foliage we had slept under the first two nights. I actually felt quite content when I awoke, most things considered. I still had a headache, but it was dramatically better than a few days ago. I now had water, food and a roof over my head. If I could but see Mary and my little boy, I don't think I would ever again want for another thing.

For several days I had been so engrossed in the act of surviving that I hadn't given them my usual amount of thought, nothing more than a fleeting nod to their existence or a briefly whispered prayer for their continued safety and happiness, and these more of habit or ritual than of true consideration. Lying now in the shelter of our hut, thoughts of home and of Mary and my little boy washed over me like a tsunami. I had but to close my eyes and see Mary, her lovely image forever burned into my brain. Bringing Johnny's image to mind was a bit more difficult as I had only seen him in black-and-white photos, hints of all he has become, yet always locked in the past. Only in sequences of photos can the subject age, gliding through time to the present. My mental image of Johnny was constructed upon two worn and worried photos and thus perpetually locked in the past. My waking dreams were pleasant at first, but a new potential catastrophe, a previously unconsidered move by the hand of fate crept into my conscious mind. Mary…I wonder if news of my disappearance and presumed death had made it to her door yet? The thought hit me like a ton of bricks. How had I been so selfish and self-absorbed not to consider the nightmare Mary would be forced to endure? I wished now more than anything else in the world that I could save her from the shock, the nondescript telegram informing her she was a war widow. The grief, the horror, the overwhelming sorrow, the fear of facing the world and raising Johnny alone without me, without a father, and all of that pain for naught. She couldn't know, despite being worse for the wear, I was still very much alive, very much determined I would live to come home to her, even if I had to swim to get there. How long would she wait? Mary was so very beautiful; it was impossible for her to enter a room without every man present admiring her lovely face and form. Every woman in the room took note of her as well, each at least a little bit jealous at having been demoted to the second prettiest. Mary could have her pick of suitors. Even in grade school, older boys fought over the honor of carrying her books while adult men noticed her, imagining what she would be when she fully matured. Why in the world she ever said yes to the likes of me will forever be a mystery. How long could she hold out against the inevitable onslaught of predatory men, wolves all burning with lust, salivating over such a prize, widow and mother to an orphaned child notwithstanding? Could I get back in time? When we signed up for this duty, the possibility of me being falsely declared dead, leaving Mary open and needful and hurting, never once occurred to me. What if I got home too late and she had of necessity moved on? If I took too long to get her word of my survival, she could be remarried. She would wait a while, but she wouldn't wait forever, not if she believed there was no hope of me coming home, nor could I blame her. I would want her to be happy and well cared for. These thoughts made me panic, catastrophic daydreaming run amok. Dying was one thing, losing Mary and the baby while very much alive and helpless to intercede would be quite another. Johnny could easily grow up knowing another man as his daddy, as he'd never once so much as laid eyes on me. That thought made my pulse quicken even more. The Allies didn't know this island existed until we stumbled upon it, landing in a rubber boat four days ago. Regardless of the victor, the war could end leaving us stranded here, mistakenly given up for dead. Life would go on for those at home. They would of necessity intentionally forget us. With great effort, our memories erased from daily reminiscence in order to cope with the pain of our loss, pushed to the periphery of psyche until at last they'd remained there smoothed and worried over so long all the rough spots, those that caught flesh and caused pain had been worn away.

This brainstorm quickened and deepened, the blackness rolling over my soul in waves. Unconsciously I was up and pacing, walking around the periphery of our hut when something caught my eye. It was Jordy, his eyes open and vacant, devoid of any sheen. He lay there motionless, his chest not rising and falling with the rhythm of respiration. Jordy was gone, having departed the pain of this world, his spirit leaving the bondage of his broken body unheralded.

"Poor kid. He deserved better than this," I thought. Doc was silent at his side, having surrendered to sleep sometime in the night, after Jordy had to death. He hadn't awakened any of the rest of us, as there was nothing any of us could do except mourn Jordy's passing. There would be plenty of time for that. I agreed with Doc's pragmatism and didn't have the heart to awaken any of the other boys with such sad and pitiful news. Instead I crept out in search of something soon necessary, a shovel or something with which to dig. A grave was in order and a suitable grave at that, not some shallow hole scratched out of unyielding earth, but a measured and considered and labored-over grave, a final resting place befitting a hero. I could run over and steal a shovel from the Japs, but it was daylight and the risk of being caught was too great. Not that the risk personally was too great, as I believe honoring a fallen comrade is worth any risk I may take, but there is more at stake here than just me. If I were to be captured, a massive search by the Japanese would soon ensue to snare the remainder of my crew. No, bravado borne of passion and sentiment over the loss of a friend had to be stifled, and cooler thought must prevail if I was to keep my promise and return my charges to their loved ones, me included.

If not a shovel, perhaps something shovel-like, I decided not to visit the Japs, but to scour the beach instead in hopes of finding something that may have washed up, metal panels off an aircraft or boat, a large can, anything I might use to dig a deep hole. The beaches of the South Pacific were, of late, widely strewn with such debris. Maybe I'd get lucky and find what I needed with almost no risk at all. It was still raining, so the morning patrol would probably be delayed till it ceased and the sky grew clearer. If the previous three days were any indication, I should have about an hour. I began walking north along the beach, careful to stay at the jungle's edge that I might be able to quickly disappear should the patrol boat or an aircraft appear. I didn't have to walk very far before coming upon the remains of a Japanese aircraft, not on the beach, but at the jungle's edge. The aircraft had clearly burned upon impact, the surrounding vegetation still bore scars from an intense fire, but apparently the accident happened long enough ago that new vegetation had sprouted and, like a scab, rapidly covered the wound. It took a little sifting and pulling, but finally I found a panel that had once served as a wheel cover. Most of its paint burned away, it still retained script I recognized as Japanese. "This will do nicely," I thought. "Too bad it doesn't have a handle." Hurrying back with my prize, I found everyone still sleeping. The ease with which I approached our encampment undetected and unchallenged alarmed me. I had been derelict in my duties, exceedingly lucky the Japanese had not discovered us. From now on I would post a watch twenty-four/seven. It would not do for us to be caught with our pants down. Officers, including myself, would share in those duties with the enlisted men alike. I let them sleep.

About fifty feet from the hut was a small clearing, five feet by ten feet and bounded on three sides by large boulder-sized stones. In the midst of this clearing I dropped to my knees, and using my new shovel began digging. After an hour I had a sizable hole, two feet by six feet, and about two feet deep. Bledsoe was up and had discovered my labors. He insisted upon digging a while. At first I said no, until he reminded me that Jordy was his friend as well, and he should be allowed to help honor Jordy by digging his grave. It had not occurred to me that the process was indeed therapeutic. It would be good and right for the boys that I let them help.

"You're exactly right, Bledsoe. Here, you take over for a while," I said, handing him my makeshift shovel. "Be careful, the edges are a little sharp and can cut you." I sat on one of the rocks and watched him dig. Soon the other boys had joined us, each taking a turn at turning some soil, digging the grave of our lost friend. We worked throughout the morning, saddened at Jordy's death, but oddly happy his suffering was over. Doc had said it was very unlikely Jordy would ever have walked again, his injury at the base of his thoracic spine leaving him forever paralyzed from the waist down. He also would have had issues controlling his bowel and bladder in addition to being forever impotent. To a man, we agreed that had we found ourselves in the same situation, none of us would have wanted to survive, facing life with those deficits. He never regained consciousness after that first night in the boat. For a short while it had seemed as though Jordy might rally after receiving the antibiotics. In fact, his fever did drop, his temperature normalizing, at least to the touch, and his breathing becoming deeper and more regular, but he just never woke up. Comatose, we had no way to give him adequate water or nutrition, and healing bodies require both, especially in such hostile environments as we now found ourselves. As Doc had stayed constantly at Jordy's side keeping vigilant and dutiful watch, he knew the exact moment, telling us it was at 2:02 am when Jordy took his last shallow breath. Doc was doing a pretty good job of hiding his distress, keeping a stiff upper lip and all that sort of thing, but inside he was dying a bit, taking Jordy's death as a personal failure, beating himself up for an event that was inevitable, an eventuality occurring regardless of the care he received. He sat silently upon a rock watching us dig.

We shared no words finishing the grave; gently lowering Jordy into it before returning the removed, loosened soil to cover him up, a strangely comforting image seeing him disappear beneath loam and humus a million years in the making, like seeing him at once become one with the ages, his body given back to the earth from which it came. Again, as we did for CJ we solemnly recited the twenty-third Psalm, the only Holy writ known to each of us, an apropos eulogy for the journey of one's spirit back to God. The psalm was especially poignant' since Jordy's fever-addled brain had repeated it over and over. Funerals, even simple ones such as this, always set the minds of men to ponder eternal questions. King Solomon said in Ecclesiastes, "God set eternity into the hearts of men." Profound words, but of what reality? Clearly standing beside a reminder that eternity is not within the realm of possibility, the wise king meant something different. Are our hearts, our souls eternal, or is it the quest for the eternal, the searching that seems to infect every man with the "eternity set in our hearts?"

After a good long while, Doc was the first to speak. Thinking aloud he said, "Do you think after all of this there really can be a God?" He looked for an answer to his question, half sincere, half facetious in the eyes of those standing around this new grave. I decided to address his sincerity rather than his cynicism and answered saying, "I've never been what you'd call devout, but I think He exists.... Jordy sure seemed to believe."

"I mean a caring, loving God. One that gives a damn about us dying here?"

"I know I prayed for water and it rained," I smiled shyly, embarrassed I was perhaps subject to superstition. Considering the events of the last week, I got suddenly bolder, "You can call it coincidence all you want to, but I think He answered my prayer." Doc nodded understanding, at least an understanding of my reasoning, but I don't see I made much of a dent in his growing skepticism. It seems in war there are two kinds of men, those who run to a God, and those who run away from a God, but nonexistent are those who don't acknowledge a God, a higher power, a deity. "There are no atheists in foxholes," was a quote my granddaddy was fond of. In times of crisis, the psyche of men requires there be a reason, if not for the crisis than for our existence, the question woven into our souls and minds, into the genetic material determining who we are as individuals, but shared, a commonality with every human who exists or who has ever existed.

As if cued by my thought, Jim said, "I think we're here for a reason."

"And Jordy wasn't?" Doc spit back incredulously.

"No, he was, but he must have accomplished whatever it was God wanted him to."

"So we're disposable like a paper cup? Discarded when God is finished with us like a piece of trash?"

"Not discarded, called home. God takes us to a better place."

"Sounds like wishful thinking to me. Fuck that! I don't think I like this God of yours very much," Doc said, angry not at Jim, but at the God his soul was wrestling with. He walked off into the jungle, leaving us awkwardly looking at one another, his vehement comments having a ring of sacrilege which, given the solemnity of the occasion, made the rest of us squeamish, not wishing to offend a deity, known or not.

"He's your God, too. God is God, whether you like it or not," Bledsoe said in appeasement, not to Doc nor to the rest of us, but to a God he believed was listening. He was right, man's belief or disbelief did little to either alter the reality of or enhance the existence of a creator God. Like the stars or the moon, he either is or is not, regardless of our acknowledgement. One by one, we broke from the grave after saying our goodbyes to Jordy, then returned to the hut for a meal of coconut and lizard jerky, both still novel enough to be appetizing. Funny how comforting food is after a funeral, even this food and this funeral.

The day wore on, and we all remained quiet save for the conversation necessary for the mechanics of living, mostly grunts and guttural utterances, the nonverbal communication routinely exchanged in the company of men. After a couple of I hours I was bored, nothing to read, no chess, none of my usual sanctuaries from monotony, nothing to save me from myself, save me from again spiraling out of control, compulsively ruminating of Mary and Johnny and what might be. The *what if* and *what might be* could prove unhealthy if I followed every lead to an inevitable catastrophic conclusion, even if only in my mind. Recognizing my need for diversion, my reeling mind needing soon to be occupied or risk going stark raving mad, I began to work. It occurred to me standing in the rain that morning that we needed some way to catch and contain rainwater. This would save us trips to and from the stream for fresh water and decrease our exposure, every sojourn away from the hut another chance to be discovered by the enemy. We still had the raft, the material of which was waterproof, so I decided to repurpose it. Retrieving my shovel, I again started digging. By nightfall I had dug a hole five by five by five, a cistern that I intended to line with rubber and canvas from the raft. I left the raft intact, allowing it to overflow the confines of my cistern onto the surrounding ground, a trap to capture as much water as possible. Bledsoe offered to help saying, "You know Major, you're still the boss. You could delegate these jobs to the rest of us."

"I know that, but my mind needs the exertion, sort of therapeutic, if you know what I mean."

After completing my task, I walked out to the ocean for a swim. We didn't have any other way to bathe, and I was covered in dirt and sweat from a day of toil in the tropical heat. After being trapped on the ocean for days I considered it my enemy. I didn't think I'd ever care to see it, smell it, or hear it, let alone swim in it ever again, but I've got to admit, the cool water sure did feel refreshing. From the waves, only my head exposed to the night air, I watched as a flight of *Zeros* returned from a night patrol, flying in tight formation, they did steep breaking turns to align themselves with the runway before disappearing behind the mountain in descent. It was probably one of those bastards that got us. He sure seemed to have come out of nowhere. The hair on the back of my neck bristled at the thought. "Fuck you, you assholes!"

I shouted at the top of my voice, a curse to be lost in the white noise of the surf and waves, but my anger and desire for vengeance, a blaze now rekindled would not be lost. Too bad we had no way to let the Allies know about this base. They seem to operate out of here with complete impunity, striking then returning to a secret island, or should I say an uncharted island? To my knowledge, this little stretch of coral was not on any of our charts. Seeing the flight was an epiphany of sorts, a spark re-ignited, realizing I had become so consumed with surviving our mishap I'd forgotten my mission, the sole reason I found myself away from home, separated from my wife and child. Past successes notwithstanding, the war was not yet won. I couldn't allow all of this to be for naught, the lives of my crew, of Lenny and CJ and now Jordy, all lost well before their time, given up for a purpose that couldn't just be cast aside because it was inconvenient. Before this was over, we would have to find a way to do more than swat at these guys, find some way to attack them without them knowing the attack was perpetrated by an enemy hidden upon their own island. We would have to be creative. We had no weapons to speak of, no explosives to end the war for them with a bit of drama. A frontal assault would be suicide as they outnumbered us twenty to one. No, we would have to be clever and secretive, subtle acts of aggression. Destroy their aircraft, but make it appear to be a mechanical malfunction rather than sabotage. Loosen propeller bolts, sever control cables, clog pitot tubes, small acts of malfeasance with no immediate gratification, no flash or explosion, our attack purposed to be discovered by a hapless pilot after a time, perhaps in the heat of battle, a mechanical mishap, inopportune, far from land and help and hope, no survival. Exactly where they left us, every Jap fighter we claimed was one less to do battle, to wage war upon my brethren, one more loyal Jap soldier dispatched to hell. My plan somehow seemed right, bringing a quiet calm to soothe my newly erupted anger, a content alignment with my sense of justice.

After my swim, I lay on the beach and considered the stars. Without the lighting of nearby civilization to dilute my senses and deaden my perception, the entire Milky Way was on display, too magnificent a spectacle to believe there was no creator. "No God indeed," I chuckled. The end of a taxing day, I was lulled to sleep by the sound of the surf and a balmy breeze drying the salt water from my skin.

CHAPTER 19

I awoke the following morning after sleeping deeply all night, undisturbed. I had a major erection, dreaming as I do every night of Mary, her warm inviting body and the amazing things she could do with her fingers. I awoke smiling at the thought and then remembered where I was. The sun was high in the sky without the anticipated rain clouds. "Odd," I thought, glancing at my watch, "It's 1030, I wonder why it's not raining?" Then I heard a foreboding sound, the low rumble of the Japanese patrol boat. My heart stopped as I held my breath, fearful to move. This is not good, Shit, Shit, Shit! Do I try to make it into the bush? If I move at all I'd risk drawing their attention. How could I be so fucking stupid? I was twenty yards away from the protective cover of the jungle, laying naked on the sand save for my military issue boxers and my dog tags, my clothes and gun in a pile twenty feet away. "Crap, my gun is over there, too." I could hear them speaking, their foreign tongue sounding more to me like gibberish than language. Had they seen me? How would I know by listening? Nothing in the timbre of their conversation suggested alarm or surprise. Would they shoot me from the boat before checking my identity? Surely not, I could be one of them, for Christ's sake. If I were standing they would have no question I was not Japanese, even from a distance my six three frame would betray me pretty quickly, but I wasn't standing, I was lying down, so they should have a lot of trouble determining the disparity of my height from a distance.

The boat was eighty yards away and not yet past my position. Slowly, using small, clock-like increments, I raise my head from my sand pillow to peer over my chest and past where my erection had tented my boxers, a quickly waning phenomenon, to see the boat pass the point where I lay on the sand from my left to my right. There they were, the same crew that passed by every day, smoking and talking and laughing, chortling loud enough that I could discern their voices over the sounds of surf and engine. An eternity and then some seemed to pass before the boat was past my right foot and again in my field of vision. Thank God! Earnest men, men not numb to their duty, not complacent from lack of previous encounters, would have seen me. These guys just motored by me, as oblivious to the semi-naked man lying upon the beach as if they were on a party boat. Still, I was not about to awaken their attention by moving, at least not moving rapidly. After they had passed to a point where they would have to look back to spot me, I began to make my way into cover. A blur of motion in their peripheral vision might be enough to betray me, so I determined to proceed slowly. Still flat on my back, not once taking my eyes off the Japs, I cupped my hands and propelled my body eighteen inches at a time, dragging my hind side over the coarse volcanic sand. My boxers, functioning like a scoop, were full of the stuff by the time I reached the jungle's edge.

"Whew, that was close," I heard Bledsoe say from the cover of a bush.

"That was stupid!" I said in confession. "I don't know how I could have let that happen. I'm truly sorry." I could have explained I was tired, I was distracted, it wasn't my intent, then I recalled what my granddaddy always said, "An excuse is the skin of a reason stuffed with a lie." Better to be a man and take the heat of responsibility than offer a hollow excuse so I left my disclaimer at "I'm sorry."

"What are you boys doing here?" I asked.

"When we woke up, we noticed you were missing and came looking. We must have walked right past you 'cause we didn't see you till it was too late.

Anyway, we were prepared to take 'em if they came ashore after you." They all still had their guns drawn and cocked.

"Thanks boys. I'm sorry I just about let you down. I guess I'm pretty lucky they didn't see me."

"I'd say they were the ones that were lucky," Bledsoe laughed. "I was thinking you might be pretty good Jap bait."

"I guess not."

"Anyway, Major, we've got more problems. Doc, Bill, Joe and Jim are getting sick. High fever. Doc thinks it might be malaria."

"Malaria? Damn it all! Did he say what to do about it?"

"Quinine! Doc said we might be in luck 'cause some of the pills we stole were quinine, but we don't have enough. He says we're all probably gonna get it if we don't have it already."

"So we gotta go get more. Do you think the Japs will have enough?"

"Doc says the Japs got it all. Before the war all malaria was treated with quinine. It comes from the Cinchona tree in the Andes Mountains of South America. The Japs cut off the world supply and kept it for themselves."

"So what is that nasty shit they give us to take, those yellow malaria pills?"

"It's a drug called Atabrine, a synthetic quinine, but it doesn't work as good as the real stuff. Funny thing is the Germans developed Atabrine when they couldn't get quinine from their Jap allies."

"Doc told you all that? I thought he was sick."

"Nope, I just knew it. Read it somewhere along the way I suppose. Think you got enough luck left in you to go get some more?"

"Seems like this is my lucky day, Bledsoe. This time I think we'll just go around the beach instead of across the mountain."

"I was hoping you might say that, Major," pleased he wouldn't have to climb the mountain again when an easier route was available.

"Well, this time we know where we're going."

Back at the hut Jim, Joe, Bill, and Doc all lay prone on piles of fern fronds Bledsoe had gathered for their comfort. Doc was dry and shivering, his temperature on its way up while the others were drenched in their own sweat. They all looked terrible.

"How do you feel, Doc?" I asked, feeling his forehead.

"Awful! I've got to get better to die. Kill every fucking mosquito you can! The little bastards are doing a better job of killing us than the Japs," he said, his sense of humor still intact. "Where the hell have you been?" His teeth chattered beyond his control.

"Oh I just took a little nap on the beach," I said wryly, waiting for Bledsoe to fill him in on all the subtleties of my comment. Bledsoe gave me a wink, but never said a word.

"Well that's just great, Major. Meantime me and the boys are dying here."

"I thought you said you had to get better to die?" He gave me his best chin-down eyes-up okay-smart-ass look.

"How much quinine we got, Doc?"

"Two days' worth as long as it's only four of us taking 'em. Think you can score some more?" he asked hopefully.

"Bledsoe and I are on it tonight. We know exactly where to look, but you've got to show us what we're looking for." He tossed me a small box with Japanese script containing an amber bottle labeled with the same script. I shook my head as I examined the bottle, "We'll never be able to read this…"

"Smell it," he said. "You won't forget it. It smells as bitter as it tastes." Opening the cap, I took a long whiff. He was right, it was not a smell I would soon forget.

"And, Major…"

"Yeah, Doc, what is it?"

"Don't fail or we're all dead." He searched my eyes for understanding.

I nodded, saying, "Don't worry, we'll get all we need." Doc rolled over on his mat of ferns, seeking a more comfortable position before adding, "Aspirin would be nice too."

Anticipating my question he said, "Think about it, you know. Aspirin smells like acetic acid." I looked puzzled, so Bledsoe responded, "Vinegar."

"Ah," I said then looking about asked, "Where's Skip?"

"He went for water, saying we'd die if we had to wait for your cistern to work."

"But it hasn't rained yet!"

"We know that. He's just looking for a reason to be an asshole."

"He needs a reason?" Jim said weakly. We all laughed at his well-timed joke, happy he could still make one.

Bledsoe and I left early for our raid, hoping to find a hiding place close to the Japanese field while it was still light enough to see. I wanted a better look at their compound and intended this mission for reconnaissance as well. We would need tools to accomplish my proposed sabotage, a plan the boys applauded. Skip said it was "Nice to see you get your balls back." He wanted to come along with Bledsoe and I, but I had seen him lose his composure under pressure before. I had to have someone capable of thinking on his feet and Bledsoe was my obvious choice. "Besides, the others need someone here to take care of them. They're too sick to leave on their own."

"Why can't Bledsoe stay and let me come with you?"

"Because if anything happens to us, the rest of the guys will need you to lead them. You're second in command here. They can't afford to lose us both." His ego satisfied, Skip let the subject drop.

We had an hour before dusk, and several hours to wait before the camp was lulled to complacent slumber, so Bledsoe and I sat hidden in a tall clump of grass beneath three palm trees and watched the sun set.

Bledsoe asked in a hoarse whisper, "So, how is it that Skip came to be your co-pilot?"

I rolled my eyes, "The guy is a loose cannon. He somehow made it through the ranks because of someone his daddy knows. I sure as hell wasn't going to give him his own ship and I didn't have the heart to saddle any other crew with him as their co-pilot. Jack begged me to let him move up, so I did and kept Skip on my crew so I could keep an eye on him."

"His daddy must really know someone special…."

"The president," I said, grimly. "He was a childhood friend of Roosevelt."

"Wow! That's what I call connected."

"Yeah, his daddy owns half of New York City. Better be nice, 'cause we'll probably both work for him after we go home." Bledsoe chuckled, but I was serious. It has always been so in the world, title and privilege have more to do with who you are, your lineage rather than your competency. You had to look no further than the royal families of Europe, for an example. American industry in the last century thrived because it escaped from that mold; bold, intelligent entrepreneurs making a way for themselves. Sadly, the secret to their success was slowly being eroded away and the thinking elite who created the companies that made America great were being replaced by half-wit or, worse yet, no-wit sons. I vowed to myself, right then and there, I would never be employed by anyone I did not respect. I would make my own way, open a business of some sort where I was the master of my own fate. I would take care of Mary and my children and someday Johnny would replace me at the helm…then I chuckled at my own thought. That's how it happens. Parents don't care about their children's competency, they only care their children and grandchildren are cared for. What better way to do that than to pass on a measure of your own success to your offspring?

"Kind of funny the things a person gets from his parents, hey, Major?"

"Yes, I suppose it is." Bledsoe's voice changed pitch, betraying his anxiety. He clearly now had an agenda, so I waited to see how this conversation might unfold.

"I remember you saying something to Lenny that day we first met… something about being Jewish?"

"Yes, Bledsoe. My grandmother was legally a Jew, making me the same, though I wasn't raised that way. I didn't even know anything about it till I was sixteen. I was raised by my granddaddy after my mother died. He figured I'd have enough to deal with in backwoods Georgia without having that label hanging over my head."

He shook his head knowingly, then asked, "So you think being a Jew is a bad thing?"

"No, not at all, But lots of people do. Look at what the crazy bastards did in Germany. We're still finding mass graves where they rounded people up and killed them. Can you begin to imagine hating someone that much?"

"Imagine it, yes! I've been waiting for years …" He stopped abruptly, not really sure he wanted to divulge his fear.

"Waiting for?" I prodded him onward.

Closing his eyes and steeling himself he said, "Waiting for someone to discover my secret. Seems I inherited something, a label, from my parents as well."

"I remember you saying you never met your father. Let me guess, was he a Jew as well?"

"No. As far as I know he was a white Anglo-Saxon protestant. It wasn't him, it was my mother, she was beautiful and smart and she loved me like no other, but she was a…"

From things he'd shared in the past I anticipated next word being prostitute. Instead, he said, "Negro."

My initial response was to laugh, as I thought he was joking, but his face, a very white face, displayed hurt instead of mirth. Here was Bledsoe, baring his soul to me and I almost blew it.

"I'm sorry Bledsoe. You're not joking, are you?"

"No sir, I'm not," he said, quickly looking away embarrassed.

"It's just surprising, that's all. There's nothing about your appearance that would have ever lead me to question for a second you're not a white man."

"I know, that's why I've pulled it off all these years, but it's quite true. My mamma was a burlesque dancer at a club in Atlanta. She started dating a white man, this lawyer who came to see her dance all the time. He got her pregnant with me then disappeared. When I popped out looking more like him than her, she hunted him down and threatened to make a big stink if he didn't help me. At first he thought she wanted money, but reluctantly agreed to pull some strings when all she asked for was a birth certificate proclaiming me white. She promised to never ask him for anything else ever again and to my knowledge, she never did."

"Sounds to me like she loved you very much and didn't want you to live with the same crap she put up with."

"That's true. At least that's how she explained what she did. She named me and told me my real mama was a friend of hers who died, leaving her me to raise. My name was different and my skin was different, so I never had reason to question her growing up. She was the only mother I ever remember. Around the time I turned sixteen she got real sick, and on her deathbed she told me the real story, said she didn't want to die without me knowing the truth. I didn't believe her at first. I thought her sickness might be messing with her mind, but she gave me my daddy's name and told me to go see him. After her funeral, I waited a few weeks, thinking I could just forget about everything, but I couldn't. So, one day I marched myself into his office in the middle of the day to confront him. He denied her story at first, and I actually believed him till I saw pictures of his other kids on his desk. He finally fessed up when I pointed out the irrefutable family resemblance and told him all I wanted was the truth."

"I thought you said you never met your daddy?"

"He was a sperm donor, that's all. I'll never consider him my daddy, so I didn't lie," he said sheepishly.

"Oh, I didn't think you lied." We sat for several tense moments in silence, me trying to digest what he'd just said, him waiting for judgment.

Bledsoe must've felt I could be trusted, confiding in me his deepest secret, a secret kept not of embarrassment nor lack of pride, but of self-preservation, a means of survival in a world hateful of any differences. Save for the legal sleight of hand performed by his otherwise uninvolved father,

Bledsoe would in the eyes of the law be considered a Negro. At birth it was clear he'd inherited from his father the color of his eyes, the texture of his hair and the color of his skin, all unequivocally Caucasian, a perfect disguise in a culture obsessed with racial superiority, but his mother really was a Negro woman, a tall, shapely beauty with ivory teeth and skin black as coal. In 1942, polite white folks used the term Negro to label her race rather than other, more hurtful terms. My granddaddy would have worn my ass out had I called another human being a nigger, even though that's the term all of my neighbors used. He said the term was best used to describe an unclean lazy person regardless of the color of their skin, but probably best just left unsaid. My granddaddy was a very wise man.

"Let me ask you something, Bledsoe. Does this change how you see yourself as a man?"

"No sir, not really. I'm the same person I always was."

"And are you a good person?"

"Well, yes sir, I think I am."

"Then why do you give a damn what anyone else thinks?"

"I shouldn't I guess, but I'd be a liar if I said I didn't."

"For the record, the Bledsoe Courage I know is an amazing man regardless of the color of his skin."

"Thanks Major, that means a lot. I guess my question is, would you have taken the time to know the man if I were…well, darker, shall we say?

"I'd like to think so, Bledsoe…but I doubt it! " He thought about it for a moment before saying, "Same here, you Jewish son of a bitch!" Initially I was shocked at his words until he broke into a grin and we both cracked up laughing.

Right at dusk, two groups of three *Zero* fighters touched down, returning spent from their mission, their exhausts glowing red hot in the early evening light. Landing six in train, they taxied to a ramp on the far end of the field before shutting down. The Japanese must have a system similar to ours, with crew chiefs and mechanics taking over the ground operation of each aircraft as the weary pilots ambled off to supper or a drink or both. The airplanes were all refueled, re-armed, and inspected, then tied down for the night, the flurry of activity dwindling from several linemen down to a single ranking NCO, the ultimate authority, armed with a clipboard and pencil, jotting notes about each individual aircraft before turning in.

Another two hours passed before the compound was at long last quiet. Just to be sure, we waited another forty-five minutes to allow anyone still awake to fall asleep. Now the only anticipated watchful eyes should be those of the sentries, hopefully the same two we encountered three nights ago. We began by searching for the pair and, sure enough, there they were, sitting in a jeep at the end of the runway, smoking their brains out. We made our way to the infirmary tent and again found it empty but at the ready, with cots made up and equipment standing by to render care at a moment's notice. Bledsoe stood guard by the door while I made quick work of our thieving. The same cabinet holding the medications was thankfully still unlocked and had been restocked. I recognized the figures on the front of the package as the same I'd been shown earlier in the day. Just to be sure, I opened the bottle and took a whiff of confirmation, then poked the package into my pocket before thinking better of it. There were four such packages so I decided to take half the contents of each, emptying the tiny pills into my pocket, leaving behind the gross illusion that nothing in the cabinet was either missing or tampered with. I then searched for aspirin, finally finding it with my nose as well. There was a single large bottle, so I took a handful, again leaving the bottle appearing intact. Grabbing a couple boxes of the Sulfa and a wool blanket off two cots, Bledsoe and I slipped out the front door. The sentries had not moved and we slipped back to our original hiding place un-noticed.

"Bledsoe, I want you to take this back to Doc and the boys."

"Where are you going?"

"I'm going back. I've got some other pilfering I need to do."

"But…"

"That's an order, Bledsoe. I'll be okay. You just get this back to Doc."

"Yes, sir." I knew he was uncomfortable with the plan, but I couldn't pass up the opportunity. I may not be so lucky as to have these two bozo guards on duty tomorrow night. Slipping through the dark, I made my way to the flight line. The moon would be over the crest of the mountain soon, so I had to hurry. If I could only get a screwdriver and wire cutters this would be a productive mission. There was a hut, a shed-like structure at the end of the flight line, I assumed was a maintenance building of some sort. Luckily, it, too, was unlocked. Slipping in, I lit a match to illuminate the dark shed. Neatly stowed upon a wall of shelves were tool bags, each with an individual's name painted upon its side. The organizational skills of these people was astounding, every tool wiped clean and stowed in its place. Opening the first of the bags I stole a screwdriver; from the next I acquired wire cutters. I'd be willing to bet the loss of each would bring dishonor to the prior custodians. Replacing the tool bags to their proper places, I turned to make my escape from the scene of the crime before realizing I'd discarded the spent match on the floor, something that would not go un-noticed. I lit another and crawled around on the floor searching for the single shred of evidence I'd almost left behind. Finding it, I blew out the second and poked both into my pocket before slipping into the night.

My safest passage back, the one affording me the most cover, was on the opposite side of the Japanese compound. Only twenty feet in front of me sat a line of *Zeros,* mission ready and tied down for the night. Tempting targets of opportunity for me, bulging as my pockets were with the newly acquired tools. The field was pitch dark, the moon having yet to make an appearance above the mountain top, the faint shadow it cast out across the water receding back to the island slowly as the moon rose. I guessed I would have maybe twenty minutes before the field would be awash in its light. Would that be enough time to pull it off? My compulsion to act was irresistible, so without wasting time I chose as my victim the aircraft closest to me. I was not familiar with the structure of the *Zero*, but hoped there would be a port or inspection plate, something easily removable through which I might gain access to the control cables. Sliding under the tail, I lay on my back and began searching for anything that might let me in. There was no light and I didn't dare light a match, so my search had to be conducted by my fingertips. Within thirty seconds I'd found, at least I thought it was it was, a five-by-ten inch panel secured to the frame with eight screws. I began removing the screws quickly as I could, holding those removed in my mouth. If I dropped or lost one my act of sabotage may not go undetected. Removing the last and retracting the panel, there was my prize, the elevator control cable. Like in American aircraft, it was made of braided stainless steel. I didn't want to just cut the cable and run for that would be too easily detected before the aircraft lifted off in flight. No, I wanted to only partially cut through the metal strands, hoping the failure would occur sometime during flight. I discovered there were ten individual strands of wire woven together to make up the cable, any one of which was strong enough to withstand the rigors of flight without anticipating its failure. "Damned engineers the world over love redundancy." It took me several minutes to dissect and cut individual strands, the whole cable virtually impervious to the small wire cutters had I tried to cut it in entirety. After thinking about it for a minute or two, I decided to make a second series of cuts about a foot forward of the first, being sure in this series to severe the single strand I had left intact in the first. Now I had a braided cable designed for failure, held together only by a single foot of overlapping braid amongst the cable bundles, its structural integrity maintained by friction alone. The cable might withstand a little stress before coming unraveled, but not the stress that would be placed upon it in combat flight, or at least so I reasoned. Pleased with my bit of impromptu engineering, I replaced the access panel's last screw just as the approaching moonlight reached my position. If I hurried, I could again slip into the darkness of the mountain shadow and escape, having accomplished more than I originally planned for this mission.

I was just about to go when I heard the squeak of brakes nearby, the sentry jeep stopping a mere fifteen feet in front of the *Zero.* "Damn! Of all the luck," I thought, pulling my .45 from its holster. I sat crouched under the tail of the aircraft waiting to spring. There could be no running away. If confronted, my survival would require I kill both of the Japs. My heart raced and my mind reeled quickly through several scenarios, all of which involved killing. It would be better if no shots were fired. Silently killing both with my knife before either could get a shot off would be ideal. The only way that might happen is if I was bold enough to take the initiative, claiming the advantage of offense, catching them by surprise. Then I could ditch their bodies in the bay and with luck maybe get away without the rest of the Jap contingent being any the wiser. Upon discovering the bodies however, it would only be a matter of time before they scoured the island looking for us. I could kill them then take a plane to make my escape. They may think it the act of a lone enemy and not go looking for my boys, but that would be unlikely. Besides, even if I were lucky enough to get the airplane off, I couldn't do it without being heard, And then the rest of the squadron was sure to follow in hot pursuit, pissed I'd killed their comrades.

Neither of the guards had gotten out of the jeep. Were they being cautious, anticipating my attack, or had they even now failed to see me here in the shadow of the tail? I sat frozen, time as still as my body, a lifetime of "what ifs" passing before my eyes. This is why I loved chess, why I was good at it, anticipating my opponent's next few moves, planning my own end game in response. Despite the appearance of infinity, the unknown, there were always a finite number of moves anyone could make and a finite number of responses. This was my forte, what I was born to do. Only the stakes had changed, instead of playing for scotch we were playing for life, either mine or theirs or both. Lucky for me, it appeared these two guys remained unaware they were even playing the game, let alone figuring the odds. Another lifetime passed before the guard closest to me stepped out of the jeep. Looking straight at me, he failed to see me. He was a kid! Sixteen, seventeen at the most, all dressed up and smoking and playing soldier, serving like so many a conscript to some outmoded Asian notion of honor, emperor, and country. We had beaten them back, defeated the best and most appropriate the Japanese had to offer. Now they sent the dregs, the last drop of manhood, or should I say pre-manhood, their last remaining males, too young to have any life skills, let alone skill at killing. This was no more than a child in my sight, a child now just a trigger pull away from his last thought. They would be simple to kill; neither of them cognizant of what had hit them, snuffing short their lives. Two shots or two quick slashes of my hunting knife, and my immediate dilemma would be dealt with. I could do it, would do it if provoked, but... only if provoked. The kid yawned and stretched and turned back to laugh at something funny said by his companion. He put his cigarette between his lips, then undid a rope belt and dropped his trousers to his knees before relieving himself into the night. "Jesus, this kid doesn't even have pubic hair," I thought. "How can I kill him?" Kill sounds so sanitary, so devoid of intent. Murder was the *mot parfait*, the perfect word to describe what I contemplated, no moral ambiguity.

Pulling his trousers up, he clearly remained unaware that I watched from only yards away, close enough I could smell his urine fresh on the sandy soil. He flicked his cigarette butt into the puddle, its last glow snuffing with a hiss, before climbing back into the jeep.

The jeep restarted and I exhaled a silent sigh of relief, perchance removed of my moral dilemma, but the vehicle didn't move. They sat there long enough my legs began going to sleep, numb and tingling, lacking circulation from my squatting position. Still illuminated by moonlight, I didn't dare move. After another half an hour, they slowly drove down the flight line before turning and proceeding to the remainder of the compound. As theirs was the only indication of life in the sleepy camp I decided to avoid them as much as possible and walk down the beach, more exposed, but further from the only eyes awake to see me. I walked unchallenged all the way around the island to the point where I had slept last night. Bledsoe sat there at the jungle's edge awaiting my return.

"Nice night for a stroll?" Bledsoe's smartass question a clue he was growing impatient at my tardiness. Concerned for my well-being, he was more upset I had acted alone than had taken so long to do so. It was easy to understand and ignore his insolence.

"Get the medicine delivered?"

"Yep, Doc and the boys say thank you."

"And to you," I said. "Anyone else getting sick yet? I'm hoping the good doctor will be wrong in his prediction this time."

"Me, too, but he's not wrong often. He said we should all start taking the pills now. Here, I brought you one," he said, offering me a pill that had been in my pocket only a couple of hours ago. I looked at my watch and discovered I was wrong about that. It was now over five hours ago we had been in the infirmary tent. 0435, the dawn would soon be upon us. No wonder I was so tired. I lay down in the sand expressing my exhausted state to Bledsoe who said, "Oh no you don't! We're not playing that game again." With that, he grabbed my weary arm and pulled me up. As we walked back to the hut I told him of my further exploits.

"Damn, Major, we need to watch, keep an eye on the planes going out and coming back to see if you scored."

"As long as the cable holds together till the plane is off the ground we got 'em. Pretty hard to fly an airplane without pitch control."

"And if it happens over the ocean they wont be able to figure out we got 'em till it's too late. They won't know what hit 'em…. Brilliant, Major! Absolutely fucking brilliant."

"I thought so," I said proudly.

Back at the hut I found a corner and curled up with the intention of catching forty winks. Before I was out I asked Bledsoe to keep a watch on the Japs, "They don't seem to go out much before daybreak. Station one of the boys in that same clump of grass where you and I waited. It seems to be pretty secluded and you can see most of the field from there. Have them keep a watch on everything going on in the camp, and most importantly, stay covered so they don't get caught."

"I'm on it, Major. Anything else?"

"Yes, be careful!"

"We'll do our best, Major."

Almost asleep I remember saying, "I know you will."

CHAPTER 20

When I awoke around noon it was raining, a soft summer rain, the same rain we had grown to anticipate, but for some inexplicable reason had failed yesterday to materialize.

"Good news, Major, your cistern holds water like a champ."

"Uhm? Oh, good," I said, still sleep-dazed.

"I hear you had a busy night, Major," Skip said. "You really think it will work?"

"I hope so. If not we'll try something different, but you were right. We can't just sit here for the duration and do nothing."

"I'm glad you see it my way, Major. Now, I've got a plan to blow up the fuel dump by…."

Now I was awake, "And how exactly do you propose to do that without letting the Japs know we're here?"

"Well I…"

"Beause if you've got a way to do it without giving us up, I'm all ears."

"I guess I haven't thought it through quite that far, Major."

"And that, Skip, is why I'm still the boss. Come up with a plan and think it through to completion, taking into account *all* the possible contingencies, and I'll listen. Until then do not attempt to engage the enemy offensively in any manner unless you first clear it with me, understood?" I could only begin to imagine all the disastrous ramifications of Skip being left alone to his own devices.

"Yes, sir," he said, much like a chastened eight-year-old. Poor kid, he was trying to be an officer. He just didn't seem to get the big picture. I couldn't afford to have him moping around here or worse yet plotting against me, so I added, "Skip, that doesn't mean I want you to stop thinking. Your input is valuable. Just keep in mind in addition to defeating the enemy, we'd all very much like to survive to go home if at all possible. It's our obligation to do both!"

"Yes, sir," he smiled, feeling validated. "I'll come up with something."

"Well, we've got water and fire, what I wouldn't give right now for a cup of coffee."

"Yeah, that'd sure hit the spot," Doc said.

"You look like shit, Doc, how you feeling?"

"Better, not well by a long shot, but better. I probably owe you my life."

"Just doing my job, Doc. I'm just glad you're on the mend. How's Jim? Feeling any better?"

Before he could answer, Bledsoe burst in, "Hey, Major, I think you scored. Six planes left in the first sortie, only five came back. Only four more and you're an ace!"

"I don't think it works that way, Bledsoe, and we can't confirm what happened to the plane. He could have tangled with one of our fighters and lost."

"You go on with that false modesty crap all you want to, Major, but I'm tellin' you, you got 'em!"

"Maybe you're right, Mr. Courage. We'll certainly go try again tonight. I thought about some other things we might try, like loosening prop bolts, but that would require different tools, not to mention leaving you hanging out in the open while you do it. Maybe the best thing is to just repeat what I did last night and see what happens."

"There are thirteen of them, well, twelve of them now. How about getting the rest of them tonight?" Bledsoe asked.

"I've thought about that. It probably would be good to get them before they're suspicious. With only one they're inclined to think it a fluke. With the second or third plane lost they'll be smart enough to know something is up. That's what I want to talk to you boys about and get your input. Getting them all will be risky. If we're successful and all twelve of them go down, we may get away with it, but if even one makes it back to report the airplanes were lost because of structural failures instead of combat, they'll know they've got a saboteur about and come looking."

"What are the odds of getting all twelve?" Jim asked.

"Slim to none," I said grimly. The group knew my assessment was correct, the weight of my words casting a pall of silence on the group as they considered.

Skip was first to break the silence, "I say we do it, but let's wait until everyone is healthy. We'll probably have to separate; it's easier to run and hide alone than in groups."

Bledsoe added, "But keep in mind every day these fuckers fly is another day they can kill Americans."

"I agree with Skip. We need to time this so everyone is healthy enough to make it on his own. Doc, how long're you thinking it will take?"

"Assuming no one else gets sick, I'd say a week maybe? Ten days tops."

"A little more time will also lull the Japs back into complacency. Any other considerations?" I asked.

"The moon was full last night. Ten days from now we won't have to worry so much about moonlight giving us away."

"Anyone have a clue as to the date?"

Bledsoe counted on his fingers, "We crashed on Friday the twentieth, three days in the raft and now five days here. That makes today Friday July 27, 1945."

"So we go next Friday, a week from today."

"August 3," Bledsoe interjected.

"So we go next Friday, August 3. Any other discussion, gentlemen?"

"Will we all be involved cutting the cables, or just you and Bledsoe again?"

"I think just me and Bledsoe. Maybe one more, I'll have to think about it. I've only got one screwdriver and one pair of wire cutters. We could steal some more I suppose, but that just makes things more complicated. Just one more thing to go wrong."

"Friday August 3?" Everyone nodded agreement, then Doc added, "Everyone remember to take your quinine!"

A whole week, seven days with nowhere to go and nothing to do except stay hidden and out of harm's way? It sounded easy enough, a vacation of sorts. Better than that, a vacation on a tropical island. "People pay a fortune for the chance to do the same," I mused. I could just visualize the poster in the travel agency window now, replete with phrases like, "Visit Paradise," or "Tropical Splendor." I can't remember the last time I took a vacation. "Who am I kidding?" I was growing bored just standing there thinking about it. No sex, no liquor, nothing to read, not much of a vacation to my way of thinking. I didn't care how beautiful the setting; I'd already seen enough "tropical splendor" for a lifetime. Perhaps I would have felt differently about my sojourn in the South Pacific if there weren't people out there charged with the task of killing me. I definitely would have liked it better if Mary had been here, alone with no one else in the entire world to disturb us or inhibit us, now *that* would be a vacation.

We spent the week readying ourselves for the mission. Those of our group healthy enough took turns observing the daily Japanese movements. Though the loss of one of their *Zeros* would have prompted increased security had their leadership suspected foul play, we observed no discernible change in their daily routines. We looked for patterns and numbers, things to help make the actions and reactions of our enemies more predictable, and therefore more survivable.

In our reconnaissance we learned the twelve remaining Japanese aircraft were divided into two groups of six, each group further divided into two flights of three *Zeros* each. Each aircraft had a single pilot who flew it exclusively. Each flight of three had a single mechanic responsible for the maintenance and refueling of the aircraft of that flight exclusively. There were two Japanese soldiers who functioned as armorers, keeping all twelve of the *Zeros* as well as the bombers, a *Dinah* and two *Bettys* armed and ready for service at a moment's notice. Protecting the aircrews on the ground was a contingent of a hundred to a hundred and twenty regular infantrymen. These men crewed and maintained four different antiaircraft guns positioned around the airfield. Soldiers from the same group also crewed the patrol boats that made excursions around the island's perimeter twice a day. These boats were also used to shuttle supplies delivered to the island via submarine, the harbor being too shallow for a sub to enter. All supplies seemed to come by sub rather than by ship or aircraft. The Japanese were keen on keeping secret the operations on this island. They had yet to be attacked because the Allies knew nothing of the island's existence. Supply ships and planes could easily be tracked and followed, so the Japs were taking no chances. Who knows how long they might have continued to strike from obscurity, returning unchallenged, had we not stumbled upon them. The crew of the *China Doll* was about to change all that!

The commanding officer, or the person who appeared to be in charge, was himself one of the fighter pilots who, obvious even from a distance, ruled his charges with an iron fist, his every command quickly obeyed with a crisp "*Hai*" and bow. The commander wore a sword at his side at all times, even when flying. Bledsoe told me the swords or *Katana* worn by Japanese officers were badges of honor, heirlooms that may have been in the wearer's family for generations, having been passed from father to son. Enemy or not, there was much in the Japanese culture to be admired, most especially the pervasive discipline and spirituality long ago lost by Western civilizations. The tradition of the Samurai, a sect of warrior monks I'd read about and admired since childhood, appeared very much alive and in practice by these pilots. Every aspect of the pilot's day was steeped in tradition and ritual; morning bathing, tea, and prayers, all paying homage to the spiritual side of being a warrior. As a westerner the discipline of this culture was a bit unnerving. Every man from top to bottom appeared to conduct himself in a life oriented toward a goal of excellence, striving and practicing every day to achieve ever newer levels of skill, and with them some greater measure of honor. An entire society imbued with this same *zeitgeist*, if I may borrow a word from another enemy nation, this same worldview was foreign and frightening to our Western way of thinking.

The thing that scared most Americans about these men was not their abilities as pilots and warriors, for they had been gifted or not in the same proportions as any other men. Nor was it the code of discipline that governed their lives. No, the thing that proved most frightening was their unparalleled willingness to die for their emperor and his cause. In April at the Battle for Okinawa, the Allies watched as over 2000 Japanese pilots intentionally crashed their bomb and fuel-laden aircraft into our ships. These suicide pilots were called *Kamikaze*, young men all, educated and intelligent, men with their entire lives ahead of them, men whose courage and unwavering dedication to their emperor, tradition, and history rendered them virtually unstoppable. Though most died in vain, we still lost significant numbers of ships and men to their heroic, if not misguided actions.

In 1281 the island nation of Japan was under attack by the Mongols led by none other than the great Kublai Kahn of *Xanadu* fame. The Kahn's invasion was denied, however, thwarted by a typhoon that scuttled all the Mongol invader's ships. The typhoon was credited with saving Japan, the storm forever after memorialized in Japanese tradition as the *Kamikaze* or "Divine Wind." The island nation was again today in peril, albeit as a consequence of their diabolical actions, and the spirit of the *Kamikaze*, embodied in these young suicide pilots, was asked to once again intervene. More young Japanese men volunteered for this sacrificial service than the

Japanese had remaining airplanes to fly, an incredible testament to service and loyalty and honor. While we hated the *Kamikaze* with a passion, we had to respect them. If you said you didn't, you were a liar.

My men were proving just as disciplined, just as prepared to be captured or die for the sake of our cause as the Japanese were for theirs. I have never been prouder of anything in my entire life than I was of that group of men. In spite of the sickness, pain, or hardship they endured, not a single one of them uttered a word of complaint. Quite remarkable, as they had plenty of time to complain, plenty of time to worry, plenty of time to decide the risk of the mission was not equal to the benefit it may purchase, plenty of time to get bored. Boredom can be a tremendously powerful poison, a phantom enemy to the heart of any man, and given our present want for the trappings of civilization, the specter of boredom hung thick in the air. We were all getting pretty sick of coconuts, but by the same token, we were very grateful to have something to eat. No one complained of the monotony of our diet. The lizard jerky still tasted fine, even good in comparison to what we might have been forced to eat, but you can only eat something for so long, no matter how good, before the novelty wears thin. I'm sure the island's lizard population will be happy when they are no longer Nouveau cuisine, the bright spot in our limited palate. We must be getting enough nutrition, for although each of us has lost weight, we all are getting stronger after our ordeal at sea.

By week's end both Doc and Jim were fever free, and the jaundice, the sickly amber glow each had developed, was fading, first from their skin, then from the whites of their eyes. I'm sure Doc would have appreciated the gesture had we delayed the mission for a few more days, perchance giving both him and Jim a little longer to recover, but neither he or Jim ever once requested such a reprieve. Fortunately for the rest of us, no one else contracted the disease. We all certainly had enough mosquito bites to have been infected, inoculated with the little protozoic bastards, but were successful at holding their proliferation at bay with the daily quinine we all took.

In addition to reconnaissance gathered of our island neighbors, we worked at other contingencies as well, anticipating the Japanese response to our subterfuge. We hid our present living accommodations beneath the camouflage of fresher foliage. We added to our larder of foodstuffs, collecting enough coconuts to keep us supplied for at least a weeklong siege. The cistern was topped off and covered with a mat of fresh green palm fronds. With any luck we hoped we could all continue to stay here together, but being realistic, we planned for the possibility of having to separate and hide, surviving as individuals rather than as a group. In this situation there was power afforded to being alone as opposed to being together, an ease in hiding, an increased mobility, a single mind to consider and obey. I would not want to live the remainder of my life without the comfort of community, but for the short term this was the only viable option. We each scoured the island, finding places to hide, keeping those locations secret. Unknown to our fellows, that ignorance gave us plausible deniability. The Japanese were infamous for torturing their captives to obtain information. Should any of us be unfortunate enough to fall into Jap hands, we could not betray anyone else, even if subjected to physical abuse because we truly did not know the whereabouts of anyone else. Should we be captured, all we were to reveal was name, rank, and serial number. We were lone survivors of a crash and had acted alone. Given my personal "wanted" status I would become Captain Carl Jonathon Murphy just as the tags around my neck would corroborate.

We predetermined meeting dates and places with the intent of rejoining each other after the anticipated manhunt died down. The Japs wouldn't search forever. Sooner or later they would return to their mission, more wary perhaps, less complacent in their guard duties and certainly more paranoid, constantly suspicious someone else was near that meant them harm, making future strikes by our little band more difficult to accomplish. We had to make this first strike count, draw as much blood as we could before retreating into obscurity. Without conventional weapons, our future attacks would not be as lethal, but would continue if only to serve as a distraction, an irritant to temporarily divert their attention away from their primary mission and on to us.

The week seemed to me the longest in my entire life, anticipating the action, steeling my resolve, waiting for the next second to click by. Bledsoe, ever my friend, secretly made a gift for me carving a simple chess set out of bamboo. The black players were rendered in red, dyed using berries he'd found, while the white players remained the natural yellow color of bamboo. Primitive yet beautiful, it was destined to become my most treasured possession. He gave it to me on the morning of August 3 along with an apology, "I wasn't able to finish the board, but I'm working on it. I already know how I'll do it, I just ran out of time." The gesture brought tears to my eyes, tears I quickly had to squelch because men don't do such things in the company of other men.

"I wanted you to have it before… Just in case…uh, I just wanted you to have it," Bledsoe said, getting choked up himself.

"Thank you, Bledsoe. This is one of the nicest things anyone has ever done for me. We can play a match or two when we get back. We don't need a board, we can just mark off a grid in the dirt and play."

"That would be great, sir. You may have to teach me a bit. I know the basics, but I doubt I could give you much of a game."

"Knowing you, Bledsoe I'm sure that's a gross understatement. You probably could beat my pants off!"

"I'm pretty sure my assessment of my skill is accurate, sir. We can have fun regardless."

"You've got it, soon as we get back."

CHAPTER 21

At 2100 hours, dusk on August 3, 1945, Bledsoe, Skip, and I left our camp, bidding our fellows good-bye and good luck, embarking upon our mission to sabotage the entire fleet of *Zeros* operating off our island. The waning moon should arise as a faint crescent at 0420, giving us hours of time to complete our task, with nothing more than starlight to betray our presence. From the darkened beach we watched the last three *Zeroes* pass at 2000 feet over our heads, inbound for the night. When at last we arrived at our "Jap Blind," the grass-enveloped site from where we had conducted reconnaissance on the enemy's movements all week, the nightly flurry of ground crew activity was reaching a peak. There we rendezvoused with Jim, who was taking his turn at the ongoing surveillance. We talked in whispers, though I'm not quite sure why as there was no chance the men being watched could have overheard our conversation.

"Only two of the other three groups were out today. Group one just returned." Group number one, the designation we had given to the flight group led by the camp commander had been out for six hours and just returned, had already been refueled and the armorers were busy replacing spent munitions on each aircraft.

"Pretty slow day, not much to report."

"You've actually told us a whole lot, Jim. A six-hour mission and spent ammo. That means these boys saw some action today, probably somewhere within a 500-mile radius if they didn't refuel somewhere else prior to returning. Good work!"

"Thank you, Major."

"Tell me, Jim, have you seen any change in security?"

"No, sir, same two guys in a jeep, three shifts for round-the-clock surveillance. Best I can tell, all they do is drive around and smoke."

"Good. That means they don't suspect any monkey business with the plane they lost last week; otherwise, they'd be all over the field with a fine-toothed comb. We just might pull this off, boys."

Over the next two hours we watched the activities of the ground crews dwindle to a lone supervisor with a clipboard, inspecting the day's labors and taking copious notes. When at long last he completed his task, he retreated to the maintenance shed and stood at the door surveying the line of fighters. Taking the last two draws of a burnt-to-the-fingers cigarette, spent, consumed to the point of pain, he extinguished the red embers by rubbing them together between his palms, then blew the ashes into the night air. Even through the darkness at a distance I could see he was a great deal older than the men who answered to him, his face betraying a great internal sadness, an emotion not expressed to his charges. He knew something, saw something, an inglorious end…the fate of his nation perhaps? The Japanese were slowly being beaten back. He saw the future, their futures, the writing upon the wall, the disgrace of defeat, a promise unfulfilled; his emperor a god, but not a very good one, leaving him to wrestle with a single unanswerable question: why? His labors now complete, he trundled off to bed, perchance to dream of better times.

"I thought that guy would never leave. Let's go," Skip said impatiently.

"Hold on there, cowboy. We're gonna wait a while and give everyone time to go to sleep."

"You're right, as usual," he said, nodding.

The next forty-five minutes passed in silence before I asked, "Are you ready?" Both men nodded affirming. "Skip, your job is to be our lookout. I expect you to keep your eyes on the guard jeep at all times. If they change positions, I want to know about it, understood?"

"Yes, sir."

"One other thing, a gun shot will bring everyone in camp out to see what's going on. If there's a problem, use your knife. Be sure they don't have the chance to get a shot off. You'll have to be quick and decisive if the situation calls for killing."

"Yes, sir," both men answered, aware of the gravity of my words. We had all killed men, been responsible for the deaths of perhaps hundreds if not thousands, but all of our killing had been accomplished anonymously, sanitarily, bombs dropped from altitude, sometimes multiple miles separated from our victims, nothing personal, this is war. None of us had taken a life up close and personal, eye-to-eye, *mano-a-mano*. The task was repugnant on the most gut-wrenching level, not an act any of us would perform lightly or without cause. War was cause enough. It had to be, or I would never sleep again.

The only detectable life in the camp at this unnatural hour was emanating from a jeep, parked presently in front of the infirmary tent, about 300 yards away. It was the same two kids I'd encountered on the night of my first act of sabotage, still smoking and talking, the solace of bored young people the world over. I was happy to see the two complacent guards again. It lessened the likelihood we would have to kill anyone here on the ground. "Be smart, kids, and stay over there, out of our way." Slipping through the darkness, we made our way to the airplane tied down closest to the shed. Skip crouched under the wing, keeping watch as Bledsoe and I made quick work of the control cables. Bledsoe held the panel and retaining screws as I repeated the same technique that had presumably been successful on the previous mission, severing the cable in two places so it was held intact only by the friction between overlapping braids of stainless wire. Within five minutes we had reassembled the aircraft, leaving no discernible trace it had been tampered with, and moved on to the next plane. Unchallenged, we sabotaged all twelve fighters within an hour and fifteen minutes, the incompetent Japanese sentries moving only one time in the same period.

Rejoining Jim in our blind, Bledsoe said, "That was too easy, kind of scary if you ask me."

"Well it's far from over. We won't know till tomorrow night how successful we've been. Who's got the next watch?" I asked Jim. Consulting his watch Jim said, "Doc should be here in fifteen minutes to relieve me."

"We'll wait and walk back together after he gets here."

Right on schedule, Doc arrived to take up his position as the morning watch.

"Keep a sharp eye out, Doc. With any luck, you'll have nothing to report."

"Yes, sir, Major."

We walked back to our camp quietly jubilant, happy with our labors, but anxious to weigh our success. Arriving, I lay down, my mind racing, recounting the details of our raid. I must have been pretty tired because I was asleep before the sunrise.

At 0930 I was wakened by a loud explosion followed shortly by two louder explosions, a crash followed by the detonation of large ordinance. It sounded like thunder echoing from the mountaintop, perhaps a storm brewing on the opposite side of the island. Within fifteen minutes, Doc was back to report, "The jig is up boys. They know or will know soon."

"What'd you see?" The guys all gathered around Doc, hanging on his every word.

"The first three flight groups made it off without any apparent problems. The fourth group was leaving when the second plane banked hard right then sort of shuddered like a stall. It rolled inverted and crashed on the mountain about a hundred feet down from the top. There was a big ball of fire then the bombs blew. It was quite a show! The other two Japs turned back and landed. One of them was the commander with the sword."

"Damn it! It's only a matter of time till they inspect the planes and find the cables cut. They got two back on the ground?"

"Yes, sir. I came back as soon as it happened. Last thing I saw was most of the Jap soldiers scrambling up the mountainside. I don't think they'll come down this side, but we'd better be ready."

"Do you think the pilot had time to communicate a problem?"

"It all happened pretty fast, sir. He hit the mountain within a few seconds, ten at the most after he began to wobble."

"Good job, Doc." Pausing to consider the situation, after several seconds I said, "They won't come down this side yet. They have no reason to think this was anything other than a stall/spin accident. I suspect there's no way to tell from the wreckage that it was a victim of sabotage. No, they shouldn't suspect anything until after they inspect the other two planes and they shouldn't do that till the others don't come back. I think we're Okay for the present. Who's got the next watch?"

"Skip is up next," Bledsoe said.

"Skip, pay close attention to what they do with those airplanes. The second you see the back access panels come off, you head back here and let us know."

"Yes, Major."

Skip returned well after dark excited to report that none of the other airplanes had returned.

"Congratulations, Major, your plan worked perfectly."

Our mission had been a military success, as we had taken out eighty-five percent of the enemy's aircraft without a shot being fired and without a single casualty on our side, a brilliant success for any strategist. Why then were we filled with such apprehension? We knew to a man once our actions had been discovered we needed to be prepared to reap the whirlwind.

"Tomorrow they'll know. Tomorrow is Sunday, August 5," I said vacantly, lost in thought, calculating our next move. "A day, maybe two and they'll come looking for us. They won't do anything tonight. Best get some rest boys, a hell storm is headed this way soon. Who's got the watch tonight?"

"That'd be me, sir," Jim said.

"Come and get me if there are any dramatic changes. I'm gonna take the morning watch myself."

At 0530 I was awakened by Jim, gasping for breath as he had ran fast as he could back to alert us, "Major!... Gasp... Pant ....Major! You've gotta come...quick." Jim looked as if he had seen a ghost. He was pale, clearly distraught, horrified was the word.

"What is it, Jim?"

"You've just gotta come see. I can't believe what the fucking bastards have done."

"What, Jim, just tell me."

"They've killed them, Major! Killed them all!"

"Killed who?" I asked, getting perturbed at Jims lack of clarity. I grabbed him firmly by the shoulders and said, "Take a deep breath and tell me what happened!"

"The Japs! They must have blamed the villagers for what we did 'cause they killed 'em all, every man, woman and child." He began sobbing as he said the word 'child.' Regaining his composure he said, "I saw the ground troops moving, but they were going away from our camp, marching on the beach around to the little village on the other side of the harbor. They were carrying rifles with fixed bayonets, so I decided just to watch rather than come and get you. Next thing, I hear soldiers shouting orders like they were rounding people up, like they were herding cattle or something. The women were screaming and children crying. The Japs spread out in a single line like a barricade on the island side of the village and marched through, driving the villagers forward with their bayonets. They drove them forward right into the ocean...." He again was sobbing. I knew his next sentence without asking, felt it arise from a deep, unlit and unvisited crevasse in my soul. My voice broke in concert with Jim's, "Go on."

"And then they opened fire. They killed every soul in the village, every man, women, and child. They even killed a couple of dogs that had followed their masters into the water."

I was truly dumbstruck. In all of our planning we anticipated their retribution, but we never once considered that it might be misdirected toward innocence. The existence of the village, the unknown dynamics between the natives and the Japanese, elements right before me the entire time, and yet I had remained oblivious to them. How could I have been so miscalculating? We probably found ourselves spared, safe from reprisal, but at what cost? Forever henceforward I would bare the weight of the souls of the natives massacred, as guilty of this atrocity as if I had ordered their execution, pulled the trigger myself, snuffing short their lives, casualties of a war not theirs to fight. Mine was not the hand of death, but his alibi.

"What are we gonna do, sir?"

Disbelief, shock, horror, anger, guilt… my emotions ran the gamut within seconds of learning of the tragedy. My initial gut response would be to meet the Japs headlong, go in guns blazing and kill as many of the bastards as we had bullets to do so, but I knew this bravado would cost us our lives, and for what benefit? What end would justify the sacrifice of my men? A response was clearly required, but a measured response, not one of passion driven by these or any emotion. Justice had to prevail and retribution would be justified by punishing the men responsible. The Jap soldiers were merely following orders, misguided evil orders, but orders just the same. They, too, were victims, having little or no choice but to do as all good soldiers do and follow those orders, good or bad. They too would be forever traumatized, seeing the faces of their innocent victims always before them every time they closed their eyes to sleep.

"Was the commander there?"

"Yes, sir, he walked behind the line of soldiers with his sissy assed little sword drawn."

"Symbolic, I'm guessing. He was taking credit for the act. Okay, we'll give him credit. Before we leave this island that man will die!"

"But what about the rest of the little yellow bastards?" Jim asked, amazed that I had not suggested we get them as well.

"They were following orders," I said flatly. "Besides, we don't have enough ammo to kill them all. They outnumber us twenty to one."

"What did they do in the Westerns?" Bledsoe asked.

"Huh?"

"Western movies when the cavalry was surrounded by Indians?"

"They went for reinforcements," Jim said, more a question than a statement.

"Exactly! They went for reinforcements. That's what we should do."

"Again, huh?" Jim said. "How do you propose to get reinforcements?"

"Major, think you could fly one of those airplanes?"

" Absolutely! An airplane's an airplane," I said.

"Well?"

"Let them repair the plane, then steal it and go for reinforcements… brilliant!" Jim said, now up to speed. Then he added, "Too bad we didn't think of this before we got all those people killed."

"We did, Jim. I didn't think I'd have a chance of making it then because all the other Zeros would have been after me in hot pursuit. But now…"

"Now there's no one to come after you."

"Well, there's two *Zeros* left, but we can disable one so it shouldn't be a problem. Downside as I see it is you boys will have to hang on till I make it back with reinforcement, *if* I make it back. Don't forget, I've got to make it into an Allied airfield in a Jap *Zero* without getting shot down in the process, *if* I can even find one of those airfields. We have no idea where the hell we are. I could take off over the Pacific and never see land again. A lot of *ifs* in this plan."

"If it can be done, you're the man to do it, Major. We have faith in you," Bledsoe said. I smiled to modestly acknowledge the compliment.

"One other thing," I said solemnly, "Just because they killed all those people doesn't mean they are not looking for us. I can't believe they won't increase security."

"You may be right, Major. We'll have to do some reconnaissance to see how paranoid they still are."

"Well, if they really do start looking for us it implies something substantially more sinister. It means the commander was just looking for a reason to wipe out the village and used our attack as an excuse. It makes his act appear to be righteous retribution, when all the while he knew they were not responsible. I'd like to think no person is truly that evil. My hope is he thinks he's dealt with the problem and nothing further remains to be done."

Bledsoe looked skeptical, "So nothing will change? I don't know if I believe that. How we sabotaged those planes was simple, but sophisticated, even elegant, not something a group of South Pacific island natives are capable of. If the commander gave it half a thought he would come to the same conclusion." Bledsoe's observations were wise as usual. Perhaps he was right, but the only way we'd know for sure was to watch the Japs and see what happened. After dark we'd go back to see what, if anything, had changed.

"I suspect they'll make a token effort to increase security, but when they see nothing it won't take long for the same sentries to fall into complacency. We'll watch, but we're not gonna act till we know what's what."

We observed from the cover of our blind for hours. The two Zeros were already repaired, and having been flown, gave me confidence my handiwork had been adequately repaired and the aircraft were safe to fly. As the sun sank below the ocean's rim we saw the carnage of the Japanese massacre, human flotsam, bloated and suspended lifelessly at the water's top, strewn ragdoll-like along the beach. The sharks and seabirds feasted upon the carcasses, the victims' blood having called out to them, enticing them to come and dine. With so many bodies from which to choose the sharks ate leisurely, no frenzy borne of immediacy. I saw no Japanese watching as this travesty reached its logical conclusion, forbidden by an innate sense of guilt to watch.

Here was nature, yet again cleaning up where we humans had so egregiously trespassed, eliminating any stench, any clue of the crime committed against humanity and the earth. Were we not here to bear witness, vengeance might have been left in the hands of a God who punishes the children for the sins of the fathers to the third or fourth generation. As humans, we feel it necessary to usurp the privilege of a God who declares, "Vengeance is mine," thinking we might better serve justice. But we saw. We knew and would not, could not forget. When the war was over, there would be justice, would be retribution, and would be more blood spilt to atone for this crime against humanity, but only if one of us survived to tell the story.

For three days and nights we kept a constant vigil, the airfield always under surveillance. The same boats and crews patrolled the island perimeter on the same schedule they had kept before our action. The same two sentries shared the night duty, patrolling the airfield and camp in an open jeep. We observed no variations in what we had come to anticipate from the Japanese. It seemed too easy. Was the commander really this daft, or was he a brilliant strategist, luring us in by appearing oblivious to reality? After three nights of watching, seeing no discernible evidence our existence was suspected, we decided to take action. "There is only one way to find out." If I was going to do this I needed to act before the Japanese arrived with reinforcements of their own to replace the aircraft and men we had destroyed. I had to play my hand, and soon, or risk losing my window of opportunity. Tonight is the night. I would go alone, the plan to be off before daylight August 8th while the Japs were all still snug in their beds. Once the engine fired up, I guessed I would have maybe one minute, two tops before the entire Jap contingent was alerted and rushing, hell-bent upon securing my demise. That the Japs would be alerted and come running was inevitable, a foregone conclusion that's only variable was how long it would take for the Japanese to respond. Two minutes was not enough time to get the engine warmed up, so I had to anticipate its performance would be less than optimal. I needed optimal in an airplane I was not familiar with. The basic controls should be the same, a stick and rudder pedals. The engine controls, however, could prove very different. Placement of the controls varied from aircraft to aircraft, even within our own fleet. There was a lot to consider before attempting starting the engine and alerting the Japs. The clock started ticking at that precise moment. All in all, this was not the best plan I'd ever come up with, but I was convinced if I could get the wheels off the ground I was home free. My only other obstacle, and it would be a doozy, was to avoid getting blown out of the sky by my own comrades. With the advent of the *Kamikaze*, U.S. military tactics had changed dramatically. The only way to stop the suicide pilots was to hit them first, killing the pilot or disabling the airplane so it could not be used against you as a weapon. The operative word in that sentence was *first*. "Shoot *first*, ask questions later," had become the instinctual survival mentality of the Allies, a mentality that very well might get me killed today, victim to *friendly fire*.

"You know you don't have to do this Major. We can just hide out till it's over and…"

"And miss out on the rest of the fun? I wouldn't dream of it. Listen guys, no plan is without risk, and I think the risks in this situation are acceptable. The greater risk might be for us to be forgotten completely after the war. I can assure you, our side wrote us off long ago. Hell, boys, we didn't even know this island existed till we found it the hard way. If the war ends and we're still here in hiding, we might never be found. I promised you from the beginning that I would see you home and I'm damned sure not gonna break that promise. I already feel like I betrayed Lenny. And CJ. And Jordy," I said, my mind's eye seeing each of their faces as I spoke their names. "I can't let that happen! Besides, I want to see my kid before he has kids of his own." Everyone laughed at my joke, but I was only half joking. My greatest fear at present was not dying, but living, marooned here on this island while Mary lingered on, believing me dead. She was young and beautiful and had a child to think of. She wouldn't wait forever if she truly believed I was dead, nor would I want her to, but going home to find her married to another man would be worse than death itself. I was going home or I'd die trying.

Bledsoe was on watch duty, but all my other men were present as I laid out my plan. I would act alone, as no one else was capable of helping me. Tonight I would steal a *Zero* and fly to an Allied base for reinforcements, pledging to return by nightfall, seventy-two hours from now.

"Captain Johnson will be in charge here." I saw Skip's smile of accomplishment. Skip was a good person, but leaving him in command scared the crap out of me. I continued suppressing that thought, "Your job is to stay hidden and stay alive until I come back for you. If I'm not back in seventy-two hours you will know I've failed. Regardless of what happens, stay hidden and stay alive. That's an order, the last I will give you until I get back, so I expect it obeyed to the letter." In unison the men responded, "Yes, sir." They then lined up to shake my hand, wishing me luck before I headed off. Skip Johnson pulled me aside at last saying, "Thank you, Major. I won't let you down."

"I know you won't, Captain. See you soon!" We exchanged salutes and I was off.

I arrived at the blind just after dusk. When Bledsoe saw me alone he knew the time had come.

"I'm sorry now I suggested this plan, Major."

"You didn't suggest anything I wasn't already planning, Bledsoe. I've just got to do it now before the Japs have time to rearm themselves. I'm kind of surprised it hasn't happened already."

"I know, I was just thinking the same thing. I wonder what's taking them so long?"

"The Allies were kicking their ass before we crashed. They know the end is near and they're retreating, preparing to defend the Japanese mainland. God help us all because that will be a bloodbath. I shudder to think how many men will die on both sides before they surrender, and that's the only thing we'll accept, their complete and unconditional surrender."

"I hope I live to see that," he said wistfully.

"Me, too, Bledsoe...me, too!" We sat silently together, contemplating that day. After a good bit I said, "I'm just sorry I can't leave you in charge here. You're certainly the most competent, but Skip is the ranking officer, asshole or not."

"Thank you, sir. Coming from you that means a lot."

"I want you to make me a promise regardless of what happens," I looked at him questioningly.

"Yes, sir, just name it!"

"I trust you, Bledsoe. You're one of the smartest men I know. Don't let Skip do something stupid and get these men killed."

"You've got it, sir. Anything else?"

"I'm guessing my chances in this thing are about fifty/fifty. If I'm not back in seventy-two hours with the Marines, I've failed."

"Marines, sir?" he laughed.

"Just a figure of speech. If I'm not back, it means I'm dead, understand?"

"Oh you'll be back, sir. I'm confident!"

"That makes one of us, Bledsoe. Look, regardless of what happens from here on out, I want you to keep the men hidden and alive. I made them and you a promise, but it may be you, Sergeant Bledsoe Courage, who keeps it!"

"Yes, sir. You can count on me."

"Funny, that's the same thing Skip said."

I lay down to get some sleep before the mission, letting Bledsoe keep watch. As instructed, he awakened me at 0330. I was deeply asleep and it took me a few minutes to shake it off.

"Are you ready for this, sir?" It was a question a priest might ask a condemned man before his execution. I smiled bravely, hoping to hide my apprehension, and said, "No time like the present. Remember Bledsoe, no matter what happens here, stay out of it. Your job, your orders are to keep these boys alive. One other thing, if something happens and I don't…well… check in on Mary for me, okay?"

"You're gonna be back here in seventy-two hours with the Marines. The clock's ticking." We exchanged salutes and I slipped off into the blackness of the night.

The first *Zero* I came upon was the commander's own mount. I figured stealing it should add insult to injury, so I didn't even consider the other aircraft tied down next to it. Slipping beneath each wing, I loosened the retaining ropes. Looking about, I did not see my friends in their jeep, nor the light from the cigarettes I'd bet my mother hung from their lips at this very moment. Not seeing them made me a little nervous, as their presence had always before been a constant. I sat for a couple of minutes straining to find them in the darkness, but to no avail, so I decided to proceed. The Japanese had always heretofore kept their airplanes armed, fueled, and ready, allowing them an immediate response to an attacker. I decided to gamble and not check the fuel quantity visually as Dave had taught me to do so many years ago. Stepping up on the wing to open the canopy, I noticed how the aluminum skin buckled, deforming under my weight and quickly decided this might not be the best tactic. Pressing with my thumb I tented the aluminum skin and guestimated they must be a third the thickness of a comparable American fighter. Looking further, I discovered a series of retractable handholds and steps purposed to allow the pilot access to the cockpit without damaging the plane. "I'm behind the eight ball enough as it is. No reason to damage the plane before takeoff if I don't have to." Perched atop the highest step, I searched for and found the canopy latch and slid the glass back cautiously, trying to be quiet as possible. Stepping onto the seat, I slipped in. "Well this should be an interesting flight," I thought, as my head, perched atop a six-foot-three-inch frame, protruded above the windshield, far too tall to close the canopy without ducking, pressing my chin against the glare shield. It was still so dark I could see nothing inside the cockpit. Having only three matches, I began my exploration of the cockpit limited to my sense of touch. Surprisingly, my fingertips told me the cockpit was arranged very similarly to the North American AT-6. Logging almost a hundred hours in the trainer three years ago, I still felt pretty comfortable with the aircraft. There were, however, some significant exceptions. The landing gear and flap controls were on the right instead of left side of the cockpit. A pump lever to the right of the instrument panel was either a hydraulic pump for the flaps and landing gear or a fuel pump, a critical difference for me at the moment. Most aircraft of the day required the fuel system to be manually pressurized, using a hand pump prior to starting the engine. As I would get only one shot at this, choosing the correct pump was of premium importance. Failing, the Japs would be on me like white on rice well before I could try a second time. On the left hand side of the cockpit, I felt a similar pump handle on the floor, near what I assumed was the fuel selector valve. It made sense this was the fuel pump and the other the hydraulic.

Okay, time to light a match and have a quick look around. Once illuminated, I could see the fuel selector had three positions, which I assumed would be right tank, left tank, and off, with the off position being presently selected. A creature of habit, I chose the left tank and began pumping the fuel pump handle, watching for movement on one of the many illegible gauges in the panel. Indeed, I was rewarded when a gauge on the right side of the panel sprung to life. When the needle stopped rising I stopped pumping and looked for an engine primer, and there it was, same position as in the Texan. Three shots of fuel ought to do it.

"Now to find the starter button," I thought, lighting the second match. Igniting a flame was a risky proposition, as I could now smell fuel in the cockpit. Finding two buttons next to the magneto switch, I assumed one was probably the starter motor, the other the clutch switch that should engage the prop once the inertial starter was running at full rpm. I put the stick and rudder through their full ranges of motion, assuring myself the controls were free and clear with no locking device. That would be catastrophic if I managed to get the airplane off the ground only to find the controls locked. With that thought I instinctively reached to check my parachute, then recalled I had none. "Selfish little bastards could have at least left me a chute in the seat," I quipped to myself. "Well, I guess this is it." I sat for a moment and brought Mary to mind. I envisioned her sitting sweetly on her mother's front porch swing in a white sundress, a glass of lemonade in one hand, her legs crossed as she bounced her free foot rhythmically, her nails painted bright red and perfect. Johnny was playing with a toy airplane in the yard. For a child I'd never laid eyes on, I could see him perfectly. He looked just like my brother Davey. It was a perfect late summer morning, the entire world cast in an amber glow. "I love you, Mary," I said aloud.

Reaching for the starter button, I depressed and held it, hearing the inertial starter beginning low, revving up over about ten seconds till its pitch reached a maximum. Releasing the switch I engaged the clutch and the prop turned in synchrony. Four blades spun past before I flipped the mag switch on, the engine responding with a POP POP POP. It started to catch then died, silent. "Shit!" I start the fuel pump and prime process again as I look frantically about. There they were, the two boys in a jeep rushing towards the *Zero*. "C'mon baby, c'mon," I shouted at the airplane as though it were listening. I hit the starter again and waited for the wind up. An eternal, ten seconds passed before I could hit the clutch to set the prop spinning again. I hit the mag switch just as the first sentry jumped upon the wing from behind. As he reached for me in the cockpit, I pull my .45 and shot him twice in the chest, only inches away, the blast propelling him backward off the rear of the wing, his mortally wounded body falling upon his partner. The second boy had his rifle aimed at my head, but his aim was displaced when struck by his partner. He misfired and I heard the bullet whiz past my left ear, thankfully missing its mark. Before he could fire again I shot him twice, his face exploding into a bloody caricature of its living form. The engine caught again with a POP POP POP then started to die. Frantically I pushed the throttle quickly open and closed, forward and back, my efforts were rewarded and the sputtering engine remained alive. The whole of the Japanese army was rushing for me if not already upon me, surrounding me, hot for my blood. I push the throttle forward and spun the *Zero* around thinking I can clear my path with the machine guns. I pulled the trigger on the stick but nothing happened. "There must have been a safety on the gun somewhere, but I had no time to find it now. "Damn it!"

In an instant, men were trying to climb upon the wings from all angles. Advancing the throttle, I accelerated into the crowd before me. Angry, frightened men, bobbing and weaving, leery of my next move, defensively scattered to avoid the spinning propeller. Just as I began to think the way would part and I'd be free, a jeep pulled in front of the plane. I tried to stop and avoid it, but to no avail, the prop stopped abruptly, eating into the steel of the jeep's rear deck. The engine suddenly silent, the shouting and cries of a hundred angry Japanese men fill the void. I realized all was lost as I was grabbed, held fast by multiple hands before being struck in the head multiple times with the butt of a rifle. Blinding flashes of pain envelope me, becoming my universe, I surrendered to my fate. With the fifth blow, the world went black and I ceased to exist.

CHAPTER 22

Opening my eyes, I anticipated seeing flames, and perhaps even Satan himself. I knew I was dead, or at least I should have been, because I vaguely recalled being beaten to death by an army of Japanese soldiers, taking turns and great satisfaction in kicking and stomping and beating the soul out of me after pulling me unconscious from the *Zero*. Yet here I was very much alive, and unfortunately, cognizant of the fact, pain an encompassing reminder of my failure to reach mortality. I tried to open my eyes to see whether I'm truly alive or dead in hell, but found they were swollen shut, light and shadows perceived through my eyelids. For all practical purposes I was blind. I was also having difficulty hearing, my ears were swollen and full of dried blood, proving no competition for tinnitus, the Greek god of loud obnoxious noises, peeling a deafening ring, echoing through my skull. This can't be hell, not the hell I learned about in Sunday school, because the overwhelming stench in my nostrils was not of brimstone, but of shit, fresh human excrement, and urine. I'm pretty sure that's what I tasted as well, the mere thought bringing new meaning to my understanding of the word nausea. My hands were bound behind me, pulled up into the small of my back by a rope, with a ligature fastened around my throat, connecting the two. Struggling to breathe, I'm unsure if it's the rope or swelling from the hematoma around my neck that was suffocating me. I was bound at the ankles as well, a useless gesture on their part as I couldn't run let alone walk if my life depended upon it, which it probably did.

After they beat and bound me, they dragged me by the ankles, finally throwing me into the open trench of their common latrine that I may be further debased and humiliated. At their leisure, they took turns relieving themselves upon me, an act in human society considered to be the epitome of degradation, reserved for only the most hated and reviled. I was alive at that moment, not because they wouldn't require my life of me for surely they would, but to be punished, tortured as much as possible before I was finally allowed to succumb. A bullet in my head would be a blessing, an act of supreme mercy, for I gladly would be elsewhere, anywhere an end to this torment might be found. Perhaps if I could hold my breath long enough I would die." God forgive me, Mary, I'm sorry, but I've got to be released."

Holding my breath, I refused to breathe, and my private hell faded to even deeper blackness. I lost consciousness only to be revived by another Jap fucker, one of a long line of fuckers to take a piss on me. I manage to say with a voice more a hissing whisper than human, "*Watashi wa amerika-jin, watashi wa anata no yujindseu*, I am an American, I am your friend." My present tormentor found my words hilarious, the funniest thing he had ever heard in his life. Laughing heartily, he perfected his aim, striking me between the eyes with his stream of urine. "How long can this last?" I wondered, spinning in and out of consciousness so many times I lost track… one world devoid of pain, black, and empty of everything, one world pain itself, endless and unbearable, a nightmare I wouldn't wish befall the vilest of criminals, not even on Hitler or Tojo themselves. I had no concept of time, lost here in this encampment of suffering. This was hell. It had to be, for God himself could design no better punishment. My only solace, my only comfort was the thought I would indeed die, and soon, God let it be soon.

I woke yet again, lying on the tarmac in the noonday sun, still bound, sputtering, coughing, and wet from the bucket of sea water thrown upon me, not only to awaken me, but to wash off enough of the vile, nauseating stench that they, my captors, might be able to endure my presence. I heard, or I thought I heard a voice, English, intelligible words spoken in a thick Japanese accent.

"Who has helped you, Captain Murphy?" "I'm not Captain Murphy," I thought bewildered, my mind reeling, trying to make sense of the strange question, then out of the fog I recalled the ruse. When I was not quick enough to respond, I was kicked in the chest, making me cough blood.

"Who has helped you?" the prick asked again. Again I am kicked. Maybe I'll get lucky and this will end it, I'd gladly give up living.

"Who has helped you?" he shouts. Before he kicks me again I open my mouth signifying my willingness to answer.

"I… Am…. Carl… Jonathon… Murphy…Captain…. 47…2630," my voice reduced to a gasping, ghostly whisper, unintelligible to anyone, unrecognizable as me. I awaited the boot blow that hovered over me menacingly, but it didn't fall, a reward that I had responded in a fashion.

"Who has helped you, Captain Murphy?" spoken in a tone now softer, mostly civil. The seawater has loosened the blood crusting my eyes; I pried them open for the first time in hours, if not days. My inquisitor was none other than the commander himself. He stood over me surrounded by other soldiers, his subordinates, underlings brandishing rifles pointed in my direction. "Okay, you fucking Jap prick," I thought, "Let's dance. The worst you can do is to kill me, which would be a relief."

"I ask you again, Captain Murphy, who has helped you?"

After several seconds I answered with the only response I would ever give him the satisfaction of receiving, "Carl Jonathon Murphy, captain, 47-2630." The boot fell again, slamming into my chest. He walked around me to display his frustration and, I presume, lack of patience. Drawing his sword, he pressed the tip into my cheek.

"I will ask you only one more time, Captain Murphy, who has helped you?" I mouthed the words, compelling him to lean closer to my face that he might hear. With the last bit of moisture in my mouth I spat, hitting him squarely between the eyes before saying, "Carl Jonathon Murphy, captain…."

In anger he brandished the sword above his head, broadcasting his intent, its metal shining, gleaming in the sunlight. Down he swung, both hands holding fast the shank, delivering the blade with enough force and speed to take my head. "Yes God, Thank you, I'm coming!" The sword struck my neck severing the ligature. A blinding flash of dazzling sparks consumed my vision, as increased blood flow hit my deprived brain cells, but to my amazement and dismay I was alive. He had lacerated my neck, leaving the faintest of nicks, but his disciplined swordsmanship had left my throat intact, my head still connected to my body. Breathing easier, I reflexively extended my still-bound arms to a position of lesser discomfort. As the commander walked away he shouted orders first in Japanese, then, for my benefit, in English, "Let him lie here in the open. They will come for him, or the sun will do its work."

"Oh Jesus, boys…stay where you are. You don't want any of this." The adrenalin rush of the encounter spent, I lapse again into the dream world of blackness.

I dreamed I was bacon, hot and sizzling in a skillet. My granddaddy was frying me up, fixing breakfast for Davey and me. I saw myself as well, sitting at the kitchen table, back in Valdosta. I was a third grader, whining about school being over and Granddaddy said, "Not long now boy, and you'll be out for the summer." His words were comforting, a promise my torment will soon be over. "Now you boys finish your breakfast and get off to school. I'll be at Mrs. Johnsons delivering her baby when you get home. Don't forget your chores or your home work, hear?"

"Yes, sir. I love you, Granddaddy," I say, giving his cheek a peck. Granddaddy patted my head on the way out the door as he always did every morning, then his loving pat turned to the sole of a boot holding my face to the steaming tarmac.

I was still here, still alive. My boys did not come for me, had not been foolish, or noble or brave, but had obeyed my orders and stayed away, hopefully oblivious to my plight, but even if they had seen, they had obeyed. For that mercy I was truly thankful.

"Who has helped you Captain Murphy? Tell me and you shall have water before I end your suffering." I did not answer his question, but heard, emanating from the depth of my being a scream as he pressed more firmly with his boot, crushing my right cheekbone. Again I passed from pain to the shelter of oblivion. Into the comfort of darkness my mind receded only to be summoned forth by a bucket of seawater.

"If you tell me, I will let them live. If you don't, I will burn the jungle and scorch the earth leaving nowhere they cannot be found. Then I will kill them, just as I am going to kill you."

"Carl Jonathon Murphy, captain, 47-2630." He responded again with his boot, this time with a swift kick in the groin. Reflexively, I vomited the bitterest of bile. Amused that he has elicited a response he placed his foot upon my scrotum and slowly, methodically crushed my genitals, grinding them into the dense pavement. Again my mouth formed a scream, but I passed out before it escaped. Again the seawater.

"Captain Murphy, who…" Before he could finish asking another question I answered him, "Carl Jonathon Murphy, captain….," again he kicked me, this time in the belly and again I puked. "God in heaven be merciful, I don't think I can take anymore."

"I am not an evil man, Captain. I do not enjoy this, but your reluctance to talk is leaving me no choice. Tell me what I desire to know and I will end your pain."

"Just like you had no choice murdering all those civilians?"

"Casualties of war, Captain. They were impairing my mission here. Just like you, I answer to a higher authority. My mission must not fail."

"It's a little late for that, Tojo. You lost your squadron and soon you bastards will lose everything."

"Amusing! You call us *bastards* and yet we know the names of our forefathers for a thousand years. We ARE Nippon, while you are a nation of upstarts and mongrels. Who are the bastards?"

"Well I guess you're getting your Nippon asses kicked by a nation of upstarts and mongrels, then." Seeing I'd struck a nerve I pressed on, "What a shame, a thousand years of honor, all lost by a single generation. I'm sure those forefathers of yours are spinning in their graves. The death of Nippon, all past honor lost for the pride and arrogance of the present generation. That's quite a legacy to leave your children, hey Tojo?" He kicked me once again in the stomach saying, "Nippon will never die," before walking away. When I was finally able to stop gasping in pain I called after him, "Nippon is already dead. You're just too fucking stupid to know it yet!" Whipping around, he drew his sidearm, hurrying once again to my side. Leaning down he held the barrel to my forehead. I felt and heard the hammer cock, the trembling of his hand transmitted through the steel to the battered flesh of my face. I was strangely calm, not afraid of the next second, for it held nothing I could neither face nor endure. "This is it then, good-bye Mary," I thought, closing my eyes. Seconds later I heard the pistol's report and felt the bullet rip through the flesh of my left thigh, shattering my femur before making its exit, leaving an even larger, exploding devastation of flesh in its wake. "My name is not Tojo….I am Yoshi Nomaguchi, the last of a proud line of warriors." Once again I lost consciousness; the last sounds I recalled were of his boots walking away across the compressed earth of the runway.

The morning sun awakened me to a different world, a surreal world, menacingly frightening as it seemed so completely irrational. The maddening roar of tinnitus provided the background music to what I was to witness. As before, I awoke expecting to find myself residing somewhere in the afterlife, reward or punishment, heaven or hell, but I was still alive, yet strangely, unbelievably, incomprehensibly everything had changed. The ropes binding my hands and feet had been cut as I lay comatose, sometime in the night, leaving my liberation unrecognized. I rolled and sat on the tarmac, taking stock of my injuries. My head swooned as I sat up, weak, spent, exhausted. Everything hurt! My face felt like a bag of mashed potatoes, so swollen I barely could open my eyes. Every breath was an exquisite agony, the pain of my ribs popping and grinding together, having sustained fractures at multiple sites. My hands were crushed and swollen, my fingers resembled sausages. My poor scrotum had been crushed beyond recognition. I was one large bruise from head to toe, very much in pain, but remarkably, very much alive. "Even Tojo's gun had failed to kill me," I thought, refusing, even silently, to acknowledge his real name. My left thighbone had been shattered by the gunshot, leaving me unable to arise and walk away from my captors.

My captors? It was not my injuries, nor my freedom I found most surreal that hot summer morning. No, it was my captors, the Japanese soldiers who had only yesterday taken such delight in my torment. They still surrounded me. Like dead men walking, they passed me lying on the tarmac oblivious, indifferent to my presence. Feigned behavior I couldn't say, but avoiding me nonetheless, I remained unacknowledged. No eyes met mine, but were downcast, intent upon escaping my gaze. They strode around the obstacle of my battered body in silence; ghost-like, bereft of joy, of soul, of emotion. The trance-like actions of men marching to a gallows, to the end of themselves, surprised at a fate, their collective fates now realized, defeated and humiliated, given over to servitude at the whims of a presently unseen victor.

They boarded the patrol boat in small groups, a launch that ferried them to a larger vessel awaiting them just outside the shallow harbor. An army on the move, yet none carried provisions or weapons, the uniforms on their backs the sole item in their possession at departing the island.

Nothing that morning seemed real, but rather dreamlike, a walking dream had I been able to walk. I struggled to wrap my brain around what I was witnessing, but it met with no semblance of logic I could conjure up. As the last group of soldiers boarded the launch, my crew came to me on the tarmac, emerging tentatively from the jungle's cloister, each bewildered at the strange turn of events, but obviously confident in their new safety from Japanese reprisal. "What the hell is going on?" I asked as they tried to help me to my feet.

Attempting to stand, my leg buckled under me with terrible pain.

"Lay him back down. Bledsoe, you and Jim run up to the infirmary and find a stretcher," Doc ordered, being in charge of all things medical.

"I sure am glad to see you, Major. Do you know how hard it was to sit and watch those pricks do this to you and not do anything?" Bledsoe asked, tears in his eyes.

"I'm glad you did, Bledsoe. They would have killed us all had they found you."

"They almost did, sir. Twenty or thirty Japs came ashore the first day they captured you. They found our camp, but we'd all split up and hid just like you told us. They burned it down and kept on looking, but never found one of us. I was in a tree just ten feet above 'em when they came through, but luckily they never looked up." He hurried off with Jim to retrieve a stretcher as Doc knelt to examine me.

"How bad am I, Doc?"

"You look like shit, but you're gonna be okay. Looks like the Japs left everything behind. They just got up this morning and walked away. It's the damnedest thing I've ever seen!"

"What do you think it means?" I asked, truly puzzled.

"I think it means we won!"

"They just gave up? We surely haven't had enough time to invade and conquer Japan since we crashed. It just doesn't make sense."

"Nothing in this war has made sense to me, John. I gave up trying long ago."

Bledsoe and Jim returned on the run with a stretcher and a box of medication. Doc gave me a shot of something that washed over my body with the loveliest, most intoxicating of warm glows.

"Morphine?" I asked.

"I hope so," Doc said jokingly, "I can't read Japanese." Loading me gently onto the stretcher, they carried me to the infirmary, and though their every step sent a searing pain echoing through my body, strangely I didn't care. Whether it was the morphine or the events of the day, I still don't know. I only know I was happy, truly and unabashedly happy for the first time since I could remember.

Awakening in a Japanese cot, bathed and clean, my nose free of the stench of human excrement I feared might linger on me forever like an odor tattoo, I discovered my wounds freshly dressed, and my shattered bones splinted with plaster. Doc had worked his magic, leaving me feeling human once more. Seeing me alert for the first time in days, he was quickly at my side with lots to tell me.

"We won! The war is over!"

"I kind of figured that much, but how so quickly? It doesn't make sense."

"Bledsoe and the boys went exploring the camp. They found a radio receiver in the commander's quarters and we tuned into Radio Tokyo. MacArthur accepted the Japs signed documents, an unconditional surrender three days ago. The whole show happened on the deck of the *Missouri*. Hard to believe they sailed right into the Tokyo Bay harbor without firing a single shot."

"They just rolled over and gave up? I don't believe it. I always figured we'd win, but not without invading Japan and kicking the shit out of every fucking Jap left alive," I said incredulously.

"From what we could gather on the radio, we did. The B-29 boys over on Tinian dropped some new kind of bomb on a couple of Jap cities and totally wiped 'em off the planet."

"A single bomb?"

'Yep! Must've been one hell of a big bomb! Anyway, the second did the trick, convincing the Japs they were licked."

"Wow! Who could have imagined that? Well, that explains why the Japs just up and left." As Doc filled me in on everything I'd missed in my sleep, a sleep that though feeling like a refreshing two-hour nap had actually consumed three whole days, Bledsoe came in bearing gifts.

"Good morning, Major. Welcome back to the land of the living," Bledsoe said, displaying a smile that stretched from ear to ear. "Here, Major, I thought you might just want these." He handed me a package wrapped in rice paper, then flushed in embarrassment as he realized I couldn't open it with both my hands encased in plaster.

"Sorry, sir! Here let me open it for you." Opening the package, he withdrew its contents one by one. First he handed me a leather holster containing a *Nambu* Type 14, the sidearm preferred by the majority of the Japanese officers corps.

"I'm guessing this is the gun the bastard shot you with. Funny, it feels kind of cheap, almost like a toy."

"I can assure you, Bledsoe, it's no toy," I laughed. "How'd you get this?"

"Same way I got this," he said, revealing the commander's Katana sword. My puzzled look asking the question for me.

"He killed himself with this. Committed ritual suicide. The Japanese call it *Harkiari*. I'll bet there's a lot of that going around today," he said chuckling, before continuing more somberly, "I pulled this out of his gut." It was fitting I should now possess the weapon used to snuff out his life. I would always feel that my words killed him long before he died plunging this sword into his own belly.

"Thanks, Bledsoe. I really appreciate the gesture."

"There's more, well, one thing more," he said removing a small, ornate box.

"The bastard played chess?" I asked, surprised and somewhat disgusted.

"He owned this, but I don't know if he played or not. Doesn't look like it's ever been opened."

"Why don't you keep that, Bledsoe? I don't think I want to remember him as anything other than a thug, a murderer who killed an entire village of civilians."

"Thanks, sir, I will, but you still owe me a game."

"Don't worry, Bledsoe, I'll never forget. We'll play with the set you made for me." His smile broadened even more. "Hey, Bledsoe, in all your snooping around did you ever find any maps?" He answered my real question without my having to voice it.

"Admiralty Islands, sir. They were right under our noses the entire time."

"Unbelievable. Intelligence assured us they had cleared every one of these islands."

"Well, they missed this one," he said, rolling his eyes cynically.

"I don't suppose we've been able to contact anyone on our team to say we're alive?"

"The fucking Japs smashed the transmitter on their way out the door, but we're already working on a solution." I raised my eyebrows questioningly, so Bledsoe continued, "Skip left this morning to..."

"Left? Left how?"

"He took off flying the remaining *Zero* for..."

"Good God, they'll shoot him out of the sky!"

"Skip thought of that..." When I looked skeptical he said, "Okay, with a little help from me. We painted stars and bars all over the thing and just in case that wasn't enough, I painted FRIEND in three foot letters on the bottom wing."

"Well done! Do you think he can..."

"Find his way back? Got that covered, too. I sent along a map with the island circled in red. Skip gets to be a hero, we get rescued, everyone is happy."

"Bledsoe, I could kiss you! You're a genius!'

"I try, sir. If it's all the same to you, you can keep the kiss." We both laughed.

"That's enough excitement for one day, Major. I want you to get some rest," Doc said to me as a not-too-subtle request for Bledsoe to leave me in peace. I heard them arguing as I slipped once more into the world of Morpheus.

CHAPTER 23

"*Captain Murphy*, that's one of the most amazing stories I've ever heard," I said, placing special emphasis on the name he had given us. My raised eyebrows begged him to consider his answer to the riddle of the day, "Do you recall your name?" I could see he was struggling, still deep, but swimming upward, slowly slipping free of the abyss, the Alzheimer's dementia holding captive all his recent memories. Though the unbounded prison seemed to be offering him a brief reprieve, the vicious malady soon would lock him away again, and then forever.

"Yes, I remember now. Actually, it's Colonel, son, I was promoted before the Army discharged me," he smiled proudly.

"And you are Colonel…?"

"Colonel John Stone, United States Army Air Corps" he said, his face betraying the relief he experienced at recalling his own identity. "My friends call me Johnny."

"Colonel Stone, you're a hero! Your story should be made into a movie," I said, sincerely impressed. "As an ER doc I've heard lots of great stories, but yours tops them all."

"Well if I am a hero, I'm one of millions. The Admiral tried to pin a medal on me saying the same thing. He wanted to put me up for the Congressional Medal of Honor, but I flatly refused. My entire generation, every last one of us, did what we had to do, then came home and got back to the work of living. There really wasn't anything special about me or what I did." His eyes welling with tears, he added, "Just think about every one of those boys who weren't lucky like me. They didn't get to come home. They're the heroes, not me."

"Spoken like a hero in the truest sense of the word," I said. The old man actually blushed at my words.

I sat in wonder, studying my patient, Colonel John Stone. Several hours ago we began a discourse, a clinical exercise purposed to discover the identity of a cantankerous old geezer found lost, wandering aimlessly in the snow. As the day had worn on, I'd discovered how wrong I'd been to dismiss him because of his advanced age. I now found myself absolutely mesmerized by this man, the nobility of his character, the poignancy of his story. Before me sat a hero of *Indiana Jones* proportions brought low by a sinister malady beyond his control, his story, a heroic adventure, very nearly lost save for a fluke, chance encounter. I wondered how many other grand stories of his generation were being forever lost to mankind, claimed by the ravages of dementia and time.

I have found it a universal truth that upon completing a good book the reader has the satisfaction of knowing the story in total, but if the story is good and noble and true, always find themselves a bit saddened once it's reading is completed. I didn't wish the story of John Stone be completed too soon. I wanted to know more, had to know more, so I continued plying him with questions.

"So, how did you get off the island?" I asked, hoping to spur him on.

"Oh, Skip came back after a day or two, I don't really remember how long he was gone because I lost all track of time after the Japs sailed away. The Army sent a C-47 to pick us up. The pilot said he still had trouble finding us even with the map Bledsoe sent along. The island was just a little bump sticking out of the Pacific at the end of the Admiralty Island Archipelago."

"And they flew you back where?"

"They flew us first to Espiritu Santo, then on to Hickam where I spent three months in the hospital while my boys got sent Stateside without me. The Army, thinking us dead, had long since shipped our personal effects home to our grieving families. My camera made it home to Mary weeks before me. She found my film and had it developed in hope of seeing images of me, but of course there were none as I was always the person behind the camera. It was no consolation to her, but I was glad I'd taken plenty of pictures of my crew. After all we'd been through together, I thought of them often, long after the war. In spite of that, the photos, images frozen in time, were all I had. I didn't actually lay eyes upon most of them again for almost thirty years. It was funny, odd funny not ha ha funny, how it all wound down. We'd shared the adventure of a lifetime together, literally through hell and back, taking care of one another like brothers, and then, without warning or fanfare it was all over, climactic and joyous in our victory, yet anticlimactic just the same. We just drifted apart, silently and without warning, like a mist that dissipates as the day heats up. Guys promised to write, had every intention of doing it *tomorrow*, but days turned into weeks and weeks into thirty years. Oh, there were Christmas cards and an occasional letter or two, but surprisingly little considering all we'd endured together."

"You said something about thirty years?"

"Yes! The *Snoopers* had a reunion in '74 in San Diego. Most of the boys still living came, of course *boys* wasn't a good term anymore, because we were all old men by that point."

"That still must have been very satisfying for you. Who of your crew attended?"

"Well, Doc was still alive and kicking. After the war he came back and finished medical school, then went home to Missoula, Montana to practice medicine. He was a GP and pretty much the doctor for the whole town. I got a Christmas card from he and Joyce every year, but didn't see him again till '74."

"How about Jim?"

"Jim Moberly? Well, word is he died of an aneurysm sometime in the sixties. He just didn't show up for work one day. I didn't hear about it for a couple of years."

"Any idea what he did after the war?"

"Jim was pretty artistic. I don't think he ever finished his architecture degree, which was a real shame, because he was very talented. Like I said, he painted the babe on the nose of the *China Doll*. He did such a good job painting for us, pretty soon other crews were paying him to paint naked girls on their planes as well. He ended up making more money at painting nudes on airplanes than Uncle Sam was paying him. I guess that skill followed him home, because instead of architecture he ended up painting ads for some big advertisement firm up in Manhattan. Rumor is he died making love to one of his young models. That really surprised us all, 'cause he was married and had three kids at home. I guess you just never really know a person...I thought I knew him then, but I guess a lot can change in twenty years," he said pensively.

"Men will be men," I said sadly. "How about Bledsoe?"

"Bledsoe Courage? The most amazing man I ever met in my entire life!" His face suddenly brightened, recalling his friend. "Bledsoe came home and started college on the GI Bill. He kept going till he got his PhD in literature from Berkley. In the late fifties and early sixties he gained some notoriety as a Beat poet, publishing several collections of his poems, a part of that whole City Lights scene."

"City Lights?"

"A bookstore in San Francisco that was the cultural center for the Beat crowd. Bledsoe was one of the originators, or perhaps *instigator* is a better word, beginning an intellectual cultural movement in the coffeehouses of California. About that same time, he also decided to publicly embrace his ancestry, officially declaring his race as black. I thought his a pretty brave act considering all the racial upheaval of the fifties and sixties. He certainly didn't have to tell anyone, as his white man disguise was flawless. No one would ever have guessed, but the ruse must have been gnawing on his soul. His poetry was full of the angst he felt hiding the color of his mother's skin, a betrayal of the most important woman in his life, and God knows there were lots of women in his life. He must have done pretty well with those books because he now has a house in the Hollywood Hills. I know for a fact that when he joined the Army he didn't have a nickel to his name. He was, and still is, an amazingly smart, introspective guy. I guess that's why the ladies all find him so attractive. When he turned eighty, he was living with a women twenty-five years younger. I guess that's his secret."

"Bledsoe Courage a beatnik? From what you've told me about him I can't begin to picture that."

"Oh, I don't know, Bledsoe thought very deeply about everything. Over ten years or so, he evolved like most thinking people do. Once he got over the race thing, he didn't much care what other people thought of him. That aloof indifference made him cool, *sine qua non* to the whole beatnik personae, so yes…Bledsoe was the quintessential beatnik. I think he also recognized a market for his talent, though I still can't fathom making a lot of money selling poetry."

"Maybe the house was his girlfriend's," I laughed.

"You may be right! He sure had a way with the fairer sex. He still does, and while lots of guys would have bragged about half his conquests, he never did, a true gentleman through and through."

"Do you talk often?"

"We do now. Cell phones have changed the world more than just about anything I can think of. After we reconnected in '74 we started talking on the phone about every other week. Now that long distance charges don't mean what they once did we talk every other day or so. I still feel embarrassed about how little we talked for those first thirty years, though."

"People get busy and other things take priority. I can see how easily that could happen."

"Point is, son, don't let it happen. People and relationships are all that's important in the end. Learn from an old man's mistakes."

"If that's the worst thing you ever did, than you've led a charmed existence," I said.

"I probably have. It's funny though, as you see the end of your life approaching, you have more regret over things left undone than over things done wrong, at least that's my experience."

I ruminated on his sage advice before asking my next question.

"How about Skip? Any idea what happened there?"

"Yep, and you do, too," he said with a gleam in his eye. "He came home a hero and fell right back into his family's money. They owned about half of New York City and several big businesses across the country. They even owned the ad firm that Jim worked for. Skip's service in the war finally earned for him the one thing he lacked as a young man." Answering my raised eyebrows, he completed his sentence, "The respect of his father! He was fine for a while in his insular little world, but after a few years grew bored of his father's money. Like most people who have all the money they could possibly want, Skip wanted something else," he stopped and searched my face for comprehension. Seeing again my quizzical expression he continued, "Skip wanted power! In the early fifties he began seeking political positions in New York. He ran several unsuccessful campaigns for mayor, congressmen, senator, and governor, hoping one of them might be a steppingstone to what he really wanted, which was the presidency. Trouble was, he couldn't even get elected as dogcatcher in New York, so he moved out West to establish residency and began to run for office there. He was finally successful in 1960, winning a congressional seat in Colorado. I got invited to his victory celebration. It wasn't very long before he was a real power broker in Congress. All that continued through the Nixon years, till people started realizing the fortune he was generating for his family and himself, voting to support extravagant military expenditures. Remember the $20,000 toilet seat scandal?"

"I do, actually. That was him?"

"Indirectly, yes. It cost him a vice presidential bid paired with Ronald Reagan."

"Wow! That's quite a climb," I said.

"Especially for a guy who was neither exceptionally bright or competent. Don't get me wrong, Skip was a nice guy and all, but leader of the free world? It would have been a nightmare," he chuckled.

"Did he make it to your gathering in '74?"

"Nope! Other than in newspapers and on television, I've not laid eyes on him since that day in the Pacific when he came back for us in that C-47. Funny, Bledsoe told me that Skip had visited him in San Francisco back in the late fifties to seek help with his campaign, corroborate his war record and all that, but Bledsoe told Skip to his face the government didn't need his incompetence. He was, of course, insulted and left in a huff, which ended any relationship they might have had. Boy, that's *chutzpah*! I would've had trouble telling Skip what I really thought of him. I guess I'm glad he stopped with Bledsoe before he got to me. Anyway, none of us ever really heard from him after that."

I shook my head in amazement before asking, "How about Joe Spencer?"

"Joe got killed in a car accident not long after he got home. 1948, I think. He and his new bride were killed in a car accident, broadsided by a drunk while honeymooning in Daytona. Killed 'em both instantly while the drunk didn't get a scratch. I don't even think the bastard went to jail. He was some judge's son and the whole affair just got swept under the carpet. Pretty sad to survive the entire war like he did, then come home and get killed like that."

"You're right! There doesn't seem to be a lot of justice in the world." I paused reflectively then said, "Let's see, I'm trying to remember everyone. How about Bill, uh, Bill Wooster, wasn't it?"

"That's right. Well, Bill and Jordy had become great friends and he took losing Jordy pretty hard, more so than any of the rest of us. He professed to getting *saved* in the fray of the South Pacific and vowed to carry on for Jordy after he died. He kept that vow and came home to become a Baptist minister in central Missouri. Over a few years, he learned his craft well. Bill was always charming and charismatic, so it was pretty natural that he would attract quite a following. By the mid-fifties he was preaching on the radio on Saturday nights on KMOX, a clear-channel radio station in St. Louis, making him well known, even famous in the Midwest. As his popularity grew, he and his family began traveling around the country preaching hellfire and brimstone at revival meetings. They had this big circus tent they'd set up just outside city limits and stay for a week at a time, preaching and baptizing sinners into the kingdom. Folks say he was quite an entertaining speaker. I wish I would have known about his broadcast because I would have loved to tune in, but I never did."

"Did you ever get to go to one of his services?"

"No. Just missed him once when he was preaching up in Dayton in '68. By the time I put two and two together, he had moved on. Mary and I drove up to try and catch them, but we'd missed him by two days. All we found was a poster with Bill's picture, an advertisement for the revival still tacked to a telephone pole at the fairgrounds. It might have been an old picture, but it didn't appear he'd changed any at all in twenty years. I kept that poster, still have it at home," he chuckled recalling the day. "It said "Free and open to all who seek the truth," but suggested contributions to the ministry were welcomed. I guess like most ministers he lived off those contributions, "Love Offerings" they used to call them. Bill must have done pretty well because he showed up at the reunion driving a big, shiny blue '68 convertible Caddy. He told me he got married right after the war and commenced to having kids, five girls, all a year apart. They sang together as part of the act. I guess I shouldn't say that, but tent revival meetings all smack of razzle-dazzle show business to me. Knowing Bill, I'm sure he was quite sincere. Bledsoe told me he'd heard every one of those girls were wild as March Hares. You know what they say about preacher's daughters?"

"Yes, sir, I know. I dated one in high school," I grinned.

"Why, Doc... I'm shocked!" he said mockingly.

"Well, of your original crew four were killed in the war. Any other crewmembers I've forgotten? That's all I can remember."

"Only three were killed; Lenny, CJ and Jordy."

"But I thought Jack died as well?"

"We all did. Had a service for him and everything, but he didn't get killed. He and his navigator, Dan Andrews, both survived the crash. They were captured and spent several years as prisoners of the Japanese. Dan died of malaria and starvation in the hold of some rusted ship. The Japs were transporting prisoners back to the main island for slave labor. Jack told me they had 'em packed in there so tight they had to take turns laying down to sleep. No food or water for days, most of the guys died before they got to Japan."

"But Jack survived?"

"Yep. Ended up losing his right leg from infection, but he lived to tell about it. He went home to New Orleans and opened a restaurant in the French Quarter, got married to his high school sweetheart and had a house full of kids. I'm still mad at the son of a bitch!" he quipped. "I believed him dead till he walked into the reunion, tall and tan and handsome as ever. He still smoked a pipe, but had advanced from the corncob pipe I remembered and now puffed on a Meerschaum. It was like seeing a ghost," he said, his face still revealing the shock and surprise he felt at discovering his friend alive after believing him dead for thirty years. "I felt so betrayed, but Jack showed up with troubles of his own. I felt sorry for him, so I got over it pretty fast. His wife had died of breast cancer a year before, and he was still grieving. Shut out of his life as I was, I never got to meet her. Knowing Jack, I'll bet she was a real beauty."

"And how about you, Colonel? What has your life been since the war?"

"Oh, a pretty good life I guess, all things considered. The Admiral managed to get Mary and Johnny flown over to Hawaii to spend that fall close to me. I still remember September 21, 1945, was one of the best days of my entire life," he said grinning, his mind's eye transported him there. "I was sitting, enjoying the late summer sunlight in the garden, playing chess with Admiral McCallister when Mary walked in with Johnny in tow. She was a vision, all in white, more lovely than even my best fantasies, and I had some pretty damned good fantasies as I recall. I stood up, or tried to stand up to go to her, completely forgetting my leg. I fell flat on my face and scared poor little Johnny so bad he cried. She and the Admiral got me back into a wheelchair and soon I was sitting with my little boy on my lap for the first time ever. He was three years old. The most beautiful child I'd ever laid eyes on and he was mine, no doubt about it. He looked just like Davey did at that age. I just sat there and bawled like a baby, while Mary stroked my hair and said everything was all right. She'd received a telegram reporting me missing in action, but said she never gave up hope. She knew somehow, someway I was okay and would be coming home."

"And then you were home," I said. This time I had the tears.

"And then I was," he said, choking on his words as my tears brought him to tears anew.

"Did you have any children other than Johnny?"

"No," he said, quickly angered. "That fucking Jap robbed us of that with his boot. I wasn't even sure I would ever again get to be with Mary in a normal marital way," he said, raising his eyebrows inquiringly, asking in effect, "Do you know what I mean?" When I nodded 'yes' he continued, "But we worked it out. Mary worked it out with lots of love and patience. It took over a year, but we finally got back to some semblance of normalcy. You have no idea how bad a man can feel about himself in that sort of situation," he said. "I'm still embarrassed after fifty years."

"You were attacked in the most gruesome and torturous manner any man can imagine. You have no reason to be embarrassed."

"You can say that all you want, but until you find yourself in the same situation you can't begin to understand."

"You're right, sir. I'm sorry…please go on."

"That fucking Jap bastard stole my manhood from me. My children. My legacy!" He was shouting at this point, anger boiling over, spewing bile at a man long ago dead. "And then he stole my vengeance, killing himself like a coward before I had a fair chance to settle the score. I hope he's burning in Hell!" I had no words for him. I was surprised at how quickly he'd grown agitated. Decompensating before my very eyes, his vehement demeanor becoming the same as when the police delivered him in handcuffs several hours prior. I considered ordering a sedative, but thought better of it as he gradually regained composure of his own accord.

"I'm sorry, son. I just can't seem to get past that sorry *sack of shit*. I guess I still feel cheated of my right to avenge myself."

"Do you still have that same animosity for all Japanese, or just him?"

"Just him now, but that wasn't always the case. I hated the entire Asian race with a passion for years after the war, right up until the time Ohito visited me."

"Ohito?"

"Ohito Ono was one of the Jap soldiers on the island. Back in ninety-five he came to the United States looking for me, bringing along his grandson to translate. Through him he said he was remorseful for things he had done in the war, the civilians he helped massacre still weighing heavy on his soul. He couldn't do anything for them, but he could still apologize for how he'd mistreated me when I'd been captured. I was the only American he'd encountered in the war, and so, hard to forget. He confessed he'd been one of the men who'd taken turns pissing on me, but I didn't recall his face from that encounter because I was, for all intents and purposes, blind at the time. I did, however, recall his voice and it made me shudder, ripping through me like a cold, cutting wind. He was the man who laughed at me when I declared in Japanese I was an American and his friend. Well, he sure as hell wasn't laughing now, standing there at my front door. When I asked him *why now*, he said he'd recently discovered he was very ill, and as it became clear to him that his time on earth was slipping away, he felt compelled to find me and beg my forgiveness, a self imposed penance to be preformed before he could die in peace."

"And did you?"

"Forgive him? Didn't want to at first. In fact, I left him; left them both standing on the front porch in the rain, slamming the door in their faces after his grandson told me why they'd come. They stood there in a downpour getting soaked to the skin for well over an hour before getting in a taxi and driving away. The next morning at 9:00 a.m. sharp they again knocked on my door and again I refused to let them in. They repeated the same process every morning for five mornings straight until finally Mary had had enough. Over my objections she opened the door and talked to them. The grandson explained they would not stop coming until Mr. Ono had either spoken with me or died. Mary, being more civil than I, invited them both in, offering them a seat in the living room. Under the pretense of making coffee, she then drug me into the kitchen to talk some sense into me. We argued passionately for at least an hour while the two men sat patiently in the next room getting quite an earful. She finally made me realize that forgiving Ohito was the best thing, not only for him, but for me as well. As in most things, Mary was right. When it finally became clear that Ohito's cause had become her cause as well, I agreed to sit and listen to him. Turned out Ohito was a good man. It said something profound that a sick old man had bothered to come all the way from Japan just to beg another man's forgiveness. Made me realize that there are good men and bad men in every race. After he showed me a picture of himself as a young man, I remembered his face. He was one of the soldiers who'd stood guard, his weapon pointed at me as I lay crippled on the tarmac, a silent witness to his commander torturing me. Ohito said that while it didn't excuse his actions, he was just a kid at the time and like me, like all of us, was just following orders, doing his duty for his country. Said he knew at the time he was wrong to follow those orders, but didn't have much of a choice in the matter. Like any soldier at war, he would have been shot if he'd refused to obey the direct orders of a superior. At Mary's request I listened quietly to his story. When He'd finished I was still mad as hell so I left and took a walk to collect my wits. After I'd fumed a bit I finally realized I couldn't very well hold him responsible under those circumstances. When I returned, it still took all my courage to become man enough to utter the words, "I forgive you." Relieved of a lifelong burden, Ohito broke down and cried. Mary and I cried too. It surprised me to discover just how liberating the act of forgiving someone else could be. I didn't realize how concretely my anger and hatred had held me a prisoner all those years."

"Wow, John. That may be the most profound thing you've said all day."

He shook his head with a sage knowing, happy to have shared this bit of hard earned wisdom before saying, "Turns out Ohito was the one who'd cut the rope binding my hands and feet before he got on the boat that day, his initial act of contrition an act of kindness to a man he believed would soon die. About a month after he'd returned home we got a letter from his grandson informing us that Ohito Ono had died of stomach cancer. As he'd died peacefully, Mary pointed out that I'd extended the same kindness to him, releasing him from bondage."

"Amazing!" After a few moments of silent reflection I prodded him onward saying, "So your first stop after the island was Hawaii. How long did you stay?"

"We came home for Christmas, and I'm glad we did. It was Granddaddy's last with us. He died of a stroke on December 27. We shared a great Christmas together. He just worshipped little Johnny and played with him to the avoidance of everyone else present, morning to night. We found him dead in his bed the following morning. Granddaddy had lost Davey, and I think he was just waiting to see me home safe before he went to be with Lydia."

"Lydia was your grandmother?"

"Yes, a grandmother I never knew, but she performed for me the greatest kindness by linking me to my people."

"Your people?"

"The Jews! I'm a Jew in every sense of the word because of her. I always was, I just didn't know it. Being Jewish is determined not by your faith, but by your mother's ancestry. Granddaddy was too practical to stigmatize me in a world that so blatantly hated the Hebrew race. He raised me up Baptist, just like everyone else in southern Georgia. Quite accidently, I found out about my family history before I went off to college. I did a little clandestine research about Judaism before the war, and then I embraced that ancestry when I got back home. Don't get me wrong, I'm what many people call a messianic Jew because I believe Jesus of Nazareth was God's promised messiah. After the war I delved into what it was and is to be considered a Hebrew....one of God's chosen people. I believe I survived the war by the grace of God. There can be no other explanation."

I nodded a passing understanding, but I wasn't sure I understood choosing to embrace a lineage so brutally victimized in that same war. He must have sensed my bewilderment, because he continued with an explanation, "Look, son, you can choose what you believe, but not who your parents are. I chose to embrace a tradition several millennia older than the nation I was prepared to die for. What's so strange about that?"

"Not strange, just fascinating. And did that community return your embrace?"

"Not so much at first, A Georgia cracker, a Baptist no less, reading the Torah, but they grew used to us," he laughed.

"Johnny and Mary?"

"Followed what I did. Turns out Mary's father's father was Jewish."

"And that makes her?"

"My wife," he again laughed.

"So you went to war a Christian and came back a Jew, Bledsoe went a white man and came back black...absolutely fascinating! What happened next?"

"Well, we got Granddaddy laid to rest before New Year's Day, then we moved back up north for me to finish school."

"Architecture?"

"Yep. Finished my degree in '48 then moved to Arizona to do a fellowship with Frank Lloyd Wright at Taliesin West. Jim Moberly had been a graduate fellow for Mr. Wright before the war. He warned me saying apprentice was a euphemism for kitchen slave, but then helped me get the position when I wouldn't be frightened off. I finished up my apprenticeship in 1950 then moved the family to Cincinnati, Ohio where I worked for a big architectural firm for the next eighteen years. Johnny grew up and followed in his old man's footsteps. He attended Harvard then came home to join me in a small practice, Stone and Stone, Architects. We were pretty successful and both kept working right up to the time he retired in 2003."

"So you practiced for over fifty years?" I asked, amazed.

"Fifty-two to be exact. Of course, the last ten years, Johnny did most of the heavy lifting. I just stayed on for consulting and the like."

"Wow, what a life!"

"I've been a blessed guy, all in all," he smiled.

"And is Mary still....?"

His eyes welled up with tears and he choked on his words, "I lost her last year."

Again I got teary, empathetic to the raw pain he still felt, "I'm so sorry, John." I said, placing my hand on his knee to offer comfort.

"She got uterine cancer. She hid the fact she'd started bleeding from me for three months. The doctor said it wouldn't have made much difference given her age. She suffered terribly there at the end. All I could do was sit and hold her hand. It took her three days to die. I never once left her side. At the end she smiled at me kind of queer and patted my hand....she just slipped away..."

"I'm so sorry, John. How many years were you married?"

"Sixty-nine, almost seventy years."

"Wow, that's quite amazing, considering the length of the average marriage today. How did you do it?"

"It was mostly Mary putting up with me. She was the best thing that ever happened to me."

"I can see that. From what you've told me, sounds like she was damned near perfect."

"Oh she wasn't perfect, son, no person is, but keep in mind I had only known Mary four weeks when we got married. I left for the war still totally infatuated, so consumed, so charmed, I couldn't see her faults. Throughout the war that's how I continued to see her, an ideal conjured up by longing and hormones and immaturity. Mary remained perfect in my mind's eye, my dream girl, hell, any man's dream girl. An unrealistic fantasy, but that fantasy helped keep me alive, kept me going through hell if for no other reason than to come home and live out my life with her."

"I don't think you were the only man of your generation so afflicted by that malady. I've been to the Air Force Museum and the Smithsonian and seen lots of pictures of the airplanes you flew. There were pretty girls painted on the nose of almost every American aircraft. Funny thing is, there can't be that many beautiful, ideal women in existence."

"I think you're right, but that *malady,* as you put it, sure took its toll on marriages after the war. Innocence and sexual propriety somehow got lost in the midst of the conflict. Men came home with unreal expectations of wives and lovers, and I was no exception. The women we came home to had changed as well. For the first time in recorded history they'd joined the workforce in unprecedented numbers, demonstrating that they were every bit as capable as men to perform pretty much any job, even manual labor. It gave them a new worldview, liberated from the notion that they were inferior to men. It's hard for kids of your generation to realize just how revolutionary that attitude was. It shocked and changed the world. As I think I told you, Mary took a job while I was overseas. That experience, coupled with her raising Johnny alone for those first few years, changed her. It's funny, but after the war, despite all I'd seen, I was the one who had naive notions while Mary's eyes had been opened. While she loved me and wanted me, she really didn't *need* me. The first few years of our marriage suffered for it as I gradually came to realize that Mary, the real-life Mary, was not that fantasy girl I'd carried around in my heart throughout the South Pacific. In her defense, no one could have been, as *that* Mary was an impossible, unobtainable ideal. No, she was an independent woman, who had her faults just like everyone else. I just didn't discover that reality till after I got home." He chuckled to himself, recalling one of Mary's foibles before sharing his thoughts, "The woman loved to drive and believed she was a good driver, but she couldn't drive worth shit," he laughed. "She wrecked my '49 Pontiac…"

"The same Pontiac we were looking for in the parking lot?" I asked. He responded, looking at me with a deer-in-the-headlights absence, totally unable to recall our search for the car, an event that had occurred only two hours prior.

"Never mind, Colonel, go on, Mary wrecked your favorite car?"

He laughed, recalling the episode. "It's funny now, but it wasn't too funny at the time. She was putting on lipstick in the rearview mirror, driving down Broadway, late for an appointment as usual. She rear-ended a humorless cop and couldn't charm her way out of the ticket. We only had one car, so she couldn't hide her little indiscretion from me. When I sided with the cop, telling her she shouldn't have been driving and putting on makeup at the same time, all hell broke loose. It turned into quite a row. She vowed she wouldn't talk to me and didn't for a week, not until I apologized, and talk isn't the only thing she wouldn't do, if you know what I mean, son," he laughed, giving me a wink.

"I'm married, I know very well what you mean."

"Well, I finally broke down and gave in, even though I knew I was right. If I hadn't I'd probably still be sleeping on the couch. Mary could be the most stubborn, headstrong, obstinate woman you ever laid eyes on," he rolled his eyes and shook his head, then smiled, remembering, "But the makeup sex was worth the price of the car!"

Surprised, I genuinely laughed aloud, "I think you're a horny old goat. I don't know how she put up with you for so long. Sixty-nine years you say?"

"For sixty-nine years," he nodded, then paused, bringing her image to mind. "Funny thing is, when I think of her now, I don't see her as that twenty-year-old fantasy girl, I see her as an eighty-year-old woman, her body ravaged by time, but still just as beautiful as ever to me. Through good times and bad times, I grew to love her more with each passing day. I'm nothing without her..."

"And where do you live now?" I quickly asked, hoping to distract him from the now and forevermore unbearable pain of losing his soul mate.

"By myself," he said defiantly, as though I'd just touched an exposed nerve. "I sold our old house in Terrace Park and moved into a condo on the river. I just couldn't stand being cooped up with all those memories in that house without her. Johnny and his wife wanted me to move in with them, but I wasn't going to have it. I don't want to live long enough to be a bother. Not to Johnny, not to anyone!" This confession was not going to make our inevitable conversation any easier.

"So, John, any idea about what happened this morning? You're over two hundred miles from home."

"I had a dentist appointment across the river in Covington. I left home at 7:30 and started driving. It started snowing really hard and I got confused and I panicked. Next thing I know I'm on the island hiding from the Japs. I feel so very foolish."

"John, anyone can get confused. Still, after we get you home, I want you to see a neurologist friend of mine in Cincinnati." Scrawling my physician friend's name and number on a prescription blank, I placed it in his palm. "I'm concerned, given what I've seen here today, that you may be developing a touch of Alzheimer's disease. We've developed some newer medications in the last few years that seem to be very promising." He smiled and nodded his head, but we both knew I was wasting my breath. He would never do anything to extend his life knowing that Mary, his other half, was so close, awaiting him on the other side.

"So, one more esoteric question Colonel. After all you've been through, what is the most valuable thing you've learned?"

Without skipping a beat he said, "Friends and family, son. Nothing else matters much, but if you've got friends and family you're a wealthy man." I smiled, accepting his wisdom, a nugget mined from the depths of a soul eighty-nine years in the making.

"Speaking of family, does Johnny still live in Cincinnati? I'd like to call him and make arrangements to get you home. He must be worried sick." I could see my words had insulted him. He didn't need help from anybody and, given their recent history, especially not his son. He opened his mouth to say so when I quickly added, "I know you could drive yourself, but we have no idea where you left your car. In this blizzard, it may be a while before the police find it." The gravity of his new situation began to permeate his thinking, the loss of independence, the loss of personal freedoms, the loss of his essence.

He sat quietly pondering his immediate future before asking, "What happens next, Doc?"

"You're pretty lucid right now, John. I believe you have some decisions to make while your thinking is clear enough to do so."

"Decisions?" he asked, already knowing the answer. "So you think I'm gonna get worse?"

"My experience with dementia, John, is we can slow its progression, but we can't stop it. It's probably wise to plan for that day."

"So how long I got, Doc?" he asked, choking back the panic.

"Don't know. I'm not even guaranteed of my own next breath so I don't want to predict yours."

"I understand that. It's not my next breath, or even my last breath that scares me. It's being alive with a dead soul that scares me. I'd rather die than Johnny have me as a burden. Surely you've got an educated guess?"

"You're eighty-nine, John. With medications and some luck, maybe a year or two."

"But will I be *me* during that period?"

"Again, John, I don't know…. I doubt it, if you want the truth."

"I do. I don't much like the sound of it, but I do."

"I think we need to get your family involved. You're gonna need some help whether you want it or not."

Again suddenly angry, he asked, "Do you realize what you're asking me to do?"

"Yes, I'm sorry, but I do. As a physician I have to be concerned not only for you, but for everyone else around you as well. You easily could have killed someone other than yourself this morning. That said, this is not a prison. I can't legally do anything against your will if you are competent to make decisions."

He looked at me questioningly.

"Yes, sir, at the moment I believe you are psychologically competent, so the decision is yours. With your permission, I'd like to call Johnny."

Colonel John Stone, American hero, acquiesced with a nod as I picked up the telephone on my desk.

"Hello, Mr. Stone, please. Mr. Stone? I'm here with someone who wants to speak with you…"